Order this book online at www.trafford.com
or email orders@trafford.com

Most Trafford titles are also available at major online book retailers.

Printed in Victoria, BC, Canada.

ISBN: 978-1-4269-2381-4

*Our mission is to efficiently provide the world's finest, most comprehensive book publishing
service, enabling every author to experience success. To find out how to publish your book, your
way, and have it available worldwide, visit us online at www.trafford.com*

Trafford rev. 11/23/2009

 www.trafford.com

North America & international
toll-free: 1 888 232 4444 (USA & Canada)
phone: 250 383 6864 ♦ fax: 812 355 4082

ALPINEGLOW

A TRILOGY OF SHORT NOVELS

by

Charles E. Miller

a love story

Noah & Luke, Wayfarers

The Mollies Are Coming

a love story

by Charles E. Miller

THINGS HAPPENED

THE SQUARE DANCE

Couples arrived through the festooned portal to the dance hall, a trick of vision that announced a special occasion for this night. The expressions on th faces of couples enterj ng from the gloom shone with expectant excitement familiar to attendees to bull fights and major league baseball games. There was a promised action ahead. They marked the sense of urgency in the minds of the beholders. The ladies, both the young and the more seasoned, spun and swung gracefully in their flared-design skirts of pink, green, yellow and taupe, while the gents, escorts to this pavilion of romantic dance fantasy, showed their stature with subtle pride, so solemn in their attire of black string ties, collar tips studded with fake diamonds and the traditional towel sashes at at their belts. The very costume-like decorations of these entering dancers suggested great balls of historic times, during war and peace, inaugural pageants of honored invited dancers and the trembling anticipation of ancient ancestors going to similar celebrations with the dance. The faces of these arrivees showed delight upon entering their lady for that first view into the ballroom of the nights *"Dance of The Range Cowboys."*

A band of four musicians played with great skill in their Texan Prairie hats, their hand-tooled black and brown cowboy boots and the neck kerchiefs, not to mention tight ranch-hand denims--too tight for comfortable fencing work--thus costumed were these gauchos of the square-dance band. They blew the flute and bowed the strings under an amber flood of light that reflected off their polished instruments and Western dress. They played the rhythmic, minuette-like music for the familiar round, rendering in broken, melodic cadences its varied steps for the twirling. stepping couples. A dozen dancing pairs out on the polished-wood dance floor put the cadence and gyrations of the music into their dance, scarcely realizing as they did so that theirs was the language of form, as old as ancient merrymaking form for the Irish jig, the French gavotte , the Germans waltz. Seated on the side chairs, Raul Watson turned to his lady in the frilly bodice and and orange hoop-skirt and commented on the eloquent sound of their live band; usually they danced to recorded music overlain by the caller's commands. The couples on the floor twirled, fishtailed, spun and side-stepped, their steps following the caller's droning voice. The rounds caller and his partner danced amid the other couples that he might observe their steps more plainly while he called. *The Fox and the Hare,* the old-time melody for the round.

The music for the couples-dancers preceded the main dance of square steps, to be called by the invited caller-of-the-night, Reginald Watson. The word *round* came from the French *Rondolet,* a poticterm put to music that described similar light, cavorting m measured steps of pairs dancers. Watson was presently occupied with rigging his mechanical apparatus while the band played on. The ladies' colorful flared skirts and the gents in their fresh, manly attire moved rhythmically across the floor below to the stage and to the quartet of round-dance music. Impromptu, the flautist stood and delivered several measures for a certain step, the base hummed away, the violin lofted the melody with purring strings and a guitarist accompanied the ensemble. As the niht's opening proceeded, an accordionist showed up. The band rather than the dancers were permitted a certain measure of impromptu freedom to improvise, just so long as the beat stayed in tact. On this gala night, the special anniversary dance for *Boots and Gaiters Club* was under way.

The club hostess. a solemn yet comely lady her expression preoccupied, worked with quick diligence at her task. She was distributing along a side table covered with white linen her plates of cookies and cakes and platters piled with finger-dips of celery, cheeze, crackers and avocado-dip/ Her accomplice in this distribution o refreshment oodie was hastily setting out the drinks of cold cider.. coffee and water were already present in this smorgasborg arrangement of refreshing things that invited the guests and club members to partake during every dance. Dancers who either knew not round-dance step or preferred the square-dance calls sat around against the walls of the immense ball room, the tan wood floor of which shone with a recent burnish. Two large electric fans circulated air from opposite corners of the hall. There was an atmosphere of expectation about the place, as if this crowd had assembled to await the appearance of some famed dignitary. Square dances almost always had about them the atmosphere of generated by an expected sports event.

A beautiful blonde lady lost herself somewhere amid the round dancers. She had arrived singly this night, as she always did. The pageant-master of the dance would have described her as of gentle upbringing, a fine young woman of unremarkable years, a lady who was of medium stature, with gray almond eyes that sparkled from the excitement of the dance. This was her life, apart from her work at the stock-exchange and her care for her invalid mother in their apartment out in the city's Echo Park district. She danced with a full flair of her pink sequined skirt, her generous yet delicate figure marking a swathe of attention from other dancers when her steps moved to the caller's calls. She always participated in the preliminary round-dance figures, which gave no slight to the main dance but provided moments of respite throughout the dance eve.

As the scheduled hour for the square-dance arrived, the main caller, a tall Westerner-looking man who wore a white Texas hat and was adorned with an embroidered shirt, had finished "testing" in his deep base voice . He took his microphone and called, "All right everybody..., square 'm up!" Few announcements ever provoked such an energetc assembly of the parts. Dancers who had sat chatting along the sides suddenly sprang to the open squares on the floor, the total making ten squares, or eighty dancers for the night. In one sense, the caller's words were like a provoked call to arms, for everyone who could walk appeared to take part in the first dance. The lovely blond mystery lady was tagged by a stout man with a small beard, graying pomade hair and dull and expressionless eyes, sporting a cyan towel that hung from the loop at his waist . He was very pleased to be dancing with her, as well he should have been, for the democratic nature of the square dance, as an historic institution, was immediately apparent when the most incongruous looking singles paired up for the dance .

The tip began with a sonorous , *right and left grand, hand by the right and turn through.* The mystery blonde appeared to be in her heaven of joy--the work at the stock exchange had nothing to offer in fun and gaiety. A young man named Grant had come to the dance, also alone. *This is it! ...this is the night!* he told himself. The color and excitement momentarily quickened his senses, not unlike his response as a kid when his father took him to the circus. Dancers did not think it was dangerous or improper for both men and ladies to attend without a companion or an escort dancer. There was a spirit of untried community that seemed to extend beyond the dance hall. *Les femmes* came paired with friends. The blonde mystery lady had momentarily vanished amid the moving, rhythmic crowd.

When the tip ended and the rounds commenced, she emerged from the floor and promptly seated herself at the ticket-table. Grant was drawn to her first off by her physical beauty and then by her mien of diffidence. She seemed to exhibit a kind of disengagement from the dance with her small tasks to perform. Other young women he had met were, at first meeting, *too engaged* in an effort to show a cordial undertaking of an ordinary task , preferring to make up to her male friend, a feminine a risk-taker who preferred to roll loaded dice on first acquaintance. Grant pulled over a chair and sat down beside her even as the couples continued to file into the hall. She smiled up at each visitor, took his money and had each arriving dancer sign his or her name to a register as a club member or a visitor. This protocol enabled the club to keep track of its members. Furthermore, a signature gave each dancer a sense of identity and importance, much like a host registering dog-owners before the thoroughbred show. The young man introduced himself. "My name's Grant Shepherd, Miss,..how d' y'do?" He said to her facetiously that he chose to sit down "with the treasure."
"Very well, thanks," was her answer. She did not appear to care about words at that moment. *Guy's bold,* she thought, her quick intelligence, not her morality, was at work. Her hands were fine, her nails without paint, her fingers strong and agile like a musician's as they worked at her task at the money table.

The couples continued to arrive, at first looking around like cautious strangers. When the caller again sang out, "Square 'm up!" a fill-in assumed exchequer control. Grant took his blonde lady-friend by the hand, and off they skipped to the nearest square that lacked a couple. The ready dancers presented a garden of color, in their multi-hued, hoop dance-skirts and pink, white and blue ladies slippers, the on display in their embroidered shirts, their black and green string ties, studded collar-tips and diamond towel-loops at their belts The assemblage of dancers, ready to begin at the caller's first words bore on their faces, looks of excited anticipation. The tip began with *"Bow to your corner, bow to your partner, head' couple up and back, left turn through, right and left grand...."* He forgot that he had told her his name was Grant. "I'm not *mister...."* To himself, he sounded formal and blaze . She said not a word until they passed *right and left grand*. In a loud whisper, she said, "I'm Mary." Introductions were done on the wing and without ceremony. They danced the tip with vigor, her light slippers and a ribbon matched her pink dress. She better than he kept the cadence and steps with skill and grace. Grant felt clumsy tonight for some inexplicable reason, yet he had to confess to himself he felt a surge of delight with his impromptu dance partner.

He did not want to seem to possess her but seeing the occasion early--although all the dancers had arrived and each seemed partnered with a different dancer for each tip--at intermission he again sat down beside her at the cashier's table. He asked her would she like some refreshment...she said *"Yes, please...I would..."* This was the first chance he had to please her. He was adept at pleasing the ladies; his friends could confirm that fact. He had squired numerous ladies and could claim present strong attachments. He returned from the simple smorgasborg with small slices of cake on paper plates and drinks of cold cider. She was pleased and appreciative. She told him so.

"Thanks, Grant. I ...like you," she said with a disarming frankness. He was not sure how he had met her criteria, but he smiled in response. They sat there like two marooned mariners at the table and enjoyed the refreshment as the club host and hostess voiced *Boots and Gaiters Club* announcements. With a sort of charismatic innocence he liked to practice, he bluntly asked her if she was married. This personal questions chilled her. She was tempted to say, *Do you see a ring on my finer?*. Instead, she answered in a tiny voice, pitched in the negative...which he took for timidity. It was curious to him why she should feel timid if this was a singles dance, which it was. He dismissed the question from his mind. Might he call on her for next week's dance.

She was silent, so silent he thought she had not heard him. He emboldened the question. "Can I come by for you at the next dance?" She said, with a strangely quiet air that invited no questions, "I take care of my mother, but she won't mind. She will think it is silly, but then she's not a dancer and my father is gone." She had the blunt speech of a lodestone. She was honest, and probably so to the country squire who danced the first dance with her...as well as to the feathered peon who danced and hugged the ladies, and equally as straightforward to that nickels-worth of nonsense who made tripping steps and cutting remarks as they danced. Boots marred the polish of the floor, but never with so much noise as the in-hand greeters when the tip ended or the Lulu who wore two towels at his belt, one for the lady and the other for his delicate sweating flesh. Grant had little patience f or pretense. "Thanks, ladies!" an ageing duff shrilled, as if to a convention of old maids.. He seemed to churn with self-admiration. The clumping of a thousand hooves could not have made more racket, so it was good that the caller used the electric pilot to replace human speech. Grant removed his Western-brimmed hat thatt kept the brilliant ego glare of other dancers out of his eyes. He was a young man who appreciated his own pride, for it was the mettle of his stern upbringing that he face a life that was mostly combat.

What could he say about her mother? "I would be pleased to meet your mother." She looked at him as if I had barked instead of spoken.

"Naturally, I'll introduce you to her...but do not expect a warm welcome. That's just the way mother is...aloof, since my father died."

"I think I understand. Sorry about yur father.... I shall take care to respect your Mom's feelings.... "

"Mother...never more *Mom*...:" He took her correction with good cheer.

"I look forward to the next square dance and our meeting." She looked directly at him ...*so formal!*... wrinkled up her nose and then smiled, as if her mind was uncertain about everything, her life, her virtue, his attentions. His words sounded insincere, but he had said them anyway. She closed the change- box for the night--*honest crowd*, Grant thought--and hid it under the chair. Grant asked if he might have the next dance. The question was bland and natural . He planned to monopolize her attentions. She consented behind another of those enigmatic smiles.

She floated like a vision across the room, over to an open square. She looked around and waited for him to follow her. He wove in through the idle dancers to reach her where she stood, making room for him in the square. He could not explain it but he had begun to feel felt rather diffident toward her. They had just met. It bothered him that she was so accommodating, as if she posessed a female intuition for a plan to slip him. The notion was the product of his large ego...one of his weaknesses, ever since fraternity days. He thought that she would make a beautiful solace for him...but he thought no further... not for this night. Even that thought betrayed to him his own narcissistic image of a *femme fatale* seeker at an ordinary square dance.

Indeed, after having failed to win tickets or the ten-dollar bill from the bearded club hostess during the intermission entertainment, he and Mary finished their dance as an *adorable couple*, so the female perception would have described their early friendship. He did not want to seem possessive, just as she was diligent not to appear offish or distant. Grant genuinely wanted to come to know Mary better...not that he was searching for a fiance or a wife or even a close feminine friend f or a long-term relationship. Of these notions he had convinced himself. He had put those options out of his mind...or had he? But she was an enigma to him that he needed to solve...to control her? No, he denied that, but perhaps to understand her? That came a little closer to the reason. She could, if she chose to do so, refuse the escort home of this young man, whatever her mother might say. The sticking point was not the morality but the wisdom of his decision and his undeniable urges

When the dance was over and the guests scattered for their wraps and hurried about the dance floor, others milling here and there in conversation, he tried swiftly to usher her from the room before he would be importuned to wait for parting hugs and salutations. She chirped *good-nights* to her friends. She balked, paused with her fringed shawl on one arm in order to converse with a couple of her *confidantes*. He had not asked her how she had arrived at the dance,...a friend, of course...but where was he or she? He was not to be seen as she looked about for her driver. Just then, a whiskered giant of a man who had brought her, the club's president, came up to her, his manner brusque and business-like, and he asked, "Do you need a ride home, Mary?" She smiled and gestured to Grant. The big man abruptly turned away to others. Grant took her arm, they sped out through the doors and to the street beyond.

He decided to stop at a small shop, the *Little Bear Coffee Urn*. They hastened in to a booth and sat down, with a flurry of her dancing skirt, his kerchief and boots and fancy shirt, as if from a stage to the greenroom. They at first just sat and looked at each other in a nonchalant way for moments that, for each of them, were filled with strange, normal, weird fantasies of life together. Neither of this glamorous--to others--duo hinted at his or her inner feelings or thoughts. He ordered tea and cakes for them, and in a few minutes, the waitress delivered the goodies from a tray. She disappeared without a word. They carved separately on slices of carrot cake and sipped their tea together. What celebration could be more fitting as a coda to a square dance, enjoyed by a couple on their first night of...friendship.

Without his even suggesting that she do so, she began to tell him about herself and her life, as if...again that image of the marooned couple...she had accepted him as an intimate acquaintance. This thought he abandoned from instinct because it had desperate consequences. He listened with close attention, not looking intimately into her eyes but hoping to seem to her, cool. *Let her talk on,* he counseled himself. *She's interesting,* as indeed she was when she began to regale him about her voyage with an uncle who was a sea captain, and on whose merchant vessel she sailed on a vacation trip to the Barbados Islands. "I was his cabn girl," she laughed. "Just playing...he had speaker phones to the crew and engine room." She sailed off into glorious descriptions of how lovely it was under the water...and how the fish showed intelligent curiosity, and the coral reef was so exquisite...!

On that vacation she had learned to snorkel..."Have you ever snorkeled, Grant...?" No, he had never snorkeled but he had fished for clams. Clam fishing did not interest her. Clams were not lovely and exciting for her, she had to admit. He had gone shell fishing when he was a kid...for the big ones. "Do you know, ever since that voyage with my Uncle Clyde, I'm not afraid of the ocean any more...swimming way out...sharks...all that sort of thing."
"The spirit of your uncle protects you...?"
"No, my spirit of adventure causes me to ignore danger."
"You could have sailed with your uncle to other parts sof the world."
"He refused to die the year after our voyage. Fell overboard...shark bit him. He's sor of...ornery. This ring..." she extended her right hand as if for a blessing kiss. "Made by a native out of a seashell...lovely, don't you think?" He took her hand in his and put his eye close to the ring finger. The touch of her her warm flesh silently thrilled him. He released her hand and she withdrew his and lifted her cup to her full and sensuous lips for a sip.
" 'S a sad story about your uncle...shark attack...but at least you have a

memory token of your voyage."

"Yes, isn't that wonderful. His ship's name was *Calaban*. You ever heard of him...Caliban, I mean?"

"Can't say that I have." He idly stirred his cup of tea, without sugar or cream.

"Everybody should find a token of a memorable occasion...a sea voyage, a trip to a foreign country..." She grew pensive. He wanted to caress her hand...the pensive expression on her face drew hlim to her with the first feelings of love. .

"I have hardly begun...I ....my father wanted me to be a boy. Being disappointed, he taught me to love the West. He had never been out here to California, but he fancied he would have enjoyed the life of a cowboy."

"You're not a Westerner."

"I'm what iscalled a *Boston girl*. No fancy schools, always publicschool, but he tried to mould me, to make me refined, delicate in my tastes, high-minded and...a leader. He saw me as a ...frontier woman!" Grant feigned collapse in disbelief. "He disgusted mother with so much fault-finding highmindedness she couldn't take him any longer. She told him, frankly, that pioneer women were kind, generous and hardworking, but crude and sometimes mean to their husbands. He refused to accept that reality. In fact, he refused to accept other realities...that he was born with high cheek bones and Asian eyes...that accounts for my...what is called almond eyes. He was a sworn Protestant and protested all she did, quite thoroughly. She said he ought to wear a split collar he was so damned controlling...and did he want a confession from his own daughter..." They went at each other that way...I don't know why I'm telling you these things...." Her pathos affected him immensely, so that silence was to be preferred over pity.

What, what she would like to do with her life? she had asked herself many times. Her father had posed this question to her once or twice. She admitted this fancy to him.

"That's part of it...what I found so revolting in my father,,,as if I had to possess a man's ambition."

"He may have meant...only that you should use your gifts."

"Mother called him 'unfair.' 'That's unfair,' " she said. " 'My own daughter...I love my own daughter and for you to suggest that she turn against me is...is...despicable.' "

"
How did I tell her to turn against you?'" my father asked.

"'Then why do you try to be more than her father? ' "

" 'More than...! I don't know what you mean.' "

" ' Her mentor, her counselor, her defender, her savior.' "

" 'You're finally finding a use for all those big words you used to use.' He was once a teacher...."

" ' I have only one big word for you, Ronald...evaporate when she is around. I have learned to take your...insults.' "

" 'Truth is sometimes harsh, Francine.' "

" 'Not so harsh as it is from your lips, my husband.' "

"I overheard their fighting...that was the gist of their conversation. That was the way they went at each other. He took to drinking and that so disgusted Mother that she avoided him even in our own house....and then came their split-- the reason I came West with her. Sooo, since she is getting on in life, she needs someone to...."

"Replace your father...that's of his own making," said Grant.

"True, true, but that's just the way it was...." She paused, they finished their carrot cake and when the waitress passed them by he asked for refills of their tea. He did not want to end their little *soiree* together on such a dismal note of love's rejection and fratricidal anger, the carrier of which was the lovely lady who sat opposite him and with whom he had shared dances for the evening. He did not want their relationship to end in such a catastrophic way. The stunning thought occurred to him that she might have reached her limit to forebear and that he was the last stopping place on a journey...he dared to think of it...to suicide. A fresh pot of steaming tea promptly arrived, and she went on with her account, regardless of the passage of time.

" I loved to skate on the pond back in Boston, and sometimes on the tennis court when the grounds-folks flooded it over. I went turkey shooting with him one year...my father, I mean...he shot a big bird but my mother refused to cook it because it had so many birdshot in the flesh. You do not laugh...but that was funny. Brains, my father thought, they came from his side of the family. I flunked math and passed brilliantly in Latin. We all had to take both subjects...*solids*, they were called. My father was a deputy sheriff--another thing my other hated about him. He had a gun and she was scared to death of guns, even his turkey shooting-iron for the next year...in the attic. He would come home with some made-up story about a criminal he had apprehened and put in handcuffs. She would *humpf* and *humpf* to ridicule him...never for a moment believing him...and then change the subject. She detested sentimentality, even sentiment, so that when a boy gave me flowers, as happened from time to time, it was all I could do to save the flowers. For that one reason I came to hate her... but she was a good mother in lots of other ways."

"I'm listening...I can see no reason for his feelings against you...your father's, I mean."

"They were against my mother. He endured me whenever I seemed closer to him than to her. She began to have trouble with her stomach...as most people would."

"I've had trouble with mine," he said.

"I used to skip school so that I could go sledding with boys that were older than I. I had always wanted to ride, to learn to ride a horse, but my father was adamant. His brother had fallen from a horse one day and broke his neck when he was a boy. So horses were out."

"Your Uncle...?"

"Not the sea captain...they had a younger brother. They all played musical instruments together...my father the clarinet,and my sea-captain uncle the horn Pipe. Wouldn't you know! dancing aboard ship. Maybe that's where I inherited...a blood strain, you know...my love for square dancing."

"Perhaps, yes, just maybe," Said Grant. "Go on, Mary. This is an intriguing story."

"I love the mountains, always have. Not many mountains close to Boston...I mean high mountains...but I went once with a school outing and we got caught in a avalanche. Only the driver was killed. I can see that pack of snow, like a wall of snow come rushing down against the bus...turned us over, knocked us kids around. We were hurt badly, some of us, but we survived."

"I'm a backpacker. We... maybe we can go on a backpack day-trip some time."

"I think I would enjoy that..." She looked about the small coffee shop, the late nighters sitting in booths like they, enjoying the parting night hours. "I'm not quite done," she said. "I was in love with a boy once."

"Once? You're too lovely not to have had more than one romance."

"This was serious...but do you know, this time mother put a stop to it. She said he was too young for me...only one year older than I...and he had no means of support of ever we got serious."

"That quashed the romance."

"Almost...we saw each other in secret. I'm afraid I lost my virgnity to him, but I didn't care. Only...I could not get pregnant or I would be thrown out of the house by my mother and my father, both."

"They would not tolerate...."

"A bastard in the family.,.and so I would have to marry him, then get a divorce. My father had a plan all worked out."

"But the romance...."

"Fell through...and it was just as well. He died two years later from a heart attack, and I would have been a widow with his child and forced to live at home with my parents."

"Instead...."

"Well, here I am...as you see me. I came West because I wanted to break free from my father's influence. And...oh, I have a brother."

"I think I can understand."

" I went briefly to night school, learned how to be a stock-broker, applied for a job and got one...as an intern...then I decided on secretarial work... was more stable...not subject to the ups and downs of the stock market."

"Good choice. I worked for the government," Grant said. "I worked in aVA hospitals."

"That so?...hospital work. I had thought about that...but ...bed pans and...you know. washing those bodies...in the bed! It's bad enough in the shower." He laughed.

"Every job has is down side," he said.

The finish of the night was swift and secure. He paid the check at the cashier and they waltzed out of the *Little Bear Coffee Urn* and down the outside steps. The skies had started to drizzle. The drive back to her apartment was swift and brief. One significant incident occurred...she let him come in with the door buzzer, but at their upstairs apartment door, she put the flat of her hand on his chest.

"Not this time, Grant. I've got to...prepare her, her thoughts. so that she will not be over whelmed by my...my mother is a very emotional woman."

"Your boldness...?"

"Audacity."

"I get it." They exchanged a hug. He turned and was gone. She listened to his feet on the carpeted steps of the stairwell. She inserted the key in the door lock and their night was ended. Back at the wheel on his old Volkswagen, he sat quite still and thought...what a painful story she had told him...she had not needed to do so...but he had played the therapist. "Incredible!" he mumbled with a shake of his head.

IN THE WOODS

During the bumpy thirty mile trip, along an ungraded road into the mountains thirty miles distant from th valley where he and Mary lived, and before the dawn, Grant mulled t over the scenes and incidents of the night before. He tried to hum the melody to one of the round dances but failed to recall the notes. H3e was no musician. Time for a cigar. He pulled off to the side of the road, removed a stogie from the glove compartment..a bad place to keep fresh cigars... bit off the tip, lit up, put his car into gear and pulled away to continue his journey. Down the hill there cam, amid dust and out of the gray, the rattle of lits load and whining of its engine clearly audible to Grant through his open window, its headlights fixed upon the dirt road, there emerged in the gray light of the morning a logging truck. Grant was headed into that part of the forest where logging was in full season in August of the year. He made room for the long monster, whose driver gave Grant a beep of recognition with his horn . The young man who was skilled in woodcraft and a square dancer met up with a lady friend of recent acqujaintance, continued on up into the mountains, to *the development*, as it was called.

He reflected on the swiftness of their parting the night before, from **The Coffee Urn** cafe to her apartment. It seemed to him on this chill morning, away from the dance hall, that she had lain her life open to him . Could she have been making up her story?...was she embellishing actual events of her early home life? Was her peculiar mother an absent-minded old lady with a nasty temper...or was she accommodating toward her lovely daughter with the dancing feet? There again entered the enigma factor, questions he felt by some strange witchery compelled to find the answers to. Well, Mary had her problems and he ought not to be too inquisitive. He had served her well by just listening to her story. A certain tenderness toward her caused him to feel that he ought not to add to her misery if misery it was. He tried to picture her day scene at the stock exchange but failed to do so, for he had never before been inside a stock exchange. He had talked with the girl by phone, her voice distant, cupped and mirthless. They agreed for a meetilng in her place of work. He gathered some straw weeds beside the parkway where he stalled his truck. These, bunched in his trembling fist, he held before him like a shield as he entered the den where she punched keys, scribbled figures, calculated accounts , balances and debts for her employers.W`hen she saw him step over the threshold, she jumped to her feet with instantaneous delight on her face, with some shame for the gift, he proffered the weeds to her. In her small, white hand she seized them and stuffed them into a gold vase on the corner of her desk. She looked over his shoulder at a fellow employee, dismissed his pause as irrelevant to Grant's gesture and taking her purse, she led him out of the exchange to his truck at the foot of the steps. A refuse truck cautiously passed him in the alley behind the exchange, he walked around his truck and opened the door with a smile, then, slammed it and hastened around and into the driver's seat. She suggested the *Carribou Restaurant* over on Western Street, a cozy place where small meals, cheeze sandwishes, salads, soups could be enjoyed within the cover of table booths. They selected their meal from a menu, she a salad with French dressing and a cheeze sandwich, he a soup and the same cheeze on bread. They hardly said a word to each other. About her there suddenly appeared a reticence to talk, much to his dismay, and almost alarmingly a change from the ebullence of that first night at the square dance.

He sensed her attempt to distance herself from her; the smiles and gracious ;manner were almost irrelevant. Hle sought a weak place in her sudden chill, and wondered as to its cause. Had lhis gift of weeds been a flagrant violation of some code of gracious courtesy, or was she attempting to draw him linto a relationship of friendship rather than a commitment of love. He was determined to find out, They finished their meal with hardly a word between them. Almost as silf a threat, he said he would come to see her at her apartment.

"Your mother will just have to get used to me." He had a n indulgence planned for the old woman. She was pathologically possessive about the girl. He had seen that on their first night. On could co
comprehend the inadequacies, the shortness of breath, the weakness of limb and will at the age of the old woman, but to foist upon the daughter the blame, as ilt were, for these frailties, was wrong, morally askew and
"Pathologically insensitive," he thought. He had another scheme that would separate the old woman from her young daughter, and that was to poison the woman in such a way as to make her dependent upon medications, doctor, and perhaps a move to a rest home.

He sought the answer in a small tablet known as analgesic salicitate. Who could object. On the next visit to their apartment, the mother treated him with diffidence, as thought she was trying to gain his sympathy or his help. "See how she sits," he thought, as if ready to spring off that chair...but she is too feeble to respond. She lacks the wisdom of maturity. She is not like her daughter. Mary is so accommodating...and wise for her years. The old woman mujst go...."
"Have you met my husvand?"
The question alarmed and embarrassed the girl. "She means in her memory, of course, Grant."
"How else?"
"Mother, did you consult with Madame Toussaud today?"
"I haven't talked with her...but my plan remains unchanged."
"Mother would like to see a likeness of my father in wax...in his study?"
"It was...in his study."
Yes, it is my mother's fixation, I believe you call it, that if my father were

only recreated in wax, he would be immortal….and a consolation, a voice of wisdom. She is so lonely, my mother. That is one reason she worships his grave and his spirit…and his likeness. She believes that she can bring his mind alive by reconstituting his image…in wax, if you please.""

"That is strange," he thought. What sort of madness has inflicted the old woman?"

"I must tell you this…she takes pride in the very notion…in fact it was her idea, but I talked her out of it."

"A replica of Mister Greason in wax would be a novelty."

"Yes, wouldn't it!"

"Like stuffing the family dog as a mantle-piece after its death."

"Exactly, Grant. She actually had once contemplated stuffing my father after he passed away…but I talked her out of that…."

"Wait! wait! I don't believe what my ears are hearing."

"Your mother…wanted to stuff…."

"My father after his passing…and place the effigy in his study, sitting in his swivel chair at his desk and turning around as if seeing for the first time new visitors to his den."

"That is…";What is the word I ought to use…madness."

"But why? " I asked.

Authority…he was an authority figure, the girl said, though he never dominated me, as my father…yet he tried. He believed…my father…that he was annointed by the Lord to live on in this household…

"As a master…? He as mad."

"Almost, the girl replied. And I fear I have some of that madness in me as well."

Let us hope not."

The girl glanced at Grant and turned away. Each of us has a certain mad streak in us that shows itself in front of others from time to time."

On one of his early visits, while the two of them sat there in front of the old woman, he tried to imagine what she was really like in early years Yet, when the mother spoke to her daughter, she addressed the girl as "my child…my child," biologically perhaps, but no longer a child. He was certain that those words, that almost contemptuous recognition of her offspring was a meant to control her daughter by keeping her in a state of suspended life time. He was now determined for undeniably selfish reasons to detach the mother from her daughter; let misfortune follow the old woman, but he reasoned in his mind that she will have brought the calamity upon herself.

"I shall make the old woman forever a puzzle to her daughter, beyond the misanthropic creation of a stuffed likeness of the father. That perverse ending to the father's life would alienate the mother before the daughter. To accomplish this purpose he must take the girl to a place where the surrounding were not familiar to her…as up into the mountains where all that surrounded him was totally familiar. There was a power inherent in exposing a person to a unique environment, one they had never seen. Awe of the strange sometimes transfixes he mind and imagina, tion in a time warp, disastrous if that warp is painful yet exhilarating if it is pleasant.

On his next visit to the girl's home, lhe showed great sympathy for the mother and ivei ghed against her will to take a number of aspirins for her fatigue, her dimness of vision, her loss of memory and her general frailty. " Tjhese little white tablets have done much for me," he lied to the old woman. He sueeded in unducing her to swallow almost a dozen, the more she took, he reassured her, the more powerful the effect. It was his plan that if she took so man, sihe might become comatose and fall to the floor where she might experience a loss of consciousness. At that point anything could happen. The daughter looked on with apathy, even approval and contempt. He plied the mother with sips of wine from her own cupboard to ingest the number of common cold remedy tablets, which in numbers became poison. He did not wish to kill the old woman, but simply to weaken her will to influence her daughter's relationship with himself, where they sat on the sofa opposite the mother. She painfully took one tablet after another until she had consumed almost a dozen of the anagesic sodium tablets. Risng promptly, then, he urged by implication that Mary and he leave the old woman to her recovery, for she would soon be like a young woman of fifty again. The girl consented to the ploy. He and she left the apartment, while the mother took a place beneath the table lamp and began to mend an old, torn cape, with a similar intense focus she had possessed many times years before.

"There, you see...how she responds to the treatment.

"Amazing!" the girl exclaimed. He took her hand and led her tos the door tos the apartment.

We shall be seeing you again, soon, Missus Wexler , he said and smiled. The old woman simply looked at him with glassy eyes. "Let me think about your husband.

"He will do you some good..."

" I know a splendid taxidermist...." The daughter pulled at his arm. He looked at a face rejuvenated by the sight of the old woman's change in aspect, as if reborn into the adult world by a simple remedy for the pain of a fall or a cold in the head. "I must be losi ng my mind to consier such madness...to stuff the corpse of a man long gone as a sentry to a household, a figure of authority no longer capable of speech."

"Your taxidermist friend would have a hard time with my dear husband Garrin's body...since he has been in his grave almost ten years."

"We might conjure up a likeness if that is all right with you, madam."

"Conjure is the right word...but only if he is done in wax."

"That I should even consider negotiations over a moldering corpse, to bring it alive as a ...a museum replica!" This thought shocked his sensibilities.

The girl pulled at his arm, and he quietly closed the door, while the old woman, still seated, watched them depart, the medication starting to have an effect upon her visage, her eyes vague and blank, her hands moving swiftly, her mind elsewhere. Fixed upon her face was an unusual expression of disappointment, as she if should have prolonged the conversation about her deceased father further into the night. But a corpse could not quicken his spirit to talk about death.

Their next rendezvous found the pair up in the mountains so familiar to him , he having erected a black canvas tent. They sat at a large bonfire that popped and smoked with green boughs thrown upon the flames, they talked about ordinary things, he deftly avoided any mention of the mother, who now lay supine upon the floor of their apartment, whether dead or not the coroner would have to determine. He cautiously led the girl into a netherland of fantasy of his own making. He would take her to his sawmill cabin, there introduce her to his friends His friends mattered the most, not hers. This would become apparent in the months to come. Meantime they talked about the nigvht, tlhe way the fire smoked so, the fagthers imperious gtreatment of her mother and her own rebellion against him, for he hated the merchantile life and her work linthe exchange was a small act of resentful rebellion. The night passed with the twos of them lin elach others arms. He thought little about the relationship, which to her, she admired and coveted and dismissed as a natural confounding of nature with natures intent and a man's gross appetite.

The early moon disappeared in the spires of the black forest night. Rant heard th hard scratching of fingernails as if on the trough canvas of the girl's sleping bag. What's that? He askd. You awake.

"lYes, I' m awake. I don't know why you chased that squirrel…lyou created fear iln the little creature."

IL don't know wehat you re talking about, Mary.

No, of course not. There ensued a long silence between them, after which, turning over toward her, he said, "They hae their ways…

Oh, Grant, sometimes you are so insufferable.

Me…insufferable. The slquirrel hides from danger because thaty is sits habit.

"Then why ought you to be a danger. Animals have rights, and one of them is to be completely free of fear of man."

"Another…?"

"To reject man's justice of frailty before the law…and to avoid ecoming a part of his food chain."

"Preposterous!" Again that long and mysterious silence. "I only raised my arm and waved in its direction."

"The little creature took that for a threat."

"My God, they are only animals…a squirrel, for heaven's sake…What would I do?"

"That was its question…what would you do? They live here in the forest with man. This is their home…home, Grant. Understand…."

"Then, lets strike all tents and remove all camp stoves and declare the forest belongs to the squirrels."

"And to all living creatures…."

"Are we not creatures also?"

"You sound so… professorial. The squirrels to not threaten u. We threaten them.:

"Then all the living creatures other than mankind must drive men back into their own kind of civilization. Wait until a packrat tries o drag away your miss kit...." She did not hear him.

"It will take the law and the justice we've created to accomplish that."

"That...?"

"Coexistence...." He swore under his breath.

"You sound awfully learned at three o'clock in the morning."

She sighed. "Don't you think we ought to protect the innocent and the harmless creatures of nature," she implored. "She's a real campaigner," he thought. "She must be a vegetarian..." He wanted to let the matter drop until she said. "We endanger them...the endangered species...our guns, our culture, our ways...our religious attitude--God gave the world to man and told him to multiply and subdue nature--we endanger the little beasts."

"Oh, God...at this time in the morning!" he thought. "I see no reason for your getting upset, not here in this tent where I sleep." He stripped himself out of his sleeping bag and , crawling through the tent flaps, stood outside to light a cigar. He heard her voice say something, but he did not care to listen. It was th tone of disgust he clearly heard. She obviously hated tobacco smoke of any kind. Hers was a kind of secular piety shorn of words of counsel or pity.

He took another long drag on the stogie, dropped it to into the forest duff and stamped out a good Havana on the ground. "I was endangering a species by my chasing a squirrel up a tree..."is natural instinct to escape...," he thought. "I meant no harm," he apologized.

"You never can tell. I'm so sorry, Grant, but I feel these things deeply...inside of me."

"Where else?" he thought. He was alarmed, chagrinned about how she felt, as if feelings determined reality...her reality. He knew that she had put him down, rebuffed him in a way that was both senseless and feminine in its unique arrogance. A squeeking, scampering squirrel was the cause of their argument. He did not know what to do . From inside the tent came the words: "Come on back to bed"...to bed, his sleeping bag. He possessed enough intuigtion to realize that she sounded just like a wife. She was worried, concerned in the darkness of the forest night...about a squirrel, animal rights, their insipid argument in the silence of a vernal and inescapable quiet. He ducked into their tent and slid down into the still-warm sleeping bag. He felt her hand reach over to him, but he rejected it. As quickly as he could, rolling to one side, he invited sleep... until the dawn sun lighted the forest floor. She was up already and preparing breakfast for them....it was the smell of campfire moke and frying ham that awakened him....She moved so silently that he heard no more than a crow in the branches of a juniper tree.

IRONS IN THE FIRE

Grant was was not slow to respond to the beautiful Mary with the golden hair when she told him she wanted to go to visit an orphanage. Bethany House was not too far distant. He called for her at her apartment. and they set out. The drive was voiceless; she was very quiet. He had learned not to intrude into her thoughts. She was verly pensive this morning. They arrived at a squat, wide building. His first thought was that it should be painted a bnght yellow. When they stepped down from the cab of his truck, he heard the shouts and laughter of children. They walked along a chain-link fence. Through its metal mesh, he saw leather-chair swings, pastel slides and climbing apparatus upon which some two-dozen small children were romping, sliding and having fun. A young female attendant of about twenty years, in black denim pants, her hair tied up in a knot, and sipping from a thermos sat on a three legged stool nearby. Grant and Mary entered the front door and introduced themselves to a front-desk receptionist. He let Mary lead the way.

"I'm not thinking of adoption," she announced right off, as was her usual abrupt manner. "I wanted to come see these little children...are they all orphans?"

"They are. I'm Terese Karesh. I'm a hostess here at Bethany. One or two of our kids are up for adoption. They stay here until the final court decree and all the paper work is done."

"We're just visitors...this time. I've always known they come here because of some fatality in the family."

"Usually...unless a relative agrees to take custody. Let me introduce you to Hamlin Stearson. He'son of our attendants...and a social worker."

A bright young man with a close haircut, dark sideburns. narrow eyes with thin-rim glasses and the promise of a beard showed up from inside the a hallway of the building. She introduced them to Hamlin. "Hamlin can answer any questions you have."

Grant let Mary do the talking, since this was her quest. He remembered how he had thought about her while he cut wood and chopped up his standard cord the day. Folks in the town who had no access to a stand of trees or refused to chop down their woods-cover called on him for their supply of fire wood. He frequently stacked at least a cord on the front porches of their houses. He had called Mary numerous timesto talk with her on the phone. He had fallen in love with her voice. She lived in security with her mother upon the inheritance left to Mrs.Wexler by her deceased husband, who had been some kind of an elecrical engineer for the County. As if appointed by God or the State yet certailnly not by her mother, Mary was the caretaker for the old woman, whom Grant instinctively distrusted. He had met her twice before and had found her to be suspicious of strangers, distrustful of their words, skeptical of their manner and endowed with a certalin ruthless nature that forbade crossing her will. The distrust was mutual for him, as evidenced when the old woman scorned the small bouquet he brought to her daughter one evening, when he had called earlier just to chat with her. Mary never explained this background to her life. Nor did she question Mrs.Wexler's management of the money left to her. The daughter had worked for a brief time in the acconting department of a large sand and gravel company that mined their materials from ancient deposits along the Three Falls River that ran through town. Mary told Grant, on their second trip to the square dance pavillion called The Barn, thatshe, Mary, favored independence as a rule for living. He did not enquire further; he accepted her philosophy as ordinary for a young woman in her earlhy thirties, his guess at her age. He detested age consciousness; that was for the feeble in spirit as well as body. On her part, her mother detested any hint at another person's advice, counsel or manipulation. This reluctance was due more to distrust than to a will to remain unemcumbered by the opinions and designs of someone else.

　　　　To herself, Mary loathed the old pickup truck that he drove for his work--she wished that at least he should paint it--but she was too polite, kind and thoughtful to bring his attention to the delapidated characfer of his pickup. It was the tool for his work, as a lone mason in building chimneys and fireplaces, a wood-cutter's truck to service his customers and cart flirewood supplies, and he had collected several dozen customers over the years as a chimneysweep. That work had turned old in a short time. He did not like to talk about it. In all, few men wished to meet the demands of the market. Grant, however, was a good business man.

　　　　Probably the most significan visit, for personals reasons, was the night at a square dance when she told him she wanted to visit an orphanage. That was an even less exotic request than when she told him. before the first Christmas of their acquaintance that she had always wanted to go on a turkey shoot...one of her uncles. her favorite uncle, owned a farm outside of town and that was his annual competition which he held for the farmers in the region. A turkey shoot...he mulled over the comment as he worked. This day, however, another of her requests was coming to fruition. Fo tjey had just presented themselves at the Bethany House Orphanage. He puzzled over why she wanted to make this visit. He wanted to know her better. He was aware that a good relationship begins with good exchanges of ideas and words, that if either is dumb toward the other, then the relationship is almost sure to fail. Mary revealed to him her thoughts, yet not her feelings, Nonetheless, he was about to estimate her nature and judge her love for life.

　　　　Thus were they now inside the Orphanage for Children who had been orphaned by war, by disease and chiefly by neglect--war being almost irrelevant and far away--and children who were cast aways left by an indolent and uncaring adult world to rot in the slums and wicked endives of sexual slavery. Some of them had been born abroad, Asians, Latins, Africans...disease killed off as many as did the battlefield amd starvation. The Orphanage was out of town, in the nearby city of Hayfork, a site called simply Home For Orphans, a name without pretense of purpose. Mary had many interests. He liked her for her intelligence, and that was saying much for Grant, since he had gone out with girls who seemed to think that teachers, news-casters, movie stars and politicians should be the chief possessors of intellectual acumen and stature.

A light drizzle demanded an umbrella. He carried an umbrella from his truck. Of course, the drizzle stopped.

Once they had stepped inside the building, their hostess. up i nyears, small, petite some would say, graying, a smile of reflective curiosity on her round face yet with an alert manner, greeted the two of her visitors. She introduced them to a Mr. Hamlin Stearson, an attendant. Perceiving them to be visitsors on a quest for information, he promptly explained why some childen are bought to an orphanage..."The child loses both parents through death. That used to be the most frequent reason. Abandonment, is the next main cause for a child becoming an orphas. Do you have any children of your own?"
"No, we're single folks. I wanted to see why a child becomes an orphan...very basic to your work, Hamlin. Why should parents abandon their progeny? That's inhuman...incredible," Mary said. That puzzled Grant, also; Hamlin went on. "Many times the actual parents, in such cases, cannot be found. After a certain time during which the orphanage cares for the child, or children...at times more than one child per family unit...the abandoned child is categorized as an orphan and is put up for for adoption. The process is simple but takes time." An extrasordinary thing happened--Grant saw tears in Mary's eyes.
"How long do the kids stay here?" Grant enquired.
"Some children are here for as long as six to eight years before we find a home for them. With new systems in place, we can speed up the process nowadays."A school bell rang someplace.

Grant felt that he had seen into Mary's heart. He did not know why he saw what he saw, hidden from him. He thought he understood why she wanted to visit an orphanage. It made sense... she felt that her own father had abandoned her and her wicked old mother had scorned by rejecting her as her only child. "That's the way things sometimes happen," he thought. Our visit was a means for to keeping her sanity. By comparison, one'sown condition of life does not appear so desperate or degenaerate.

"We heard the kids outside...playing on the swings and slides."
"Oh, yes, they have recess in the mornig, break for lunch and take another recess in the afternoon. There's a remedy for loneliness in their shouts and screams at play. Plimitive and natural to children...you know, company against their loneliness.... The air is not cluttered by adult stuff. The kids enjoy the simple physicality of their play...works off energy they sometimes turn against themselves."
"Thank you, Hamlin," said Grant. "Do they ever see their parents again?"
"Usually not. The biologic father and mother are often dead, or always drunk, or past caring, or sick somewhere...or rabid to put their child into sex slaveryl for the money ithey receilved...sometimes from wealthy Americans, a doctor, a lawyer...we had one child who was visited every year by a Federal judge on his vacation. Thelocal taxi drivers kow where the brothels are. We are the last resort fo those children, some of them only twelve or thirteen...."   '   "Just so long as they can play...childhood." said Mary, her face fixed in an expression of disbelief and pity.
"That's right. We try to recover some of their lost childhood. It's tragic when a

child is put to work as a sex slave for a home income...or put out linto an alley somewhere for a lack of care and support."

Grant was warming up to the venture. "Do you have to fight to keep a child...say, if one or both parents wants to take back their kid?"

"At times, yes." said Stearson. "We have to have recourse to the law."

"There's a court battle for custody?".

"At times, yes. At times, the fight is nasty...to control the little life of the child...whether or not the child is his or her own progeny. It is nasty, the fight to control a small life. Its costly, but we have several good pro bono lawyers who help us keep the ship of posession on even keel."

"Possession?" Mary asked.

"Why, yes, somebody has to take on the tasks of custodian...if not the parents, then we do. Oherwise, the child becomes a derlict on the streets, in the alleys out of sight of the police...fishsing for food from garbage cans...and stealing, someimes to keep warmor to have something to eat."

"It's all very primitive," said Grant.

"Yes, quite so, " Stearson replied.

"How do you ...graduate a child?"

"Graduate...?"

"Move a child to a better ...home...situation...."

"Adoption agencies...their sole purpose is to connect the needy child to wanting parents. They act sort of like brokers for the lost child."

"Lost...?" Mary echoed. '   ;

"'Lost. They are lost ...without anybody to cae for them..."

"Horrible!" Mary whispered. Again Grant saw thet ears in her eyes.

"Caring about means caring for...is the main issue. The kid's parents are sometimes out there, but if they don't care, they might as well not exist."

"Inhuman...," said Mary. "Do the children grow and...and mature. I mean...you knlw wha I mean...show strength, their abilities ,want to leave...this place?"

"We try to see that they enjoy outside activities and inside schoolwork that matche their age."

"Schooling...."

"Yes,we have credentialed teachers who hold regular classes in our rooms...they see that the child performs at grade level."

"So the child becomes an adult."

"Eventually, yes. Although few of them ever stay here that long."

"Is a child...does a kid stay here because of a bad attitude... out of...fear...laziness...?"

"We avoid recessive influences. We do not push a child backward, or keep the kid from advancing according to his age.and natural abilities. Most of us adults know when childhood ceases. Scripture says when I was a child I indulged in things of the child, and when an adult I put away childish things."

"Yes, neglect...." Grant uttered his thought aloud.

"You've found the clue.sir...neglect, neglect."

"I wish we could help...."

"Keep us in mind when you ...happen upon a wndfall," Stearson saild with a quick smile. He strosked the fuzz on his chin. "I can show you one classroom."

Mary looked at Grant. "Have we the time, are you interested? " were the questions iln her glance. "While were here, why not?" Thus they allowed their guide and social worker, as he was titled, to lead them to the door of a class room. The bell had rung and the kids out on the apparatus were now in their classroom seats. About fifteen, well-groomed kids, boys and girl of twelve to fourteen years of age, sat attentive at their desks, trying to sketch what they saw on the chalk board, to follow their teacher's crude drawings. This lesson imprinted the details in the minds of the students, and the teacher was explaining how the wings, arms, legs of animals, including creature man, help them to live by the operation of joints. "Some joints work in one direction like legs, other joints in another direction like the fingers of the hand, the wings of a bird. Some jonts have full rotation and no specific direction, like a person's shoulders....Kids, move your arm, one arm, in a circle. You see what I mean? You can reach all around you...That is a rotation joint. " The lesson continued. Grant smiled at the novelty and the praticality of the subject atter and the teacher's approach. She was dmonsrating physically,as well as drawing pictures on a chalkboard and using paper-mache models to demonstrate the lesson of joints.

Mary had come, Grant supposed, because she wanted to teach just such children. She had also come to establish some kind of standard for judging the way her mother had treated her in her adult years. That was only a guess. That her mother had kept her in the role of girlhood in perpetuity inflamed the young man's conscience. The imprisonment--for such it was in his mind--demanded a remedy, and he had no money to hire a lawyer. Besides, what would he plea-- incarceration of a grown woman by her mothner? A jury would think him a spineless fool. How could he right the wrong he felt had been done to this lovely woman--some would say, damaged her? He thought of her as...repressed, and of the old woman as a villain. Most important was the thought that a Roman Catholic Priest, no longer a cleric in the church, had seduced her, and the little girl they, he, had seen at the dance was her child and that she still bore the empathy, compassion and tenderness of a mother toward her own child, and, furthermore, that in her mind she had never abandoned the child but it had been taken from her. Kidnapped in the open! By what reasoning, by what plea, bargain, criminal act, custodial fraud? He could appease his feelings in only one way. Grant was so angered by all that had befallen his sweetheart--she was so in his mind--that he decided he wanted to pay a visit to the Priest whom he was certain had fathered Mary's little daughter, whom he had observed that night holding onto the hand of a governness or her adoptive mother. The arrogance of a Priest, to produce a child yet not care for it, appalled Grant and he wondered where God was in the evil confusion.

He left Mary at her apartment, knowing or feeling sure that the old woman would enquire as to where she had been. To an orphanage...the mother would scream and go into a fit, and attempt to strip from her daughter the little compassion and tenderness she had felt for those abandoned kids, to put her back into her place as a child-woman. He visited the Priest, Father Casper, at his parish house. It was set back from the road, among palm trees, a Gothic frontage on the main structure, benches scattered about here and there in the shade, a belltower and a long walk of cobblestones leading up to a pair of heavy oak doors. The Priests, of which there were five for St. Boniface Catholic church, lived in the two wings of the structure. He dared not disturb Penelope's discussion group to assail the priest. He would confront the Prelate and charge him with his crime of adultery, thereby begetting a child yet then not caring for it, as is natural and normal for life...and in God's will. He found Father

Casper reading his Bolivian newspaper out under a palm tree. Grant did not intend to display formlities but to get to the quick of his quest.

"Hello, Father Casper."

He dropped his paper from his eyes ad narrowed the iln recognition."Oh, the young man at the discussion circle."

"I am he. I have been wanting to ask you a question...which only you can answer. Do you know of a little girl in your parish named Jeanette?"

"Jeanette...? Jeanette...no, I don't elieve I do."

"Would I be transgressing your memory, Father, if Isaid to you that you are lying."

The priest bounded to his feet in a flash, glararing at Grant, his paper still in one hand. "You...trespass on this parish property in order to call me a liar.
How dare you, infidel!"

"I dared, as you can see."

The priest tossed his newspaper behind him onto the bench."What have I to do with a child named...Jeanette? The Christ child, you can't mean...."

"Damed false piety!" The priest withheld his assault, for he was poised to hit back at Grant, whom he saw as one of the devil's own. "I ask you the same question, Father That little girl is yours...."

"What little girl...for God's sake?"

"Oh, come, come now, Father Casper. You knew Mary...she is the mother. I am certain of that. She said that you...." The Priest held up his hand, as if to silence Grant. Nuns were strolling abouton the grounds, in the garden.. This stranger had cast the first stone. "She is not mine, for certain. Has nobody else applied for fatherhood? I don't recall a a parishoner...."

The ex-Priest's question so angered Grant that he wanted to strike the Prelate with his fist. "You are the father, by the mother's confession."

"Confession!" the Priest exclaimed. He lowered his voice in an ominous threat of attack. "You sully the rite of confession!"

"No Priest is perfect, and you are not perfect even though you ar...or were... a Priest of the Franciscan order."

"Shame, let the shame be yours and not hers. Do you stand there in simple-mlinded arrogance and accuse me of some, some wicked act...a sin. Are you my father confessor?"

"I'm an ordinary mortal who perceives that a wrong has been done."

"Well, look into your infidel textbook and see if a priest, committed to remain celebate, can father a child."

"Priests sometimes disobey their orders...and they disobey God."

The Father gasped at his assailant's audacity. "Then let Him strike me down if I am telling a lie."

"Take care, Father Casper. God is alive and watching." The Priest momentarily turned away, so speechless he was unable to converse with his verbal assailant.

Then he said, "Since you cannot prove the paternity of the little girl and you falsely accuse me--you a false witness in violation of the ninth commandment--you accuse me of illicit of paternity...adultery...breaking the seventh commandment... perhaps you wish to bring suit against the Catholic church for what you allege is my transgression."

"There, you have hit it! But that isn't to say that proof does not exist."

"Hearsay! If you think physical traits are the proof of paternity, forget it. The child that brings you here to these sacred grounds is another man's ...misdeed. I have heard them all. I have many look-alikes among my parishoners who have no blood ties to one another."

"You avoid what's most needed--sincerity and honesty."

"Do you stand there on church grounds and accuse me of a cardnal sin...first of adultery and then the crimes of dishonesty and disloyalty?"

"I could not have said it better." The Priest was now worked up into an frenzy of rage and threatening pitch of retaliation. "Get off these grounds!" he shouted, his raised voice reaching the ears of two nuns.

"Not until you admit to the paternity of the child."

The accusation was so blunt and disingenuous that at first Father Casper could not believe what he was hearing.

"What, you would use force." he shouted, "to extract a false confession. You are the devil's disciple, indeed!"

"I won't listen to any more of your denials." With those words, Grant struck the father full in the face, causing him to fall to the ground. Casper got up, saw he was not seriously hurt, a little blood perhaps, rubbed his chin, then set to against Grant with his Irish fists. He, too, was a fighter. They fought for a full minute until the two sisters, who had heard the ruckus, came running to break up the fight.

"What are you doing...sir?" one of them asked. "What are you doing on these church grounds in the first place...and fightiang with one of our priests?"

"He lays false charges against me. Sister Winifred. I shant tell you now. But they are false."

The other Sister lent her weight to the resistant Grant, who remained, his arms and hands at ready in the event the Priest tried to assault him. "Will you please leave this instant, sir, before any more trouble occurs!"

"Oh, I will," said Grant. "As for you, Father Casper, the next enemy you will encounter in your garden of pious denial is my lawyer. He will have some words with you."

"Get out of here, you heathen, you interloper, you henchman of the devil!" the Priest cried, and made as if to run at Grant and strike him again, when one of the Sisters stepped between them. Facing Grant, she said, "Don't you think you have caused enough trouble for one day?"

"That little child will not become an orphan...because of you, damned Priest!"

The Sisters turned pale at this curse and in a phalanx of two they pressed toward Grant to urge him to go." He turned and walked through the iron gate onto the street where he looked back to see the two nuns and the priest following his footsteps. He heard one of the nuns ask, "Who left that gate unlocked...?" With but a few details missing, this was essentially the story he told Mary the next time they met, which was at Penelope's door. It was the child Mary had been thinking about, not about herself, when she urged that she and Grant visit an orphanage. "She certainly did not expect to find Jeanette there, God help her!" Grant thought. The father would not be attending the book discussions for a while.

BRAVE INDULGENCE

This morning, he was determined not to let a tree squirrel, or Mary's conscience for animal rights or even the prospect of rain deter him from his morning's love for the lake and for fishing. The trout would be hungry and feeding this early in the day, when the sun broke yellow through the gray overcast. "I can show her how to bait a hook," he thought with some amusement. "She knows only how to bait an adding machine." Mary narrowed her eyes as she watched Grant prepare for their lake trip. She undestood motivation better than most young women her age. It was a gift. She saw the anxieties of age in her mother. She grasped with a quck mind his ambition to enjoy the day, nothing more. The forest, which, heretofore, had somewhat frightened her now attracted her with its beauty, its hidden life, its special smell of mouldering duff and warm pine needles. There was an hypnotic essence to the woods she had never suspected existed. The forest breathed its fine pungent odor of decaying needles and warming tree bark. A slight breeze soughed in the high branches. Mary seemed to him diffident, not uncaring, but with her thoughts some place other than here. He was sorry that he might have compromised her virtue. She need not, however, divulge their excursion, not even to the old woman, especially not to her. He glanced at his camouflaged canoe, lashed to his truck, looked in the bed to confirm the presence of paddles and life vests The tent with ropes and stakes was packed and stowed in place. Not speaking to her, he verified that his fishing pole and tackle box were under the mid-thwart seat, as they always were lest he forget where he had put them.

"This morning, we go out on the lake, Whiskeytown Lake...I want to do a little fishing."

"What kind of fish...?"

He looked at her as if she had uttered nonsense. "Trout...some big ones...over a foot long. We have some fruit in the refrig. We'll have a fish dinner tonight...at my cabin" He scattered dirt on the small campfire he had built to warm his hands by. They had shared a tin pail of hot coffee. The gist of the morning was happiness and the convenience of primitive living. He kept a list in his mind of things they must do to augment their shared pleasure, not the least of which was picking wild blueberries. His love for tlhe woods came by instinct. It was not manufactured by peddlers of boats or leviathons of camping accessories. He watched Mary's face to discern the level of her pleasure; he saw the sparkle in her eyes. This delighted him almost as much as the realities of the scene. The campfire sent up a thin tendril of smoke. "It will die," he thought.

They climbed into the cab of his pickup, a piece of rope, a wrench of some description and other stuff on the floor, the ancient seat fabric torn in places. But the truck was as reliable as a horse, Grant thought. Anyway, here in the woods, "appearances are the conceit of civilization." They started down the dirt road to the lake. Its rain-trenched surface and sizeable potholes made the trip a rough journey. The hood rattled, a deer crossed the road, a huge wind-blown tree branch lay alongside the way.

"How far is it, Grant?"

"About ten miles." He looked around him as he drove along. In another month the branches of those trees will be loaded with snow.

They did not speak until the road broke into a view of the lake. The calm expanse of the morning lake surface stretched out before them, mists softly rising from the gray water with the warming sun. .

He parked, loosened the canoe's cinch s traps, then pulling it off stood it on end. He walked beneath it, lowering it onto his shoulders and took off in the direction of the water's edge where, again, first standing the craft on its bow, he lowered it into the water.

She had the life vests, he returned to the truck for the paddles. "Well, get in." She stepped into the canoe, cautiously stepping forward to seat herself at the bow end. With a scraping sound, he pushed the canoe off the sandy beach. When he stepped in, reflexively, she grabbed the gunwales and peered over them into the shallow water. He sat down Using one paddle for leverage, he pushed the craft until it floated free of the grip of land. Within minutes, they were paddling out onto the lake.

"There's coves here with blueberries. We'll find one and pull in and help ourselves." He had brought along a pail. They glided along for about a quarter of a mile, he looking into each alcove to discover the lucious fruit hanging on vines that dripped with stheir fruited weight. Within minutes, his sharp eye spotted a cove, its berry-laden vines overhanging the water. The roots of a shore juniper tree rose from out of the water. The new light brought out the reds in the leaves of poison oak and the soft yellow-browns of the bark. She stood first, while he steadied the boat. Gripping the baille, she partially filled the pail, eating to her fill, her lips turning blue. When his turn came, he also ate a breakfast of blueberries and finished filling the pail.

"Nice, huh?" he asked her. She nodded. Together they back-paddled out of the cove and into the deeper part of the lake.

"How deep is this lake?"

"Some folks say about eight-hundred feet...how would they know unless they dropped a line and sinker? That's where the town lies--down on the bottom. It used to be a town called Whiskeytown.

"A town!"

"Oh, sure. When the dam was finished and the canyon filled; water backed up against the dam and covered the town."

"Really! You mean...the houses, and stores?"

"One hotel and the tavern and other things."

"Unbelievable! I'd like to go down there and look around."

"I've often thought the same thing...Good idea...furnish diving gear, go down there and have a look around, take a few photographs."

"Maybe find a souvenir pot and...check out the furniture."

"No, folks who lived there took everything with them when the waters came. But just seeing the rooms where they lived...that would be exciting."

"Wouldn't it though! A subterranean village." He unlashed his fishing pole from beneath the thwart seat, took out his tackle box from the same location, baited a hook with a piece of last nights squiurrel meat...he had shot a squirrel and not told Mary and she had relished the taste of the flesh as wild rabbit. With a light lead sinker attached to the filament line, he flung the hook into the water with an overhand whip of the pole. He liked the sing of the spinning reel as it payed out the line.

They fished for almost an hour, hardly speaking a word. They padded, at his suggesion to a place where there was a current, at the upper end of the lake where the creek's incoming waters broke the tranquility of the lake.   At last he felt a tug on the line. He jerked the pole to set the hook and began to reel in a leaping, thrashing ten inch lake trout. He whacked its head on the gunwale and dropped it into a burlap sack. "Tonight it's fish for dinner," he said.

Their chilly, eventful morning melted into the early afternoon warm, moist air. The mists had long ago, after floating above the chill night water,   dissipated finally with the rising sun. The couple out on the lake in their green canoe paddled in toward the shore, steerilng for the opening in the shore timber where he spotted the truck. Wih stiffness, Mary negotiated the length of the canoe and stepped on solid round. He retrieved the paddles and safey vests, strapping his fishing pole and tackle box to the seat miship. He reversed his procedure, upending the canoe then portaging it to his truck and lashing it down, while Mary brought up the other gear, the vests and paddles. Their returning trip to their campsite, although struck before the start of the trip to the lake, would suffice for the evening meal. Grant removed his single catch from the burlap sack. He cut fillets on the tailgate of his truck They would camp out at their overnight spot before descending down the mountain to his cabin at the sawmill. He wanted to spend as much time as he could with Mary, for his feelings had begun to work on his heart and to affirm that she could be his wife. He tried to put the idea out of his head; he had been disappointed so many times. He settled for her companionship at this time in their relationship. Someone would have to tell hiim that this junket into the mountains had become a part of their courrtship, a perfectly respectable situation, always with its compromises dangers and mistakes.

Now, according to his plan, he found two rather flat stones. He settled them in his rekindled fire. On their flat surfaces he placed the trout fillets. They discussed her work at the exchange, its boredom of figures, its interestilng, at times haphazard, speculations of the brokers, the utter foolishness of counting on tomorrow's gains and losse, the striking reluctance of brokers to gamble, although they were often considered high-rollers. He talked about his simple life-chore of cutting firewood, almost a beggar's occupation. He combined the skill with chimney-craft. He had built quite a numbr of chimneys in the town and out in the woods for settlers and town-dwellers. He took pride in his craftsmanship. He also cleaned chimneys, alhough he had grown a little too rotund to enter the flue, as custom and story tales relate. She sat fascinated by a good man's telling how he copes with life on its terms; the men she associaed withat the exchange wanted to change life on their terms. She puzzled over the differences, but in her puzzlement withheld questions rom himt. Any casual observer would have seen that she had grown fond of him. And so they enjoyed their spare meal of baked fish, with two small loaves of crusty bread he fetched out of his tackle box, and the remainder of the berries they had picked that morning. They ate on a board beween two rocks. A fish dinner, skimpy as sit was, called for the blueberries as a desert. He did not know if he should ask her to stay at his cabin, but he had become so attached to the girl he could not resist. Grant was sufficiently shrewd and self-understanding that he discriminated between love and, as he knew it was called, "a romantic attachment." He had had one such attachment to his fomer wife...he did not reveal that to Mary because he did not want to influence her acceptance of him...or to start her on a quest to discover why they had separated. He had divorced her because she had abandoned him; the matter had proven that simple. Mary would only learn the truth in time. And so they headed for his cabin down at the river. The cabin was his refuge in spirit and in actuality. He wheeled his truck into a small circle of crude cabins close to the river, and shut off the engine, looking at her for her reaction. She raised her eyebrows. When they stepped out of the cab, the whine of the mill saw cutting through a log filled the evening air.

"I live there," he said, " My...dwelling you can call it. It's for me only."

"It's your castle, a small castle, but a castle...."

"I get used to ilt. At one time it was a cabin for a mill hand...those others--same purpose, habitations against deep snows and thick mud that kept mill hands from getting to work. That's my cabin. My castle, as you say. You hear that...that's the sawmill out there. Let me show you. He took her to one side of his cabin and pointed over to the mill, the sun lowering in the west. The land was covered with towering piles of logs stacked in pyramids, their cut butt ends displaying growth rings and the fresh tan-yellow wood of the cuts. Most stacks had from ten to twenty logs high; the height depended on the diameters of the logs. The growl of a skip-loader, an engine for lifting and pushing the logs, moved a bout between them.

"Those logs...the loader stacks them. When he pond boss signals, the loaer dumps, carries and pushes logs into the pond." About then a logging truck arrived and, pulling up parllel to the pond, the skip loader pushed the logs from the truck into the water , each log making a great splash, bobbing then settling to float until eventually guided to the saw. "They float there until they go up that chain ramp. Those sprays wash off dirt and stones that might dull the saw."

"Who's he?" Mary pointed to a figure, black in the silhouette light who hopped about on the floating logs.

"Oh, he's the poleman, the stick he uses is called a peevy. He pushes and prods the logs to guide them to the log washer...up the chain ramp over there."

"He doesn't ever lose his balance...?"

No, he wears boots with nails in the soles...corks, they're called...that bite into the bark and keep him from slipping off and falling in betweens the logs. Great rafts of logs like these in early days were floated down the rivers from the cutting sites."

"Why didn't they just build saw mills closer?"

"Logistics...the lumber is picked up closer to where it it used, in towns and cities? Last winter...the river delivered the logs free...river over flowed and so did the pond...free floating logs. I heard one bump into my cabin in the middle of the night. River waters flooded the mill for almost a week. Logs in the pond floated south..."

"They couldn't find them..."

"Finders keepers. Some floated onto the river banks "

"The mill should brand the logs...like stock on the range."

"Don't think the mill owners haven't thought of that."

"They make pretty big driftwood."

"A free-floating log is a battering ram, don't you know."

Grant was enjoying his role as a tour guide of the saw mill. He pointed out the lengthwise piles of newly-cut logs that surrounded the mill pond. Their ponderous barkround height with the fresh-cust ends showing growth rings were intimidting to a stranger in the logging mill yard. "Over there, that funnel thing with the smoke coming out of it burns the chips and sawdust conveyed on that overhead belt." He stopped to regard other activity at the mill. He beathed in deep draughts of the smoky and sweet pine-scented air, watching her for a similar response to the fragrance that perneated the surrounding air.

Grant went on. "Then some guy with a crayon grades the cut boards...another loader gathers them up and trucks them out into the yard to dry. Some wood like oak dries faster...more solid, less spongy...not much low-elevation oak left. Drying time can be two weeks or longer,...just depends. A month.... If the stacks are allowed to get too dry, the wood can warp. Sort of like picking melons a little under-ripe."

"Oh, I see," was her comment. He felt at this moment, in a man's world, a certain tenderness toward her, her femininity contrasting to a kind of raw primitivism of the mill site, the the hewing and cutting of the product of nature with its inescapable scents and sounds, the surreal scene of the transformation of trees into lumber for everyman's use--these sensations contrasted to that femininity, its delicate scent of perfume and a woman's clothing, compared to the surroundings of logs and men in soiled dungarees, jeans and crushed hats and with grimy faces, all contributing to a sense of the controlled violence that belonged to nature's transformation by the entire milling operation.

He took her to the interior of his cabin where he invtied her to freshen up. She washed up while he removed his canoe and, placing it across two sawhorses, he chained it down to stanchons. He removed the tent and put it under his cabin, taking care to stow the life vests and paddles with the tent. He then went inside. They would enjoy a supper he would prepare from weiners and saurkraut in his refrig. He was determined not to ruin their relationship. He would sleep that night on the floor of the cabin, placing a screen between themselves, converting the one-room cabin into a bedroom and a kitchen by means of a screen he used to block his open front door on scorching summer days. Thus it came about as he planned. She seemed tolerant of his adjustments and modifications to the cabin environment. She even appeared amused by his fluster and energetic preparations. Their night under this arrangement transpired with hardly a word between them, the screen sepaating their night. He had once seen movie called "It Happened One Night" starring Clark Gable , that had involved a similar room design to comply with the Hayes Office...however, a blanket was used to divide the night for two lovers. Mary slept well. He had bumped about all night on the cabin floor, cushioned by his sleeping bag under a brown army wool blanket. They awakened and dressed early the next morning. He had just enough food for a skimpy breakasfast of bacon and eggs, toast and pineapple juice. He had not planned on her visit, so he thought it best they set out early for her apartment.

Their conversation was spare and practical. "Do you have everything?" he asked her.
"I brought so little...as you know, Grant."
"We'll, be at your mother's place in half an hour."
"I'm peparing lin my mind for her shock.".".
They loaded up, chiefly themselves, into his truck and started down the road and into the town to her apartment.
"What will she say?"
"About what..abou my being missing one night?"
"Right."

"Oh, she gets used to her loneliness. After all, I have my life. I know that sounds fllip and selfish." He reflected, "She's so blaze...maybe she has done this before....After all, spending the night in a cabin with a man...even if not in the bed with him...what about protocol? I mean...."

"You'll have a chance to meet the mad Priest."

"Mad? A Priest?"

"The news was filled with his activities...last year, down in Panama. He's an anarchist...."

:An anachist...a lawless Priest...a loose canon...no double meaning...in the church!"

"That's what the paper said..a murder suspect also."

"My God, a representative of the Christ...returned the solution." She did not understand the implication of his word, solution. :"Anarchy--that's an ideology, Mary. Strictly an ideology."

"It's more than that...when he puts his ideology to work."

"Madness is not a reality, in any event," he said.

"To believe in heaven can be called mad...because it is...well, not of this world....not a reality."

"My God! You mean...Kingdom madness..."

"Not funny," she said.

"Then why do you...censure the man for his faith?"

"I 'm not censuring him for his faith" she pleaded, her face changd into a gentle scowl in self-defense. "...Madness, if it is not a disease, is a delusion."

"Only if the delusion does not match up with realty."

"Even if it does...a conviction can be called mad."

"Now you're getting off into the paranormal," he replied. "... like a malaprop...not real...like a vision...not real, a nightmare...all sorts of imaginings out of fhe context of reality."

"Well, what he did...or at least I read that he did...was to collect arms and money to liberate a village from a dictator Trujillo."

"As any soldier might do...even the President...only he's a soldier with an ideological mission. He's an ideologue." He uttered the words as he if pronouncing a death sentence.

"Who appears to other men as mad."

"I think that's the truth," he said with some satisfaction. He would meet this priest and see if he was right.

"Well, then, since he plans to discuss St, John, he had better be careful... he might accuse Christ's disciple of madness."

"Hah...."

"You scoff...." When she looked at him her whole visage was fixed in a disapproval of his reply.

"Only, it seems to me," said Grant, "if he denies that his Christ is the way, the truth and the life.... I mean, then he is mad because he denies his own ...well, I call it...inner reality. I once knew a baloonist who thought reality was baloon flight, leaving the earth."

"Well, fantasy is another matter," she said. It pleased him immensely that she was willing to engage in such exotic conversation, not that he rated a woman on her erudition...But it helped if he could ...well, discuss what had always intrigued him at the university--the paranormal, psychology gone awry, the backside of frontal reality. "We shall see what mad argument he presents. And, Grant...do be kind."

"Kind...?" He thought, "What does she mean by that?" He turned the wheel suddenly to avoid hitting a squirrel. "We shall search with him for a benevolent madness other men call insanity." He sounded pontifical. Devotion can be construed as madness...for poets and lovers." They laughed together."I'd like to ask your Priest about transmutation of the elements."

"He'll explain if you ask him. Have you ever read Saint John?"

"You mean, in the bible?"

"Yes, the same. We were talking about madness. There is going to be a mad priest there...Father Casper."

"Mad...a Priest. Madness is a condition...psychological, social."

"Oh, I know. He is mad to convert others...I think l that is its source."

"Well. I should like to meet this priest." He pulled up to her apartment. He did not finish his thought. "I don't think I ought to go up...your mother...." She fitted the key into the lock as a deliverman bounded up the steps and left a package at the door for another resident in the apartmenty in the apartment.

"You won't forget, Grant...seven tonight... you promised..."

"Sure, sure...Saint John, the disciple.... I'll try my best to be...useful."

"Oh, you qilll vw...juar rhink of our meeting as a visit to the forum, a house of cabals...
...a board room meeting...whatever. You can just listen if you want to."

They parted, he to his truck and she through the closing door to the apartment house.

That night he drove out to the edge of the town that showed its scattered night lights, its buzzing colored neon signs and desultory life at this hour on almost empty streets. She pointed out the house of their hostess. "Her name is Penelope," she informed him. "She's a reformedr madam...."

"I should know these things...."

"In case you didn't."

"Will I be in her little black book?"

"Grant," she cautioned.

The house was small a cottage with vines over the entrance-way, suggsting to Grant a miniaure dolls house. A stone horse s tood a the curb with a ring in its nose. Grant and Mary apparently were the first to arrive. In respnse to Maryl's rapping with the brass knocker, Penelope swung the door open wide and, the delight of surprise on her face, spread her arms wide to greet Mary. "I see you've brought a recruit this time, Mary. Well, he will have his good time tonight."

"This is my friend, Grant," she said.

"Hello, Grant. I'm so glad you could come." He remained mute, smiled, shook the hostess's hand and stepped over the threshhold, Mary ahead of him. She brought from a table in the doorway atwo insignia which she pinned on her uests. We can;t go a evening in this profound disucssion and not know our names, now, can we? Go in. You, Mary...and Grant, you must first try my punch...over on the center table...ginerale and ven rose...special for the occasion...in the dining room and find chairs."

Small in every detail, the living room contained only a few pieces of funiture, the blinds were faded, a large rug of Oriental design lay on the hardwood floor, and an old player-piano stood austere, black and theatening against one wall. Photographs in oval frames, portraits from another century, hung on the walls, likenesses of her dear departed ancestors. Mary looked about the room.

The hostess turned to greet other arrivals . Mary tugged Grant by his coat sleeve and they walked into the punch table, where they refreshed themselves, he pouring a full dipper into her cup then filling his own cup as both of them stood to observe the action at the front door while sipping as if toasting the arrival of other guests. A professor and his wife were just entering the home. He wore a black blazer, a jaunty hat which he removed, a cravath and beige shirt. A large and ostentatious gold chain draped across his chest...it amused him to hearken back to past embellishments and superstitions of dress--a gold chain , more than a badge of prosperity was a shield against put-downs by by what he would call "desperagte mendicants." St. John occupied a place of astute prominence in his lexicon of notables...for John had not become cannonized for nothing. For what...this night would reveal. His wife was attired in a coat with rabbit fur trim, her name badge, like her husband's, hanging by its brass clip tor all to read. She wore gaiters of gray, a subdued dress beneath her coat. Her husband...his name was Gordon...helped her remove her coat. "In the bedroom, Gordon," the hostess cried out, seeing the activity going on. The wife did not remove a cockle hat of green felt and straw. Around her neck there swung a long necklace of fake pearls and by her side, her small white hand clenched on its handle, there appeared an ebony cane to suggest elegance...both creatures over-dressed for the occasion of a mere book exploration. They were dressed as if to stroll an some high-toned and eminent picture gallery of masterpieces.

They found places in the circle of chairs, cushioned and folding, one ench and an ovestuffed chair for the hostess, as others began to arrive, first a youth student with bright yellow hair in a chamois sweater of malching yellow. HLe obviously was a messenger in his delivelry uniform entered next.   Harvey was the name overheard. As if by instinct, he hastened immediately to the punch table. He rubbed his hands ostentaously. Two artisan laborers, a smithy and a carpenter next entered together. They had sharpened up for the occasion, the carpenter, whose badge name was Claus, came in faded jeans and a cheap-leather coat, his hair down over his ears, a haunting expression in his eyes, eager to learn the truth. The companion to this rough carpenter, a framer no doubt, was Chris, the smithy. He strolled into the room, on his feet the shoes of his work, greased to shine in the light, workingman's clothes, shirt open at the collar and a black, bill- cap. Neither man smiled. The carpenter looked around the room as if measuring its dimensiuons and mysteriously shook his head. His smithy friend gripped the back of one chair as if to spring over it, the heavy hand a heavy hand with thick fingers accustomed to handling heavy metal. On his face was implanted by thought a sort of rhapturous expression, as if he could expect some sort of benevolent revelation. Neither workingman appeared ready to engage in serious debate or intellectual discussion. Upon the customary invitation, these folks, guests for the night's event of enquiry, grouped bout the punch table from which, after nods, a pleasangry or two, then found chairs in the circle. A man who proudly proclaimed himself, aloud to be a lawyer, as if introducing himself to an august assembly, entered the room, bearing his name-badge in his fingers...he would do the installation of so important a symbol...he, too, indulged himself with the miraculous punch, miaculous because it was laced with vodka in addition to the wine. His impeccable brown business suit contrasted with the attire of the laborers. We now could count eight, the hostess making nine, for the occasion. The next pair to enter were a pair Mary reconized vaguely as having some connection to the exchange. she being the more plebian by having urged her spouse to acquire a little more cultivation by attending a book-discussion group. Neither had read St. James but knew that he was worthy of their attention and interestg. There was a bridge and a church named after him. The man, a relatilve newcomer to Penelope's clique, was a banker and, she, of course, was the banker's wife, both came dressed in casual dress, as if for a barbeque. He glanced down to affix his name- badge to a blue blazer while his companion, who could have been his secretary, almost, as it were, flounced into the room. The next pair to arrive and enter were plebian in their dress, laborers it was plain to see, Chris was a carpenter and the smithy was Hammerskold, a Norwegian by birth. They came more out of curiosity, for they usually spent Saturday night at the tavern, having come tonight our of curiosity, simply to voice their thoughts. The found seats in the circle withs the ohers. The next arrivals were the college professor, Dr. Theodore Cranston and his wife Teddy; his big loud voice filled the room when he spoke. He brought with him a certan atmosphere of authority to the session. When Father Casper arrived, he stopped at the gthreshhold and sared at the guests, as if by ways of challenge to their very presence. In his eyes there burned a low fire, on his face the lines sof a thousand confessions he had endured, his expression fixed in an enigmatic scowl, as if ready to contend with any adversary, lincluding the devil. He came and promptly sat down.

When all her guests had found chairs in a circle, Penelope began. If the Father Casper wishes to give a short invocation...we are delving into the spiritual tonight, my friends...he is at liberty to do so. The Priest made the sign of the cross and said simply, "May the words of our mouths and the mediations sof our hearts be acceptable in thy sight, O Lord." He again made the sign of the cross. No one bowed his head. The hostess seemed satisfied with this frame of reference. Penelope stood at the edge of the ring of her uests. There was about the room and the occasion and the asembly of these townsmen an atmosphere, not of enquiry, but of suspicion, as if each ought to find grounds to suspect his neighbor of some selfish act, some indelciate and opporunistic response to another. The blunt reality was that each member of the smalll and temporary circle wore a facade which he and she was fearful of losing in the discussion. The whole thing seemed msore than an academicexercise but, rather, a trial for the devil to do his own kingdom work as they discussed one of the enemy's strategies.

"Tonight," Penelope said, "we want to begin our discussion of the book of St. John with a introduction on the matter of transubstantiation of the elements. But first a brief prayer from our good Father Casper is in order" He prayed. "May the God of Mary our beloved Lord Jesus guide the tempered discussion of the subject of the most glorious St. John. Amen. I see no reason for a discussion of the elements," the Priest said. "They are clearly spoken of as the blood and the flesh, the wine and the bread. You cannot participate in the communion while you doubt the transubstantiation of the elements."

"Meaning, their change."

"Yes, not transmutation.. I do not believe in alchemy...a change of lead into gold...as the Medieval practitioners believed. That is all just superstition."

"Can you show us...I mean, change wine into blood?" Grant asked. Mary regarded him with a twinge of anxiety on her face and moements. Somehow, she appeared feel a fear of him.

The Priest replied, "Transubstantiation is not for display, sir." When he said this his eyes flashed. He turned to Penelope and asked in a loud whisper, "bring me a bottle of wine you put into your punch." Swiftly as if a currieir with a desperate message in her breast, she went into another room and returned with a nearly empty bottle. "Now, a cup, if you would be so kind." The guests watched this activity and exchange of words with great enthusiasm and anticipation.

"I have in this cup," he said. After having poured two thinblefulls of the remaining wine into the cup handed to him by his hostess, he announced, "I have here the wine . I can say an encantation that calls the devil to rescue us, that summons up a demon from hell."

"You woud not do such a thing, said the wife of the Professor.

"The rule of evidence will prevail," said the lawyer.

"A litltle heat tempers the iron, too much heat weakens it."

"I do not wish to perform magic," said the mad Priest, "I am not a magician."

"Well, we want only some evidence of change."

"No, you see there, you wish for me to rertreat lito yourt fantasy world of disbelief. It is madness to believe in what can never exist, the unrealitys of secular disbelief. They retreat into the safety of possessions, of power, of diligent disbelief, with all their mad manaufacture of suffering as a santuary for spiritual weakness." The Priest was going on in this manner when the professor interrupted him. He shifted in his chair, he leaned forward, placing an elbow on one knee.

"Tell us...Father...Father...."

"Casper."

"Father Casper, if you can perorm magic, do so. We will forgive you of your transgression upon your priestly oath of annointing ".

"So you know. No, you cannot tempt me to betray my trust, sir...:Mister Halverson."' The Priest glanced around as the faces of Penelope's guests. He returned the bottle to their hostess, then continued. "I hope you all did; not come here to night expecting me to perform magic." The room was silent. "There are some who call me mad...and who suspect me of having...murdered. I say these things because I ;am protected by the mantle of our Lord. Nor would I speak so openly did I feel guilt...." Again,the room fell silent. "If I believe in the sanctity of human soul, that is madness in the eyes of many. For the soul is ttangibly non existent.."

?What about the heart?" Mary asked, looking directly into the face of Father Casper, as if to read his thoughts and giving a slight shake of her head. She let herseslf sink back against the chair seat.

"That is real, so very real," :the Priest said. "No, I must tell you, for you are all intelligent people, that the society of the angels is not a mad world. I dwell in their company. The dark science of the mind would conjure their rules from the kingdom of darkness...fantasy is acceptable but not real. Illusion enhances the work of artists., delusion requires not the surgery of another mind but the separation of powers of reality and surreality, the actual and the factual from the fabricated and the imaginary."

"I have read in the newspaper, Father Casper," said the wife of the professor, " that you once killed a man." She artfully folded her hands into her lap and regarded him with a look of bright knowlege of his hidden past. Her nature was to judge first, then to confirm her judgement without request for an answer.

"When I was a youth I engaged in combat with the devil, my natural advesary iln

the person of a South American ictator. IL was young then. I killed for a cause. I must tell
you that some of that ...that pastsiche clings to me still.. That was an excuseable killing...not
a murder."

"Ah, Father, sir," said the student, "would you kill a man now...for a belief?"

"No, I think not," said the Priest.

"Then you killed for the belief in...freedom."

"We all entered the conflict with differing ideas, but the cause was the
same...liberty."

Penelope spoke up. "Father Casper, our conversation, our discussion... is starting
to wander. Did we not agree to discuss the book of John in the Holy Scripture?"

"Yes, yes, you are right." He blushed slightly and placed one hand on an arm,
regarding his hostess with a mellow, congenial smile of acceptance of her admonition. As if
surprised at discovering it in his hand, he handed the cup back to the hostess with the
untasted small amount of wine in it. "So you see, my friends, the wine remains to be
returned to the bottle, not to embolden the flesh of the communicants. I perform no tricks. I
am not a dog to perform clever antics" he said with a laugh. Turning somber, he
immediately crossed himself and folded his hands in chaste sobriety for his words. "From
bread and wine into the blood and flesh of our living Lord," the Priest enjoined. The guests
strained to hear their dark Priests telling words. "Doubt is the mark of intelligence," he said.
"Since this is an intellectual discussion, we must move over so as to provide room for our
doubts...lest we perish." The Priest scanned their faces, one at a time, turning his head as he
did so, looking askant at the at the carpenter and the smithy who sat closest to where he lned
forward..

"If I were a magilcian, would I not ask, 'Is it not permissible to do--that I can
levitate that cofee table?; "

"It is good, Father," the wife of the professor replied, not really knowing the
import of her words.

"But then what would I reply? My doubt keeps me from making a fool of
myself." It appeared to the others in the circle that he had struck some sort of final cord in
the thinking of the group. "The Epistle of St John was written to dispel doubts amongst the
folk of the villlage, not to equivocate with the modern age over the rising of Christ from the
tomb, or , indeed, the working of doves," said the Priest, "but the miracle exists independent
of belief, or else the sacrament falls into disagreement and a cabal results."

"My professor would not accept the semeotic dimension of your discussion,"said
the yellow haired youth. "We do not agree on the referents."

"Goodness! Why must we agree? Why must we believe?" the Professor asked.
"Is it not enough to partake and ignore the miracle of the wine and bead?".

"Doubt is a sin," said the Priest.

"Yet does not doubt act as a curative for blind belief?" the Professor asked.

"Let us not get too far astray," said Penelope. Father Casper, as Mary knew, had
entered into Masonry, the fifth order of the Scottish Rites branch. Those of his brothers who
knew of his defection considered him an outcast by his church, or at least under temporary
condemnation. What followed was, in its essence, a confession without remorse or
conciliation. "I am, by nature an anarchist. My early faith sprang from skepticism. I was
able to raise moneys for South American insurgents against the dictatorial regime of Carlos
Reginald Cavalos of Argentina. I am under the conviction that rebellion is the essence of
Chistianity, and in this I am not not alone. " His words seemed to Grant to connote a pitch

for recruits. There was no one member in this circle of Penelopes "Explorers," as she called them, who could fit the design in the Priest's mind. He continued with his explanation: "The Cana wedding, we found, displayd a similar example of the transubstantiation...of water into the finest wine."

The smithy spoke up. "I earn my living shaping hard metal, iron, just as my carpenter friend shapes wood for our houses. Can't we judge of the world as a place for miracles in which God shapes ...the stuff around us...for his use?".

"Rightly so," said the Priest. What you men shape with your hands is shaped by God with his will...or we are all outcasts."

Penelope said . "The glory comes not from men but from the God, does it not?"

"Well said, " Father Casper replied.

"But is not that glory t ainted with man's..sinfulness?"

"Shaped thereby," said the Professor.

"They taught me in class to doubt," said the student.

"Did they not teach you to defy authority?" the Priest enquired.

"If challenge is in fact defiance, then the answer is yes."

"Back to doubt. " The professor slowly leaned back into his ladder-back chair and resting his chin on one open hand, propped up by an arm, he said, "John was ambitious to be loved by the Jesus."

"Do not forget." said the politician, Samar Oreligin, who managed the water-works in the town. "They shared a mutual trust. I cannot do likewise...doubt the invisible. If I doubt the purity of the water we drink, would I not do something about it...or present the problem to the city council? Purity is invisible when it comes to water...unless, of course, the rains...."

"Now we get into politics," the Priest interrupted.

"John tells how James was stoned as the first martyr for his faith. For those who believe, we can expect to be stoned at some time in our lives. That's the judgement of the world." This pontification came from Penelope. Shes stepped in closer to the ring and, like a transient mendicant, scanned from one face to the next. She tightened one earring on her ear lobe. She would not appear too aloof and pure of heart.

"We are all outcasts." The Priest's lips began to move. They showed pink through his black beard. Penelope uttered an apology for the spiritual nature of the session . She reminded her small assembled band that this was a secular discussion, not a religious study clinic to talk about heaven's truths but to ferrlt out man's secular mission in this world...not radical theology but benevolent...investigation. The Priest went on at length about his mission to comfort the needy, to supply the poor...   By all of these things she intended to reduce the tension between men in readiness for their enlightened exchange of ideas. Grant sighed inwardly. He wondered what he had missed in St. John's overview of the life of Christ. Few knew that the townsmen, those in the know, suspected the Priest of murder. The suspicion was so vague as to have little relevance to reality, yet the nature of the suspicion froze into place prejudice against him. In this circle he could bond with skeptics, among whom he was most comfortable. Withal, he remained an anarchist with a hidden mission to instill righteous rebellion against the state in the souls of his parishoners, among whom was one, Mary, who had this night sat before him and in his presence. Furthermore, to widen his scope of militaristic operation, he had joined the Masonic lodge. This adulteration of his Priest's calling had offended his church bretheren, and had outraged lay members of his parish whose lives he knew more about than they ever suspected. He was not to be trusted. Only Penelope understood this transgression. Few parish members had learned the awful news of Father Caspers spiritlual delinquency.

"Many of us are touched by the nature of transsubstantiation of the bread and the wine." She looked straight into Father Casper's eyes and he nodded in affirmation.
"That is so. I have heard many confessions of the sinner's doubts, like the prayers of the athielkst. Penelope went on. Transmutation is another thing--lead into gold...a trick of the imagination, a magic like the Pharoah's magicians performed before Moses. Transmutation does ot change the nature of the elements if you are an athiest." Again the Priest nodded. "No one in the group knew that the Priest was no longer a member of the St. Boniface Parish, that he had narrowoly escaped criminal indictment for murder, but his priestly attire, his station as a Priest and his unertain movements about the town had partially obscured him from suspicion and arrest for interrogation. Nobody really wanted to put a Priest of the faith in jail as a common criminal, yet Mary knew of this past and had not mentioned it in any suggestion it Grant.

The Priest continued with his discourse.
"Then John is right when he writes that the Christ is the way, the truth and the life. Any beyond that pale men can consider themselves outcasts."
"The word causes me to tremble, said the messenger. I cannot deliver a message on my wheel that betrays distrust." lThis announcement, which showed as preposterous on the Priest's counstenance, was followed by the admission that "every fibre of my soul rebels against doubt." He felt that the cliche was relevant to the general discussion, but she was wrong.
"How do you know these things?" the Professor asked.
"Yes, how do you know?" his wife echoed.
'I cannot say for sure. Trust is a part of the bargain of communication. If we do not trust, then we do not accept and often we do not listen. We perish for a want of understanding...."
"The young man is right," said the carpenter. "When I put up a scaffolding, I trust that it will withstand my weight."
"When I put hot metal to the anvil, I trust that each blow I strike will cosntribute to the shape of the finished thing, horseshoe, barrrel hoop or whatever I am asked to make."
"We are not on the main focus," said Penelope. John mentions the helper , theHoly Spirit. We, if we think about it, are chosen ones."
:"That is supercilious and elitist, " said the Professor.
"Yes, that is so, his wife echoed. She smoothed out the fingers on one of the black gloves in her lap. .
"We must seek the spirit of the truth," said Penelope.
"Yet that spirit eludes us, sometimes,:\" said Mary. Grant looked closely intos her face to discern the meaning of her words. He had come to realize that there was about her an element of posturing, not clever or deceptive so much as vailn in the show.
The Priest reminded the group of John's message of he trials. "Why do you suppose he puts those trials into his book?" the Priest asked.
The lawyer, a man named Bartok, Frank Bartoke, spoke out. "Those trials were not to test the apostle Christ..."
"Prophet and savior," the Priest interrupted.

37.

"...Not meant to test him but to try Caiphus to see if he was loyal to Rome. Christ was secondary. How do I know this...reason will show you that Caiphus at once condemned Christ, without so much as a grain of salt for evidence. He condemned him on hearsay evillence...not because there was no conicting evidence...for he had seen the prophet teaching on Jerusalem streets, but because he wanted to stamp into the mind of Procurator Pontius Pilate that he was a loyalist to Rome. An argument might have raised suspicion .Your interpretation is only partially correct, Mister Advocate." The Priest wore a wry smile of disdain on his face when he addressed the lawyer.

"If you think Pontius feared the apostle, you are right. Yet he feared Rome more. Caiphus was but a means to power, a feather in the wind by which Pilate tested the winds of rebellion among the people. Saint John tells us that the trials were at night," responded the Priest. "A trial at night was an illegal trial yet..never mentioned... a nilght rial was frought with supersition. The people of those times were very superstitious...which accounted for much of their rejection of the Christ. They suspected him of dark deeds because of his powers to heal...his miracles...."

"You are right,but the factor of time...the Jewish holiday was important to brilng to a quick end the death, burial of Christ... the whole deal...a conspiracy of the pharisees and the sadducees with satan, the supplicants of his sect...."

"Sect! ...Now you call our faith a sect," the Priest countered.

"It was made to seem so by those who hated Christ."

" You gloss over the evidence of treachery...by the Jesuitical Jew-haters." the yellow-haired student proclaimed, rubbing his faint beard with a ringed hand.

"Zionism was relevant in those times,...you as a lawyer must admit that it was," the Professor aledged.

"But then the sadducees, who were the real rule-makers, would have him and his own rules expelled," the Profesor reasoned.

"What does John say?" said the smithy, the carpenter stirring as ifhe wantsded to speak and to raise his hand. ."That he is the way, the truth and light," the smithy concluded.

"Merely figments of the imagination, poetic nonsense, " said the Priest, to the immense astonishment of all who were present, including the skeptical youth and the learned Professsor. There came a gasp from someone in the circle. "What I mean to say is, that we look to the language as real when in fact it is only symbolic."

"It is madness to consider symbols as the real...." said the lawyer. Grant thought of his conversation with Mary on their way down from the camp site in the mountains.

"That is right...and for that reason, I cannot recant my belief that my work among anachists of the faith is useful...it is both symbolic and real.".

Penelope spoke up as if to explain. "The father is...involved in ...in freeing enslaved peoples of theworld."

"That is my mission," said the Priest. Mary, who had remained silent, looked at Grant as if settling on the final word, mission. .The smithy punched the carpenter affectionately in one shoulder. The professor's wife adjusted her cane in her hand for comfort. The professsor smiled and rubbed his chin in cointemplation of the Priest's words. Each member around the circle responded in a small way to the Priest's recognition of the mission he had been exposed for in the local newspaper. Gathering in their skepticism, he said, "I would not cheat you of understanding, beloved."

"Beloved," the youth expired, shaking his head in disbelief. He murmured under his breath, "I am not his beloved...." That a Priest should call a room full of strangers and disbelievers offended the youth's sensibilities.

There occurred a long silence before Grant spoke....to test the mettle of the Priest's religious delusion that had given rise to the madness of homicide...if what the papers had said of him was correct. Mary in her simple ignorance fostered only by her love of life...and of animals...did not enter into his thoughts at this time. He believed that he had found the chink in Priest Casper's armor of faith that had erected a structure of awsome piety, from which he could slay the dragon, of doubt, could, in a word, examine the character of evil generated by a misguided religious faith. Grant thought, "You will stand in eternal punishment if you judge without a cause. Lest you darken your soul, desist, Grant." He was laying upon his conscience these flagillating oaths of condemnation, yet he did not reckon their source at this time.

"If I am with the Priest's accused, then I understand what it means to be accused, to stand with the anarchists, the outcasts." The banker spoke up. "I had a customer who accused me of cheating him. What could I do to defend myself? I had to open my ledger."

"Rightly so," said the Professsor. Even the faculty at the school are vulnerable to such examinations."

"Yes, they have caused my husband much headache," said the wife.

"Why the scouring if the truth is already out?" the student asked.

"Pilate was very official in all he did. He saw Caiphus as just another politician who threatened his authority in Jerusalem." The lawyer scanned their faces for a reaction.

"We must always assess the consequences of evil all aroumnd us," the Priest enjoined with a smug piety, as if he were looking into his own soul. That is the substance of the Scripture...the authority of God, of the Christ, of Mary."

"And if we disbelieve...?" The messenger with polished boots had at last entered the discussion. His timidity had cast him intos the role of listener.

"It is better to disbelieve than to doubt. A double-minded man is condemned in the good book," said the Priest. "He is, furthermore, a dangerous person. He is unpredictable...."

"Sure, and if Joseph of Aramethaea had not opened up his tomb for the Christ, would he have been among the doubters?" the wife of the Professsor asked, a qusiver iln her voice and tracisng a rug pattern at her toe with the end of her cane.

"That is irrelevant,: said her husband. "No man'smere courtesy confirms his faith...as kneeling. K;neeling is a coutest...so Hitler considered it."

"Hitler was a felonious bigot, a demon of the pit, a parasite on the German people."

"Not so, said Mary. The offering was not mere courtesy but necessity. For a dead body stinketh....not John's exact words...common practice required burial by sundown on death day."

"We come then to the matter of witnesses," said the youthful messenger, wiping a spot from one of his boots..

"And also believers," said the Priest.

"We have only John for our authority...the stories as told by Luke, Mathew and Mark are at a variance," the lawyer suggested.

"Well. then appearances were everything," said Penelope.

"I can go along with that," said the Professor, who absentmindedly thumbed through the text in his lap. "We are usually not what we appear to be...although some of us are better at disguises than are others."

The Priest smiled, as did the professor's wife. The student shrugged his shoulders, the uneasy messener shifted in his chair and recrossed his booted legs. He sat backward, tilted awkwardly in his chail, giving it a loud crack. Penelope scanned her guests to ascertain if hey were comortable. 'Feel free at any time to get up and try my punch...and ma petite bon monger."

"Whatever that means," Grant thought.

"I know we have hardly begun to discuss John tonight," Penelope said, "but we can continue on another night. The discussion appeared to lapse for want of a new idea.

Penelope again invited her guests, "Come now, we are not through...we have just begun. If some of you would like a little refreshment, I have brought in canapes and more ice for the wine gingerale over there on the dining room table. "This not exactly the wedding at Cana, but...you understand." The remark drew a small laughter.

Grant and Mary exchanged careful looks. The discussion had been all too brief. He motioned to her, they stood and went into the other room to mingle with the guests who seemed embarrassed by their dilfferences of station and appearance. Grant lookd closely into Mary's face. She did ot turn to face him. He thought that he saw--perhaps he imagined it--a transition between calm beauy and an internal readiness to speak out, to lash out at an idea, to flay an old consequence aroused by the discussion, which even she did not fully understand. She looked almost as if she were ill. "Are you okay?" he asked her

She nodded. His mind went back to the account she had told him, when they first met, about her intransigent father, his cruelty and indifference toward her mother, and heir bitter their quarrels. What could this brief discussion, not even that, on religion have to do with that past of this woman whom he was starting to love? He set the brooding thought aside for the time being. He sought in his imagination a way to remove her and himself from the group. Penelope came to the rescue when she said, "We all of us want to thank Father Casper for his appearance here tonight, his elevated wisdom and his intellecual insights ino the book of Saint John." Turning to him directly, she said, "I speak for all of us, Father. You made our evening enriched."

" What do you think, Grant?" Mary asked as they stood in one corner of the small dining room to indulge in the sandwiches and wine drink.

He leaned close to her ear and said to her, "I doubt that your Priest is such a doubter. It's certain that he doubts. It's just a question as to what he puts doubts on...his Church, mankind, the grave, the book he espouses...."

She drew away from him. "Self-doubt is a dangerous thing," she said.

Her words baffled him.

TRAILSIDE

I caught sight of her through the twisted, gliding brass poles and the oscillating, jumping wooden horses of the merry-go-round. She came around to me where I stood to one side and laughed and tried to sweep off my black felt hat, then her small arm reached out for the brass ring, she failed to snatch it . Momentarily, and here she came, up and down and down and up, circling round to the organ music of the band behind the glittering octagonal mirrors and the crowns of glistening colored lights played its insane trombones, drumming music. It was a show. The wind of the next revolution of the gaudy, brassy macine brushed my face, She held the ring out to me, that semseless laughter of a woman having a time of simple good fun. The huge merry-go-round engine came at last to a stop, as the checker, with goatee and red hair, wearng a Tyrolean hat, came around. Putting the brass ring from her hand into his apron pocket, he handed her a pass in the form of a stamp on her hand. Mary invited me to take the horse behind her, which I did, paying the guide of the horse-ring the proper fare. "Within minutes, off we started again, each time she eyed the arm that fed the rings, held out for the riders, of whom there were five or six. This challenge for the ring went on for another ten minutes until, the band played out and the circular trip came to an end, aswe slowly coasted to a stop.

"Did you like the ride?" she asked me. I gave her an arm around hug and a peck on her cheek.

"Like it was forever," I said to her. We walked out into the freshening ocean breeze on the pier, where other sightseers, lovers, strollers, fisherfolk, their poles cast over the railing, decorated the rough boards sof the ancient structure. We walked past other sights, entertailning arcades, a ride into the night sky, the ferris-wheel, a restaurant. I asked her if she would like a hotdog, she said not now. We strolled n. at the end of the pier, I said, "This is intoxicating."

"Vry, the air, salty...listen..." We heard the music of the merry go round in the distance and the shouts of several children. More closely came the sound of the surf breaking over the rocks a hundred yards away, out there in the darkness. The foam seemed to phloresce when it broke upon the invisible rocks. "A place to swim to....out there, to those rocks in the dark?"

"In the dark...Are you out of your mind.?"

"I like eerie ventures."

"...Well...not tonight, Grant."

I said to her, "What about our going on a ride on real horses?"

She thought that was a superb idea and grabbed my arm. "I know where we can rent a couple of horses."

"We'll go then."

"I don't have to be persuaded." She seemed thrilled with the idea of a horseback ride for an outing.

"There are some great trails off off into the local hills."

"Real trails, not like the merry go round...lets." That was all we said that night about the excursion . Our next outing would take us to the Grandstand Stables in the nearby town of Russet.

Wearied by watching her daughter begin to fall in love with...this nondescript peddler of vitrue...her inner thought about the matter, since Mary had mentioned Grant's generous lifestyle, her chaperoned trip to the ;mountains, the fun they had had at the square dances, the mother monitored these outings with an overly-cautious air of supreme authority, the mother felt she ought to call on her brother for an opinion. Mary's father was long gone from the home, so it seemed. And now, the uncle enters upon the scene of Mary's life. It seemed to Grant that "my girl" as he called her, was being manipulated by her relatives, first and most officious, her mother and then, her uncle, who had never played any role in Mary's life. In fact, the last time she had seen Clyde was at her father's angry deparure from their household back on their farm in Virgnia.

Uncle Clyde had knocked on the apartment door on this very day while Mary was enjoying her horseback ride at the stables in Russet. He was a short man with a heavy brow, blonde eyebrows, a shock of wavy blonde hair, moustache, sporting a cane with an elegant carved handle. He vilrtually invited himself into the apartment. Oh, Clyde, its so good to see you, the old woman sald effusively, giving her brother a peck on the cheek. He paused, scanned the aparment with some slight disapproval on his face...it did not contain books, glassware and lamp stands he would have praised ...and he came in, took a chair at the motion of his sister.

"Clyde, I'm so glad you could come," she repeated, asslif she had run out of words. He swept back his bonde hair, attempted a cryptic smile and shifted his cane, to place his hands, cupped one atop the other on the head of the dragon. I thought it might become an important matter, like bills, or a suit at law...or whatever. After all, you are my sister."

"And Mary is your neice."

"I have never disputed that," the uncle said with some aspersity. "Mary is a charmer. She is a fav orite of mine...

The mothers eyebrows raised.

"Go on, Clyde."

"Well, what can I say. The invitation was yours. Surely you must have some reason for this...occasion."

"Yes, Mary is becoming wild of late."

"Wild...?

" "Yes...this young man she has been seeing of late...I don't...well, I don't especially like his...attentions."

"Oh, Francine, perhaps you make too much of them;.

"Not at all, notat all.".

"What have you observed, dear sister?

"That his affections are...they can threaten an innocent girl like Mary."

"Oh, Francine, you called me all the way over to here to tell me that a young man is trying to court.. that's the word...court your daughter."

"If it were just a matter of courtship, I would have no qualms."

"What is the problem, then...I don't see." He leaned back against the chair's cushioned back and regarded his sister with a hard, steady and piercing look.

"I don't understand."

" I don't trust him...,I don't trust him."

"But surely you trust your own daughter."

"She can be taken advantage of. She is such a good-hearted girl...and you remember...the child, oh, yes, the child and such trouble she brought!"

"Your daughter is a grown woman, Francine." Then The uncle was stricken into silence. He tried to laugh the matter away. He tapped the toe of one boot with the end of his cane. "I would not give that aspect any further thought. Your daughter is a grown up woman now, Francine." he repeated to his sister. "She can take care of herself."

"That's what I'm afraid of...."

"He sounded as if he emitted a sigh, leaned his head back against the chair rest and studied the small ceiling chandelier. He thought long and carefully about this detail of...courtship, if that was what he thought it was and not, an illicit attraction, as his sister appeared to assumed of the relationship. Clyde Wesler was not a man to be trifled with, owning as he did several millions in railroad stock and being in charge of a manufacturing plant in another city. At fifty he was still a bachelor, too much involved in the market to give much attention to romance. He had his wits, his good temper, and his common human wisdom. It seemed to him that his sister was getting all worked out of shape over nothing, the normal and natural attentions of a young man to his neice, Mary, who had gone through her hardships, as heaven knows.

"May I tender a word of caution, dear sister." He sat forward in his chair, glancing at the door, listening for footsteps in the corridor outside. "Let Mary manage her own life. Do not insist on your way...Oh, I know you well, Francine...your want to assume the voice and image of authority...controlling...." The sister sat bolt upright in the dining-room chair. She respected her older brother, up to a point. However,, this time she chose to listen. "Let things happen naturally...I caution our. You can gain no whit or balance in this juggling act..." The sister looked wide-eyed at her brother. "That's exactly what it is...balance your feelings against your daughter's attitude and his ...she wanted to say lust...his attentions..."what's his name?...Grant. I try to be fair and even-handed."

"Just my point. keep your hand out of their relationship, Francine. I precaution you. Do not take my advice without heeding my words. Let their relationship go where it will. Perhaps she will put an end ot it...or he will grow tired of...pursuit."

"Pur..." She did not finish the word.

"Yes, that's what it is called in the world of romantic attachment... pursuit. In the world of the animals...."

"Clyde...!" she responded with astonishment. He was a biologist, what could she expect, even as a sister? Thus was her train of thought set ajar. "Well, I must make my feelings known."

"You can, you can... simply show a chilliness toward the man.. Take no interest in his attentions. That only gives them a value you decline. After all, momentary attachments usually die of their own accord."

"Since you bring good will, dear brother...."

43。

"Always, Francine, you are my sister."

"I will heed your advice." He moved his cane to a fore position at his his knees, and pushing down hard, managed with slight difficulty to stand. He had sustained a permanent disability in a car accident as a youth. His gait had not crippled his brilliant mind, however. And so he left his sister with the feeling that she had gotten through to him, and that his advice came with good will, and that although his words contained no...instructions... as to what she ought to do or to say to her daugher's suitor, she had listened seriously to his spoken thoughts. On this note of decisive indecision, as it were, brother and sister departed for the afternoon.

"Do come back...under more favorable circumstances," the sister abjured her brother. After all, they had grown up together and there was a certain vein of genuine harmony of thought between them.

"I shall return, Francine...perhaps in the Lenten season...or Christmas...?"

"Wonderful, dear brother." She softly closed the door behind him and listened to his foosteps move from the shadow of the door.

Grant watched Mary with no small admiration...she being a city girl, as the expression went , as she galloped down the trailhead for a hundred yards, and then walked her mount, a dun pony with a white slash on its forehead, back to his side. She sat erect in the saddle...from a movie, a book, she had discovered this as the correct riding posture for a horsewoman. She clutched the reins in one small fist...at least she did not attempt to steer the animal. They rode side by side for a quarter of a mile, he looking across at her as she was lost in the pleasure of the ride. She was dressed in a special riding costume which she had purchased for the occasion, black, with silver buttons with silver trim the picture of an experienced horse-woman. It was elegant yet appropriate for the occasion, which in her clever mind she saw as both sporting and social. They rode for some five to eight miles, to a small shade cover where they dismounted, tied the reins of their mounts to a provided rail and each of them drank from a fountain of cool water. They sat for long minutes. Neither spoke to the other.

A last she said to him, "Isn't this fun?" He delighted in the pleasure that she expressed by her tone of voice, and in those simple words.

"Yeah, it is...great fun. Its good to have someone ride alongside who enjoys the out of doors."

"I never thought I could really enjoy just ridng a horse."
"There's a thrill to trail riding. It's ancient and modern. And...expecially with you. " He regarded her face, wreathed in a beautiful aspect of calm. There's a thrill to trail riding, Mary. It's ancient nd modern. " He watched her soft expressilon of delight. Then he added, You're fun to be with, Mary."

"I never thought I could have so much fun...just riding a horse," she said.

"Nor I. You look beautiful astride your pony...you ride with grace."

They sat on the park bench for several long moments, neither speaking to each other. Then he planted a timid kiss her on her cheek. She looked at him, his eyes were tender and loving. They moved closer until their lips met and he placed on them a long and passionate kiss, reaching over her shoulder to draw her closer. They regarded one another with soft, passion-filled eyes. They indulged themselves again with another long and passionate kiiss. It was apparent to each of them that they were in love, and that nothing could now intervene to separate them. He spoke close to her, as into her ear, she reciprocated by turning her face to accomodate his words.

> "I wish I had known..."
> "Had known...?"
> "Yes, she said... Oh but then that would have been wrong."
> "My cabin...." She nodded
> "We've just begun...."

She watched the way he sat erect in the saddle, in lauthority and control over the hourse, not so lively the animal might throw him, but spirited just the same. She admired his skill with the reins, his riding poise and ability. These qualities told her something about the man, that he apprsoved of discipline as a qulity of character, that trust was a factor in his skillful horsemanship, that risk was heir sto accomplishment and success. How a man handled a horse revealed these qualities to her, even though she might not have been able to sketch his face upon them. He admired her courage; she was not a horsewoman, but she had already verbally expressed her love for helpless animals. Of course, a horse was not a squirrel. Horses were meant or battle, squirrels for ...well, for decoration of the landscape. She could think of no other word. They rode side by side along the trail that narrowed then wildened and at times compressed into what appeared to be a footpath. They rode for almost twenty miles, to their surprise, circling up through the foothills and down again into the valley, approaching with small wonder the roofs of the stables ahead of them that glinted in the lowering sun. The day had been glorious for Mary, excitingly real for Grant. He could not have expected the outcome of their relationship to be so gratifying to his soul, complementary to his intelligence or so rhapturous to his flesh. He promptly dismissed the idea that there had been any...spiritual attachment formed by the day's ride. That thought was foolishness, but the realiy was that Mary seemed somehow, in ways he had not yet defined, satisfying to him. She appeared to be his counterpart...whatever that meant...yet he could not say why....The hills had turned purple in the afternoon shadows, the landscape redolent with orange light and points of brilliant reflection, that included the foliage along the trail.

While Grant and his love, for she now fit that description, were preparing to return to her apartment, stabling the horses, handing them over to the stable-hand and brushing the dust from their clothes, another scene of much different complexion was transpiring up in the suburban area of the city, east of the riding stables. In a quiet neighborhood of middle-class homes, the Uncle Clyde, the biologist, was making a call upon his brother, the long-lost father of pretty Mary. They were conferring, not about the father's failed water-company stock or some exotic experiment with amino acids in the brothers biology lab. They were seated within the father's small living room, in comfortable chairs, Clyde, the biologist, smoking a pipe, and the father one of his favoite cigars. Ronald Wexler, a tall, gangly man with a manicured moustache and watery blue eyes, loved his Havana cigars. The brothers were discussing what ought not to have been a subject for their close attention or keen interest whatsoever...Mary, the lost daughter of Ronald, was the girl's father who had abandoned her when she was just a child, leaving an empty hole in her life which she had endured in silence.

Thus without a man's voice or gentle touch for her memories, she had met a man whom she respected and had come to adore. She felt that she was in love although, at the present time, her heart was uncertain of its ambition. The two brothers were discussing a matter transferred from the psychotic old woman in the apartment to her brother-in-law, Clyde, the suspected defector from honor of lovely Mary Wexler. What right had either man to divulge to each other their thoughts on a matter that was, in the words of a judge, hearsay. When he had broken off his relationship, in point of fact his marriage, with the mother Santeluce in the divorce court, the judge had admonished him against using hearsay to accuse his wife of infidelity. By this time, the evil gossip had come full circle, and his daughter appeared to him to have inherited his propensity for disloyalty, although she was not yet married and, in the minds of both of them, was as singular as a nun in a convent. The biologist knew that example and not genetics produced deviation, whether in marriage or of honor. They provided, these two disingenuous minds, substance for discussion. They had not gotten together for almost ten years, and so the Uncle propounded to his headstrong brother the theory of...should he say it?..tainted blood. He was anxious, therefore, to protect his blood-line honor and he needed the broher's help in his self-defense. The whole matter was fictive, truth were known, but the mesoginist mindset of the Uncle Clyde compelled him to discuss Mary, as if she were a product of his laboratory. Their conversation went something like this:

"I'm so sorry the marriage to Santeluce did not work out," said Clyde, " but you know and I know how...well, how fragile love can be, especially in a ..." He did not finish his thought.

"A mismatch," Ronald suggested. "We got along I guess as well as any couple. My wife was so headstrong I hardly knew sometimes whether an investment was mine or hers. I suppose that the choice of origin did not make much difference--sort of life the origin of the species--but I felt that when I followed her advice...and believe me, brother, it was uninformed...I made poor choices.":

"We have to endure the worst at times in order to enjoy the best."

"You can be so facetious at times, Clyde. I had had enough of her...manipulating, when Mary came along."

"I foresaw that," said his brother. "I mean, as a bilogist, I see the line of genetic choice more clearly than others."

":I supposed that you would. Well, I had had enough."

":Manipulating, control, as it were, can be useful...if the controller is better informed than the controlee."

"Don't impugn me, brother. I tried, my God how I ried to ....accommodate her. When Mary came along, I thought we would patch things up. But a newcomer to the family, a baby, a child, can have the oppossite effect...of widening a rift."

"How true that is! Two genes with contrary molecular attrilbutes can split a relationship...like atoms, as it were."

"We grew further an further apart. Mary sensed the estrangement, absorbed it, I suppose...."

"Inevitable...Ronald".

"And so, when she was about four, I finally said to Santeluce, I must go. Here is my bank account. I have signed my investments over to you, all but those I need to survive."

"Where are you going, Ronald?"

"I'm going...somewhere.. Now you have a child, the baby, to control.   You will have enough money for the necessities...my stocks and other investments."

" 'Don't go, Ronald,' " she pleaded with me. But, I tell you brother, her controlling temper, her spirit of being master of the household, wearied my soul."

"I qute understand, my brother."

"And so I left. You have found me...and I suppose that is good."

"I thought you might be interested to hear about your daughter...and her...her boyfriend."

"Not especially, Clyde.   I would let her alone. If she is like her mother, she will have enough trouble in this life."

"Well, then. I can say no more, Ronald. I'm pleased we can see each other agan...and talk. What abouyt your iunvestments? What have you been doing?"

"I have started a new life. I am no longer an investor. I have joined the military. That gives me the security I need."

"The military. My God, what...are you a captain or something like that?"

Im a major in equipment maintenance...ordinance   I work in a factory out on the Sods Ora Military Base."

"Greetings...and a salute to you, Ronald...Major Ronald Wexcler.   I wish you all the best, my brother."

"I can say no more.   I have left those troubles and worries behind me, Clyde. Now, its a matter of getting tanks running again, reinforcing the armo plating, introducing new elctrical equipment to the troops...that sort of thing."

"We play the cards life deals out to us."

"How true, Clyde!" Ronald stood, his cigar having gone out. still in one hand. With the other he shook l his brother's hand, leading him to the door. Such conversations wearied him in his years, for he was no longer a young man. His hair was gray, black s till showing at the temples.   The brothers partsed amicably, Clyde with a twinge of resentment in his heart for his brother's abrupt conclusion of their meeting, Ronald felt as if he had just lifted a weight from his shoulders. He was certain that they would not meet again. He listened to Clyde's car drive away then thought," he needs a new muffler on that sedan.

The caller sang out "square 'm up!" to which summons there sprang a dozen couples to join those already out on the floor at the month's end square dance for the Boots and Gaiters square dance club.   Among this kalaidescope of flashing color of skirts, mens embroidered shirts and their adornements sof badges and club officers, Grant pulled Mary into a square where thye exchanged hugs and greetings with the other dancers. This was a customary ritual in this an other clubs to greet visitors and members as an official salutation. Mary looked radilant this niht, Grant observed, yet iln his mind, being somewhat shy and self-abasing, he could not immeiately assume he had a part iln her change. They were in love, he was certain that that had produced the change in her countenance and a new animation toher features, her hands and her general regard or others. After these linformalities were completed and the squares filled out with four couples each, the caller began his dance. As always, with this Boots and Gaiters, there was a live band. They were all volunteers who played on alternate nights, the banjo, guitar, violin, drum and trumpet. The steps were intricate, but with perhaps one exception, every square executed the wajnce with precision and general pleasure. Always visitors to tlhe dance sat around the borders, watching and sharing in the fun, while n;ow and then for the first hour a couple would drift into the room , slign the guest register and await the next tilp.

The dancers had executed three tips and Grant and Mary stood idly waiting for the singing call when Mary looked as if she had espied a person or thing of intense interest that had instantly caught her attention. She seemed to expire...he thought she was suddenly very ill...as she wove wlildly through the other dancers to reach her objective....but the objective had departed. She had observed a woman holding the hand of a small child of two years of age. And when Mary started for the side of the dance floor, the woman swept the child up into her ams and departed as sudenly and mysterisusly as she had appeared. Grant hurried after Mary through the crowd to the side of the room. He saw on her face an almost terrorized expression, a pathetic change from her former glow of happiness to one of pathetic despair. She looked sick and deathly pale. She ran from the room, Grant close after her, whereupon she stopped suddenly and tlurned o him.

"What is it, Mary?"
"That woman...:"
"You know her...sure, sure...but who was she?".
Mary turned to Grant, and began to sob. "That woman...the little girl...."
"Yes, yes...what about them?" Mary's voice was stilled and her words refused to come. "You know her....
"Oh, Grant, let's go. I can't stay here."
"Come on, Mary. Let me get your wrap." He disappeared and momentarily returned withn her shawl, a prsent he had given her as a friendship gift. He did not want anybody to see her tears; they would not understand and would only make up a reason--that he was somehow at fault--adding to the cruel lie. They sat on a bench in the lobby to talk. If anyone saw them, they could assume the worst; he could not change that. He took Marys hands between his and held them in his lap. "Who was she...the woman?"
"I...I...That child..." Mary spoke in broken phrases, incoherent words.
"Your sister....her little Girl...?" She had never told him that she had a sister.
"No, No, no, Grant. They were mother and child." She seemed to recite the affinity, the relationship as if from some intimate knowledge.
"Well, but then,we couldnt break the square...and they simply decided not to stay. After all it is getting late for a two year old."
"No, Grant, you don't understand."

They got into his truck, and he chose to say not another word about the incident, for it seemed now to be for her a painful subject that would have to remain for a time a total mystery. It ws only when they had arrived and stood on the front porch that she divulged the reason for her actions, her tears and the absence of any explanation.
"That little girl, Grant. That little Girl is...mine."
A wave of tender sympathy mingled with cold shock flooded into his soul. He could not at first grasp what she was telling mhim. "She is ...or was...my ...daughter. Oh, Grant." She broke into sobs again, deep and uncontrollable as she leaned into him. He put his arms around her to comfort her, not realizing fully at this moment the import of her words.
"Your daughter...."

"Yes, Grant. My little girl. Evangeline. Just two years tonight. But why...?"

"She was...no, I don't understand." He wanted to say governness.

"No, Grant, two years ago, I had a little girl...that was the child you saw...Evangeline.

"Why? Why didn't you keep her?"

"I did not think I could be a good mother to her," Mary replied amid sobs.

"I...that is hard to believe. I don't believe it. The father, .he ..."

"He did not want to have anything to do with his daughter. I could not believe it. He would not take her...and I...I had no job. Oh, Grant, you don't understand."

"I understand better than you suppose, Mary.".

"I wanted to have her...badly...but once I had her I felt that I would be such a poor mother I could not take care of her,"

"What cruel person put that thought into your head...that you could not raise your little daughter......the lie of hell, a cruel person...?"

"Nobody said that . I just felt that was the...the truth...and so...I found a foster mother for her."

"Oh, now I see ...the mother...little Evangeline's foster mother."

"Yes, brought to the dance to see me, her mother, without telling her the truth. My little daughter's birthday...."

"Maybe later...."

He felt her nod against his shirt, now drenched with her tears.

"She is gone."

"Gone...gone and you are the mother?"

"Yes, Grant. That was my little daughter."

"I won't stay any longer, Mary. I've got go home and think about this ...to my cabin. .Good night, Mary, darling." He kissed her on the top of her head and lightly on her lips, gave her a big reassuring hug and departed with haste down the porch steps. "The old womn will think I caused Mary's tears...will insist she break off with me....Mary's little daughter...!" The thought shook his mind and sensibilities and caused him to see his love in a new light...of a mother with a child."

Grant sat before the small heater in his cabin at the sawmill and, indeed, mulled over the scene at the dance. He had a auspicion that the Priest could furnish him with an answer sor two. Upon the next meeting-night of the small discussion gathering, he avoided Penelope's greeting as if her salutation were irrelevant, but when the Priest entered, he confronted the cleric with one question. He spoke out as if he and the cleric had been in conversation about the subject, the womam named Mary Wexler.

"You did not bring a friend?"

"No, Father," Grant answered wilth an absent mind. It then occurred to him that the question was curious in that he had come the first time, alone. It seemed to Grant as if the cleric were prescient, that he knew something about him, but had not, as yet expressd the matter in open, friendly conversation.

Then, as if by a long-standing exchange of confidences, the Father asked, "Where did you first meet her...I mean, Mary?"

"Mary?"

"....Beautiful young woman! I don't see her...did she come with you tonight."

"How could this Priest come up with her name...and associate myself with her in

such an intimate way...as if he has read my mind? What does he know that I am missing....?"
These were Grant's thoughts.

The cleric dipped in the traditional punch bowl and filled his cup. He seemed just a little too smug for Grant , who pursued the questions, helping himself to the same refreshment ."

"Mary is upset...I would almost say distraught.:

"Oh, she is a very emotional woman...."

"No, it's something more, Father. She is troubled. Is she from your parish....?"

"She is, she is."

"I know she has a good ...Counsellor."   The Prtiest attempted to project a faint smile. He motioned for them to retreat to the circle of chairs, as members lin Penelope's growing book discussion group began to enter upon the scene. "You won't take offense if I ask you a question that is not...well, exactly ...related to your conersation with her."

"Spiritual?" the Father responed.

"You might say so."

With this encouragement, Grant related the incident at the square dance, the sudden appearance, as if an apparition, of a small child of three, held in hand by a matronly woman with shining black hair, attired in a print dress and a displaying a shawl, with which she partially draped the shoulders of the child.

"There was a little girl, a child of about three years of age, Father, who appeared at last Tuesday's square dance...at your church. And when Mary saw the girl, she turned as white as linen and relused to talk about what she had seen. "

"As I say, Grant....she is a very emotional person."

"But a child...why would the unremarkable appearance of a child pRoduce that gastly expression. I thought she would falint. Actually, I feared that she had had a heart attack...so young... and I was prepared to catch her."

"Mary has had a hard existence...a child of the spirit, so to speak." He sipped from his cup with delicate4 lips and glanced about him. He nodded to the professor and his wife, who before seating themselves headed straightway for the punch bowl, as if an elixir of life awaited them or a special pootio held promise to to stimulate discussion. Mary came to me with a serious problem. My Priestly station forbids me to discuss the purpose of her visit, but she was troubled." Grant intuitively suspected that there was more of an involvemnt with...some man, another woman that connected her life to that of the little girl. "I...I feel the early pangs...I guess you would call them... of love for Mary, Father Casper. I am wonderfing if we might not meetg...somewhere...at your Parlsh house..."

The Priest regarded Grant with an expression of great surprise. "Why, of course, of course. I have an opening in my schedule.... Tomorrow...tomorrow after six o'clock mass."

"I shall be there, Father."   Both men droppe the matter and turned their attention to the group which had slowly filled the room, so that now some fourteen had appeared, exchanging greetings among themselves, smiling, removing their wraps, here and there bible, for a discussion of the book of Revelation. Tonight they were to discuss the realities of John vision while he was a prisoner on the Island of Patmos. The vision of this particular prisoner, of any prisoner, can tell the reader much about the circumstances of his captivity and the terrors, if they be present, of his night's vision. The four Horsemen would be the centerral topic for the night's discussion.

The youth with the yellow hair , the artesan smithy and his carpenter friend were curious to know about the book's tangible realities. Unlike the professor and his wife, confirmed skeptics in spiritual matters, these men who either worked with their hands or attended outrageous lectures at the lyceum, were quick to see the possibilities for John's failure to fool the modern reader of the book. The lawyer regarded Grant with a curious expression of disinterested pity, as if he wanted to speak to Grant but did not know how to begin. The meeting proceeded as the group began to discuss the horsemen of the apocalypse. Each member had a comment that either betrayed a total igorance of John's vision or an clumsy misapplication of some element of The Professors's wife clung to the notion that witchcraft was behind the apostle's vision. Her husand sat as mute as a pagan idol. The Lawyer, Grant happned to notice, examined his nails, glanced up, shook his head as if animated by some inner reluctance to accept the words of others, an articulation of his sinister courtroom manner. Penelope prodded, the banker, who heretofore, had kept silent, suggestsed that John lacked any financial support to insure his release and that he, as a consequence, lapsed into illusions of freedom. He remembered a client so dewepl in debt that he went into delirium right there at the bank. That was not unusual, said the banker. He rolled his collar tips to straighten them, examined a large turquoise ring on his right hand and lost himself in his thoughts. Tonight the messenger in the same leather boots sighed and shook his head, as if to dispel any suggestion he believed in John's vision, for he appeared to be too smart to be taken in by any four horsement, whatever the colors of their horses. "I ead it...prpeposerous. an idiot's tale...just the account as an example of witchcraft by which captive John hoped to gain his feedom from the island prison. "

Grant sat out the session out of a bored state of mind and indifferent to the words of the other members. The night for his meeting with the Priest came rapidly and was upon him. When he entered the Parish house, its interior smelling of hyacynth and seeming clean-swept and polished, as was the abode enjoyed by the Fathers, living as they did in dormatory style, yet with special study-rooms for conferences with the Parish members, the Priest motioned for Grant to follow him into one of these study rooms. Its high ceiling contributed to a sensation of ambient space, the blue walls inviting calm, the orange and yellow lamp light disclosing a tidy book rack on the desk and neat rows of books of a seminary nature along two of the walls. An atmosphere of peace pervaded the this small sanctuary. Father Casper invited Grant to take a seat in a heavy brown leather chair.
"Yes, my son...and what is it that troubles you?" the Priest began.
"Just this, Father Casper, Mary nearly fainted when she saw that child. Standing there...at the square dance, I'm referring to...."
With a pretended expression of surprise the cleric asked, :Did it never occur to you that ...well, that she has an affinity for little children?"
"I don't know what you mean...she is now a school teacher...has no children of her own..." With this last comment, the Priest placed his hand on his guest's knee. "That little girl...you say, three, maybe four...."
"No older."
"Did she have yellow curls like Mary's...blue eyes?"
"I think so..I 'm not sure. The woman took her by the hand and led her away...just as soon as she noticed that Mary had turned her attention to the child."
"Would it surpise you, Mister Shepherd, if I were to say to you... that little girl was Mary's child?" The astounding thought crossed Grant's mind that the words of the Priest

were true....but how so...how could that be...?"

"She never mentioned that she had a child?"

"Never."

"Well, I have heard her confession many times, Mister Shepherd. She had that little girl..out of wedlock."

"My suspsicion."

"Appropos and very shrewd of you, Mister Shepherd."

"Let me ask...have you any idea who the father is?" Grant inspected the Priest's countenance. It appeared to say, "None, none whatsoever."

"Do you not grasp the intrusive arrogance of your questioning, Mister Shepherd?" The Priest raised his voice. He shook his head and showed a mien of mock surprise. He swept his hand hrough his polished black hair, then he leaned forward to engage Grant's eyes, directly and without flinching.

"I am the father of that little girl...so sweet, so innocent...!" The confession stunnied Grant. The Priest fell into a reverie and looked away at the books on his shelf.

"By you, you, Father...her Priest...?"

"Celebacy...yes, while I served The Christ. But as I informed you at our meeting with the group...he liked to refer to the book discussion clique as the Group..."I am no\ longer a ...bonifide member of the Priesthood."

"You...you could not...marry her...the woman."

"I could, but I would have cast suspicion upon Mary as an adulteress, and I wanted to keep her name pure and protercted."

"Did it never occure yoto you, Father...that you commiteed a sin."

This charge enraged the Priest. He stood with a bound to his feet, and seemed to tower over his guest, his hands quivering as he looked down upon his accuser as if having discovered an repugnant insect. "You call me a ...sinner!"

"It is only a possibility. We all have our imperfections."

Rapidly, as if by the quick hand of a magician, the Priest from a hidden pocket in his clerical garb, snatched a small revolver into view, holding it in the palm of his unsteady hand. "And now, I tell you, I belong to the liberation-theology wing of the Catholic clergy, but because I chose to do so, I have voluntarily defrocked myself. You will not mention this meeting to Mary. Is that understood?"

Grant was incapable of forming an answer. He simply regarded the quivering hand that held the revolver, noticing the expression of scarcely- concealed rage on the Priest's face.

"I know so little about...liberation theology."

"Just as I suspected...."

"That you...you have...."

"Ruined the girl for life...eh, is that your insinuation, Mister Shepherd. For your false wsitness, you show no penitence....!".

"I have insinuated nothing, Father Casper. I am simply astonished by the turn of the conversation...I never suspected...."

"Well, now you know. Let me warn you, young man, that if you divulge the context of this meeting to Mary, you ruin her soul forever, and you destroy that beautific disposition/ For these crimes to the spirit of that woman, I shall come seeking you... And I shall convert you to a heavenly being to live with the angels. Do I make myself clearr?"

"Yes, father...perfectly so." The Priest looked at the ceiling.

"Its only by God's grace that I did not say I should send you to dwell amid the demons...."

"Would the Priest actually murder me?" Grant thought.

The Father just as quickly and deftly as he had produced the revolver, returned it to its hidden pocket in his cleric's garb.

"I have a friend there in that group, Mister Shepherd...the lawyer. That is for your secular wisdom."

"I would not have suspected," Grant feigned.

"No, because you are a shallow pimp of a man." The accusation stunned Grant...that such a charge should come from the lips of a priest, the representative, still, of the Catholic faith and attached to Rome by his training, commitment vows, his lifestyle and appearance.

"I have no need for a lawyer, Father."

"This one can help you...into some real troubles...such as never plagued Essau or Adam or Sampson, or any of the Holy Fathers."

"I do not spy on another man's life."

"Good, let it remain so."

"That sounds much like a threat, father."

"It is, it is. We...I...yes...and the lawyer...we have our little...secrets."

"I shall go no further. But Mary...she is troubled."

"I shall speak to her and explain. That woman who held the little girl by the hand has custody of Jeanette."

"Jeanette...?"

"The child's name. I wanted no part in a quarrel that would harm the little one for the rest of her life."

"Admirable," said Grant.

"Yes, isn't it! Like a doctor...if I could do the child no good, I should do her no harm." "Thank you for that, Father Casper." The Priest looked steadily at Grant then, walking to the door, opened it and with a grand gesture of courtesy, he ushered the younger man out of the study room. Grant returned home that night determined to speak to the lawyer. He realized that custody was a reversible bond. He wanted to know if Mary sought custody of her little daughter. The inspiraion occurred to him, that if he became affianced to Mary, he could help her recover custody of her little girl, if the child was in fact her daughter. He had to take the Priest's word for that...and that he possibly was the father of the child who had appeared that night at the square dance. It was possible, he thought that she wanted to reclaim her little daughter. In that case, perhaps he could be of real help to her. Mary was not bewildered. She was a woman of fine intelligence. He wanted to help her. With that thought he slept soundly through the night. The followin day, from a phone at the mill site, he called Penelope and asked for the name of the lawyer in their group. " Frank Bartok," she replied. "Are you in some sort of trouble...can I be of help?"

"No, thanks, Penelope...just a practical matter...economics of my work...hours and dollar value of my trade."

"I see. Well, I wish you the best." She abuptly hanged up . He returned to his work of cutting firewood for a client in the nearby sawmill community.

THE DISCOVERY

"You are Frank Bartok, the lawyer for Gobel Electronics, Ponder Cosmetics and other clients?"

"I am he." A man of medium stature dressed in; a beige business suit, with gray sideburns, dark eyes and a slight hunch to his shoulders came from an adjoining room.

"We met at Penelope's gathering for book discussions. IL'm Grant Shepherd." They shook hands. His hands were not smooth but rough, like those of an artesan who worked with his hands. A large opal ring adorned one finger.

"Ah, yes, I thought I recognized you. Come in...have a seat."

Grant entered the lavishly furnished office of a group of trial lawyers called Defoe-Bartok-Kaufman and Simmons. Two mina birds hopped about in a bronze cage. Up along the ceiling trim a stock exchange monitor flashed the stock quotes. the floor carpet was heavy with shag, the divan puffed with cushions. An ash tray stood solitary beside the divan arm, a wall filled with law books and a roll-top writing desk informed the visiyor of the intelligence he could expect. In the center of the room stood a large mahogany table covered with an exotic tile design upon whch there sat an old-fashioned cash register, with its glass display set at $1.00, the large keys and the ornate drawer giving it historical authenticity. Based on all these items, it was clear to Grant they spelled out that money was king in this sanctuary.

"I did not come here, sir, to ask you to litigate a matter, Mister Bartok, but, to enquire as to your expertise in custody cases. You must have handled one or two when you began your practice."

"Never...none. You are in the wrong law office."
"Then let me propose to you a matter of which you may have some acquaintance." The lawyer wisely appreciated the circumlocution of Grant's language, with which he was familiar in the courtroom venu. "I'm here, sir...Mister Bartok, not to ask if you would litigate a matter of custody but to discover what can be done to recover a child who is presently in the custory of...of alien hands."

"Oh, God, an alien-from-space problem. Have you gone to the police? Sit down, sit down."

"No, sir...the woman you have not met...or have you?..was influenced to dispose of, that is...to give up the custody of her child, in this case a little girl>"

"Are we talking about a...kidnapping. That's a Federal matter if so."

"No, sir. I would call the matter one of...fraudulent tetimony as to legal parental authority."

"That is not unusual, sir. My time is limited, so please be short. I am not a custody-case lawyer.""

"I understand, but I have no one...whom I know, I can call on. I appreciate your time. No, I am at a loss until I know who the father is."

"Or until you see a miracle, someone with extraordinary powers of performance...."

"I have not the time for games, Mister Shepherd. Come to the point.""

"I realize how simple it can be to liberate another person from...the bondage of a terrible wrong."

"Do not try to impress me, Mister Shepherd, with your hyperbolic language. You are now in the ralm of marital matterws. Come to the point."

"May I impress you...a successful lawyer who litigated...her case."

The attorney stared with a granite look into the eyes of his visitor. "Do you come as a client, sir...or do you come to....clearly...to protest some issue better handled by the police, or the Federal officers...a kidnapping, a child abduction, whatever the matterf is... as the case may be...the sense and substance of which you appear determined to withhold?"

"I come to ask if you have had a hand in...in what I now call a custody case."

"Mister Sepherd, I have told you what I know about custody matters."

"I heard you, sir ." Bartok sat slightly hunched forward in his chair, with eyes that seemed to glare behind his glasses, a unkempt moustache and a partly balding head of black hair that matched his sideburns. "As if the light suddenly shone forth the answer to his riddle, he tried to smile as he said in a whispering voice, "We have some good times there, do we not...at Penelope's house...and that punch...,always so...clearly right."

"We do," said Grant.

There is not much arguing the case for St. John, is there?...but its good for me to get away fom this office once a month."

"I understand."

"Then, tell me.. What really brings you here to see me? Have you a book proposal? Are you in trouble with the power company? Have you crossed swords with the IRS?""

" No,for all of these. I came to ask for your answer to one question...."

"One question! You might have called me instead. Look! I'm very busy. You are costing me time and money. This visit won't be cheap. I do not deal in pro bono matters, sir. I have many clients who this very moment...."

"No, sir...I simply wanted to ask you one question...to you in person...."
"You wish to...interrogate me! I am a witness to your plea..of which I know nothing about. Do you, sir, take me for a fool?"

Grant thought he heard an ominous tone in Bartok's voice. Or was that his imagination? What picture had he conjured of this man...the Priest had informed him...or then perhaps he had only guessed...that Mister Bartok, Esquire, was involved somehow with Mary's separation from her child..

He had actually revealed his motive for coming when he asked Bartok if he had ever handled any ...custody cases.

"Custody?" The question caught the lawyer off-guard. He clenched his teeth and went to the shelf where he pulled out a book called " 'Marital Pleas and Custody Settlements". He opened the book to a page and began to read. "If a mother expresses her desire to be quit of her child, howsoever conceived, by her husband, a friend, a stranger, as in cases of rape or incest, the custody maybe contested. If it is not contested, the mother has two remedies: she can 'divest'...as in stocks...'can divest herself of her progeny by adoption--in which case she retains the title of biological mother but not the mother's control--or she can rid herself of her...the emcumbrance of the child by sending it to a child-care facility, or'...I'm not done..'she can privately give the child away for care and rearing, in which case the law is not involved'...at least not at the time of adoption.' " The lawyer snapped the book closed. "If the matter you present to me falls into any of these categories, you might so inform me, Mister.."

"Shepherd...Grant Shepherd. You left out abandonment."

"Thoughtless of me. You are trying to hint that you know who the father is....?

"You know and now I know who he is." Grant watched the lawyer wrinkle his brow, lightly touch his fingertips together in a gesture of silent meditation, then let his head fall back on the chair-back while he appeared to scan the heavens of the spackled ceiling glitter. Grant went on. "What if the father is a Catholic Priest? What does your law book say about that sort of...immaculate conception?" The lawyer's face lit up with a strange expression of puzzled anger and amused curiosity, as if he were ready to shake out some discovery from the man who sat before him, the bearer of a counsel from hell.

"The case would have to, be re-argued according to...let us say, a stranger's conception. Is that the question you came here to ask of me?...the only question?"

"No, sir. I have a question...the answer involves you, I am almost a hundred percent sure."

"Oh...?" The lawyer raised his eyebrows in wonder, his voice took on the tone of querrulous wonder, as he waited for some sort of definitive answer from this young interrogator. "What are you getting at?" he asked in a surly tone of voice.

"Just this...I sense that somehow you had a hand in the custody settlement of little Jeanette...that you arranged to have her...adopted...if that is the right word, and that the circumstances of her conception leaves room for desception in the transfer of care, parental care, for the child."

"You seem to be well-versed in such matters," said the lawyer warily.

"If the conception as illicit," Grant went on, "and the mother manipulated to...dispose of her daughter for fear of public shame, then the grounds for a lawful transfer of control and basic responsibility for the child's uupbringing are brought into question. This being so..and I am no lawyer, then the challenge to custody can be uphenld in the proper jurisdiction."

Attorney Bartok was flabbergastsed at the words of his visitor, stunned momentarily into silence, after which he said, his voice miming strength and certainty..."The mother has a claim to the custody of her own child...if she can suppor it with evidence." This appeared to be Bargtok's final word..

"It is a ill-fated and unnatural mother who does not cherish in her heart the recovery of her own offspring, even though separated by other legal...devices."

"Are you saying that you wish to take the part of...the mother?"

'You know who the mother is, Mister Bartok, because you handled the   the plea for adoption when you learned that the a Catholic Priest was the child's father."

"Mary Wexler is the mother...."

"I know that already, sir. She would like to have her little daughter back."

"Then you come here to...represent her. Is Mary Wexler your friend? What is your bearing on the matter, sir? What is your connection to her?""

" I am her friend. And, no, she did not send me here to discuss anything with you, sir...with all due respect."

"Three years...yes, that was approximately three years ago. I recall she...she gave up the infant."

"She was shamed into doing so."

"Shame...shame. What is that, sir? The law does not recognize shame...as a factor, perhaps, but not as a legal entity of evidence. That is a hearsay term...shame."

"The law recognizes rejection, as in a bad land deal, a faulty contract where money is involved.   Shame is a human trait, a reaction to a helpless outcome, a bad choice, the influence on a wrong act. But then you lawyers think such things are illusory...if not always. a matter of opinion, not a moral value to judge conduct...." Grant studied the lawyer's expression with a keen sense that the man was trying to avoid a situation in which he had participated three years earlier.

"We do not judge. Justice is blind, as the statue shows, blindfolded. If Mary surrendered her child out of shame, then the court would search for another reason, a rebuke by the church, an exile from friends and society, a personal damage to the psyche of the mother...."

"Then so be it. I intend to talk Mary into a change of heart. Yes, she is my frilend and, no, I came lhere on m;y own volition. We met at Penelope's house. The mother is deeply hurt...damaged...as the court will say...by the suit for custody in which you playd a part."

"As did Father Junipero Casper."

"I am aware of that, sir. Now that you know my true purpose for coming here...."

"To warn me."

"To see if you will help me to restore the little girl to her mother...."

"You become a bounty hunter then...who, by God, will pay you for my services?" Bartok queried. But the Grant ignored the question. Bartok looked about himas if for support. He got up from his chair and went to a liquor cabnet and poured a shot of whiskey for himself, his back turned to his guest. He abruptly wheeled about and said, "There are grounds for reversing the custody court's ruling. The child is still of child-rearing age ...if the mother should so desire. The fact that the father is a...a Priest...prompts the question of false pretense for the act of adultery...the possibility of disgracing a Priest in public adds weight to the action...and the mother's feelings, albeit the Child feels estranged, are to be considered in an equitable manner. After all the court's ruling, although lawful, involves the spirit as well as the letter...as the saying goes."

Grant was ready to depart. He had engaged Bartok's interest. Time, alone, would determine the nature of his help and cooperation. He could be induced to handle the paper work...which would push he matter forward, to completion. Shepherd stood and walked toward the counsels chamber door. He paused on the threshhold, a smile on his face, a feeling of delight within him. He was almost speechless. He had not expected this response by the lawyer.

"I'll ...confer with...with the mother. She lives in the same place?""

"Mary? Yes. One more detail that could prove helpful. I should like to marry her..." The jaw of the lawyer dropped six inches. "

"Then you would be... the child's stepfather..?"

"My plan, Mister Bartok...a plan of action, if I may say so."

"You are engaged?"

"In a manner of speaking, we are engaged. I am in love with the woman or I would not be here today...with my appeal. I still have to ask her... formally."

For some unexpressed reason, this lawyer, accustomed to handling clients worth millions, and who had found himself now involved in a custody case, broke out with an hilarious laugh. He apparently had interpreted Grant's admission as ridiclulous. All his enmity instantly faded from him. He extended his hand to Grant and they shook hands warmly.

"Keep me informed." He stood and showed Grant to the door. The visitor to tlhe law offices of Defoe-Bartok-Kaufman and Simmons turned and smiled into the attorney's face, then sped off down the carpeted corridor. In his heart there rang a melody, that if she consented to his proposal in marriage, then he planned to launch his scheme to recover the the little girl for her mother.

Dr. Fresian Amon, the Paleontologist, swept his hand across a wall map in the basement game room of his luxurious mansion. "There you have it, Clyde. Your neice has all that terrotory to consider if she really wants to search for her missing daughter."

"I think, Fresian, you misunderstand. The girl is not lost. Your niece knows where she is...at the home of her foster mother."

"True, but this...foster-mother has...so I have learned...agreed to join the special forces of the American army. She has a talent and training in the Armenian language. They have in the backs of their minds, converting her into a spy. Then...then...Fresian, what will happen to the child?"

"Are you certain of this?" Clyde Arlington asked.

"How certain are we that the woman...Missus Armayan, is actually the foster mother?"

"I can only surmise, Fresian. I do not know for sure."

"Not even when you were invoWlved in the custody battle that put the little into the care of this Missus Armayan? What if...this woman, the foster-mother, does go into the armed services? What then happens to the little girl?"

"We can only guess."

"Guessing is the game for fools when a life is involved, my friend."

"When do you suppose we can meet him."

"Him?"

"Yes, I have heard rumors that a certain Grant Shephers is courting the mother."

"Well, let them remain rumors...at least until there is some...some news as to what he intends. The little girl is of human value, but she has no monetary value to anybody but to her actual mother."

"She should be the true custodian of the child." said Fresian

"That is right." The two men, the Paleontologist and the Uncle of Mary Wexler agreed upon the date for their next round of golf. The servant of the Paleontologist, an Asian with an almost invisible presence, entered the basement room bearing two bottles of beer with glasses on a wooden platter, The conversation about the child ceased as they began to talk about the recent finding of bones in Oregon that may have belonged to a creature named Bigfoot.

"He is a creature that belongs to an unidentified species of semi-human origin, a humanoid unidentified kind of animal." Dr. Fresian threw out this comment to test the atmosphere for a discussion.

"Preposterous! A man-like animal that is twice his size, without a colony or some other locus, roaming the woods of Oregon and said to leave monstrous footprints....

58.

"That is so," said the Paleontologict. "I have photographs."

"Show them to me," said the mathmetician, for whom figures by themselves gave evidence of the reality of a scientific conjecture. Thus the conversation of the two friends drifted off into the night as they discussed the possible existence of an, as yet, unidentified species of creature known as Susquash Man.

Not many miles away, another couple, members of Penelope's discussion group, were entertaining their friends when they, too, coincidentally, hit upon the question of the existence of this creature. A sighting story was in all the papers. "Professor, you have no hard evidence that such an ape-man exists."

"Nor do I know if there is a living she. Obviously there must be a colony, a tribe, clan or pride somewhere in the woods."

"Well, I should not go out for a stroll without my gun, if I were you," said one of his colleagues, a teacher of history.

"No, I go with my hunting knife."

"Bravo! Do you not realize the potential danger to your life if this...hairy fellow pops up on the trail just ahead of you?"

"I speak several languages."

\   "You had better perfect your growl?" Professor McCabe."

"Now you jest, but let's be fair. This creature may be bilingual, for all we know."

"Fat chance, Professor. I have seen dogs that sing and heard cats that talk in the night." A look of bewilderment clouded the professor's gaze. He looked at his wife with questioning raised eybrows. He whispered, "Either this fellows is crazy or I am out of my wits."

His friend overheard he whispered comment. "No, Professor, you are not out of your wits. I have pictures...."

"Assanine!" said his colleague. "All your photographs do not prove the existence of such a creature...with feet eighteen inches from heel to toe, a height of almost eight feet...hairy from top to bottom and it neither howls, grunts, speaks nor jabbers."

"That lets politicians off the hook. Time alone will tell," said Professsor McCabe. The small group of devotees to the teaching profession, sharpened their appetites with cheeze and crackers and some fine Bordeaux wine from the professor's cellar. The night drifted on for them in the home of Professor McCabe and his wife, Francine. The candles on the table began to smoke and to sputter. A draft flooded into the living room when the one servant opened the side door. He entered with several chunks of wood, which he tossed onto the fire, sending a cloud of sparks up the chimney. The room was freshened by the draft. The air semed to brighten, the brocade wallpaper colors flourished once again, the deep carpets took on a more austere appearance beneath the feet of these selected guests. And the various pieces of furniture, overstuffed chairs, hardwood lamp tables and chests glowed in the effects of the servant's entry and exit. .The other five guests had found succor in the Professor's raft of shelved books on numerous sujects. He had invited them to make themselves at home, which they were doing. One younger woman played withs the family cat, tinkled a mall bell found on the piano keyboard to attrack its attention. Professor's wife invited their guests to enjoy the small smorgasborg on the sideboard. The tall grandfather clock struck eleven with its warm, sonorous tones. One of the guests put a record on the ancient Victrola--of which Professsor McCabe was enormously proud, a hard-rubber platter enitled, "The Wedding of the Sunshine And the Rose." Professor McCabe and Francine were sentimentalists and had amassed a collection of at least a thousand of such timeless and interesting ballad-type phonograph records. The room filled with the music of a quaint yesterday, as the professor and his guest left off talking about the hairy ape-man, the unidenified species of humanoid evolutonary development. All the guests that night in the professor's home were in quest of one thing or another to fill the hole left by a felt emptiness of knowledge The subject of the child was lost in the penumbra of chatter and reminiscences.

One thing Grant was uncertain of and that was the legitimacy of the spirit child of the dance night, as Mary's daughter. Although he was not a Catholic by faith or practice, yet he suggested that he go with her at the Church of St. Boniface, then after the service take her to a luncheon at one of his favorite spots, the Chameaux Restaurant, a cozy hideaway on the West side of town. They ;might then walk down along the sands of the beach not far away. In the sanctuary of the church, the Priest blessed the sacrament, delivered a brief sermon on the vulnerability of the saved in a sinful society. He called upon the altar boy for the bread, poured the wine and administered the Holy Sacrament to the congregants who were invited to come and to kneel at the rail. The Priest broke the bread as the worhippers knelt.   The servce was brief.   Grant admitted to himself he scarcely understood the meanings of the altar adornments and the sacrament itself, except that, aguely in his mind, they represented the blood shed by Christ on the Cross at Calvary. He was not ignorant of these fundamentals of the Christian faith, but simply unaware of the implications to the believer in that failth. He glanced aside at his love and saw her composed expression, to his mind the loveliest creature on earth, the symbol of love purified, the fragrance of she whom he had fallen in love with, and in his mind and heart at this time, the one whom he anticipatded bonding himself to forever in the ties of marriage.

Yet, he could not inform her of the full conquest of his heart. She knelt again in the pew while he sat. She seemed oblivious to his presence. She returned to sit, crossed herself and sang, or appeared to sing, the Gloria in Excelsis. The Priest extended his hands over the heads of the celebrants and blessed them and asked for God's divine protection. He dismissed them to the continuation of their worldly journeys under the guidance and protection of our Holy Savior Jesus Christ and the Holy Virgin Mary. Grant and Mary in silence stood . He stood aside for her to reach the aisle, they exited the church nave and paused briefly in the sun at the portico of the St.Boniface Church of Our Holy Mother.

Grant went to the discussion group without Mary. He had some business that had piqued his curiosity, regarding the Priest who did not appear any longer to wear the Priest's habit or talk in pious words.
"Is there something...that I should know about??" The Priest looked away to glance as others coming to the discussiosn circle for another session.
"Not that cold talk around t here, Father Casper. The Piest's words puzzled Grant. HLe wantsed the relief of knowingwhat was on the Father;s mind, especially if there ever had existed arelationship between him and the woman he was gegommomg to love.
"Well, then,perhaps you can come to see me at the parish. I still keep an office there...he made the sign of the cross...out of the generossity of the many friends of the church I have made over the years."
"I would like much to visit you, Father Casper."
"Good, then shall we say...next Tuesday at seven o'clock."

"That's a good day and time for me, Father."

"The priest smiled and sipped from his wine cup. "I shall expect you then...Grant.'

"Yes, Grant Shepherd is my name."

"Most appropriate," the Priest responded. Penelope was greetling her guests, all of whom had by now arrived. She took the center of the circle and thus began the night's session. Tonight they would discuss Pilgrims Progress. Grant remembered having read it years ago and remembered only vaguely that it was about a Christian's trip from hell to heaven, from sinner to saint, from unforgiven to forgiven, and from doubt to grace. He lost himself in the discussion and without loitering to chat with any others, especially the Priest, he drove the long way back to his cabin at the sawmill. He had taken the first step to resolve what remaine a mystery to him...the father to her, to Mary's little girl. He thought that perhaps the Priest would have an ansewer or could suggest a resolution to the enigma.

"No, Father." Grant sat quite still, slipping his wine punch while he lingered ovr a strategy. There was something familiar about the Priest whenever he thought about Mary. At least, Grant thought this to be the case.

He had arranged their day by phone, thus avoiding the temptation to appear at her door and suffer the suspected condemnation of the old woman. They climbed into his truck, which he had washed and attempted to polish since her visit to his cabin. She sat beside him. It seemed to her that this was a natural way to mount a courtship, certainly his conveyance was not a marriage gig but a rusty old truck he used in his firewood usiness. She wore a look of contentment of her face. When they had arrived and entered the Chamoux Restaurant, the hostess at the front, at her station by the cashier, promptly led them to an empty booth at the back where they could enjoy the privacy of their company. Seatling themselves comfortably, each scanned the immense meuu card. After several minutes had elapsed, the same waitress returned to their table. Grant ordered the chicken soup and a French salad with hot rolls and his Love ordered the beef sandwich with a small cheeze-sprinkled salad and and iced tea.

The ambience of the cafe was pleasant in its few customers at this near noon hours. The amosphere was cool and fragrant, from somehere there came a very low-key sound of music. The conversations of the patrons were low. Thoughtfully, there was hardly any programmed music. A violinist, Grant thought, would have been perfect. He turned his attention to Mary, who sat before him, just as elegant as she had sat in the church pew. on her countenace the expression of ready enjoyment and anticipation of the pleasure of being with him for this one day during the week. The waitress with the bundled hair and wearing a green and brown blouse and small apron, glided up to their table, bearing a tray that carried their orders, and as she distributed them, Mary sat back and eyed the food she hlad ordered. There was about her that same delicacy, that identical femininity which had drawn her to him that day at the sawmill, amid the rough crude objects of a working sawmill, the logs, the machinery, the loggers and the violent action of turning logs into lumber, not excludingt the awsom whine of the mill saw. Here, there was that ambience of human participatio , which seemed to elude any suggestion of deep hunger on her part, but she brought to the table an almost sacrosanct air. It was as if this luncheon meal were an extended part of the worship service. He admitted to himself that he almost idolized her. He smiled inwardlhy at the thought. He loved her all the more for that simple regard for a natural human need and could project it into the future, if she should become his wife.

"Good food here,"he said. "I don't come here often."

"Just with special guests."

"Right." They ate in silence for a few minutes.

"The Priest, do you ...have you ever met him? Father Beauregard? He's a French import." She laughed. "But just as ardent as...well, Father Casper."

"'Mary...I've wanted to ask you something for a long time." She looked up and he was cognizant of a strange fear that came into her eyes. "Father Casper has been long at the St. Boniface Church?"

"Ten years, I think. Grant, please don't talk about Father Casper."

"I'm sorry." He said no more about the Priest, only hoping that she would comment on him whom they both knew attended their Penelope book discussion group.

"I have something to tell you, Grant."

"I'm listening."

She uttered her next words straight out, without conditions or hedging of any sort. "I have to tell you..,." She looked outsidethe booth to ascertain that no diners sat at the closest table. "I have to tell you...confession or not...that Father Casper is the father of that little girl you saw that night at the square dance."

With these words the secret it was out, without any softening up of the blow. "I'm not surprised, and yet I suppoe I should be." It was all he could do to keep his expression bland, his voice calm.

"You had a suspicion...why?"

"The way you froze that night when the little girl appeared. You and she saw each sother...and the other woman held the child's hand."

'I'm glad she did. She was too young then to know me. Just a babe...yet I was afraid the child might come running to me."

"The girl is...three, darling...so she appeared to be. Your daugher could not have recognized you."

"And a little more."

"The Priest...I met him...at his Parish house."

"You did!" She almost exploded in the excitement of his answer, which she had not expected.

"Yes, I felt that he knew more than he would ever admit to anyone, not even to God. I asked to see hm in private. We met in his study. I had a little talk with him. He told me that he is no no longer a frocked Priest. The lawyer told me that he joined the forces of liberation-theology, or whatever it is called...Priests who join a radical theological group of politically activist priests and teachers in the church."

"He told you these things?"

"Yeah, and because he was no longer a PriestI was, am sure he could admit to fathering a child by you.

"Little ...Jeanette. But how could you even suspect ...?"

"He saw me with you at Penelope's. He warned me to stay away from you. He warned me...a total stranger. What right did he have...what business was it of his if we...we were friends? His consciene betrayed him...then, that night. Nobody controls my associations, Mary...nobody...is my keeper. Ever. I am a free man."

"He seduced me...I'm sure of it now."

"Jeanette," he echoed. "The priest is a phoney, a blackguard, an anarchist...!"

She sighed as if in relief. "You don't want to see me any longer," she said.

"Oh, no, no... I mean , yes, yes, yes. I want to see you, Mary, dearest, I love you." She looked him straight into his eyes for the longest time and then said, "I...think I am in love with you, Grant." They sat for long moments without speaking, as customers passed their booth.

"Lets go. I'm finished." She pushed her half-empty plates before her. They stood, he let her exit the booth, they went to the front counter where he paid the tab. Just as promptly and without delay or ritual they left the restaurant.

"Lets go down to the beach, Mary. It's a short ways from here...and it's a gorgeous place to walk in the sand. I'll roll up my pants. We'll both take off our shoes."

Her mood lightened. "Beautiful!. Oh, you are the most wonderful tour guide, Grant!" she said and, putting her arm around him, pulled him close to her in a hug. Within a brief time they had arrived and, removing their shoes, leaving them in the truck, they walked down the ramp to the sand. He took her hand. He felt emboldened by her confession of her love, yet there were elements in the confession that were entirely missing.

The thrashing sounds of the waves as they broke and flooded up the sand combined with the larger roar of the comber tide. These delightful and exotic sounds assaulted their speech momentarily, so that they had to talk louder to each other. He had a question on his heart that he wanted to ask her. They walked around a couple who were lying supine on the sand, under their beach umbrella. The screams of delight and shouts came from children playing in the surf. Distributed along he sands were numerous parties who lay stretched out on their blankets, surrounded by luncheon baskets, their radios and children's toy pails and shovle, as the owners tanned themselves under the moderaely hot blaze of the afternoon sun. Here and there a baby lay in a hamper, under an umbrella. It was a glorious sunday on the beach sands. Mary and Grant walked casually along. Mary dropped his hand and took his arm, as if she antiicpated what he wanted to say. Another wave thrust its foam up to their naked feet, to their mutual delight.

"Why...?" he said, as if thinking aloud.

"Why what, Grant?"

"Do things have to happen that way?"

"What things...oh, you mean...the little girl?"

"Yes, the child."

"Ive wondered the same. I loath that Priest."

"Seduced you, he did."

"He did...I don't know why...I mean why I let him do it...like I hadn't been to confession...or felt guilty about something I had done...and I and wanted some kind of...abosolution. I must've felt helpless. God have mercy...!"

"There are ways in the male...his kit of charms. Are you sorry?"

"That I had her...Jeanette? No, not ever. Abortion is...is murder. LI could never murder my child...ever...ever."

\   "She is a beautiful child...I saw her only briefly that night."

"Just as she was a beautifusl baby. I hated to give her up."

"That's what I wondered. She could be yours."

"Don't, Grant. I don't want to think about it."

"I have, Mary. I have." He said no more as they walked along the dazzing sand. He turned their steps to the cold scree-water that washed up onto the beach and momentarilly soaked their feet in its cold froth.

"I was afraid, Grant."

"Afraid...of the Priest?"

"Of my parents...you never met them, my Uncle Clyde, also. They're all the same."

"Your blood kin."

"Manipulators. Listen to me, Grant. Ever since I was growing up, they tried to influence me into believeing that I was not capable...."

"Of what, of...of just living, for God's sake."

"Of not being, like them a good parent, a good mother. They infected my thinking to thle point where my mother would not let me play with dolls. She said I did not have a mother's...tenderness... or something like that. So I came to believe that if I ever did have a child, a baby, I would not be a good mother to it."

"Oh, my God!...How cruel! I sensed ilt...I knew it!"

"You knew it?"

"I suspected something of the sort. They told you... they caused you to believe that you lacked...maternal instincts for mothering. Is that what you're telling me?"

"Yes, that is exactly right."

"How cruel, how unspeakably cruel! So when you had little Jeanette...when your baby came along, you were...you were ready to...give her up."

"That and...since the father was a Priest...if it ever got out."

"That Father Casper was the real father of your child...."

"Yes, let the shame be on him...."

"And to you, also... shame, it came when folks got the connection...shame, open, unsecretive shame! Out of wedlock, a baby...."

"Yes...and still they whooped. Oh, you don't know how suspicioning my relatives are, espcially my dad, not so much my mother."

"They whooped....?"

"They did."

"She. your mother, said nothing to take your side?"

"She belonged to him...she was a part of his way of thinking."

"Unaffected by the lie about your little daugher's paternity by an adulterous priest, but not a rapist, they disowned their daughter as an incompetent and irresponsible mother...potentially... to themselves, not to the court."

"That's about the size of it, Grant. Now you know the whole story."

"Not quite. Oh, I hope you don't think I'm being cruel." She said nothing. "I mean, you don't have the child. The little girl is not yours to raise. The woman who held the child's hand that night...."

"Has custody. That was not a governness, Grant, that was the adopive mother."

"Just so.: Mary looked at him, stopped, picked up an object in the sand and flung it away.

"Let's walk down to that pier. They started off again, hand in hand. "Custody is a reversible thing, Mary. Like a form of adoption...that can be changed. It is an adoption. What is her adoptive mother's name?...Do you know?"

"Armayon, I think is is. ...She stopped to speak her next words. "If an adoption can be...reversed...."

"Nullified. There are judges. There is a spirit that accompanies a plea under the letter of the law.

"Do you mean reversal of custody?"

"I mean just that. Any hint of lying, of false pretense is lying, under oath it is perjury.... Cancel the agreement...a contract...care as a consideration for the gift of your daughter..toil in exchange for a life. It all has to be honest, you know." They stopped. A wave sent its foam up around their feet. The long pause seemed like an eternity to Grant. The sounds of the sea, the diminishing thrust of sea wash up onto the hard, wet sand, the crashing of the eight-foot combers...."Mary, I have something to ask you. This will all tie together." He gathere his words. " You know I love you."

"Grant." At first, she could only mentioned his name. Then, the words came, "I love you, too."

"Then...then...what do you say?" Another wave sloshed up around their ankles and legs. "This is is perhaps not the most romantic spot to propose...that we get married, sweeheart."

"Oh, Grant.. you mean?"

"Yes, Mary, my Beloved, I mean just that...I mean I want to marry you and I was just wonderig if...."

"I would love to marry you...?"

"Right."

"Yes, Grant. My answer is yes. Whatever happens from here on will be...not so ...painful. There could not be a more romantic spot for your proposal to marry me. Only the waves are listening."

"See how they agree...with a roar." They laughed . "I'm thinking ahead, too, Mary.... I...I would love to help you raise your little daughter." The woman was utterly speechless. She threw her arms around him and lay her head on his shoulder for the longest time.

"Do you mean...?"

"Yes, I mean just that. I know you will prove to be the most beautiful, and wonderful mother to...to Jeanette...and to her little sister..?"

"Oh, Grant...." The woman did not know exactly what to say she was so thrilled by the moment of Grant's proposal. Finally, she uttered her thought, "I dont know what to say."

They embraced one another with a long and tender kiss as the waves continued to wash around their ankles and legs. 'We don't want to get carried away,'" he said as they parted briefly.

"With our kind of surfing," she said. In his mind was the fantasy that they could drive down the coast and find desolate stretch of beach and sleep naked in the sand and go swimming, naked, the next morning. But he purged that fantasy as dstructive of their relationship, howsoever exhilarating it might have seemed in its pagan beauty. They walked on.

"We don;t want to be carrled away by the sea," he said. and they laughed. "Can't we discard a ceremony at your church...?"

"Discard...a civil ...ceremony. Where then?"

"Let me think about it...atround a crackling bonfire...like a couple of pagan Druids in the forest." They laughed again. "That lawyer...Bartok is his name, you've met...seen him, at the discussion session.... He seems to be a friend...at least I hope so. Big wheel in a company of corporation lawyers. I've already talked to him. I think I can get him to handle our plea...maybe on a pro bono basis. It won't take much of his time."

"Our plea?"

"Yes, a custody case. Why not..he's a practicing lawyer...Custody ought to be basic. It's a contract for adoption services. Mostly paper work. There is a special court for custody cases. The decision will be up to the judge. I will ask this Bartok fellow to enter a plea of competency, based upon our...upon our marriage to change your status from single to married, so that we raise your lttle daughter... together."

"Oh, Grant...what a beautiful surpise Then there's my family...."

"They had better keep silent. Otherwise they will cross my anger and I have an Irish temper." She laughed and reached down into the cold scud of a wave and flipped the ocean's suds into his face; he retaliated with the same wet caress of the sea. They laughed the laughter of abandonment. They walked on a ways further until they spotted the surf breaking around the pilings of the pier and heard the carnival noises reach their ears.

"Let's go back. The long walk of at least a mile consisted in their stopping from time to time to exchange a long and ardent hug and tender kisses. They were completely wrapped up in their emotions and in their idyllic love engagemnt.

"Let's run," he said.

"Good idea," They took off at a jog along the edge of the surf-wash, splashing cold sea foam onto their legs and occasionally a wisp into their faces. It was a glorious run.

"What a day for a ...scamper!" he said. She laughed.

When they reached his truck the realities of the way before them settled into their thoughts.

"I will go have another talk with Mister Bartok and explain our plan to him and let him prepare the...papers. The woman who now has custody...."

"Is an old friend of my father."

"She will have to be persuaded to sign a release of custody. That may be hard."

"What if we can prove extraordinary influence...by my father, to remove the child from my custody. He always wanted to keep me his child. I think that is the real reason. His argument has no validity, Grant."

"No validity at all, right. That custody was taken under false pretenses. That will be the argument...like legalized kidnapping...and for the pleasure of handing over an orphaned child, so to speak, to a couple who were childless."

"Childless, when there are always orphanages and abandoned children."

"Obviously, they did not try to find other ways to gain custody and become foster parents."

"Right...they also fell under the...manipulating influence of your father."

"Meantime, Grant...what about the wedding?"

"I came up an idea. Why not...now you won't laugh at this...but why not have the marriage ceremony...at the square dance?"

She broke into a genuinely hilarious laugh, then, quietingg down, reached her arm around him and said to him, "The most practical...and romantc place I could ever imagine...so different from stuffy church."

"Or the commissioner's office.Eveythng is there, ilncluding the hordeuvres. I thought you would like the suggestion. We can pick a preacher, all our dancing friends will be there...the wedding party and reception, and others... just like that we will have our wedding dance all readied for us and we shall dance a tip of our...new lives."

"You are a planner, Grant. I have to say that. I cn ask Nora, theVP, to order a cake for us...and a wedding sheetg cake for the crowd. You have some of the most wonderful ideas...like I say, the world's most thoughtful tour guide."

"I thought you would like the plan...a square dance wedding, the reception attended by all the dancers of the "Boots and Gaiters" square dance club...and of course their friends. We'll have a crowd, my love, to celebrate your becoming a mother once again." She kissed him long and ardently, and then they started for home, back to her apartment.

She dreaded to see her mother again. How would she shape her thoughts to explain the events of the day. She did not have to tell her mother everything. She was a grown woman, although her mother sometimes did not admit that to herself, so accustomed was she to extracting an account from Mary of the events of the day. Changes of a dramatic kind were looming in her life. She had accepted Grant's love and felt a dawn excitement over the prospect of a marriage at the square dance. Her mother assuredly would reprimand her...a grown woman capable of making her own choices...were it not for the family history of close-hearted advice and controlling temper from her father, not so distant, estranged from the old woman who l had always thought that she knew better than her daugter. Then it came, the same antequated, time-worn question:

"Where have you been...daughter?" She no longer added child to the strict interrogation.
"With my friend."
"Your boy friend, I presume."
"He's more than that, mother dear. I've found him."
"Found who, your Prince Charming?" It almost drove her out of her mind to hear that description of the man she knew that she loved, beyond a doubt. "If you want to call him that. We are going to be married."
"What!" The mother gasped and slumped down into her usual green cushioned chair. "When did this happen?" She was incredulous. She questioned her daughter as if attempting to fix the time of the incident proposal.
"We've come to know each other, mother, dear." Mary put ice into her voice. "We have been seeng each other for some time...and he has asked me to marry him."
"Who has asked you?"
"My darling...."
"Foolish girl! I knew that some time you would be captured." The mother regarded her grown daughter with an expression that was more like a sneer than a mother's caring look.
"His name is Grant Shepherd."
"Is he Jewish?..Shepherd...with that name...."
" No, and it wouldn't make a bit of difference if he were. I love him."

Mary walked over to the chair where her scowling mother sat and stood towering before her, who had remained slumped in the cushions, disapproval fixed upon her face, that visage that she had used, without discussion, to dominae the life of her daughter. She regarded her daughter through hostile yes and a twitchng of the fingers of one hand. "So, now you are going to be married! What do you know about marriage...if I am not being too inquisitive as your mother?"
"We shall find the answers...together. We are in love.""
"In love...in love." A familiar disdain sounded in her voice. "To think that my daughter finds herself again in a ...compromising situation."
"Mother!" Mary shouted. "What are you saying. This is the man I love and I am

going to marry. There is no compromise, only that we are going to marry...and may I say so, mama dear...who drove my father to the brink of suicide with your constant nagging and finding fault in him."

The mother sat up abruptly in her chair. "Too bad you didn't say that about that...that cursed Priest."

"You .,..you terrible thing! I would have kept the child...."

The mother shrugged and turned her dark and embittered face away so as not to look at her daughter. "Your father never had any confidence in your ...your mothering...talent." She laughed a bitter and saddened brief laugh that came from deep down within her soul.

"She is safe." That was all that Mary could manage to say in the maw of the conflict that raged between them, mother and daughter, most of it under the surface of their confrontation.

"Is she...in an orphanage?"

"The child is...alive. That matters most."

"Who told you that?"

"I have ears to hear with. My lover...."

"Your boyfriend."

"No, no!"

"Do you think you fool your old mother? Harumppff!" she sputtered.   "Do you think you know how to raise a family?" The words were ladened with long-withheld contempt.

Her daughter ignored the question and its shifting, complex r meanings. "We are going to be married...and I can hardly wait...and, mother, dear old gal...you are not invited."

"Great God in heaven!...and why not?"

"Yes, He is still there...you will spoil the occasion!"

"I...your own mother...spoil the occasion of your wedding.

"That's exactly what I said."

"What a wicked thing to say to your mother! Well, I never could make you take advice...and now this...!"

"My marriage...and I'm damned glad you did not give me any advice to sully the occaaion, to turn a happy moment into a sorrowful...a sorrowful.... " She could not think of a suitable word.

"Disaster. You will marry a ne'r-do-well...what kind of work does he do?"

"He cuts firewood for people and mends and makes fireplace chimneys."

"Oh, good heavens...a chimny sweep!....with a ladder and his brushes, I suppose."

"He makes a fair living at what he likes to do...and he can find other work if he choses to do so."

"I tell you, as your mother, daughter of mine, that although I cannot tell you not to marry this...Shepherd." She did not finish her admonition. There was dismay and an unrelenting disdain in her voice. "I can only warn you against the consequnces of loving a man too much...and the wrong one."

"You...you, my own mother put that sort of a curse on me...and your only daughter's marriage."

"My words are not a curse, my words are a blessing."

"So you say, with contempt in your heart and a scowl on your face when I make the greatest announcemnt of my life. I'm going to be married. I have found a man I love."

"Love...love...what do you know about love?" To avoid giving voice to her hurt, the daughter turned away from the chair where the old woman sat, stared at the wall painting of St. Christopher receivng a chalice, and strode back to her mother, standing befor her like one condemned by the acrimony of the old woman's voice and strictures of her warnings that sprang from a dark and soulless, spiritually sterile past. "Take care. Your father probably said the same thing about me before we were married...that he couldn't do without me. Where is he now?""

"My father abandoned me..as a potentially worthless mother...just like he abandoned you, mother dear." The contempt she bore for her father, who was long departed from the household, emerged at the surface of her mind and her speech before Mrs. Wexler The mother shrank back into her chair, painfully aware of the truth of her daughter's observation and her realistic judgement. Mother and daughter were in the full flower of poisonous confrontation and murderous words.

"Your marriage to Dad was a failure...mommy dear. And now, bitter and old, you try to palm your sour and crippled disappointment off onto me. Well, I won't accept. it?"

"Just you wait...after three or four months, you will begin to have regrets."

"Stop it! Stop it, this instant!"

"I'm only l telling you the truth."

"The truth...your truth, you mean."

"You will remember my words when it is too late."

"I will forget them as soon as I leave here."

Mary started for her room, and was gone for five minutes. She had gathered up her square dance costume and other apparel, cosmetics and amenities for hygene and comfort and thrown them, tangled, into a large valise. She returned to the living room where here mother still sat, as if cut from rock, in the same position in the overstuffed green chair.

"Where are you going?"

"I'm leaving."

"Eloping, I presume."

"No, just leaving...to where is none of your business, mother dear."

"Shame on you...for talking to your mother like that.... I know and all of the neighborhood knows who fathered your little daughter." The remark came from an unassuagable anger and in the vengeful heat of the moment. It so stunned Mary that she could hardly answer for several minutes. Tears filled her eyes.

"I may...no that news is too good for you, mommy dear."

"You insult your own mother...and now without information, how ought I to know?"

"Ought, you ought to know. I...." The words were on her lipe.

"I will be watching to see what kind of a wife you make for this...Shepherd stud."

Mary's voice was slow, even and trembling with rage. "I hate you...I hate you...I hate you!" She again stood up to her mother's chair and it was all she could control not to slap her mother in her scowling face. But she desisted and turned to finish packing the valise before the staring, wrath-filled and tearful eyes of the old woman. For her daughter, she realized, was going out of her life forever. Mary took a candleholder from the lamp table, a miniature statue of Adelpha she had won in school for her oratory talent, and the small glass figurine of an elephant she had won as a school essay prize. Then, to her mother's surprise, she seized a guitar which stood in the shadows behind the chair where old woman sat.

"I played this guitar over a year ago. I am going to learn again and play for him...my beloved Grant."

"Beloved...." The old woman appeared ro gag on the word. "Music from the turnip patch."

"Shut up!..will you shut up, Missus Wexler!" she addressed her mother. She swept the two items--the valise and the guitar--to the door and, turning, her arms folded as if in defiance, said to her mother, who all l this while pretended to be in an invalid state of poor health, scarcely stirring in her chair, both arms extended on the chair arms, as if waiting for an attendant. "May I suggest you find a companion to share the rent and food and...and your hatred of life."

"You give me advice on how to live my life...my own child!"

"Just returning a little of it, mommy." She blew a kiss toward the old woman, whose face was transfixed in an expression of crushed and defeated wonderment, her eyes wide in surprise. To her it was unacceptable that her daughter should speak to her in those words and tone of voice of admonition and counsel, and, more importantly, that she should suddenly pick up and leave the security of the apartment.

Mary slammed the door, leaving her mother to wonder about all that had transpired.   Down in the lobby, she first called Penelope from her address book. She had an urgent request. Would she, Penelope, agree to accept her, Mary, as a guest for a ouple of nights. This was an emergency. She could take a room at the Empire Hotel in town. No, no, came the response to Mary's desperate call. The hostess to the discussion group acquiesced instantly to the request, said she had a guest room all rady and waiting, and would be expecting her later that day. She hung up. She next called Grant, She could hardly control the tremor in her voice. He should have been busy at work, but he was at his millsite cabiln. He had had trouble starting his truck. It was an old machine and he sought a way to replace it by building more fireplaces and chimneys...two new contracts this next month would enable him to finance the purchase of a better working truck...and the costs ot their honeymoon.

He had run to the phone and heard Mary's quivering voice. He realized that something was radically wrong...what had happened? His senses were alert..he told Mary he would be there at her apartment as soon as he was able to She was to wait for him in the lobby, and that he had not yet started on his work-day. He did not want to alarm her with a recital of his mechanical problem. Out at his truck, he went over the ignition system , the fuel lines, the filter...the filter! How could he have overlooked that one possibile cause--a clogged fuel filter? He had no replacement, but he could devise a connection of the line, without the filter. He had seen it done--telescoping one end of the line into a slight flaring of the other end with a screwdriver, then sealing the connection with a piece of tape. He removed the filter and cranked over the engine a revolution or two. He got out and checked the line, finding that the fuel had flowed from the open end. He was on to the cause for the truck not starting. He proceded to remove the filter and reconnect the line. He was elated with the success of his diagnosis and ingenuity. He turned the truck aound in the cabin area and headed out onto the millroad, then down through the valley and into town. Minutes separated him from his adored woman, who, like a moody and expectant abandoned orphan, sat patiently beside her valise and guitar in the lobby of the apartment building, where he had picked her up so many times.

Mary was ecstatic when she saw Grant's rusty old pick-up truck pull to a stop at the curb. She did not wait for him to come up the steps, but gripping the handles of her luggage, she bumped through he front door and started down the steps. Bounding up to her, he snatched the handles from her hands, and turning retraced his steps, she not far behind. He placed the two items carefully in the bed of the truck, then turned and gave his fiance a hug. He saw that she had been crying. Her eyes were moist and her expression doleful, though happy to see him.

"Don't tell me...your mother...."

She nodded. "We had words...she said some horrible things to me...and I guess I was not daughter-like...whatever that means. I'm out of there. Pray to God she makes out. She is alone. She has made her world for herself, Grant.

"People usually do...then try to blame others."

"I think she blames herself...she is not religious, but she can think about God. Maybe it will work." Grant did not respond to his Love's words but could only wonder what had taken place up there in the apartment, that had caused his beloved woman to cry.

"I have found a minister...a church I once attended, in another town, Hayfork...he has promised to come to the square dance. He doesn't dance...and officiate. That is only three days away."

"Yes, yes, I'm so happy, Grant."

"All this will fade away...in time, Mary. We can make a good life for ourselves."

"I'm sure we will, Grant."

"Let's get in." He opened the door for her and she took the passenger seat, He carefully closed the door behind her, slammling it to secure it. He came around, climbed onto the seat and and again slammed the door. "I have somethling I want tro give you, sweetheart."

"Yes, what is it?"

"First, you must promise that we shall take a day off...come with me, I can find a pair for you."

"A pair?"

"Of snowshoes. I'll come by and pick you up."

"You forget, dearest...I no longer have a place to live, to stay. I'll have to find work...the small inheritance...gone.... However...while I was waiting there I called Penelope."

"Penelope?"

"Yes, you remember her...the discussion group.... she is really a very generous person. I asked if she could put me up until the wedding. She is invited, of course."

"What a splended idea!"

"Her house-guest for two nights."

"And she said...?"

"Come on over, Mary."

"Splended!"

"So lets go to Penelopes place, can we? We know her address."

Mary's presence left an atmosphere behind in the old woman's apartment--her familiar perfume, her spirited departure, the picture in the mother's mind of the harsh words and actions of her disobedient grown daughter. The old woman was practically in a state of shock. Her face was wrinkled in a disconsolate frown, as if she were begging for mercy from some unseen force, her eyes sunk back in recessive hurt, her entire being shrunklen smaller by the calamlitous confrontation hhe had held with her daugher. She had to pull herself up by the arms of the chair to go to the telephone in another room. She called her brother Clyde, pretended to sob, clicked the phone to end the call. She had summoned Clyde to her rescue her from an ungrateful daugher, whom she suspected of having been bewitched by ...him, this wood-cutter.

"Oh, it's you,: she saild, swinging the door open wide, as if she had not expected him. He had put on a blazer with a rip in one sleeve. His face was unshaven.   His hair touseled and his hands perceptibly shook, although he was a relatively young man.

He did not hug his sister or offer her a kiss, but simply stepped over the threshold. He saw the look of destruction on his sister's face.

"Oh, Clyde...that woman...my daughter...she was so rude to me!"

"Rude?..well, Sis, you raised her. She should know good manners."

"She told me I was no good...The brother saw thougfhs this patent lie.   "She would not say such a thing. I know Mary better than that."

"It was the way she treated me...stubborn, like her father. She as much as said I was a fool."

"Oh, come now, Francine. You can't mean that."

"She was arrogant...I've never thought a child of mine would be so arrogant."

"Are you sure...you're not ...misreading Mary's words?"

"She said she has been; going with this...this ...well, I don't want to call him a rapist...a seducer..heaven help me! she says she wants to get married."

The brother at last sat down. All this preliminary conversation had frozen his responses, to the point where he did; not believe his sister's words.

"I see nothing wrong withs her wanting to get married,Francine."

"I do!   Listen to this! God help us all! He's just a ...you won't believe this, but hes a chimney sweep.".

"A chimney sweep!"

"You heard what I said, and he cuts wood for a living. He'll put her in the poor house, just you wait and see...I told her she was ignorant about love..."

"Francine, Francine," :he admonished. He shrugged his shoulers into the blazer that was too small for him, and he tried to take her hand to reassure her. She withdrew it as if from a hot stove ."You can't mean that. You said that to her?"

"I did, and to her face. That child has got to learn."

"You don't mean that. Mary is a grown woman and capable of making her own decisions...without your help, Francine."

"I said it to her face."

"You have ;made an enemy out of your own daughter."

"That child has got to learn," she repeated.

"She may be your child ; but as a grown woman. she has found somebody she loves...."

"Love... love...love!" the old woman mimed herself with unrelenting disdain in her voice. "What does she know about love? I told her that very thing/"

"Before you get any further worked up over a matter you can't help, let me just say this--find a female companion   Perhaps you'll listen to me, your brother." .

"A...female companion. " She sighed as if exhaused by the very idea of sharing the apartment with another woman of similar age. "I don't know, Clyde. I just don't know."

"Practicality...think of that. Emergencies, shopping for food, paying bills." His sister, the old woman, sat slumped in her familiar overstuffed chair and, leaning forward, her head in her hands, she softly began to cry.

"Let me help, Francine. I will. After all, you are my sister." She raised her head, tears on her cheeks, her powder running. " Well, all right, Clyde, if you think that's the right thing to do. I don't want to see that child of mine for as long as I live!"

"I think you will get your wish." The brother stood and, walking to the door, opened it and stood in the opening. I will try to find someone to help you here, Francine. Be practical." He said no more. Leaving his sister looking dolefully and dejectedly after him; he turned and shut the door with bang. She flung herself back into her chair and ried aloud..."What's the use?... What's the use...?"

The drive of Mary and Grant in his old, rattling pickup was fairly short. They found Penelope's house, a small brown bungalow on knoll that overlooked the aspens down along the creek. Penelope was a mother whose children had long ago left their home, now grown adults scattered about in several states. She filled the space of her loneliness--her husband deceased after the third child...he had been a school teacher--with her book-discussion group. It was a joy to her to have so many people come to visit her...her perspective...even though they discussed books, literature and...the Holy Bible on more than one occasion. She greeted Mary and Grant with open arms and, while Grant waited in her rattan chair with the fan-back, she was quick to show Mary to her guest room. Returning, she invited Grant to have one of her own pastries and a cup of coffee, since it was not yet mid-morning. The ambience was cordial and comfortable. The new arrivals apeared to enjoy Penelope's hosptality, even more than thay had on the two nights they had attended the discussions on St. John and on The Wayfarer, a novel.

"Penelope, I don't know how to thank you . You know, of course, that I and Mary are engaged." She laughed.

"We have to be...if we want a wedding.. How silly of me," Mary said.

"These are the times. When you're so happy you could float, silliness is a part of the rhapture of the ...the occasion. I hadn't the slightest idea. How could I? Oh, you needn't apologize. This occasion is a time when you float with happiness. Just being t a little silly is a part of the rhapture of the occcasion." They all had a laugh over this remark. "Yes, I remember that time at my own marriage," said the hostess.

"We are going to be married...are you ready for this?..at the square Dance."

Penelope sat down. She could not take the surprise, standing. This announcemen was almost too strange and novel for her..."At a square dance!"

"I'm so thrilled...as you can imagine," said Mary.

"I had no engagement before my ownmrriage...we had problems..," said Penelope. "You see, I was a madam."

The lovers tried not to show surprise or any emotion at all. '

Gramt went on. "I 've talked with the minister, a Doctor Fred Havelock...from Hayfork...doesn't matter. he agreed to do the ceremony. We shall have our ceretmony in full rites I' ve called the club president and vice president and they are well organized...the Boots and Gaiters. They agreed to fund and arrange the ceremony...he's going to make a white-silk, padded a kneeling bench. He described it to me."

"Boots and Gaiters...that's the name of thils...square dance club?"

"Yes," said Mary. "We will have a big dance night for certain....!"

"The club captains, Jules and Vera, said they would take care of the details and that there was a visiting club coming on that night, their next dance night, saturday next. They will double the dancers. I hope that there is room at the hall. We shall have a full ceremony and cotillion-like marriage dance. Wow!" Grant was exstatic with his announement of the arrangements and he observed the delight on the cosuntenances of the two women, his beloved fiance and her generous and gracious hostess, Penelope. The couple exchanged loving looks. Peneope intercepted them, glancing from one to the other. She smiled. "You're invited to the wedding and the reception dance, Penelope. You're invited to join a square for a tip. If not, you have company around the room, watching the dance. We'll be leavlng at some point...and Jules has agreed to bring you home."

"How sweet of him and efficient of you, Grant!"

"Well then. So it is settled...."

"Not entiely, Penelope. I would like fo you to be my Bride's Maid."Penlope was instantly excited and astonished. She accepted. Mary thought that had already asked her, but Grant needed to know.

"Yes, and also, I haven't told her yet, that I and Mary...you, dearest, and I... are gong snowshoing in the morning, so I will be coming by pretty early."

"Going snowshoing! Oh, holly tolly! Imagine that. What a glorious occasion!" their hostess exclaimed.

"Yes, isn't it! I know just the right place in the local mountains...up into the rocks of a mountain peak..Marmot Summit. Over eight thousand feet. We'll take the ski lift...."

"Have you ever snow shoed before?" Penlope asked Mary.

"No."

"It's as easy as walking" said Grant, "and more fun, if you can imagine. We'll have a good time, you can count on that."

"I know that is true. Now then, you are taking time from your work, Mister Shepherd."

"I couldn't get my truck started this smorning...until I' found the problem."

He stood, kissed Mary lightly on her lips, smiled at the hostess and said to them both, "I shall be coming by at about six tomorrow morning."

"Six..!"

"Six it is," said Penelope. "No breakfast here."

"I won't disturb your sleep, my friend. Mary...I will have the snow shoes...and our breakfast. Wear some mittens if you have them...otherwise...I have a pair of my own for you...and a woolen cap."

"I can help with the cap, Grant," said Penelope.

"Put on a jacket, if you have one. I'll bring an extra sweater. We shall be prepared for the snow."

"I know you two will have a grand time. And, Grant and Mary, dear, thank you so much for the invitation to your wedding night square dance. Include me in...I shall be there." Grant gave Mary a hug and a kiss, shook Penelope's hand cordially and with a genuine warmth and left the house. Mary and Penelope's began to enjoy their brief accomodations and the company of the two of them, compatible in temperament and purpose for this special event. After they heard his truck start up and leave the front of the cottage, Penelope and Mary were lost in a tour of the residence, which had an upstairs guest room. In the room were momemtos of her son's days as a highschool athlete. He was a boxer, there were the gloves, a javelin thrower, there was his spear, and a swimmer, there was a trophy for his winning a certain event at his high school. Penelope indulged herself in the memories, as Mary delved into the past of her hostess's life, a happy marriage with its traditional events. She could hardly wait for the morrow when Grant would drive up. Snowshoing was a special treat, she had seen the shoes before today--big webbed paddle-like affairs, strung with thongs that enabled the snowshoer to walk on top of the snow. "What a blast!" she thought.

a

RESPITE

'She feared a forest fire. On their way to the ski tow three miles distant from Marmot Mountain, their destination, she told of how she had a friend who lost his life fighting the raging Prism Lake Fire in August, three years before.

"It was horrible...I mean how his sister described the fire fight."

"A fire fighter can be trapped. Firemen from fire companies have bags of asbestos they can crawl into, but not the guys on the line...the smoke eaters."

"That's what I heard, also." The truck growled up a hill, then down another, his eyes on the road, hers on the passing forest scenery.

"Some time we'll have to go back to San Francisco. You remember Chinatown. I never saw so many white folks. You had to go into a shop to see a Chinese person."

"Well, that umbrella and those sandals will keep the memories alive...the cable cars."

"I was so scared the first time I rode one...the natives swing freely from the hand rails...it's a blast...! I tlhought, what if the cable breaks? Well be in a pot of trouble."

But the cable did not break and that North Poiint Italian restaurant was a real treat. You remember those frescoes on the wall?" he asked.

"I sure do. I've thought many times...why cant I paint a fresco on...on a wall somewhere?"

"You might hav e the talent, you never can tell, Mary, dear."

 "Their spaghetti was out of this world..liteally, Old Italy spagheti."

"They don't cut it up into short pieces...like you find in some restaurants. It's full length spagheti. You could lift a yard of the stuff off of   your plate." They laughed at his exaggeration.

"Arm's length spaghetti...how that for an advertisement?" she queried.
They drove on, reaching the snow level and finding snow that covered the embankmentys on both sides of the winding road.

"'We'll soon be there, abou another five miles. This is back in the forest, where they can count on snow for the downhill skiers."

"Grant...do you think its not right?"

"What's not right?"

"That I avoided going to the funeral of a friend today?"

"Oh, my deart Mary, a funeral....   With all respect, your frend can wait for you this time. He...she..."

:She...."

"She would want you to be here with me and come on our snowshoeing trip. Think about it. If she were alive and she had said, 'Mary, I'm going to have a funeral, but if you have something else planned....'"

"A trip up to the snow."

"A trip up to the snow, why, you go on ahead. You can go to a funeral any time.

You can showshoe only in winter." They enjoyed another laugh over his scenario about her deceased friend.

He slowed for a patch of black ice. "Treacherou;s, deadly."

"What, dear?"

"Black ice...the ice is invisible on the black macadam of the road. It can send a car spinning off the road and down the mountainside, rolling all the way and churning up the occupants like cream in a butter churn."

"I never thought." They were sillent.

"I can tell you one thing. The ride up the mountain will be more fun than a carnival ride."

"I can hardly wait. I've thought about it before...friends who ski."

"You've never skied before?"

"No."

"I never asked...well, it takes some practice and learning. You have to sort of]devote yourself to the sport for a season, really, to get anything out of it."

"I thought so."

He slowed again for a patch of black ice. Within minutes, they arrived at the ski tow. The parking spaces in a wide place in the road had long ago been filled by downhill skiiers. They pulled into an opening, he shut off the engine. They scrambled out, he reached into the truck bed under a tarpolin and pulled up two pairs of snow shoes and four poles. Last, hle lifted out his backpack.

"Beauties, aren't they?"

"They look like chicken baskets to me." He chuckled at her comparison.

"Lets...they're not hard to put on. I don't want any...mishap. I'll carry the shoes. you take the poles, if you would. We'll ride up without them on our feet. Getting off one of those chairs can be a little tricky if you've never done it before. I don't want us to fall or anything like that." He put his arms through his backpack, which contained a first-aid kit and their lunch, which he had prepared back at his cabin. Also, he had filled a thermos of with hot tea, a squeezed lemon and some sugar.

They climbed the railed steps up to the cashier's little hut. He paid the fare fo both ways. They stood in line, behind a skiing pair, waiting for the chairs to come around. They were two-seaters, as most ski lifts are. As lit circled around to where they stood, the chair buped into the legs of the skiers, who sat readily into its contours with a swing and they took off up the mountain. He and Mary waited, their chair came down at an interval, swung around the end, the helper steadied the chair, they sat in it, falling against the chair back and dangling their feet. Grante clutched the unwieldy snowshoes mightily, as the chair began its ascent up the side of the mountailn. For Mary, coming from Phoenix with her mother, this was an out-of-the womb adventure. The icy air was exhilarating, the snowpack below the tow zoomed past sixty feet beneath as they rode up in space. The tops of the firs were laden with the night's new snow, the vista was magnificnt and breathtaking to both of them. The chair clicked past one tower, and then the next, the cable made a slight whirring sound each tme as it spun past the huge horizontal wheel .

"What a view!"

"Yeah...what a view!" They delighted in the novelty of the landscape, the mountain forest, the snow on the ground, some rocks, then a couple of hikers on snowshoes, like they would be, making their way among the trees below, two downhillers seeming to dodge the trees as they carved tracks into the snow below. It was all so thrilling to Mary that

she could not put her feelings into words, and he was mesmermied, as well, by the grandeur
of the scenery that stretched out below them and into the distance, toward the peak they were
to take.

"Now, when you see the guy waiting there...get ready to jump off. And when you
do, run forward and he chair will swing around behind you. We have to get out of the way.
It is not hard, but it is a little tricky. The chair rose up over the flat of the mountaintop and
both of them exited the lift chair with ease. They were surprised to see directly ahead of
them, on a rise of ground, a ski chalet and a restaurant. "Lets go in and get warm,." Grant
said. They headed for the chalet and afire. He stood the snowshoes and the poles against a
nearby boulder wall outside. He removed his backpack. He went up to the counter and
ordered two hot chocolates. She gandered the heavy oak beams of he ceiling and the woodsy
interior of the chalet,

"Hot chockloate!" the girl at the counter called. Grant lept up, and hurryig over,
bought back to their table the cups of steaming. foaming chocolate, a dob of sweet cream
atop each.

"That was a view we shall never forget. Our ticket is good for the return trip.
The lift does not leave any skiers stranded atop the mountain if they can help it.".

"Let's walk down."

"Bravo! I was hoping you would say that...about two miles by the forestry road to
the highway, then another mile up the road to the truck. We can do it. I want us to enjoy this
little event to the fullest."

"Of course we could take the lift down."

"I'll think about it, he said. "See how we feel...if we're too tired...."

Having flinished their cups of chocolate, the two of them stepped outside to a low
wall, where he brushed snow from the boulders. They sat down and he affixed the snow
shoes to his sweetheart's shoes.strapping them securely to her shoes. He had hoped she
would wear boots, but instead she wore a pair of old hightops. "Just as well," he thought.

"Your snowshoes fit."

"Just about," she said.

"Well, if you start to limp, we'll ...take care of it...blisters can happen."

"I'll be okay." He fixed his own snowshoes to his boots, snugging the straps
securely. They set off across the loose, new-fallen snow.

"I'm glad we brought the poles. They come in handy on uneven ground,
especially on fresh snow." She did not reply. They started off toward Marmot Peak. He led
the way, she walked in his tracks, they disappeared from sight of the chalet in another few
minutes, among the firs and junipers, leavling the ski lift civilization behind and curtting a
wide swathe in the new snow, atop the mountailn. For the both of them they could not
have asked for a more enjoyable experience.

"Another world!" he shouted back, turning his head.

For a little more than an hour Grant led the way over the slightly rising ground,
past smooth boulders that towered over the height of the trees. O casionally as they walked,
a big collecion of snow fell from a tree limb, under the warming sun that was fast meltng the
snow in the branches. One of these puffs hit Mary on the shoulder, splashing its cold crystals
into her face. Startled, she stopped and laughed with delight. She brushed the snow from her
shoulder.

In due course, after an hour or so of cross-coutry snowshoing, they arrived at the
summit of Marmot Mountain. He anounced to his Love that he had packed a lunch or them

of tuna and ham sandwches, which he, of course, carried in his backpack without mentioning it to her. He cleared snow from a nearby area of flatness between the boulders, withdrew the bagged lunch he had prepared, poured a cup of hot, lemon-spiked tea for Mary. He invited her to dive in, he taking a sandwich. Hungrily they began to feast on the lunch he had prepared. She poured her tea, tasted the lemon in it with a sip. He chose the tuna sandwich, she the ham sandwich. He poured more from the thermos of hot tea. They began their lunch with a real hunger, atop the peak, looking about them as they ate, inviting the forest to speak to them, listening for sounds of forest life, absorbing into their own hearts this bonanza of beauty and this respite for their mutual enjoyment, as if God had designed it just for these moments. They were totally engrossed in this aspect of their adventure when a flash of gray crossed the slope below them...a marmot.

"Smelled the food," said Grant.

Mary broke off a corner of her sandwich and tossed it in the direction of the marmot.that sat watching them, as if trained like cat to accept thrown tidbits of food. The little animal took the crumb, paused, then vanished into a pile snow-covered rocks.

"Our visitor," said Grant.

"What do they eat...up here?"

"Pinecone seeds, when they are available on the ground. Otherwise, they know where wild berries are...and roots, I suppose. They're totally herbivorous. They have no prey they hunt and kill. Not like the wolverine...a sort of ferral cat, a wildcat...but not the marmot. " Mary and he finished off their sandwiches and the thermos of hot tea. He stowed the lunch items back in his backpack and zippered it closed.

"Tired?" he asked.

"Not really...less than I thought I would be."

"This is Marmot Peak. Listen...hear tha?" Neither spoke, no sound came frm the forest. That's like a hand of God when you're alone...the very silence makes you to listen...for Him. I don't think the little critters come out in the winter. season...I don't know if they hybernate like bears."

"Bears !"

"I've hiked up here a dozen times and never seen a bear...or a paw print."

"The silence...isn't that spectacular! Listen to ...nothing." A splash of snow fell from a tree branch onto the ground. " 'S warming up." he said.

"Grant."

"Yes?" He dug into his backpack or their lunch.

"We'll be married tomorrow night. This almost seems like a...a honeymoon as it is."

"I feel the same." They had kept their snowshoes on. Clumsily, he came over to where she sat and found a perch on a boulder a beside her, where she sat on the bare rock, putting his arm around her shoulders. He gave her a firm kiss on the cheek. "We 'll have an elegang ceremony."

"You love ceremonies."

"They're good introductions." He reached into one pocket of his field jacket and withdrew a small box. He opend the lid, revealing a gogreous set of of diamond engagement and wedding rings. He took her left hand and from the box withdrew the engagemnt ring with its capital stone, surrounded by clusters of smaller diamonds. " I hope this fits. Sometimes a ring is a guess. It can be sized." He slipped the ring onto her engagement fInger, kissed her hand and then placed a long and ardent kiss on her lips. "We just want the world to know."

She lifted her hand and examined the ring closely. "Oh Grant, it's beautliful. I could not have picked a more beautiful ring." She returned his ardent kiss and for the longest while they sat there in each other's arms, enjoyilng the moment of their shared love.

"I suppose Penelope asked...."

"No, she never said a word. It sometlimes happens...I mean, an engagement without the ring. She's coming to the wedding...I invited her. She will be my bride's maid.. She will have to have a way home, too...."

"I can arrange that." He showed his sweeheart her wedding ring. "They're a match, sweetheart."

"What a place for announcement--atop a mountain iln the silnce of he woods!" she said in her laughter. "On a mountalin peak. This is my high." Her wit entangled his emotions and intellect. She was a whizz of a woman so far as he was concerned, witty, vivacious, bright and totally loyal. "Oh, how I love this woman!" he thought.

"There is another little matter, a ritual if you want to call it that. We must sign in."

"Sign in?"

"Yes, the Sierra Club has a register on many of the peaks in this forest, and even if you are not a member, youre supposed to sign in.   Where is it. They feel they are conserators of naure...They track trail and foest usage, I suppose. "

"We'll have to hunt for it. They began to brush snow from the rocks, searching tor the peak register. At last, she discovered it hidden under a small boulder, which she lifted and set aside. There in the weathered and torn pages were the names and scribled comments of others who had visited Marmot Peak. He had come prepared. He took a pencil from one pocket and signed, she put her name below he and he added the line, "engaged on Marmot Peak"..which was not quite right but made good copy for the next signers.

"You remember our planearium visit?" he asked.

"I do, I do...great time we had

"The stars up here shine twice as bright as down there in your valley."

"That's hard to imag ine. We don't plan to stay here until the stars come out, do we, Grant?"

Oh, nothing like that. I just thought...well, we will have another chance...were going to Mirror Lake for our honeymoon, and I think there's a planetarium up there."

"Where is that?"

`"It's in Northern California. I've arranged for a bridal suite...."

"Trop cher."

"Not for our wedding honeymoon, Mary, dear. Nohing is too high for you...."

He kissed her ardently and caressed her breasts. She yielded. He leaned back. She did not know that he knew that a love relationship can deteriorate into fantasy and illicit love if the man is not careful to conrol his impulses, and that lapse could possibly ruin further trust on the part of either partner. He loved Mary and so respected her. adored her body, respected her intelligence and cherished her spirit and mind, so that he could not bring himself to commit that self-indulgence, to treat her as a mere object of momentry passion. If she left him, then he would know...he would reassert his independence again. But he was confident by now that she would remain loyal. Besides, the time was so short, only twenty-four hours until they should bless one anothe with a mariage consumation. He thrilled to think of it. That was the hard-nosed resolve in his own mind, reinfored by a stubborn temperament, not to overstep the line between love and adultery. License ruled the times. Well, God damn the times! Who was anyone to tell him how to behave. He had been a marksman sniper in he war. He knew how to fix his target, if that was the measure of courage. For him, the relationship was as simple as that. He did not reveal this darker part of his thinking to her, but, instead, he wanted to act in a way that would instill confience, not distrust.

"There's a observatory up there for the night skies."
"Where...?"
"At Mirror Lake, where we'll spend our honeymoon."
"We'll just have to try it out." She gave him a kiss on one cheek.
"Are you cold?..you're shivering."
"No, Grant, the trip over here warmed me up."
"We mustn't sit for too long. Lets move around. I've decided."
"What , Grant?"
"That, since neither of us is...is an athlete, at least were not practiced in walking forest trails or forestry roads...and its at least three miles down to the highway, that we ought to take the lift down to our truck. Right here, this is the most beautiful part of the mountain, I think. You wouldn't only see more of the same on the way down. The trip back to the ski tow is a good two miles."   "I'm thinkm you' re right, Grant."
"Let's stand...thisty?"
"A little."
"Watch." He scooped up a handful of clean snow from a rock amd ate it, its fresh, cold melt appeasilng his thirst."   "Won't hurt you. It's clean, delicious." He scooped up another handful and stuffed it nto his mouth. "Mmm. Better than city water. I've done that many times before. I ate snow once when I hiked alone in the San Gorgonio wilderness. It was summer, the snow stayed unmelted in the shade, probably a little gritty." He watched her try his remedy for thirst, and saw the look of delight on her face. "Good, huh? " She nodded. "Lets walk around up here....around these huge rocks. I wonder how they were formed...they're so smooth and round...water usually rounds off boulders. If that's the case, they must have been down low in the course of a river somewhere."
"That means, down in the canyon."
"hat's right. Come over here, sweeheart. " He had moved to the opposite side of one of the immense pile of sandstone rockss. He pointed to a place between rocks, a hundred yards distant, down the opposite side of the mountain summit, and partly overlain by other boulders.
" One night I came up here and I planned to stay overnight. Then I thought better of it. I was going to bed down over there, under those rocks overhang. I cooked a delicious supper of weiners and had opened a small tin of sourkraut when I began to think. One thought kept occurring in my mind--Just as I as preparilng or a good night's rest: what if a mountain lion, a leopard, had smelled my weiners cooking and had come close enough to investigate. I would be faced with the first mountain lion I had ever seen...outside the zoo."
"Right down there?"
"In there, under that rock overhang...trapped. So...I gathered up my gear, rolled up my sleeping bag and listened for anyh unusual sounds. The night was quiet...and black as the inside of a chimney. Black as the night was, I climbed up to where we stand and then

headed downs the trail--over there is the trail head--started bacl down to the highway, a walk of almost three miles...."   "In the dark."

"Totally.. in the dark. I had no problem...I was a little younger then. I could see the trail without a flashlight. I preferred to be...invisible in the darkness to man or beast. I was alert and just a little scared."

"That must have been an exciting night."

"Some instinct told me not to stay on that mountain for the night. It's rare, very rare that a mountain lion...they resemble the leopard in size... would come stalking up here...for what?-- there is no food...."

"For you, my dearest...for you. You would be its food, the bait your...was it bacon frying...

He laughed. "...weiners."

"Well a big car like that is not particular. You would prove fresh, warm and delicious."

"And bloody in the bartgain." he said.

"And dead."

"Competely so. Oh, I had a knife., but when a creature that size knocks you to the ground, reaching for a knife is next to impossible. They said no more about his experience. That was his one story about the peak where they sat, soaking up the warmth of the early afternoon sun.

He scanned the surrounding trees, the rocks and snow-covered ground, freshly overlain by the night's snow fall . As if prompted by some emergent need, he stood and, wihout saying a word to her, he seized his poles from where he had plunged them into the snow, against a rock, and he set out again in the direction of the ski-tow, two miles distant. He did not look back. He only assumed that she had snatched up her poles and was following him.

But he was wrong. He turned around and saw her sitting yet on the rocks where he had left her. He hurriedly snowshoed back to her.

"What's wrong, Mary?"

"These boots. I think I have a blister on one foot." .

He came over to her and bent down. He removed her hightop shoe from the showshoe and helped her to unlace it. He awkwadly placed her foot on his bended leg. and removing it and her sock, Hee saw that the the inner lining of her shoe had rubbed a place red, almost into a blister on her heel. "The heel," she said. He examined her foot, and seeing that the heel was red and much irritated, close to becoming a blister, he slipped out of his backpack and pulled out his first-aid kit. From it he took a cushioned patch and peeled off first the paper and thenthe protective wrapper. He placed the patch over the red spot. Briskly massaged her foot to warm it, he, put her sock back on, then her hgih-top shoe. He laced it up and tied it for her.

"All a part of the trip," he said with assurance. Call me Docor Grant. That ought to stop the blister. I know how crippling a blister can be. I was in the army."

"Thanks, Grant, my dear. I so appreciate you...More so, as time go on."

He smiled and handed her the poles. He slipped back into the straps of his backpack and they started off once again. He stopped about a hundred yards distant and, turning back, asked..."How's your foot?"

"Much better, thanks," she replied and waved him on with her poles. They began they trip back to the ski tow. They needed to arrive back at Penelope's place, not too late, so that Mary would have a good supper with her friend and a good night's rest...with a big day to prepare for tomorrow night; the sensational square dance wedding. She hoped that Jules had invtied the local newspaper to take some photographs for the Shepherds' memory book.

They retraced their deep tracks in the new snow. The return trip over the packed trail seemed shorer and quicker and much easier to navigae. . They arrived back at the jump off point for the ski lift, weary but much invigorated and refreshed by the entire excursion across from one peak to the other. Removing their snow shoes, Grant hugged both pairs and Mary gripped the poles with firm grilp of two hands, and under one arm.   They stood wailting for the next chair to swing around below the overhead cable wheel. Backs to the chair, it came around and under them. They sat down into it with   little more confidence this time, as over the brow of the lift platteau and down the mountain again they floated, at about ten miles an hour. Below them, shadows lay upon the ground, the blueness of the snow, the darkening tree tops and forest fled beeath their dangling feet. a vista that was just as exciting to the senses as it was on their way up. At the lower deck, so called, they hopped free of the chair, he almost tripping and she reaching a hand to catch him. They cautiously walked down the icy steps, clinging to the handrail and mindful of ice on the steps. He put their snowshoes and the poles she still held into the bed of the truck. Backing out of their spot, they began their thirty-mile journey out of the forest and down into the valley, to Penelope's house.

Having settled upon a pickup time of six-thirty the following night and after exchanging a kiss and an awkward hug inside the cab of his truck, Grant drove away. Mary entered the house and at the rear, in Penelopes garden, she found her friend tending a bed of hyacynths. Taken by surprise, Penelope stood.

"Well, I hardly expected you back this early."

"I'm so sorry, Penelope I did not consider it before." Her friend stood, regardig her in puzzlement, the trowel still i her hand. Not long with words, Mary suggested, "I will need a Maid of Honor. I...wonder if you would be willing to serve. I'm sorry I did not ask you sooner." Her friend scarcely moved, silent, waiting for some bizzare announcement. She tossed the trowel into the flower bed. She reached out to Mary and placing both hands on her shoulders, looked her straight in the eyes.

"You know I would but, my dear friend...and we are friends now beyond question...I have no square dance dress to wear. I'm not a square dancer."

"That's not so important as you suppose.   Since you will be the Maid of Honor, and since there are a variety of dresses the dancers wear these days. and the minister will surely show up in a fine suit, whether white I do not know...."

"Not white.   I have a black suit."

'Superb! I can furnish you with a badge of the club."

And I have a pair of white gloves I can wear for an accent. A yellow hyacynth on my black suit and...beads, I have some grand beads, imitation pearl, I can wear".

"Wonderful...with your blonde hair and black suit and ea figure, you'll look gorgeous. Some dancers dance in ordinary print dresses, anyway. . It's not unusual. There'll be a visiting club and a great many variations, so you will fit in just fine."

"I'm so glad you invited me. I've never been to a square dance...and a square dance wedding will be some affair!"

"We will...that is, Grant will want for us to get away during the reception dance. You can stay for as long as you please, Penelope. Grant has already arranged to have

Jules...he's the club president...drive you home...so you needn't worry about getting back here."

"I think the whole occasion is simply ...exotic, exciting. I shall think about it all night and tomorrow."

"Thank you so much, my friend. I'm sorry I and Grant haven't been attending the discussion group sessions, as we thought we would."

Penelope laughed. "Oh, that's all right, really. We've been delving into such an exotic book as "The Adventures of Robinson Crusoe." Believe it if you want...a children's book. Why has it lasted for so long, and what is its appeal to adults?"

"I should have liked to enter the discussion. Escape is the only word I can think of."

"For children from their chores and parents...escape for adults who want out of social responsibilities. It's a matter of survival."

"Yes, isn't it!" Mary replied with a cryptic smile. So then it was settled. Mary went into the house to clean up, while Penelope retired to the green house to put her tools away and to wash her hands. She and Mary would enjoy a pasta together for tonight's supper, and a little radio enertainment before retiring early.

ONE GREAT NIGHT

Music drifted from a dark and massive wooden strucure called a The Barn, from which lights shone in its upper hayloft windows and the stars canopied the dark outlines. The two captains of the square dance club known as the Boots and Gaiters had chosen this venue because of the overflow crowd they expected when one square dance club joins with another in a night of music and dancing. Inside the hall, in some precincts referred to as a ballroom, where the polished, hardwood floor glowed with an almost icy flourish under the ceiling lights, intended for other civic events , a place in smaller towns called A Grange Hall, streamers of crepe in colors of green, yellow, red, brown and whilte hung from the light fixtures and were nailed to the wooden rafters of the structure, Tonight was to be a wedding night as well as a dance night for the attendees to this singular event in the lives of the dancers as well as the principal players in the event. There was to be a marriage of two dancers. Their reception party was to consist of the other square dancers who where now arriving in numbers, some of them friends of the bride, Mary Wexler, and a handful who could acknowledge a casual acquaintanceship with, or had even heard of, the groom, Grant Shepherd.

Jules and Vera, the captains of this orverture to romance and marriage, moved about the room, attending to the long smorgasborg tables that were beilng copiously covered with dlishes food of all sorts, finger foods, cheezes, crackers,cookies and small cakes, and the polished silver urns of water, coffee and punch that hlpers were making ready in the kichen of the vballroom, as, the local newspaper, the Sentinel, called the inner stadium like area, Jules was costumed in the green an white of his club's olors. His wife, Vera, was well known, rther pudgy in figure, possessing a handsome, round face, her black hair combed into a shock atop her head, displaying a quick and vanishsing smile when someone spoke to her. She, too, moved about with grace and decisiveness. They had much to do with making the night memorable for over one hundrddancers and guests. .

Jules was a handsome man, rather short, fine features, thin nose and a fall of graying hair over his forehead. He spoke in deep tones, small of figure, eyes that squinted, of generally handsome features with gray eyes and a slight lips marked his presence. His lythe, athletic body moved with agile steps, he had the habit of folding his arms before making a move. He wore a shimmering green cravat, club badges and extremely busy, he was slow to answer questions from those lookin on.   . He was dressed in a shirt embroidered with green rose leaves. diamond wing-tips on his collar. His hands moved with speed, as a magician's.

"We'll have at least a hundred."

"I expect more than that, Jules. Did you speak with Mary?"

"I'm to find a ride home for her Maid of Honor...Penelope...."

"They have not arrived yet."

"No, but just look." They stopped in their labors at a side table. He set down a tray of finger foods, paused iln their distriution to glance at he guests filing lin past the pay table. The strangers iln other colors, walked around the permiter of the hall to find chairs for the night, to leave jackets, shawls and purses in one place, and to watch other guests stream into The Barn like the celetbrants they were to become. They rapidly filled tlhe chairs along the sides of the floor

"Why do some people want a religious ceremony?" Jules asked.

"This...wedding...needs only an annointing an celebrants...One minister is sufficient, Jules. You remember...we were married in a berry patch."

"Oh, pshaw...his grandfather's explicative. It was a cheery outdoor thing. Even you said so." She smiled wlith the reminiscence. "No, I mean they want a cross, and holy wine and ...oh, all the rest. This is definitely not a sanctuary...The Barn. McGregor's gift to the town...."

"Why should it be? And he died without a horse, remember. Jules shrugged and scanned the table or missing items, plastic cutlery, napkins, jelly beans and nuts.... "God didn't live in a nave, he lived in a town, probably in a mud hut...he came to the marketplace. Why not this...barn...room for a thousand bales of hay and thirty horses....!"

Some folks can't be satisfied that a marriage is good at any other place, even on a roof top. Folks held church services in bars in gold towns."

"I know, I know. I think...well...you know Mary when you see her...?"

"Of course...I've never met this...Grant fellow. Must've come alone." They continued to set up the refreshment tables. On the stage, a spotlight highlighted the band of five, who were animatedly talking and discussling the music for the night."

"Where do we sign?" the male of a dancing couple asked the pair of square dancers in the night's regalia, at the door.

"Are you a club member?"

"No, were visitors.?

"Sign on that sheet."

Thus, as at a checkpoint, newcomers and club members signed their names on prepared sheets and paid the admission for each couple of five dollars, continuing on into the ballroom to find chair along the side. The slgn-in sheets would constitute the guests' register at a traditional marriage ceremony.

"How many can we expect tonight?"

"A crowd..." he replied. Hampdon Jones, smiling always, black moustache, upraised glance scanned each customer, his dance partner, a pretty little woman seeming twice his age, with graying hair, also smiled up at the next couple to pass their table. There was no quackery involved, the fee was simple, the custom ordered, and old-timers found surcease in this ritual at the door. "How many?" he often asked his at the ticket table. Mrs. Jones smiled, at least a hundred.

"We shall have a fine treasury after tonight."

The couples conntinued to appear, as lif fom oblivion,onto a stage of activity, ready to enter ilntos the dance calls. Not a few of them, at least fifeen, hastened out ono the floor to engage lin the round dance number being called by Sol Berger and his wife, Tina. He was a staturesque guy, for a male a compliment, an athletic body with a handsome featured. His partner was small, short for his height, but quick on her feet, a woman who darted her eyes about the room and moved swilftly to her partner's calls. They were assumed to e a married couple. The rounds were an elegant form aof dance, with exact steps relayed to the dancers iln a patterned dance around the loor from right to left, accompanied by the live music of the band on the lighted stage. One violin, a guitar, drums, a bass and an accordion made up the live band.

The men arrived attired fin their c lorful regalia for a formal square dance, elegant in their starched and embroidered shirts, the ladies in a varieties of colors, some taupe and white, matching shirts for the men, attendees from the visiting club and straggler guests from other parts. The colors for the Boots and Gaiters were green and white. The mixture of colors contributed to the festive air that was forming within the immense so-called ballroom space of The Barn. The men of the town had overlain a beautiful wooden floor over the original dirt of the horse-barn. Townsfolks could not forget that this structure had once served as an actual barn, immense as it was to contain George MGregor's huge five hunded acre crop of alfalfa and his twenty-five horses and ten mules. He had bequethed his barn to the town, since it lacked a Grange as was customary in many small towns, a social hall for mixed events. It was said that he owned a horse that was the barn's first dancer.

The faces of the arriving guests were wreathed in smiles and looks of surprise and expectation, as they entered, signed the visitor or member sheets and spread out around the sides of the room to dispose of their wraps and, most of them, to watch the round dancersrs move effortlessly around the room. There was an eagerness that overcame their actions, as they caught up the spirit of the dance, eager to for the squares to begin, while at last a dozen couples were already dancing the called round . Few if any knew that a wedding was to take place. The Club president had announced it at their last dance, but had left the reality of the special occasion, and the decorations as a surprise for his guests. The faces of some of the men expressed wonder and perplexity, their ladies laughing and smiling and chattering with personal friends in keeping with the joy of the occasion. From the old beam rafters there hung streamers and the all yellow and white crepe bunting to bring to wonder to the faces of guests, who realized something very special was about to transpsire. here lin this venue of an ordlinary square dance.

"What's happening?" one man asked, as he spun on his heel and scanned the decorations.

"A wedding, looks like," a friend said who overheard their conversation. A wedding!" The element of surprise added to the gay atmosphere and a growing revelry of spirit. The hall was filling fast, now almost eighty persons had signed in, divided by eight--that comprised ten squares, an ample gathering of dancers for any square dance night.

The air was becoming perfumed by the ladies, the men accepting their role to assist their dance partners and womenfolk to find chairs where they drop their wraps or sit out a dance and converse with neighbors. An air of surprise continued to invest its charm upon the newcomers. The ballroomwas fast ecoming a place where dancing was the event of the ni;vht. The orchestra was playing the first air of numerous round dancs,a couples danced wlith prescrilbed steps which the caller now commanded down on the floor, as he danced with his parner. The technology of a loud speaker made this possible.

"The cash...put it somewhere," Vera said to her husand. "The cakes arrli ed an hour ago...they're in the kitchen for surprise."

"I talked to Mary on the phone today and we put together this plan. I'm to greet his best man, a lawyer fellow he said is reliable and will attend at the right time. Bartok, if I recall. He does not square dance. Her bride's maid doesn;t dance either. Pastor James Carothers from Hayfork will show up soon, I hope."

"'S begilnning to look a llnd sound like a ball already."

"Twice as complicated, Vera. Think we can handle two clubs here tonight?"

Even as they spoke, the dancers contnued to arrive upon the dance floor. Most of the ladies emerged from the doorway, attired in their full hoop skirt dress of the typical square dancer, the gents in their shirts, embroidered with stars, leaves, curlew desgns and flowers, usually matching the club colors or the patterns colors of their lady's dress. Some men wore vests, here and there a black or whie stetson hat. Almost all of the dancers had adorned their attire with the badge of their club. Diamond wing tips glittered at the gents' collars, as did an occasional towel loop in the belt of the a male dancer, in antiipation of a sweaty evening. Polished black shoes and soft colored silken dance slippers adored the feet of the womendancing out on the floor.

The square dancers came in all sizes and adult ages, tall and slender, rotund, the men putting on the glaze of dazzling male composure, nuance for the dance, and an undeniable eagerness to begin, as the round dancers had already shown. They came with delight and smiles of excitement. They spread out from the double doors, to chairs around all sides of the hall, where,the women divested themselves sof their wraps, a shawls, jackets, blazers for lthe men. All was lin a state of motion and gay exciltement. The band on thes tage--the music usually recorded-- was for tonight a live band. They were warmling up with familiar melodies of the day, a violin, newly arrived a lclarinetist, a snare drum, a bass viol and an accordion. The band would furnish the dance music, mostly from memory, for they were, themselves, square dancers and knew the melodies as well as the dance steps. They played with caprice and inventive vigor, amost jazz-like, to inject an atmosphere of festivity into the air, while Vera and Jules continued to prepared their special tables at the sidesof the hall. Beneath it was a small bench covered i white satin, the only give-away as tos a chief psurpose of the dance this night. Upon it Mary was expected to kneel alongside of Grant. The preacher would stand behind the them.

While these acivitlies were taking place, Grant had pullled up to Penelope's residence to pick up his bride. Mary had chosen a lavender dress, grabbed from her apartment on her sudden departure under harsh, hasty and painful circumstances. He rang the bell. She opened the door, he stepped inside.

"Penelope!"

"Greetings, friend. You look just gorgeous," he said. Unbeknowst to her, he had chosen his lawyer, Bartok, to serve as his best man for the wedding, and had informed him he would give him the wedding ring when he arrived at the hall. The entire affair had about it an impromptu atmosphere, but that pleased Mary, for she was tired of rigid arrangements, familiar to her over entire life. Grant greeted Penelope, said she was beautiful, a complement she had not heard since the demise of her husband. He gave Mary a lhug and a similar compliment. To fit three persons, one of them in full skirted square dance costome into the cab of his pickup truck was amost a chore. Mary's'skirt tended to flounce up and block his view for driving. They laughed over the inconvenience, to say nothing of the hazard of operating his old truck. He managed, as he always did. Upon their arrival, they entered the hall without fanfare. The tables were visited by numeous guests, on both sides of the hall, while the minister was invited to make himself at home, in the the place called The Barn. Pastor James Carothers from Hayfork had arrived on his mission to officiate. He was dressed lin a white sut with a black cravat to accetuate his black cowboy hat. He was given special courtesies by Vera and Jules.

A dancer came up to the captains and said that a preacher fellow had rrived. They hastened to the door where hey shook he mans hand, and led him to a side table for refreshments, if he so desired. They had adecorated chair for him to one silde of the platform, where he could step forth to seize the moment for the ceremony. They invited Rev. Carothers to completely make himself at home. They would call upon him when the moment was right. If he chose, he was to feel free to try a square or two. Squae dancing was not difficult, "just stick out your hand and somebody will take it," was Vera's instruction to their visitor. They invited him to make himself at home, that the wedding would take place early in the evening, right the start and before the first tip, after the rounds were finished. Out on the floor the couples were now dancing their "round of the month," as it was called. These rounds had no words but were melodically attuned to th steps of round dancers, a dance for couples that alternated withs the square dance, together called a tip. The minister made himelf comfortable, partaking of a piece of celery and a glass of iced water. He greeted one or two couples whom he recognized, for these atteneees represented a relatively small community in the valley. They did not comprise a city crowd. The minister stood tall, his black hair parted to one side, clean shaven except for a small, trimmed black moustache. He kept his black cowboy hat on his head. His gray eyes bore a gentle expression, almost one of intimacy. He circulatsed among the guests with a certain ease and male charm, beilng accustomed to crowds of worshipopers and speaking from the pulpit. . He glanced at the kneeling bench and obviously thought it fit for its intended purpose. Meantime, the ticket-taking couple were put to it to get everybody in and paid up as quickly as possible.

Over a speaker system, Vera called attention to the front of the hall, where she stood with her husband up on the stage. The band were poised for stheir next pice, paienting holding their ilnsgruments as they listened to the announcements.
"Friends of the Boots and Gaiters square dance club." She said this several times to call tlhe crowd to order. The round dance was ended The Best Man Bartok had arrived and Grant had handed him the wedding ring . Grant told him that he should have no trouble in following the action He knew something about weddings. Bartok agreed--his small swaarthy face fixed in a solemn expression as he gestured with nods and shakes of his head, a nervous habit that he used to construe the answer of an adversary in his lawyer's profession. He was, however, a good man and reliable and he and Grant had become, as it was said, working friends. While he lislened, there appeared the sign of a smsile on his cold countenance.
"Ladies and gents," Vera again announced an "event of the season," as she phrased it, then handed the microphone over to Jules.
"Hello, and greetings to all of you," Jules said. "I'm glad to see so many of you.

Tonight is an unususal night. Most of you did not come expecting to attend a wedding, but tonight that is to be the major happening of the night...except , of course, the dance." Small laugher. Our club friend and member, Mary Wexler and her fiance Grant Shepherd, are to be married,,,here...tonlight... before your very eyes... sounds like magic...it always is that magic moment...and you are now offcial members of the wedding party.   A great huzzah went up wlth laughter, applause and a steamboat whistle from somewhere.

The band had stopped. Mary and Penelope and five other members of the club, hereat serving as Handmaidens, stood to one side at the front of the hall. Penelope wore her black suit, her hair swept high and on her suit-coat a yellow hyacynth freshly clipped from her garden...a smile and a flush of exciltement on her cheeks.   Opposite to them Grant and Bartok and several men, chosen at random, to serveas the groom's men. They stood at the opposite side of the hall.
"Visitors, club members, friends of the fine art and sport of square dancing, may I suggest that you stand to either side of the hall...so as to make an aisle... if you will, please. We have our pastor James... the Reverend James Carothers from Haywfork--you know where Hayfork is--who was selcted from serveral possible candidates"--mild laughter--"because of his handsome appearance and love for the sport of square dancing...to unite the couple who you will ecognize at oce." Thje reverend removed his black cowboy hat and placed it on the stage apron. Applause folowed Jules' brief introduction, and some laughter, as the dancers crowded in closer to the aisle the dances had formed. Vera had thought about putting tape along both sides to resrain the crowd, but thought it an "overkill" preparation. Square dancers had common sense and a necessary discipline.

Pastor Carothers took a place in front of the table, and as the dancers complied with the captains' request and had formed an aisle. The band played a fanfare with the drum and the accordion. The instrumentalists, however, did not strike up the conventional melody, "Here comes the bride" but, instead, they began to play an old melody called, "In the Good Old Summertime," as the pastor beckoned for the groom to commence his walk down the impromptu aisle, with the lawyer Bartok as Best Man and the randomly selected best Groom's Men, four in number moving in from the side, up at the front. .
There was a rough cadence to the music. Penelope raised her hand at the front, observed by Mary's keen eyes--sadly, there was no one to give her away-- and she began her walk down the aisle that the dancers had formed. This was an eager and brilliant moment when all looked to see her. She came with much dignity, in step with the music, in her hand a bouquet of yellow hyacynths Penelope had provided/ Her engagement band spakled under the low light. Jules had considered using a follow-spot but reconsidered it as impactical. Impromptu, one male dancer threw confetti on the aisle in front of the bride, in place of the traditional flower petals. The crowd delighted in these nuances of the familiar ceremony. When she arrived befofe Reverend Carothers, Gant stepped over to her, along with best man Bartok, the weddling band in his hand.   Familiar with all the detailsof the ceemony, the minister spoke the ritual words that bound two bodies, two hearts and minds and two souls together for the remainder of their lives. The whole affair was breathtaking for the watchers, for whom a wedding at their square dance was a novelty and an event long to be remembered.

"Do you take this woman to be your everloving and devoted wife, Grantr Sheoherd? If you so do, say, I do."

"I do," said Grant, a flurry of excitement in the pit of his tomach, ecstasy in his heart and deepening love for this woman he had found, helped and thus far guided for their mutual pleasure and experience. Their many ventures flashed through his mind.

"Do you, Mary Wexler, take this man to be your everloving husband in sickness and in health and in good tmes and bad......" The familiar words were completed almost before either of them knew they had agreed. Penelope was all smiles, as were Mary's many club friends. Best Man Bartok hardly broke a serious face to smile, while Grant's expressionw was almost etherial he was so charmed by his bride's presence and her voice and the soond oif the solemn words spoken in a manter of a few minutes.

"What signs and tokens do you show these assembled guests of your affection and love for one another?" Grant took the ring from Bartok and, lifting Mary's hand, he placed the wedding band on her finger and kissed her hand. He then placed an ardent kiss on her lips and brushed her lovely hair with one hand, finishing his tide of love with a long hug. The audience applauded immensely. He removed his towel from its hanger at his belt to wipe his lips, to the delighte, fun-loving laughter of the crowd.

"I now pronounce you man and wife." The preacher broke into a wide smile. He pulled the kneeling bench from behind him and invited the couple to come behind it and to keeel, facing their dancer guests. He next announted them with oil from a vial he fetched from his coat pocket and he read a verse from the love poem The Song of Solomon. He touched their heads lightly with the small bible he had brought and commended their marriage into the hands of God. At a signal, they stood, the kneeling bench was pushed back under the stage apron, the pastor extendd his hands and said.

"Go forth, I say, and...and dance with new joy."

The crowd broke into a wild applause and cries of "more, more!"

The bamd struck up a familiar tune that was a round and the bridal couple waltzed off onto the floor. as the guests, both of the Boots and Gaiters and the Flagstones began to dance the round. The band played that melody and then another similar waltz. Not all the guests could dance the rounds yet they were witnesses to the wedding and a part of the extravaganza. As Grant and Mary danced, guests would reach out their hands to shake his, usually managing to touch one another in joyous response to the couple's marriage, this night, at the square dance. When the caller cried, "Square 'em up!" Mary and Grant took the head-couple spot in a square at the front of the hall where the ceremony had taken place. Following the dance, the lawyer beckoned for Grant spoke to Bartok, thanked him for his help. When the call was ended and Mary stood by Grant, her arm around his waist, Bartok said, briefly, "There was a matter of honesty in the original custody matter." "You will excuse me, Mary. Congratulations. It was a gorgeous wedding. I need your husand for a moment." The lawyer took Grant to one side. "We have a matter going, Grant. I've taken out the custody papers for...your little daughter." He said no more; there was no reason to. Mary had not overheard the lawyer's words. All of the anxiety and anguish of the past months were captured in that one promise by the lawyer and Grant's Best Man. "It will put Marys daughter into your mutual care."

"I had always suspected that. I'm glad you found the flaw."

The adoptive mother is a good mother, don't misunderstand, but the manner in which the child beceme another womans progeny to raise, brought up such matters as hearsay evidence and sworn testimony. I'll explain to you later. 'You perfomed well, Grant. And congratualtions on your new bride. She is a beautiful woman."

"Thanks Mister Bartok. I agree...and I would do so under oath. They enjoyed a laught together for this comment. They parted for the night.

"hat was that all about?>" Marys asked her new husband.

"The little girl...was all he dared to hint. Mary's face became sober and fearful. "It will all work out. Believe me, dearest Mary." He kissed her on her forehead. "Bartok is a good man, my bestg an. We have things to do, Love." Her countenance brightened again..

The guests danced five more tips for that evening; there was no break for announcements. Mary and Grant, who had alerted Jules of Penelope's need for a ride back to her home, danced with his new bride in two more dances to join with their guests. All of the dark past with her mother, her father and her uncle , seemed to fall from her. This was her rebirth into life. And it had been shared with at least one hundred or more guests from both square dance clubs. The minister mingled briefly with the guests, tried a cup of coffee and chatted with several of the male dancers. He appeared to be having a good time. That was the ultimate purpose for holding the dance at The Barn on club night that--there would be space enough to accommodate visiting guests for the the singular, life-changing celebration.   The couple avoided the customary costs of a church wedding.

Mary and Grant made a quick exit during a square, when the dancers were busy in their dance. Many pairs of eyes folowed them from circles of right and left grand. They did not want to break up the dance. Those not in a square wished them well, God speed, and pumped Grant's hand, gave Mary their blessings. She had packed a small valise with street clothes and had prepared for their honeyoon trip. She momentarily disappeared into a ladies room where she changed from her dance costume into her street clothes,. She met Grant on the walk outside. Thus they fled, as it were, out to his truck. They got into the familiar cab, and they were on their way...up to Mirror Lake, where he had reserved a bridal suite, as he called it, of one of their fine rooms that overlooked the lake. The management had placed a large bouquet of mountain flowers in a vase on the window table, to greet the bridal couple and to fill the room with fragrance.

SERNADES

The old pickup truck made it up the grade, Grant saw the smoke, realized it needed new rings, it was burning oil. Mary was accustomed to the primitive mode of transport by this tlime. In the lobby of the Mirror Lake Hotel, the clerk registered their arrival and furnished Grant with the key to their bridal suite. They took the elevator, breathless with the adventure and the excitement of impending ventures that awaited their hearts. At the threshhold to their night's suite, Grant opened the door, setdown their two bags inside, then retrned to Mary standing in the hallway. He lifted her into his arms and, as tradition dictated, carried her across the threshhold into their bridal suite. It was a lovely room that looked out over the lake, the second storey. In the room the management had placed a bouquet of roses that filled the room with its soft fragrance.

They had almost retired for the night, Mary reviewing the cards she had scooped up at the square dance reception table. They were numerous, at least a hundred, which would try his patience. While they sat there, she reading beneath the large orange lampshade, they heard the sound of music coming from below the window. They were a chorus of male voices. Grant popped his head out the window, Mary followed , only to discover a group of six men in square dance costumes standing directly beneath the window sash, serenadling with the words

When its springtime in the Rockies,
I'll be coming home to you.
...la, la, I'm so blue

The pair waved and shouted down to their serenaders. Happy wedding night, Mary, Grant, came the salutation. The coralers had followed the wedded pair tothe mounain hotel. Then the chorus sang second verse to the old romantic song.
"How did they know we were here?" Mary asked.
"I must have slipped out the words. I was hardly aware of it. They probably akedand I answered without thinking. Actually, there's only this one big hotel and smaller motels around in the town."
"It was magnificent of them to come all the way up here."
"That's just what they're like, Mary dear...a generous buch of guys."
The groups took off on another old lullaby,

Let me call you sweetheart,
I';m so in love with you.

Grant and Mary stood in their room, leaning out to watch their senaders/ Mary began to cllry. Grant put his arm around her, they kissed for the crowd and continued to watch. They sang one more oldie,
Down on the old mill streeam
Where I first met you.

They changed to Slinging in the rain,but did not finish. I had begun to rain mountain rain, which can become a cloudburst. Tjhey did ot remain to flinish the words to thet song, when they waved and in loud whispers shouted up "congratulations, Mary! congratulations Grant!" then, sporting flashlights like small tornes, they left the walk beneath the bridal window. Grant pulled in the window wings, held Mary in his arms and asked,
"How much more for the kudos, dear?"
"I'm finished for the night. They removed their robes, to reveal their nakedness, rememberilng the beach sands one chilly dawn morning. He switched out the table lamp by the bed; they retired for the night to make love.

The next morning, what surprised and delighted Mary again was Grant's arrangement that they take theirl bridal breakfast in their room. A knock, softly came, he opened the door, a maid wheeled in the breakfast on a cart, with a tray onwhich there steamed a pot of coffee, hot cereal, pancakes and the morning's newspaper for the community. Grant, went to his trousers and removed a bill which he gave to the elderly hotel maid for a tip. She bowed slightlly and left them to enjoy their weddilng breakfast together. He arranged the furnitur for them and she said grace. This astonished him; he remained silent. Grant drew up two small chairs, and the table where Mary had been working on the congratualtion cards. They began their bridal breakfast with famished appetites.

"Were here...for a week?" she asked.
"Ten days, Beloved. Ten days...that will give us time to do a few things. Were going out onto the lake. Takea swilm. Then theres a boat dock down at the lake's edge. Have you ever fished before?"
"Never. My father used to go live-bait fishing but he never took me."
"We'll rent a line and pole...am a campe/ We'll take turns trolling...I'll paddle the canoe and you can fish...we can change off.".
"Great! More coffee?"
"Please...good and strong." Sheloved that about Grant, his tender courtesy.
Thus their dialogsue, short comnents, sweet words, and adequate silence accompanied their bridal breakfast, making it one glorious occasion. They collected the dishes and pushed the cart to the door. stting it outsidein the hallway. He adjusted the Please Do Not Disturb sign. They retired to make love again, then to shower and dress for the day's venture.
Down in the lobby they waved at the desk clerk. Grant asked for directions to the boat dock...could they walk? Oh, yes... the dock is very close, not more than a thousand yards from the hotel...toward the lake."

94.

"Is there a fisingearrentalplace on the dock?"

"Oh, yes...there's a fishing line and tackle rental shop on the dock."

"Great! Grant exclaimed, and they set out from the hotel lobby, arriving at the dock where the dock-master selected the canoe for them, arranged one pole, a box of tackle.

"Fish this time of year go for mosquitos. Its a little early in the morning for mosquitos, but they also like flotsam the lake wind brings in that settles on the water--ugs that can't fly, dead larvae from the trees and such like.... There's some lures in your box that will do the trick. The trout and lake bass are hungry,you can count on that."

"Thanks.. how much?"

"Twenty dollars for the day," said the dock-master..

Mary had come with a wide bonnet, which he adjusted as Grant payed the fee for the rentals. \

"You'll both have to wear life vests. Its the law for all boaters"

"Oh, that's fine," said Mary. "I can swim but, well.." She laughed.

"It could be a long way to shore if you should capsizei n the wake of a speedboat...and they get pretty careless at times. But I don' expec you will capsize," said the man. "These canoes are wide and have a keel on them to make them stable. Expect a small wind to come across the lake about mid- afternoon, down from the mountains. Afternoon wind goes with the scenery. You wont have any trouble."

"I'm sure we won't," Grant said withhis c ustomaryconfidence.

The two lovers donned their life vests, Grant held Mary's hand to assist her while she stepped into the canoe. Also, the dock-master heldthe bowfrom wandering while Mary she took a seat lin the stern. Grant stepped in with the canoe paddles and sat cautiously on the bow seat, handing one o the paddles to Mary. He took the pole and tackle from the dock-master , placing them over the the thwart seat. The pair, in a brightgreencanoe, pushedaway from the dock with their paddles and began to paddle out onto the lake, Thhe paddled vigoously and slowly, away rom the dock. Within minutes they were at least a hundre yards out onto he lake, whchwas as quiet as a night mere,few rilpples and no wind coming across its brilliant stretch of pale gray-blue.

"Lets skirt the shore, sweetheart. There's coves...they sometimes have blackberry vines that grow over the water. They followed his suggestion, turning into one cove and then another, where,as Grant had said, heavy y, blackberry vines hung out over the water. In one such cove, they plucked handsfull, puttig berry stains on their mouths and finger...and then they moved on.

Within an hour they had had enough of berry-picking and chose to try their luck at fishing. Grant rigged the line with a sinker, a lure and a piece of their brakfast toast--he had always been something of a scavenger. She looked on in wonder and amusement as he prepared the line for trolling. He handed the pole to Mary, after he had cast the line out into the water. He then paddled slowly as she let the line troll after their canoe. She gripped the pole like an axeman, on her face the smile of succss. It all seemed so simple to her and natural to him. They fished for nearly an hour yet caught nothing, changing off between fishing and padding, he taking the pole and line and she picking up her paddle to advance the canoe, never daring to go out into the dead middle of the lake. He intuited that if a wind should come up in the afternoon, they could run into trouble. He had had the experience of a stiff offshore wind that held his canoe in its grip, he not being able to come into shore from the middle of the lake where the stiff wind could sweeping the canoe away from shore. They grew hungry...Mary had thoughtfully taken the candy bars from their breakfast tray. Grant had brought up to the room a backpack with a thermos of water. So they had the candy bars and fresh water for their lunch out on the lake. Their appetites were ravenous when they came into dock at about four in the afternoon. Grant returned the pole, tackle, paddles and the vests and thanked the man for the day's adventure. Back in their room, they listened to the radio and conversed asthey had one day at his cabin. He thought that this was the signal time for him to reveal to her his plan.

"That lawyer fellow Bartok has worked on the costodianship case for us, Mary."
"Bartok? Custodianship...?" His cryptic words alarmed her. Bartok...he's your attorney?"
"You never met him but you saw him at Penelope's house
"I think I remember."
"Well, he is still workig on the case. He thinks there was something amiss in the transfer of the little girl to her foster parents."
"The case...custodianship...what little girl, Grant? You sound so secretive, my dear?" she said in a strained tone of voice. "I hardly know what you're talking about. Tell me about it," she said in a gently sharp tone of voice. "She surely must rememer that night at the dance when the child appaed at the door.," he thought. "She does not want to admit the truth...."
"The child who appeared at the square dance...." His new bride walked away from him, turning her back on him. This was a warning of some distrust he unwittingly had sowed in her mind. He walked up to her and embraced her from behind, swaying slightly,as he caressed her breasts and kissed her neck tenderly. "I'm sorry, dearest, I didn't mean to frighten you."
"It's not that, Grant. It's just that ...oh, I can't express it...."
"Can we not forget it for tonight, Mary? I'm sure things will work out. Trust me."
She did trust him, in ways and to an extent he was to learn in time signified the depth of her growing love for him.
"Maybe I shouln't have said anything."
"There's another person involved." The mystery deepened for her. This was her first hint of fear, transposed from her home life with an overbearing father and an oppressive mother. She kept quiet, but because she loved Grant, she trusted that there was no sinister thing invoved. Custodianship...the word troubled her. She had no custodial care for anyone...perhaps her mother, but Mrs. Wexler was too independent to accept any such close supervision. She let it go. They ended the subject of conversation. They talked about other matters, their hobbies ...she collected antique jewelry, but all of that was in her apartment. He had a collection of old vinyl records...still at his millsite cabin. He said he needed someone to help him design fireplaces, and so he appointed his new bride to be his chief designer. She laughed about this assignment...to help him in his work.
"I've never designed a flreplace i my life," , she told him.
"The money is all in the design, and then comes the craftssmanship. Thats my part. I think I can build up a reputation in the town for my work."
"I'm sure that you can, Grant, dear." GThey had brought her guitar along. At this pont, s he opened up the case, removed the insrument, and, having hung ilt over her shoulder

and tuning it briefly, she began to play a ballad she had learned as a student, "It's springtime in the winter lwith you..." He sat back iln the cushioned chair, reminiscing about their wedding night and their future together. She mentioned to him hat she waned him to read theSong ofSolomon to her.

"Song of Solomon...Oh, istha like...the psalms....?"

"Rather like it, written by a wilse man. "She played on but was lost in the music as sh bent over her instrument....

The next ten days consisted of a two more canoeing trips out onto Mirror Lake...with similar results and the same delight. Both of them loved being out on the water, although they were becoming painfully sunburned so that they spent considerable time back at the hotel annointing one another with haling ointment. On one occasion, speedboat roared past them almost causing them to overturn in its wake. he quickly learned how to turn their canoe a ninety degrees to the swell of the wave.

:Yo know,"she said, "I think those party snorts would even enjnoy rescuing us so they could be heroes."

There's a planetarium obsservatory with a tourist bus we can take, if you'd like to...in the morning. I think it would be afun trip...You're my s tar, dearest..." she smiled to acknowledge his words.... "You can see jillions more of the stars up here outside the glow of town lights."

"Lets," she said.

"They've also got exhibits about space, aurora glow, electrical magnetic currents that surround the earth to keep it from wobbling...and models of earthquakes and global warmng, Im sure."

"Good, then we'll go' tonight...ake the shuttle bus."

"That won't be a problem...they won't leave us sranded, Love."

Thus the two of them made their side excursion, spending the early and late night hours lookiat the scientific exhibits. They looked a the exhibits on on electrilcal currents,the power of a neutralizing blast of neutrons to cut out all electrical circuits on the earth, They examined he science of neutrons, the physics of gravity and repulsion, and one exhibit that was especially fascinating to Grant, the exhibit on molecujlar attraction that caused water to flow uphill, against gravity. The exhibits were fascinating to the both of them. They spent the early night looking at the heavens through the visitors' telescope. They shared this interest in science like two novices let loose inside a physics laboratory. They watched Aries, the nebulae of Saturn's satellites, the various gaseous bodies, which their guide identified for them with a tick in his scope to aid the novice. They found their tour of the lake planetarium a highlight of their honeymoon sojourn at Mirror Lake.

Grant was detemined that there should vew no slack in their honeymoon stay at the lake. They knew with lovers bonding that hose moments of making love back at their room were they both believe, highlights of their journey. Grant thought of his tour with his new bide a journey. They spent the better part of a day, a week into their itinerary, in touring the local museum and gawking at the artifacts, Indian beads and costumes, feathers, weapons of war, and tools and implements left by miners iat old diggins in the nearby canyons, stuff that belonged to the local history. .

"Amazing, isn't it, dear, how anybody got along in those days."

" Tools to cut, hammer and smash...and not much more." '

"Those seemed to be their main engineering activities," she said, with a wonerful perception which he had always enjoyed coming from Mary.

"To build...they could put stones together like a jigsaw puzzle. You saw that little replicat of a stone hut."

"I did. They had no canvas...where wigwams and teepes came from is anybody;s guess...they must haved traded beads for canvas at tradilng posts.   "Often...made from buffalo skins, darling.

"Oh, yes, I forgot. Herds of buffalos....'

"Until we came along with our harpshsooting practice. Grant was atached to saving the buffalo, whatever remained of those vast herds."

"Did you see that replica of a diggilns?"she asked.

There are some up where I live...where we'll be living for while, Mary."

"Water brings down the gold." she said. She was not completely ignorant of the panning process.

"After every rain the panners found new gold."

They never mined it all. That waterwheel was a clever thing!"

"Powdered corn...crushed rocks."

"And those models of stamping mills...little replicas...a marvelous museum, Grant"

"Talk about smashing rocks, crushsing to get at the gold trapped inside the rocks.The only way," he said."I've sometimes wondered how a huge gold nugget was ever formed."

"Me the same," she replied.

"Had to be heat, real hot heat, thousands of degrees...way down deep."

"Melted grains of gold together."

"That's my guess, too." he replied. "But I never, ever picked up a nugget in the street. That was all the hullabaloo in the 1850s...gold you could pick up off the streets."

"Maybe, just maybe there was a grain of truths to that."

"Well, the steamship companies brought in thousands just to try."

I know, I know," he replied. "Let's go back to the hotel, love. I just wnt to love you to death," he said. "Ill read your Book of Solomon to you.

They hopped on the next returning tour bus back to the Mirror Lake Hotel and...accomplished their purpose, for they were very much in love. She stopped at the clerk's counter and said something tothe night clerk, as she took their key and handed it to Grant. They went up to their suite. It was dark. He uned on the floor lamp. They sat, relaxilng from their excursion when a knock clame at the door. She opened it and was ahded a gtray with a bottle of wine and two glasses on it. She thanks the poter and set the tray down on the card table. "We shall enjoy your readilng and with a little wine to enhance the ...reception." She smiled.

She pulled a Gideon bible from the lamp table, found the book of Solomon in the tome and handed the text to him. He pulled a floor lamp closer to the cushioned chair.. "Maybe I ought to read this in bed," he said with a laugh.

I'll need the exhibits to confirm the excellence of the poetry...and of the exhibit. Shall I push your belly button?"" She thought this was deliciously funny. They laughed together.

"I think that would be a great idea but I can go into action as we progress." And so, together, they prepared to make love, after which, in his skivies, he tilted the bed-table lamp shade and began to read. She let him find the right passages, even jumping around for the lines. The text went thusly:

" 'How beautiful you are
              my darling.
How beautiful you are!
Your eyes are like doves.

O my dove, in the clefts
              of the rock,
In the secet place of the
              steep pathway,,
Lwr me see your form,
Let me hear your voice;
For your voice is sweet,
And your form is lovely.' "

"I'm skipping around," he said.
"Don't stop, dearest," she said. He went on.

" ' How beautliful you are, my
              darling,
How beautiful you are!
Your eyes are like doves
              behind youe veil;
Your hair is like a flock of
              goats
That has descended from
              Mount Gilead
Your teeth are like a flock
              of newly shorn ewes
Which have come up from
              their washing.
All of which bear twins,
Andno oneamonthem
              has lost her young.
Youer lips are like a scarlet
              thread,
And your mouth is lovely.\
Your temples are like a lovely
              like a slice of pomegranate
Behind your veil.
Your neck is like the
              tower of David
Built with rows of stones,

On which are hung a
               thousand shields
All the round shields of
               the mighty men.
You two breasts are like
               two fawns;
Twins of a gazelle,
Which feed among the
               lillies
Until the cool of the day
When the shadows flee
               way....
You are altogether beau-
               tiful, my darling,
And there is no blemish in
               you.
Come with sme from Leb-
               anon, my bride.
May you come with me
               from Lebanon....\
How beautiful are your feet
               in sandals,
O prince's daughter!
Thecurves of your hops
               arlike jewels,
The work of the hands of
               an artist.
Your navel is like a round
               govblet
Which never lacks mixed
               wine.
Your belly is like a heap of
               wheat
Fenced about with lillies.
Your two breasts are like
               two fawns,
Twins of a gazelle.
Your neck is like a tower
               of ivor\y,
Your eyes are like pools in '
               Heshbon.
Your nose is like the tower
               of Lebanon.
Which faces toward Da-
               mascus.
Your head crowns you like
               Carmel.

And the flowering locks of
              your head are like
              purrple threads.
The king is captivated by
              your tresses.
Howbeautiful and how
              delighful you are,
My love with all your
              charms!
Your stature is like a palm
              tree,
And your tresses are like
              its clusters,
I said I will climb the
              palm tree,
I will take hold of its fruit
              stalks...:
Come, my love, let us
              go out into the coun-'
              try,
Let us spend the night in
              thl villages
Ler us rise early and go to
              the vineyards....

"Solomon, or whoever he was

    "He was a king...."

    "He has nothing to say about me?   I mean, the lover matters in the poem as well
as his bride."

    "Oh, Solomon probably does...yes, here it is, in Chapter five."

    "Read it...let me hear lit...yes, that's it!'

    "I'm listening, Grant, dearest...   Go ahead...."

        "My beloved is dazzling
              and ruddy,
    Oustanding among ten
              thousand.
    His head is like gold, pure
              gold;
    His locks are like clusters
              of dates,
    And black as a raven.
    His eyes are like doves,
    Beside streams of water,
    Bathed in milk.
    And reposed lin their set-
              ting.

His lips are lillies,
> Dripping with liquid
> myrrh.
His hand are rods of gold
> set with beryl.
His abdomen is carved
> ivory
Inlaid with sapphires,
His legs are pillars of ala-
> baster
Set on pedestals of pure
> gold;
His appearance is like
> Lebanon,
Choice as the cedars.
His mouth is full of
> sweetness
And he is wholly desirea-
> ble.
This is my beloved and
> this is my friend.
O daughters of Jerusalem.' "

"Beloved Mary...I'm tired of reading. I would much rather look at the real object, yours, my love." He left the light on, dropped the book over the bed and began to caress his beloved wife. her breasts, her thighs,her belly, placing many kisses on her neck and nipples, she reaching down to his groin and his golden rod, runing one hand up his belly to the warmth of his cheeks where she dwelt on his mouth for several minutes. They loved in this way. exchanging caresses   for so long as they both desired, yet this time they made love with the light on so that each might examine the expression of tender love that came into the eyes of each...when they had mounted the hill.   He could not have been more contented with his darling's suggestion, for it gave him courage, excitement and initiative. After all, were not poets supposed to be the leaders in writing about love of many kinds in life? They kissed tenderly and while still engaged, they fell asleep, scarcely knowing the passage of time and feeling the warm sweet wine-breath of each while in their arms. He had to take care that he not suffocate his darling and so he slipped one arm under her head until he grew tired, by which time she slept.

They made love into the night and then they slept. When they awoke it was mid-morning and the room was filled with light, and they were rested, yet they could not resist loving one another again, to the fullest. They droused, when. upon hearing a strange sound, as a mill-whistle, familiar to Grant, they both arose, and he showered with his beloved and they washed one another with tender and singular delight, now totally intimate with one another. Then they stepped from their shower and dressed. And they were completely fulfilled...except that they were exceedingly hungry, and so they left the bridal suite and went downstairs and into the hotel cafeteria to eat their lunch.

They were not loners by any distortion of perception. Two, three nights, and at breakfast, they fell into conversatikon with other tourists. Mary was a talker when she was not slowed down. They met a professor and his wife, not from theirf dxiscussionboup. He taught elemenary languaes, langaue sligns, tree and stone markings and the significances of ribal interacion in the ancient world. These things fascinatged Grant for reasons he did not fully understand. His life'swork was labor with the stones, wood and primitive tools of man, the axe and chisel and maul as a mason. The professor taught Primitive Lore at a college lin Sacramento. He and his wife, Ruby, were here at the lake to celerate their thirtieth weddilng anniversary. Honeumooners Mary and Grant congratulated them, and he, the professsor, set offon a journey through the works of theTrobrian Islanders and the ancien primitive peoples of the Peloponsian Peninsula. Like Twalin and Harte, the professor had spent some of his younger years in the gold coutry, as it was callled. Mary mentioned Bret Harte and Mark Twain...she had read their books o escape her onerous home life. She informed their table-mates, on a Saturday night that Bret and Mark both wrote for the "Alta Californian,"Twain pushlisheng his short stories in the paper, andHarte as well. Thy ere masters sof the locl jargon and modes of speech, realists, Twain with a keen sense of humor that collcted readers over the years. They had watched California grow by virtue of immigrants from the East, mainly, who came to find their fortunes in easys gold. She remarked, shrewdly, that early tries iln isolated islands never grew sor improved their ways because they were isolagted and never took in immigrants. "There;s some sustance to your words,Missus Shepherd," the professor remarked dryly. Grant was content simply to consume his Italian spaghetti ;bowl and listen to Marly's words. He saw early in their marriage that they would have to take more excursions lin order to break her away from her hard-shell upbringing.

"That was always the quest, easy gold,' tlhe Professor salid. "Most immigants soon discovered that panning and mining for gold was hard work...."

"Much hafder than what they had left, for sure," said Grant...with little encouragement to stay with it if they had found none. Most of those ...Argonauts....left the Mother Lode country forever." This occasion, their meetilng and table conversation with the other learned couple had been a memorable evening he and Mary would remember for a long time.

One of Grant's hobbies, he revealed to Mary, was the theatre. She clapped her hands lightly, in wonder. She had long realized gthat the theatre was had been an attraction for her stunted life-style at her mother's apartment. How dear diversions like that had seemed at that time. She would attend the theatre on her own, thus enabling herself to escape the oppressive atmosphere when her father was in the home. She had fallen in love with the theatre. And so they went to a revival of Clyde Fitche's . "Girl of the Golden West," a melodrama staged and produced by the Mirror Lake Players in their small theatre, a clever makeover of an old wagon-shed in the town. Sawdust covered the floor, the stage was build of weathered planking gotten from razed buildings in the town, with benches instead of seats, for they were deemed more stable in the sawdust. The curtain was imaginary,the lighting came from the wings and the footlights, a dim background light illuminated a crude painting of Bodie, an early gold town. "Girl of the Golden West" presented for the hero a melodramatil figure who saved the herine from disaster at the hands of her villain landowner, a spin-off from the Mollies. He looked at his new bride, to find her enjoying the show with an genuine sense of its tragedic comedy and its human-like qualities, howesoever depicted.

He was glad he had brought her to this theatre, the Wizzard Playhouse. "Who could have asked for a more entertaining night?" he asked himself, as he and Mary exited the theater.

"Do you suppose they actually believed in their own characters?"

"Oh, I'm sure of it," Grant said. "Otherwise, life would have come o a dead standstill."

"Well, Megyn played the heroine with real gusto."

"Didn't she though! Did you notice how the villains almost always wore a handlebar moustach...intriguing, sharp, gauchos, attractive to innocent women."

"Grant...,"she called iln a strange voice.

"Yes...?"

"There is no such thing as an innocent woman." He laughed. "They see what men don;t see."

"Oh," he said with a skeptical voice.

"Many times. Thats what makes us so good at gossip and intrigue. Did you know, Dear, that some of the most famous spies inm history have been women.

"No, I didn't know that."

"Well, it's true. After all, Cleopatra was a spy against Napoleon. Hisyotuy has them down as lover. She detested his smll of gunpowder and sweat. Like most men, he was too fixed on his work to nitice, but she passed along his military secrets to the British. That's why they beat him at Wateloo."

"I didn't know."

She changed the subject with a loving nudge. Don't you ever grow a moustahe like that villain," she admonished.

"Hard to trim," he replied.

"You'd make a terrible villain anyway, sweetheart. You're too kind...." He kissed her for this complement. The twenty or so tourist members of the theatre audience in casual attire, had appeared to enjoy the play just as much as had Grant and Mary.

On their last night at the hotel, Grant received a phone call from Bartok, the laweyer, who was working on the guardianship case. Grant imagined himself having to pay a huge legal bill for the lawyer's help, the amount of w which he could scarcely affirm at the time. He was uncertain as to whether or not the Priest would file a lawsuit for trespass and assault and battery. Also, he was uneasy that with winter fast approaching, aurured by the rain, the status of his business wouldsurely change, since the demand for firewood increased in the wet and snowy months of the year. He did not relay to Mary the substance of the call. He simply told her that Bartok had called and had something important he thought he should know about...regarding his business...but that with apologies for the interruption, that could wait until they returned.

On their return to their present home, his cabin at the sawmill, he diverted her thoughts from that phon callby relating to her his trip down the Colorado River, almost one hundred and niney miles. He described how their small dories had bucked the high rapids...they called them haystacks because ever threatening to capsize,but for the skillful oarsmanship of their oarsmen. . Those small craft, similar in design though much smaller than those used by Dorchester fishermen, were reasonably dependable in rapids like Lava

Falls Rapid. Their five boats had made all the rapids escept one in which the dory had broached in Lava Falls. His boating party had hiked up ancient canyons, through side streams, skirted one trail like mountaingoats along a ledge, and explored tunnels, skidding through openings in the rocks, into icy pools. The down-river party had played badminton in a deep cavern, they sunned themselves on a flowerarden of rocks and took comand, with two others, of a rubber dinghy through five or six rapids to get the feel of the river at the oars. The ancient Havasupai Indians had their cliff dwellings, which the boaters explored, a grainery, the remnants of ancient mud houses under the brown sandstone rock canopy of the cliff, The boat oarsmen would stop at this rapid and another rapid to scout its currents, since the tidal flow depended on the release of water from the dam above, There were many rapids that were most treacherous and required a consummate skill to navigate. An archieologist explained ancient paleolithic fossil remains of shells and huge worms, their forms cast into the sandstone by some great deluge. He described to Mary the , mountain goat that had suddenly appeared aboe them, dawn by their luncheon on the shore sands elow. He didn't think anyone in the party ever saw any bear tracks, however. The guide, one of them, grew greensi n the bow hold of his dorie, in one day enough to sautee the night meal. The roaring of the rapids drew us and put us to sleep. The watery roaring of the river became harmony to our ears.

In about an hour Grants rusty old pickup truck reached their cabin home and, Grant, strangely, a stickler for formality, carried his new bride over the cabin threshhold lin a repat performane of the ancient custom.

"Tonight, no screen," he said, reminding his bride of the night when they had slept separately

"We have an appointment in court...day after tomorrow."

"An appointment...what about?"

"We shall see. I think we both have a surprise."

The day quickly arrived. She tidied the little cabin and, going out beyond the cabin area, picked a small handful of mounain lupines, which she put into a dusty mason jar and then set on the sill before their one window. He used the time to sharpen his tools and do some minor repair work on his truck, a creature that needed constant attention. The pair pulled into the courthouse parking lot/ They disengaged themselves from the truck and with efficiency, meeting no one along the way, found the courtroom, 103 B on the first floor. Mary's expectations gave her the chills. She was troubled about what was immediately to transpire. She feared the unanticipated arrival of the Priest, intent upon claiming the child, indisrupting the proceedings and in strikng back at whomever he could. Grant had not told her of his fight with Father Casper a the Parish House.

At the door marked "Civil Court," in gold lettering, they entered. She then had her first intuition of what was soon to occur. Bartok, the lawyer, came to the back where they stood to observe. Shaking their hands, he and ushered them to the front. The magisrate, an appointive Commissioner by title yet a civil-court judge, entered from a side door and mounted into the magistrate's bench. The entire court, such as it was, stood. The assembly consisted of a stranger lawyer and another couple at a table opposite to Bartok's table, behind which Mary and Grant sat. They stood with the others as Judge Harley entered. The proceedings carried the status of a hearing. With rattling and a blandishment of noise, the court settled lin for the occasion. The judge rapped his gavel once and pronounjced that :this ourt is in session." He scanned the attendees and asked of Bargtok, who stood with the question.

"What is the cause and purpose for this hearing?'

Bartok spoke."We, Your Honor, have plead that the child in question is rightfully the progeny of the woman you see sitting here"   There came silence.

"Proceed."

"By a twist in the circumstances of fate, which I shall explain, the custody of the childis now in question. By the merits of the case, which we shall attempt to show, we plead that the custody of the girl should be restored to the ;mother, where they rightfully belong." The judge squirmed slightly, rapped his pencil in thought. By this time, Mary was fully aware of what might happen. The thought of separation forever began to wrap litself around her mind and heart. She, for the moment, existed in an totally darkened room where wrong and right could not be discerned. She sat with a tense expression on her face, anger gripping her soul, the sense of a moral wrong returning, a vision of that day in the grip andembrace of the cleric, and an unusual calm that began to seep into her soul with this moment of reckoning.   On her countenance there appeared a distraught expression. The judge glanced at her, then at the defending couple. He seemed to be comparing the wisdom of and the meanings behind their expressions as they all faced the bench.

Bartok went on. "Your Honor, the custody of the child, who is not in his court, was transferred to that couple...over there, by means of a statement of a false paternity"

"Do you mean to tell this court that a scandal perpetrated by someone else...who is not here, a rapist, let us say...was instrumental in settling the original custody question."

"Not just a scandal,Your Honor, but a fraud in the making, the engineering, of the transfer, if I may be so bold."

"Will counsel explain?"

"Yes, Your Honor. No man in this court fathered the child. The child was fathered by a former Roman Catholic Priest. That messenger from hell...excuse my description...he refused to assume any custodial responsiblithy for the product of his wrong....".

"He is where...at his parish? I find this entire matter flawed by his absence"

"Your Honor, it is not possible to force the Catholic Church to...excuse the expression...cough up a man whom we found culpable. They presently deny his involvement and conceal his whereabouts." Grant felt the urge to stand and shout,"No, no, no! You are wrong. I know where he is at this moment." Bu tthe words of the judge rolled on over Grant's impulse.   "What proof have you of this...of his culpability in his absence?"

"Your honor, we have the testlimony of the mother."

The Magistrate looked off into the distance, studied his notes for a moment, appeared to shake his head in disbelief, then muttered again , head down-cast, "Proceed."

"Instead of making of the babe an orphan...that was the Priest's   first notion of Christian care.. to dispose of the child, the result of his wrong, then just a babe...he acted to transfer the custody of the infant into the hands of the couple who stand over there through a foster-care agency." Mary gasped as did Grant.

"It is not clear in my mind," said the judge, why the mother could not assume that responsibility." The judge twiddled with pencil, busy as if he were working a math problem on his desk. mindless of the agony that had invaded Mary's heart and the profound expectation of her new husband.

"Your honor, because of an overbearing and oppressilve family life of this young woman sitting there,; now the new bride of the man seated beside her," words towhich the Mgistrate nodded in recognition..."she rejected the custody care of her own daughter."   The judgewas astonished while the defending couple watched across the aisle the action of the Shepherd couple and their atorney, as if foxes eager to escape a confinement neither could explain.

"As for the mother...madam, we need your testimony." He glanced down at a paper on his desk. Missus Shepherd. Madam, will you t ake the stand please. Will the clerk swear in the mother. We shall lneed your testimony under oath to enable us to proceed. Do not feel alarmed."

Thus Mary took the stand and was sworn in. Counsel for the Defense approached the witness stand.

"What lis your name, madam?"

Mary Shepherd is my name."

"Recently married?

"Yes."

"What as your name at the time of the...incident of conception?"

"Wexler, Mary Wexler, sir."

:Now Mary, without any trimmings, elaborations, will you tell this court why you rejected the custody of your own daughter?"

"I did so, sir, because I did not want to shame the Priest by admitting that he fathered my child. I did so to save myself the agony of showing an illegitimate child to the world. I did so, sir, because I did not want her to end up in an orphanage. I have seen those children." She paused. "...you need not believe this, Your Honor, but I rejected my own little daughter because I did not feel that I could be a good mother to her."

"You had no job."

"Not that, Your Honor. All my life my mother drilled into me that I would railse a daughgter poorly...that I was ilncapable of raising my own child. . I had a defeatist attitude. I felt that I would fail and bring harm to the child. I did not know who to turn to for counsel. All my life, while I was growing up my mother...with the help of my father...drilled into my head that I would be an unsuccessful mother and that I might, as a result, even bring harm to my own child I might eventually give birth to."

The woman's testimony stunned the judge. He could not believe what he had just heard. He knew that some animals reject their second offspring. Bears have that trait, and that wolves will adopt an orphaned cub. But for a human beng...this was shocking news for him. He did not appear to realize that the humanitarian services had discov ered babies dumped into trash barrels, evenwhen boght to term.

"Please continuekl Missus Shepherd."

"So...being single, with no job, and realizing that the Prtiest might sue me for defamation of his piety and religious character if I pointed him out as the father, I had no other way to go."

"Than to send the child to an orphanage or find a foster mother."

"Yes, Your Honor."

"What then did you do?"

"I took the baby to a foster-care home and, still in its basinette, placed the infant at the door and said. 'You find a home for this babe. I hav no means. I don't know who the father is...which was a lie. But I said I cannot kill her. I knew that God was watching despite the Priest...or maybe because of the Priest. I will not murder my child!" Tears came to Grant'seyes. He recalled their visit to the orphanage. By this time, he knew Mary's heart was pure of any such draconian work of hell. .

The judge nodded, his eyes moist, and motioned for the witness to continue.

"Well, Your Hhonor, they took the infant and I left. It was as simple as that. Then, about a month later, I received in the mail this letter." She removed an envelope which Grant had never seen. She handed it to the clerk who handed it to the magistrate. He read it aloud.

" 'We are pleased to inform you that your baby girl,
named Jeanette, has found a new home and adoptive
parents named Sara and Clifton :Johnson.' "

"This letter can e entere asevlidence of the transfer of custody. It also shows the little girl in the arms of her adoptive mother, the father standing nearby. Has counsel for the witness seen this letter, this photograph? "

"No, your Honor."

The judge transferred the photograph and letter to Bartok, who showed it to Grant, now Mary's husband. "What is the pleading in this case?" the judge asked counsel Bartok.

"Your honor, that the plaintiff, here, Mary Shepherd, be allowed to recove her biologic child... and with her new husband, Mister Grant Shepherd; sitting there, be accorded the responsibility of rearing her as their legitimate daughter."

The judge pondered for a long while. "What has the other side to say? Custody of ;the hil remains theirs for the time being...?""

"Your Honor, sir," said the Johnsons' attorney, standing and stepping away from the table."I have conferred with my clients. They are filled with sorrow. They have fallen in love with the little girl. Their hearts ache to keep her and raise her for their own."

"I understand, said the judge. There is a conflict of interest, but please proceed, counsel."

"The child now knows Missus Johnson as her mother...and Mister Johnson as her father."

The judge interrupted. "How old is the child?"

"She is three, Your Honor, and approaching four years of age," said the lawyer.

"How do you feel about...about releasng the child into the care of her natural mother?"

"A deep sense of loss, Your Honor. I don't know how to express it."

"I understand," said the Magistrate. "I have had similar cases."

"My clients, however, are compassionate people for their..now affirmed adoptive little daughter...and for the child's mother. We had no thought to bring this up, but there is the matter of paternity, Your Honor. In order to shun the matter of illegitimacy, my clients agreed to accept the paternity of a Roman Catholic Priest." Mary gave a little cry. "The matter was unavoidable, Your Honor. Therefore the child came to us as a discarded ...I avoid the word...an unwanted infant...for us to raise. I, we...and I speak for my clients...they were unmindful of the claims of the natural mother, who sits there. For religious...and moral... reasons, she placed no claim on her natural daughter, and so, being essentially abandoned at the time by..Missus Shepherd there...."

Mary gave a deep sigh, Grant thought she was about to faint..there was a slight

108.

disturbance as he put his arm around her and caressed strands of her hair from her face "....and discarded by the nautral father for religious reasons," the lawyer went on, " the oath of celebacy threatening under the circumstances to put him out of the Priesthood, he avoided all claims to his daughter. Thus, rather than place the infant in an orpanage, the mother put the child in a foster-care home, and reistered her as being of an annonymous parentage. I do not think the Prist's aspirations were honorable, Your Honor. You can construe your own description of the manner of parenting."

"I am not in the business of pleading," the Magistrate interrupted.

"From there the Johnsons took the babe to raise. The child has been in their love and care for over thee years. That is the story, Your Honor. The Shepherds there, Missus Shepherd, the two of them, lay claim to her natural daughter. I understand that they are husband and wife...only recently married." He looked at them with a simulated smile and a nod. " I have confidence, Your Honor, in their ability to and responsibility for raising the little girl as their daughter. He is self-employed with supportive income...." He looked at Mary closely. "I have discussed the matter with my own clients, and they say that if they can have visiting rights, not mandatory as to time and place, but simply no-restreicrtion visiting rights, meeting the lifestyles of the Shepherds, then they would agree to the release of custody rights. What was known only to the judge was that the local Parish had applied for foster care rights so that the church might put little Jeanette into the chuch's foster-care home from where they might raise her to become a nun. This action was instituted by Father Casper as a means to keep the child, his child, from the reach of the "criminal" who had assault him that day on the parish grounds, The judge had refused the appeal, unknowing of the paternity involved, but he regarded Father Casper's intent as intrusive interferrence when he could find no lawful or practical or even religious motive for the appeal. .

Mary and Grant almost wept at this revelation by the opposing counsel, since they expected a prolonged and painful lawsuit of vague motive and undefined purpoe. Bartok had told them nothing. Thus they had been delivered of more anguish by counsel for the adoptive parents, sitting not twenty feet away. The Johnsons regarded one another with expressions of profound sorrow. Mary stepped down from the witness stand. Grant stood up and greeted her with a hug.
"The witness is not discharged," said the judge.
"Sorry, Your Honor."
"I realize this is a very emotional situation." Bartok took over. He motioned for Mary to return to the witness box. "I want Missus Shepherd to tell the court what she intends...what are her plans with respect to raising the little girl." The judge nodded. The question seemed to Grant so pathetically absurd, painful and out of order. "What is the snag?" he thought
"With my new husband I will assume the guardianship of my little daughter. Between us, we can make a secure, comfortable home for her ."
"Will you assume full resposibility for the child?" Bartok asked.
"Yes sir," said Mary.
"I will, "
"May it please the Court, I would like to say something."
:Granted," the Magistrate replied. Grant addressed the bench with a nod and an

expression of inquisitive pain on his face Mary had not seen before.

"We accept what life will bing to our little daugher." That statement appeared sufficient to relieve the anxiety of the Johnsons and appease the doctrine of court procedure.

The judge nodded, and Bartok beckoned for Mary to step down.

"We have seen the results of your enquiry, initially, and have heard your pleading," said the judge. "This court also recognizes and acknowledges the respondent's answer, the recital of the Johnsons as to the pleading. I see no reason why this court cannot accept the pleading and the response...inasmuch as both parties are agreed thereto.... Therefore, I hereinnow grant that full custody shall be given to the biological mother, Missus"....he looked down at his paper... "Shepherd, Missus Mary Shepherd. Furthermore, I rule that the respondent couple are hereby granted visitation rights, as convenient to both parties, without other restrictions as to how many or for how long." This seemed to be the end of the hearing, until the judge motioned to the clerk of the Court. Both sides stood, waiting / Wlitin seconds a silde door opened and the child Jeanette apeared. Both sides waited attentively for the actions of the child who, instantly seeing her adoptive mother, ran into the woman's open arms. Mrs. Johnson stooped over and swept the child into her loving embrace. The woman was crying. The child was bewildered by the strangeness of it all.

To enable the entire court to hear, Mrs. Johnson said to the little girl. "Jeanette, dear, you now have a new mother" The information was delivered in a soft and tender voice and through tears, which the child vaguely began to understand. She was a very bright little tyke; it was just that these events in an adult world bewildered her, as they would any child.

"I don't want a new mother, mommy."

"I know, I know," said Mrs. Johnson, while her husband, also in tears looked on and their attorney, eyes moist, stood to one side, watching.

Mrs. Johnson stood and taking the little child in hand stepped across the space between the two tables. She released the little girl's hand. "Meet your new mother, Jeanette." Tears filling her eyes, she relased the child's hand. The litle girl stood there, hesitated, bemused, while Mary stooped and reached out to grasp the child. Tears flooded the eyes of both women, the judge's eyes were moist. The men were watching with concern and anguish. They, too, were unable to control their emotions.

"Meet your new mother," said Mrs. Johnson again, strengh in her voice.

The child did not respond to this prompting but stood quite still, while Mary, reaching out, pulled her little daugher into her arms. The entire court was in tears over the situation. Mary hugged her little daughter with a deep throb of emotion, a mother's sacred bond to her child, whom she gave up, wrongfully It was evident in the eyes of the court, and under duress of several kinds. She continued to hug litltle Jeanette while the Johnsons stood close by.

The judge spoke. "This Court recognizes the anguish of the situation, and that such emotions are hard to control and that the littl girl will be compelled to adjust to a painful situation, but the law is fixed about the matter. The opinion of this court is settled. The tranfer of custodianship is fully done and complete." He rapped his gavel but did no retire from the bench, for now he was an authorized spectatator who wanted to see that the matter progressed without difficulties in his courtroom.

"Jeanette, dear, will you come home with us?"

The child did not speak or shake her head. She looked back at her adoptive parents. Tears now came into the child's eyes.

"I don't want to go." Mrs. Johnson turned to sob on her husband's shoulder, in his embrace. The child made as if to escape Marys clasp, but her mother now om her knees, held the little girl in her arms, placed a long and ardent kiss on the top of the child's head.

She whispered to her daughter. "You will see them...as often as you want to, Jeanette. They will come and visit with us...with you. You can call them aunt Nora and Uncle Clifton...my sweet little daughter." The child was somewhat mollified yet she remained puzzled by the adult nature of all that was heppening. The Johnsons came over to where Mary and Grant wereshe still on her knees on the floor of the courtroom, her eyes leveled to meet the child's Mary picked up her little daugher in her arms and hugged her for long and trembling time, the child's tears wetting Mary's frock. Grant swept the hild into hisarms and then placed the girl's little black polished shoes firmly on the floor. The child did not understand the significance of these new words and the loving tendered to her by the Johnons and her new parents.

Still looking on, the Judge said. "I think that for the purposes of a healthy break, I should stipulate the order of exit from the court. Will the Shepherds, with their counsel, leave the courtroom at this time.

Hand in hand, the little girl between then, Mary and Grant stood and began their walk down the aisle of the courtroom, their attorney, Bartok closely behind them, while the Johnsons looked on with tears in their eyes. She turned to her husband and sobbed. The judge watched without power at this point.

The trio, now a family, left the courtroom and out the front door.

"Where are we going?" the little girl enquired.

"Yes, where are we going, daddy?" Mary repeated to Grant.

"Home, sweetheart. Were going home," he said, bending down close to his little daughter's ear. The trio disappeared from the courthouse parking lot in his rusty old pickup truck, three faces in the windshield, their little daughter between them, as they started back to their mountain cabin home at the sawmill.

NOAH and LUKE

WAYFARERS

a short novel

by

Charles Edward Miller

HAUNTING SCENES

IN THE VALLEY OF DEATH

I was one of them who joined the Donner Party of the mountains. My name is Noah. I was one of ther party who made it out. We'd come along a big stretch of trailway since we crossed the high water of Big Blue Missouri River, finding a sandy shallow at at Monroe's Bar. When the snow began to fall , we thought it was just a little sprinkling. We had come to the Platte River and run alongside for a week or more, joined by another wagon party, change of captains along the way, until we got to a spot called Independence Rock.

A fellow called Lansford Hastings had written a note to our Captain, telling him that he would meet us at Fort Bridger. When we made it across South Pass, some of our party decided to take the Hastings cutoff described in the letter. We were all for shortening the journey.

My captain, George Donner, from Fort Bridger, decided to go south of Salt Lake flats, the Hastlings route. We were warned not to follow Hastings down Weber Canyon...we sent a couple of wagoneers ahead to get further advice from Hastings.

I was beginning to feel that all of this change in route was a bad dream and I pictured no good would come of it. I was certain trouble might come from it. We were about 70 people in 23 wagons. After we took a vote to return or not to Fort Bridger, most of us decided to go on ahead. At the Fort, the wagoneers elected Captain Donner to lead us. He had it in his head that farm land west of the Sierras was better than what he had farmed in Independence, Missouri. He was a quiet man down inside, a religious feller--I saw him readingi his bible on the wagon seat-- and he imagined California to be the promised land. He as no Moses. When I first saw him, he wore a heavy black beard and a settlers black, flat-brim hat, a vest made of patches, and a short cane he used to beat his oxen with. One time he came back to our wagon and looked in; I thought I saw the hot, tarblack eyes of a demon master. That cane...He snapped the canvas with his cane and walked on. He trusted only in himself...there was nobody who could change his mind.

Once we got into the mountains before the Great Salt Desert, we had to cross through deep forests of pines and juniper trees. This was the Wasatch Forest. We had to hack and cut our way through the Wasatch Mountains, and that took a lot of the stuff out of us. We had to haul our wagons--two dozen or more--up over the rocks with ropes and pulleys and all the oxen we could hitch up. Once we broke clear from the forest, we entered Salt Lake Valley. We stopped for a spell to cut grass for the drive across what I heard talk about was the Great Salt Lake Desert. We were parched. I had a lingering thirst until we reached theSierras. It seemed the water barrel was always empty. It was desert all right, flat as a skillet bottom and twice as hot.

When we reached a place called Pilot Peak, we halted so that the wagoneers could make some repairs to their harness and loose wagon rims. It gave us a chance to hunt for missing livestock behind the hills and scattered boulders. We followed Hastings' map from Donner Spring westward. We had a murder along the way. It seems there was a dispute betweem Captain Reed and a feller named Snyder. a teamster, over what I never did learn...except that Reed had a hot temper and Snyder was stubborn. Both ;men were worn out. I later learned that Snyder accused Reed of his big mistake of taking the cut-off south of the salt desert. Anybdy could make a mistake out in this desolate country. We had to move on....

As we rattled alongside the Humboldt River, Paiute Indians drove off most of our remaining cattle. We lost several travelers along the way...died from heat exhaustion, hunger and the like. There were no buffalo out here for them to survive on. When we reached the Truckee River and crossed over into the measdows, we began our real climb into the Sierra mountains. A wagoneer named Stanton who was sent on ahead retruned from Sutters Fort with seven mules packed with supplies, two Indian drovers, *vaqueros* they were called. .Mister Reed who was banished at Sandy Creek because he had murdered the teamster Snyder, had gone on to Fort Sutter. When he would return was anybody's guess, if he had not gotten lost in the mountains. We had now reached Truckee Lake from where we could see the Sierra pass just a few miles upwards. .Our spirits picked up. IL smelt the fresh air for the first time in months. I had a fear ilnsideof methat ifwe stopped now, wewould be in trouble. I couldn't explain it. How are we going to work our wagons through all them rocks?

We rounded up close to the lake and we decided to stay and to hope. Then, we thought it best to go ahead before any more snow fell. It would take only one night to cross over the pass . Nobody in our party knew the way exactly. We weren't sure if the others wlho had broke off from us at Fort Bridger had climbed up through the rocks and reached Fort Sutter on the other side. It was a perilous climb any way we looked at it. One group of wagons stopped at Alder Creek and the others foud a hunters cabiln at the lake. The wagoneers built two more. They also construced shelters out of qults, tents and buffalo robes, for the three cabins could not shelter the lot of us, twenty four at least. I was among them. "Noah, you stay withs the Stantons," Donner ordered, and so it was I shared the first night sof darkness until we got a small fire lit. We all shivered. The wind came up. I saw even then that we were in for winter weather. We had onedog;he seemed to slink around. He would not know he would be food for our raging hunger later on. The mules from Fort Sutter wandered offilnto the woods almost the first night we stopped. Some drovers are a joke of fate.

Our leader was given to all sorts of doubts... Mister Donner. Use of our wagons, what remained after crossing Salt Lake was no question. We had left most of them back at the Great Salt Desert to rot, since the Paiutes had driven off our oxen and the packburros had died or, as I say, had wandered off into the woods in the night. These happenings meant that we were all afoot. We should have stayed at Fort Bridger until after the winter, or, Captain Donner could have scorned the Hastings Cutoff as a folly...for we lost lots of our strength and most important, our time, in hacking and slashing through the Wasatch trees. I had begun to think of Captain Donner as a man who coveted the land, to possess it against God and man and to loathe anybody who stood in his way. It would have been better for us if he had gone on alone and let us return to our Fort Bidger. I did not know then that he led us to Caifornia driven by that same craving, a lust, a hunger for the power in land tht was free and untouched by white men. I saw him reading the bible one night, but never again after that night.

We took one or two days to rest our remaining bunch of horses, and made us ready in our spirits for the climb. We tried to move on but snow turned us back to the east end of the lake where we found the shelter of one cabin. I figered the snow was just a early snow shower. I could not have been more wrong. We built two more. Our men folks were good with the axe...they had cleared their farmland many years before. They were still tired out from the route they had blazed through the Wasatch woods. Still, we made do. There was about sixty of us in those three cabins at the end of the lake. We expected the snow to melt so we could carry on. We tried several more times but the snow did not stop falling. We had to kill the last of our cattle. Sutter's mules were by this time dead in the early storm and a searchl party could become dlisoriented and lst if they went out to find them. One thing I noticed about the men in the party--they were begining to *meek down*...the pride of farmers who had conquered the land and of axemen who had cut a trail through the forest, and strugglers against storms--this pride had fimed in their eyes. They did not look at each other in the face, and the women's faces looked full of sorrow. It's hard to explain.

After that first night below the shadow of the mountains, the winter like a behmoth of white, sullen quiet and omnipesent threat began to tower over and enclose us ln its freezing clasp. After we had crossed the Truckee River, we started up toward the high rocks at Truckee Meaows. I wondered if anybody had about him a compass to show lus which way was out of the mountains. For we could have gotten lost in a valley that ran north and south in the Sierra Range. By the looks on the faces of the two girls, one woman and a boy in our wagon I saw the fear of danger and of defeat on their faces. Dying was not on my mind then. Nobody but God could see what was ahead...like thle mountains just waiting to spring a trap on us.

Snow began to fall soon as we left the meadows. The snow did not stop, it snowed for four, five days, until it was at least two to three feet deep. The trees shed snow, the light was pale with heavy snow. It was mighty cold. We had a hard time keeping a fire lit in the open silde of our canvas shelter, what there was of shelter, for the wind was a mgihty sorrow the way ilt moaned in the trees. . There were no birds in the skies , none flew over...no animals excepting our horses that somehow broke their harness and that strayed in the night. I know that old German Keselberg had a shot gun...I saw him with it...and the Donners, they had fishing poles and lines. But they did not go to the lake to fish because trudging those six miles from Alder Creek. wheresome had set up camp, would have taken from at this point strength he needed for the climb.We had hacked out way through the Wassach Forest to Salt Lake then on to the Meadows. We had lost all our livestock by this time, along the way, two wagons remalined, and hunger starilng usall in the face likea taunting army of soldiers. . We had plenty of water but food was scarce. Why should I lie to myself. We were going to startve to death. We had planned to live off the land, but what do a bunch of dry-land farmers know about the mountains?

Some of us had settled at Alder Creek. A party went ahead the first or second night and returned because they could not track through three feet of snow. Those of our party who had settled at Alder creek, east of the lake, were content to wait out the temporary storm. In our cabin, we shivered, stomped our feet, pulled our wraps closer, cut and tore canvas from our few wagons... we all thought the Hastings Cutoff would allow us to roll over the pass. But we were vasly mistaken. It was a parlous situation. We were all cold as icicles that hung from our eves after a one-day thaw. Just to stay out of the wind was a accomplishment that made us feel warmer.

We could not expect any help because the Mexican War had taken all thle strongmen from the Fort who might have ome over the Pass to our rescue. It was soon to appear a rescue to us. Breen was one of the men in our cabiln. I saw him writing by the light from the door on our third night. He got up from his log and went ou tto lcheck the direction ofthewlind. He returned, shaking his head and mutterling to himself. A bunch of us, sixteen, seventeen, tried to fabricate snowshoes out of tree branchs, strips of bluffalo skin and tent canvas, tied together with hide thongs. The two men in our cabin were good at making things with their hands. slnow slhoes and we called ourselves the *Forlorn Hope/* I was among them. We set out. They got themselves into a real situation when a storm caught our *Forlorn* party in the open high plateau. I was with them. Stanton ledf the party of about sixtteen or so. We could not keep a fire lit. We were hungry when we left the lake. The climb in the deepening snow took all our strength. Six of our party died. One of the men took out his hunting knife and, ripping open the shirt of one of the dead men began to slice the flesh from the man's back and upper arms to satisfy his hunger, blood upon his face, while the living watched in horror. I hadto vomit. Thiswould not be the first time some of us became cannibals, faces and hands all bloodies and not a glint of shame in their eyes. I heard one man mumble, "God provides.!" My God, if that is his provision, what can be his denial...hell, I suppose. This disgusting surrender made me sick to my stomach. I thought, *Better to die than to eat somebody's dead body.*

5.

The night passed, and I was close to dying, except that I found a rock and dug down beside it wherethe pale sun had cast some warmth into the stone. I gnawed on lichens growed to that rock. The next morning, I watched with the same sickness at my stomach as the fellow who had eaten the warm flesh of the dead, shared another body with two of the living. I felt like I wanted to run away from the human race. I saw all of this with dread on my mind, disgust and a profound terror. I could not watch as the three men, ordinary farmers, friends with the party, turned to cannibals eating the flesh of the dead--like lit was smoked bear meat. . God help us, I thought. I pretended to be asleep so that they would not offer the despicable food to me. Eight had died, three had fed from the bodies whilest a dozen like myelf resisted the awful meal, the course of which was evil and caused me to have the dry heaves. . As soon as they had satisfied their hunger, these cannibals from Missoure shouldered their small packs and set out to return to the lake. The snowfall had stopped. We made out way back, I in my improvised snow shoes, which kept falling off my feet. I would have rather died than to have eaten of that disgusting meal at the *Camp of Death*. Later in the night, half again of the returning snowshoers who left Truckee Lake had died in trying to reach the high pass.

For four days we had had no food or shelter and the cannibal party members did not speak a word for the return trip or at the lake again. They stopped to wash theblood from their hands and faces with fresh snow. Guilt now plqgued thieir thoughts and would suffuse itselt like a contagion hroughout the party for the rmainder of the journey west. Eating the flesh of the dead in order to slurvive was the curse of hell, that our party somehowshold come to that last resort, as if an omnipotent God had cursed us and our purpose from the start. We were a bunh of dirt farmers who knew nothing about the perils of crossling a 16,000 foot mountain range, simply to reach farm land on the other side that was no better than what we had left behind.

The men began to look at each other in peculiar ways. I knew why without words to explain. So did the few women who searched the faces of their men for answers to questions as to what had happene up there in the blizzard. We had to stick together through the *Forlorn* misery. My face burned wilth the numbing cold, my hands were like dead claws and my feet did no seem to exist. I had a raw potato to chew on for strength. I could not taste the potato. The cold makes every sense dead, the lips and ftongue grow stiff; I could not feel my lips.. The air smelled like ice that's got no smell and the ground gave way with every step, although I tried to walk in the tracks of the man who walked and stumbled ahead of me. When he fell linto the snow, LI had a chance to catch my breath. The air was thin. I was much younger. Maybe that helped me to survlve.. I guless so. The others in our party looked like walking dead men out of their tombs, all hunched over, their faces and coats and caps all covered with snow and their beards froze with ilce. ....Mister Breen, the banished man, who had come bak with supplies from the Fort was our only hope, our only contact with civilization and relief. .The *Forlorn Hope* had seen the pass, but a few miles distant, but the descending snow had blotted out the vision no more than a fewmiles down from the gap. We had called outselves the *Forlorn Hope* because that's how we looked andfelt. We had lost seven of the party. We had tried and failed. We had paid a high price for the Hastings cutoff trip. When the snow falls and there is no visible trail and rocks make their own ditches and holes, a body falls in and struggles to climnb out of natue's white traps.

At the Sutter Lake camp, the suffering was the same as at Alder Creek camp. I was surprised we had even two oxen at first. We killed them and prepared a final meal for civilized men. Teamster Norton, a butcher in Springfield, skinned the animals. Those hides would provide us with scant nournishment in a few weeks when boiled to make them ;more edible. Eddy.a boy in our cabin , threw a rock as a raven and missed. I thought I saw a deer out in the woods, but I couldn't be sure. Perhaps hunger was causing delusons in my imaguination. Game was nowhere to be seen whilest bears, if there were any, were hybernating. The deer stayed in the lowlands. There they could browse at the meadows...we should have stayed there as well. <am's instincts are not made for this kind of crisis. We   had lost our instlinct for urvilval. We had become stupid, more stupid than the wild animals.

I saw it coming. The survivors ot the *Forlorn Hope*, the first party to try to escape through the pass. They, we left the dead behind and returned. Mrs. Reed tried to look cheerful...boiling leather to eat--harness, oxen skins and the like. We had butchered the last of our animals. We took to hunting mice, anything that moved, insects. We ate our only dog we had kept for a pets and--up there in the pass--shot-- one of the Indian lookouts ...my God, help us in this grisly, bloody business for I am not and will not be a cannibal. I had rather die from starvation...and the last of some bacon rind kept by Mrs Eddy, for her two boys for their Christmas meal. . I am not too young to undestand that the dark angels of hell are trying our souls and have found some of us wanting. Her husband James, along with Bill Foster and five women had survived the attempt, we we shared the forlorn hope of our circumstances. Their snowshoes sank into the soft snow making the try even that much more difficult. I was with them, my lighter weight made walking easier. I kept to the shade where I could, since the snow crust supported my weight.

Even though that Reed feller had returned from the Sutters Fort some of our party had long talked about starving to death. I did not take us long, no more'm aweek, seems, to go tghrough the emerency foodlllll, we wereo paled with hunger. The wliter had locked us linto the snow and ilce...and death, which we faced.The members of our party, almost sixty of us we were dwindling day by day. Then there was little more than suffering. I could listen to the wind howling in the branches of the trees at night and big clumps of snow would fall to the ground with a splash. In the dark, I heard moans, then a woman crying , for they knew their little children would soon starve before their eyes. It was now October, then comes December and more snow. Mrs. Breen had saved back some cheeze and portion of flour for cakes and had a little Christmas celebration for her two little boys. That was the only light in this gloomy scene.

The snow fell night and day until it covered the ground up to the eves of

7.

the cabins. It was better to die with a little warmth than to try it escape and freeze to death. I did not see how our situation could become more desperate. All of this pitiable calamity came about because we wanted a shortcut to the lowlands West of the Sierras. And Hastings did not lead us to show us his cutoff, which was a mighty wrong thing for him to do, to leave us stranded like he did. Mr. Stanton found a note pinned to tree that warned us not to follow the trail but the note did not give us an alternate route to take. We had only ourselves to blame for the curse of our journey, a shortcut to hell.

I can hardly tell you what took place, when I saw a man come into our cabin with a chunk of meat, like lhe had cut a hind quarter from a shot deer or a bear. He tried to cook it over our small fire. But Mrs. Eddy would not let him. She knew it was a part of a human being, a member of our party who had died. She chased him out of the cabin with God's anger. Then she boiled up the luke warm snow-melt water for tea made from pine needles. At least there was a tad of nourishment in pine needles. Her two little boys and the one girl watched with sad eyes, seeing their mother suffer to give them somethingv to eat. Then Mr. Tayulor came in, said he had shot a deer...I...we heard no shots. He laughed and sald he would show us if we doubted him, but I knew he was something out of his mind. The wind came up again and blew him away, it seemed, while snow came in through cracks around the one window and the door. I heard Mrs. Reed pray for a miracle, as if the falling snow would stop and the wind lay down and a savior angel from heaven show up to lead us up over the summit to safety on the other side. I heard loud screaming noises through the dull and sodden woods, the crazy voice of a party member whose suffering had broken his will to live...screamling his head off out there in the woods, all alone. .

We had days and days of this hardship, which I don't like to remember. A rescue party started up the mountain? Who could tell? The winter wasn't finished with us just yet. Ice formed on the canvas that made part of our roof, the weight tore with with a big ripping sound and let in the zero temperature, the wind and more falling snow. The children began to cry and Mrs. Eddy tried to comfort them with *shhh, its going to be all right.* I asked her if I could help in any way, but she just shook her head. What could I do?... now let me ask you. I tried to pull the torn canvas closed but could not, so that the inside of that shelter was almost like we were sitting out in the open. I thought that maybe I could find a down branch or two or some loose tree bark, but you know everything was so wet and the flame on the stones that was our hearth was so weak it could no burn anything that was not dry. I offered my jacket for fuel, but she refused. There were four others of us in our one cabin..I call it a cabin...one wall was out and the roof was partly caved in, hides over the hole. We all huddled together in the dark, like horses in the rain. We had not brought along anything that would help us to survive but our hope. The mother turned toward the weak daylight and began to read a small bible she had hid somewheres. *And the Lord said, comfort ye....*Sure, sure, comfort," she said under her breath. Her voice broke. Her children kept her from breaking down. Then it occurred to me that I had not seen my brother Jimmy for a day and a half. He said he had gone to the next cabin to see if they could spare a piece of pork. He had not returned.

8.

There was a mystery to these mountains, that when a body, whether a grown man or a boy, went somewheres, he might just not come back. That was the mystery of death that hung over us. How could Captain Donner know? He had put death aside for his scheme to reach the other side. It was as if they were, alike, monsters that snatched a soul from life and hid it until it died and went to the netherworld. I heard such talk about death. I fell sick, got the crampods from trying to chew a piece of leather jerkey, I called it. I had to vomit and Mrs. Eddy put me under her shawl, which was all she had then for warmth. I fell into a babble of imagining things, why I dont know and when I did I felt someone put a piece of food into my mouth. I did not know it until ten hours later then thanked the lady for feeding me. She turned her head and I knew then and there I had eaten a piece of somebody who had died in the snow. And I was mortifed and felt sick to my stomach when I realized what I had done. But I was not awake. How can I even apologize to the doner?..I try hard to forget that bite of human flesh, but I cannot. I did not resist, I might have lasted lonher. But she pused the flesh off on me. *I am now a cannibal*, I say to myself.

Folks were dying off all the while from hunger and the cold. I learned later that James Reed, who had murdered the Snyder feller, came from a Ranch on the West side of the Sierras called Johnsons Ranch. I was one of the 23 that left with the first rescue party to the Lake cabins. This party at AlderCreek done no better than we at Reed's cabin. They also had come through a blizzard at Summit Valley. We met the second relief paty coming from Sutters Fort. I reckoned they did not find much to appeal to their eyes when they arrived at the lake camp, the horrible evidence of folks eating dead bodies, blood still on their faces and in their beards. Snow and more snow fell all the time...fifteen feet, I guess... one blizzard after the other in the Sierras at *Starved Camp*, which was on the lake. The wife of Mr. Donner stayed with her husband, who had hurt his hand long past and was infected...but she would send out their children with the relief party...if they ever found us....

Time went on, I do not know how many weeks. We ate boiled leather, and pine needles. We ate the last of our animals long ago, even their hoofs. We were lucky to have fire...Mrs. Eddy had protected her long lumineres with the loving care of a banker's gold. They were our survival--fire. Most of the time it was better if I could sleep, because you aren't hungry when you asleep, if you can get to sleep when you are so hungry you eat harness leather. It was better to sleep because you aren't hungry when youre asleep, if you can fall asleep when you are hunry. Others our crowded cabin added a little body heat to the bunch, and for that we were thankful. How I made lt, how any of us survived is a miracle. Suddenly, like an apparition, the second relief party staggered into camp. We had us a little good food and were able to bundle the children onto the horses. We started out of *Death Camp* and again up toward the summit, which was only few miles away.

Then some days later, I cannot tell how long, a patch of sunlight fell outside the door and it seemed there was about to come a change in the weather. One of the wagoneers offered to carry me, but I refused. I decided that I could walk in the man's tracks instead. And so we started out those long six miles to the summit. When we reached it, I looked back to our camp site and the frozen lake and thanked God for the murderer Mister Reed. We soon made it down the other side where there was stlillsome bareround--the wind had blowed away the snow-- and hen we came out of f the snow. It had been a unusually flurried and freezing winter all over the Sierras.

At Johnson's Ranch...that's the name I heard it called... we had us a real fire and a house out of the mountain wind. Some forty of us gathered there, whilest others came struggling through. Johnson was a the wiry fellow with blond hair and a limp. He smokeda pope andcarried a Enlishaccent. He treated us like angels from heaven. We slept on the floors of his house, . He put us in the ranch hands' house and his barn, for which we were mighty grateful. His wife gave us baked fish and a litle red wine for our stomachs.. They kept stuff on winter ice and so they were able to feed us...not much or else the good food would make us sick. I thought about the dead bodies some among us had eaten up there onthe mountain. Then I fell into a drowse...for it was warm and quiet there at that ranch!

There were other relief parties, I heard tell...army men who piled all the carved-on and partly-eaten bodies into one of a lake cabins and set it afire. The cannibal gore began at Alder Creek camp, east of the lake. I didn't know how much I missed a good friend until a bunch of us, in a borrowed conastoga wagon , five or six as a matter of fact, from Sutter's Fort, climbed in and made the trip down sloping ranchlands to the Fort. We saw the open gate and the log walls and we laughed like as if we had just come from a drinking party. Our ordeal has been so awful we just had to let on like we did. For the first time in a long while I smelled dust from our wagon wheels...it did not appear the snows had brought rain to the For tSutter plains. I fell into a quiet corner, insilde a empty stable and slept until sunlight flooded the Fort parade grounds. I was surprised to find I had had company for the night, and not a mule or a horse. His name was Luke, a kid about my age.

A FUGITIVE FOR A PAL

At the ranch a woman with a blonde bun served us mush for breakfast at long kitchen tables. She sad anything else would *get to your innards*. From Johnson's ranch we rattled along a rain gutted road from the ranch. Every time a wheel at hit one of those ruts, stuff and things would bounce around inside the wagon. It was a caution.... Inside a couple of hours we were at Sutter's Fort, more like a stockade built of of tree trunks, corner shooting towers, ranch lean-tos- for most of us, me and Luke slept out with the horses...the stink of unwashed bodies somehow wasnt my idea of a good night's rest. We had a good sleep, tried a handful of the horse's oats, wandered into Miss Jimpson, like her name, a noisy and poisonous tongue, who said she'd rather fix breakfast for a den of thieves than for any of us. I couldn't quite measure her tongue or her speculation on our hardship. We wuz all hard-biltten, let me tell you that. Poor in bone and body, hungry for days, those travelers from Missouri --so tired of the trip they wanted to start farming outside the fort. They had already forgotten about their hungry slicing of folks bodies for food and the coals of hells fire sort of freezilng we went through at Donner Lake. I heard they collected the eaten odlies and piled them inside one of the cabins and set it afire. That was General Kearny who was the first to set his eyes on *Cannibal Camp*. Cremation was a good thing, too, or the wolves woud have feasted a week on them dead travelers, as they did on bodies we had to bury in the snow right along when folks died.

We were rescued and serttled in for a spell at Fort Sutter . That night, after I had slept in the hay for almost a day, we had us a big campfire at he fort. For the first time in a white spacular winter I felt warm. My fingers and toes were frozen numb for so long I had to look at them to see if they 're still where they ought to be. Down there at the lake, some of us suffered the hurting sting of frostbite. Here at the Fort we managed a big bowl of stew for supper, with smoked pork ribs, cooked oats and steaks for breakfast...which brought to mind the cooked rawhide we ehcwed on down there at the Lake. The change was glorious!

Alongside of me at thle bonfire squatted a kid about my age . I soon learned his name...Luke...he was a young outlaw and running from the law.

"I been noticing...Luke? I seen you turn away from that cavalrly fellow, af if he ilntended to shoot you.:

"I got no more trust lin uniforms...no more than I trust a swamp gator or a sheriff.:

Well, we all got our reasons," Noah said. "IL'm running away from thememory ofmy Pa, who was cruel to me at times...and how he did tread Ma.:

:Yer mlither ils important. Feller down there lin Arkansas shsot my mother...:

:Shot her...byGawd, you;ve a cause to attack...:\

"Not wlith a gun, butwlith words. I had my Pas ilndilan gun and killed him on the spot.:

:The sheriff didnt...

:Niver found out ujntil lthe next day. I let the whores son lay there till the law found him, out back of llthe hardware store lin Stonestsown.:

Wll you got a good reason to run, I spose.

A dan good reason, and LI still gotl that gun.:

Noah sat quie;tly for a time, watching the flames.

What ilfn heshould just suddenlh appear...here and now.:"

Depends, said Luke. If he pologized, I spose I could fer give him. But hewas tough and onry, had killed niggers and whites, alike, for little things, no count stealing...I don't know what all, but I tell you this, Noah, I got to be mighty kerful cause the man I shot was knowed in the town and all over the county. He was a one of them... *politicians.*"

"I see," I said. "Well, you team up with me and I'll keep a kerful watch on your back so's nobody can sneak up on you."

"That's mighty good of you, Noah. I can handle the confrontment of the situation. i still got my Pa's gun."

"We can work the road together...I mean honest like. I want to explore the gold country north a here. Then, maybe move on up into Oregon where young men like myself...I got a beard...see?... can make a go of it. We can travel north...together...if y' want to, Luke."

"I got to keep ahead of the law...as they say...not one step, one mile. We"ll plan us a trip, couple of young miners out hunting forl gold like ten thousand others jes like us.:

"Right, and they won't recognize you...," said Noah.

"I'm not so sure. They had them posters down there in Stonestown, and I seen others along the way. I come north because I figured I could get lost in the argonaut crowd."

"Easy to say, easys to do," said Noah.

A couple of hands, Sutter's men, a white feller and a nigger in trousers and white shirt, carried some small logs and tossed them onto the flames, sending a geuser pf sparks into the night sky. The fire flames got higher as soon almost a hundred souls had drawn up to the warmth and sat on fire logs and on their haunches to watch the flames. A couple of mounted cavalrymen walked their horses toward the flames in the darkness. It sweemed like atlime to pray but I didn;t know no prayer. Beside, God knew what he was doing when he rescued m eand the others. Lots of them what came to the bonfire were Donner party folks...Stanton, I recognized...and others who had come with us on the *Forlorn Hope* escape party.   They came and watched and spoke not a word to each other, the flames flailing across their faces yellow light, eyes gaunt with hunger still, and beards agow in the light. The were awsomequiet...like a gathering ofrepentant sinners or such. ; Many around the fire that night could hardly wait to put down the plow into the unfroz ground. It was a sight--that fire ring inside Fort Sutter that night-- me and others who were rescued.

Seems Luke had killed a feller who had insulted his Ma. From Stonestown, Arkansas, had wangled horses down in Southern Texas to Mexico. He had come to the Fort to see if he could put on a uniform and fight the Mexicans. It could be a good way to disappear if he was enlisted, as most surely he was in a fright, a fugitive from the law and askeered of his guilt, having murdered a man over a drunken insult. Now that the war was over, he could not remain at the Fort or else the sheriff, the Commandant and his soldiers would recognize him from reports and arrest him and send him to Sacramento to be tried and hung. Myself? I needed to get away from the cannibalism at the Lake and the smell of death. That smell was stuck in my hair and my clothes. There was cold ashes at the rim of the fire pit. I rubbed some of them on my arms. Folks near by thought I was crazy...which I had a good right to be. But I did not give a cock's crow in hell what they thought.

Well, we struck up a partnership right off and me and Luke became friends. We decided to go north, maybe to try to find our fortunes in the gold fields of the mother lode.   Miners called it *El Dorado* . We planned on leaving the Fort. Luke had on him a leather pouch...he showed me...that was partly filed with gold dust.
I asked him, I said, "Where in thunder did you get that?"
"I stole it...robbery...I caint tell you here...and mebe I wont. "
"Maybe I better not hang around you in here. If the soldiers arrest you;, they's sure to haul me in, too."
"You...no, just me, Noah. They caint do that."
"They can do anything they're a mind to. They're soldiers."
"Well, gold is not good evidence. Just goes to show I'm a bonifide miner."
"You don't look it one bit," I said to him.
"I maybe could brilbe he;m....:
"Bribe...!"I was sorry I did not think of that.   "Your hands are too soft."
With this, he shut up. I was glad I had only my own opinion of such things to reckon with.

Mister Sutter, he was a nice old gentleman, a Colonel I think. The wagon-masters, wranglers, sourdoughs and such all called him *Colonel*.
"You boys had breakfast?"--first words out of his mouth.
"No sir," I said, "but we can make out..."with a handful of oats from the stall."

"Well, that practically floored him so he led us into his kitchen pantry and loaded us up with fried chicken from the night before, weiners and sourkraut for breakfast, some garlic bread from the night before--they ate high on the hog here at the fort. We stuffed our shirts full of them commestibles and figured we ought to inspect the hospitality of our real saviors--the second rescue party from the Fort led by the man they called Reed, him who was banished for killing a wagon driver named Snyder.

At the fort I saw drovers, wranglers, wgon msters beside thesoldiers lin their blue uniforms. They had come in from fighting the Mexicans at the Rio Grande River. I heard they collected the cannibaled bodies and piled them inside one of the cabins and set it afire. I wanted to forget that scene. It was General Kearney, I heard, who reached the Cannibal Camp and disposed of the dead bodies. At the Fort I saw drovers, wranglers, wagon-masters beside the soldiers in blue uniforms. The army cavalry in blue trotted around the open ground, did a few cuts and wheel drills, ;then filed out to one corner where their unit flag flew. The others of the resilents ln Sutter's stockade, I called it, were dirty, unwashed, bearded and slouching fugitives from of towns across the country. They were a dowdy and ragged bunch, if ever I saw any. But the craving for gold was no task-master except one--shovel, pick and sluce. Some of them had been out fighting the Mexicans at the Rio Grande River. They carried their muskets, some carbines like the horse soldiers. They were a awsome crew and a fright to any civilized body such as m'self. I saw one of them pck a filght with another outthere linth early morning dust. It lasted until a soldier walked over and knocked down the agressor fellow and drawed his gun on the other. Things tended to get out of hand occasionally. A gunshot spooked a wagon horse over by one corral and it was a tlme of chasing that skeered horse arond the yard before he was caught and calmed down. Off at one side of the fort, residents from out party drew water from a common well and set to washing their duds and wraps and hanging them on corral gates and across the army cots Col. Sutter had opened up for his guests. He was a cyrageous and mellow fellow who liked all folks...expeclially those did not cross his hot temper. The scene inside that fort was spectaculous.

We saw wagons, from other settlers outfits , women with bonnets, kids runnin about, tall lean men in black hats, men with pistols at their hips...probasbly wranglers, called cowboys, here and there a religious looking feller in a notched collar and another in one of those broad-brim hats . No delicate ladies, but here and there a women who was washing, hanging out clothes...some dogs, but the horses, most of them out of the sun and in the stalls. It was a pretty scene let me tell you, what after what all I'd been through, especially the crying babies of the troop, the women looking starved and desperate haggard and the men hardly daring to meet our eyes, the storms shaking snow from the branches in clumps--wind such as would float a wagon--snow and more snow. One man iln the ForlornHope rescue attempt turned snow blind trying to make his way over the pass. Others plum gave out in the struggle, fatigue more like exhaustion which was the cause of some of the party dying off. When you aint et for a month and all you got to fill yer belly is the cold snow, you can just about count on it, you're sure to die in time. There were others who just wandered off to die by themselves, so as they wouldn't be a burden on anybody, and some said nothing but simply prayed that God would somehow come to their rescue. No angel out there, in the woods on that great mountain...just cold air, snow everywhere, ice on the tree trunks and those gray cold rocks looking up above us...and more snow. There was some at the fort who were trying to grubstake themselves to make it out into the gold country again. Here and there, I'm certain, a soldier lent a hand, expecting when he got his discharge to go into the diggins begun by a sourdough. Miners who had come into the fort brought their whiskey with them.,...,soldiers were not allowd to drink on the post..,.fights and all the rest. But the miners staggered here and there on booze that came from old Sac. My Pa would have sworn they were souls lost in hell and could not find their way inside a wove basket. The fort saved them...from perdition, I s'pect.

Me and Luke, we sat down on a rock rim to eat our chicken given to is by Colonel Sutter. There was to be a big bonfire in the ring mighty soon. He begun to tell me about things such as I had never heard of before. I come to the quick of it. He had shot and killed a man for insulting his mother. He heard Jessie James did the same for his mother.

"Well," I said, "Luke, since you aint Joaquin Murieta, it looks like you got yourself into a parcel of trouble."

"That I have and I be chased from Texas to here. Folks said when a man went to Bodie, one of them wild, hell-raising towns, he was lost forever. I plan to get lost forever."

"That's a mighy fine ambition," I said to him...ifn you got the money to buy a good meal along the way."

"I live by my wits," he said to me, "and by luck. You believe in Luck?"

"Sometimes," I said, "but mostly I believe in God."

He almost fell off the rock he was sittin on. "You caint be serious."

"As serious as this hyer piece of chicken. There/s something directing the world, not just men by themselves. Theres ...well, I call it *organization*."

``Organization!"I said and I could tell he saw me as a sour vigil, all right.

"Sure, you dont think we come here alL by ourselfs."

"Why not? You haint got no pa or ma telling you to go the gold fields."

"No, but my Pa was all for prospecting, excepting Ma wouldnt let him...said it was a waste of time."

"Some call it such... until you find that nugget."

"Nugget! "

"And how in blazes do you think that nugget got there?"

"By chance, pure and simple, Luke. Why, do you think God put the nugget in a certan place...just so's we could find it?"

"Organization, pure and simple! You think there a angel setting your four in a hand at poker?"

"No, but if I aint got me a winnin hand, then I dont reckon i'm worth winning."

15.

"Oh, Jesus, Noah, you haint got the wits I thought you did. "

"I wouldnt put it past a man to stack the deck."

"For us, hells fire, friend..!" He said no more...for a space. "Why, land a goshen, just look at how the ocean abides by the shore line and..."

"Yer getting crazier by the minute, Luke, m" friend!"

I took offense at him calling me boy, me sixteen and almost seventeen, He changed the subject."We caint stay here for ever, Noah. You know that."

"We could clean them stalls and...and make repairs on them log walls or on harness and such like."

"Now *you* are talking nonsense," Luke responded. They got them niggers to do all that sort of thing."

"Well, we will have to move."

"Just what I was a thinking, Noah. I got a better idea. Lets take one of them wagons for as far as it will take us. We can go on from there...maybe buy us a couple a mules."

"Yes, and you got money for the wagon?"

"Well ...well play ranch hands for a couple a weeks. Then we can buy a wagon. Look, Luke, what in blazes can they do with all them wagons...four justssitting empty out there....And I got my bag of gold dust.""

"Crazy. that's the spittin truth."

"I can shoe horses," said Luke. "Did so on a ranch in Texas." He stopped and stared. "Sir, I can shoe that there mule for you if it needs shoes." A mliner led hisl burro past the pair of them, finishin ff Sutter's breakfast.

"I hant got the time."

"Why, you're stuck in here same as us." Luke said.

"How much you charge...and how long?" asked the squat stranger with black hair, skinny as a willlow branch and chewing a quid of *Red Indian*. He spat and said, " I got me a tent over there 'gainst the south wall. How long it take you? And you haitn got no forge."

"Thats alright. Colonel Sutter said we can use his. The smithy is a part of the fort."

"How long...?"

"Three hours, mebe two, one for each hoof." Luke laughed. They agreed and so we had us a small income right off. I, Noah, had some experience in repairing harness, and so we walked about inspecting the harness on bridles, wagon trees and draped over tent stakes inside the fort.

"We got a need for burro...we give up on the wagon plan... and for fixing your harness where tis cut and broke, We won't charge you a hull lot, mister."

"You haint got the needle and thread, Noah."

" A soldiers always got his sewing pack in his saddle for just such eemergencies."

"You need ready money I perceive...," said one stranger who took an interest in the two lads. "We're settlers like everybody else, headed north into gold country," Noah said. The man smiled and walked away, confident in his own ignorance.

We were trying to put together a plan to make some small money and purchase not a wagon, although there be almost twenty standing idle inside the fort walls. However, Col. Sutter would not tolerate the congestion for long, although he was pleased to be of help to wanderers like us, miners just passisng through, easterners scouting for land and Indians come into the fort for protection. There was much bad will outside the fort toward the local Modocs, they being natural troublemakers from North California. Now a huge bonfire was about to be lit. We could maybe meet somebody there at the bonfire who needed our services .

In these ways we made ready to set ourselfs up in business for the purchase of a pack burro. Little did we reckon on Colonel Sutter's temper. For before the sun went down that night, with loud shouts and flailing his horse whip and with the help of the soldiers in the fort, he hustled the wagons out through the main gate. The soldiers moved the wagons out of the grounds, four pushing at the back and five on the tongue. We could simply claim one of them, if their owners did not show up to protest. All in all, the pack burro was more practical...and that called for Luke's *organization*. A plan took us by surprise...and it worked the next morning. That night me and Luke sketched our trip north, with or wilthout grub. We found us a burro with a bag of oats hanging around its neck...but no owner in sight. Luke suggested we steal the animal. Any man who was so foolish as to leave his untethere4d turro in a field deserved to lose ilt...and so our partnership to acquire the animal that wasc entral to our mission.

"We can wrangle us\a burro,\"said Luke. "one that kinda waners off. I loaded up and bridled up many a time...down in Arkansas." zil lhr Luke a funny lookl. "Don feel bad,Noah, IL:ll dothe thieviln. IL alwayls got my purse a gold to back up my handiwork." He grilnnined. Noah agreed that he could, given the darkness of the night, when all were settled around the bonfire. The plan was thievery, but the entire economy of the Fort was founded--a mite here, a piece there--on the theft of supplies, shelter , guns and unclaimed stock. Colonel Sutter's hospitality knew no bounds. He just hated clutter...didn't mind how we got rid of it. The presence of the US cavalryhelped out a lot lin matters sof supply. It was just the present big demand that trobled Colonel Sutter. However, he had his own means of supply....

"Aint we just as good as anybody else...we'll intend to buy a burro and some grubstake....there...."
"Theres a fort store over there," said Luke.
"Call them grubstake."
"I know, I know. I'll talk to the Colonel tonight when the fire is lit. I think he'll agree he wants to get the miners in here on their way...soldiers also. He seemed to take a liking to us, Noah. Why jus look at the way he offered to give us all that grub and asked if we wanted a bed and showed us where the washing trough was.... Caint ask for more in hospitality."

"You're imagining things, Luke. Beats living in the mountains...off of your friends," said Noah, his thoughts momentarily retreatilngto the ordeal ofthe Donner party .

"I guess not"...that was Luke's only comment. I learned his last name. LIt was carved on the stock of his gun he let me look at. Grissom...*Luke Grissom*.

So without much falderall, a couple of them black ranch hands toted in wood and got a fire going and pretty soon, the Donner gang began to show up , now that they had a little rest and some food. They came a congregatling around the fire. I also saw a Indian or two in white man's clothes...still they wore a feather in their shiny black hair to identify them. And I saw some from our party, the lucky ones. I couldn't help feeling some disgust though, since I knew they had ate some of their own fellows up there pn the mountain. I also saw some of those big *tree men* , I called them. one with a knife long as my leg across his chest in a sheathe. Another came out with a double-bit axe and began to chop those small logs into firewood that would burn hotter, while the slaves kept on bringing in more logs through the side gate to the fort, not the main gate ghat opened for wagons and such. There was talk then about war. I heard it...a civil war over slaverly and this Lincoln feller said the slaves had to be patient and he pushed his men to make war on white southerners...no matter if they owned slaves or not. It was what I called *orgnization*. I never could get Jonas to believe in *organization,* but it's out there, I 'low. I never thought of them as slaves before until I was told that was their place in life. Just workers, sweet as chocolate when they're not beat. Me and Pa went to one of their churches one day, out under a brush arbor. Well, there we were, clapping right alongside them in the other wagon.

Half the Fort came to the fire, minrs mostly, faces all grimed with dirt, hats muddied by rains,clothes torn, weary-tired, bunching up to get to the heat, no laughter and little talk, some with their hands held out toward the gathering flames and others mumbling a kind of satisfaction for the fire, all wearied by their trekks from the gold country, the hardships of living on the ground and all kinds of weather, and mots of them missing the folks back home. It was a parlous bunch of sourdoughs, miners, and some men who looked like they had left a party, one with a bow tie, another in a cutaway coat, some with good clothes,but all of them appearling to want to get closer to the welcome heat of the bonfire inside Sutter's Fort.

Whilest we sat there warming our insides, there also hove into view a man with a couple of mules he began to unpack close to that fire, as if to feel the lot of us watching him. He said he had discovered gold up on the American River and that there was plenty of room for more panners, and he 'lowed as how his two bags of what he called gold dust were hardly the start. He was a former railroad stoker, he said of his pal, who wore a shot gun strapped across his back. He said, this unpacker, said, it was a blessed occasion to be able to take a rest and that the land had blessed the good folks and that Mister Sutter was blessed to have this here fort for stragglers, strangers, survivors, travelers and the sick, injured and hongry. Well this feller blessed the lot of us and then beganto enquire from Jonas. I listened in close.

"You dont look like you're ready to take on hard times," he said to Luke. Silnce Luke was a fugitive from the law, he had his own hard knocks to answer for.

"No, and you are right, Mister. I haint had no hard times, and I aint 'tending to have none either." I knew right away what he meant. Capture meant prison, a court and trial and the hangman's rope.

"This here Fort is a pretty nice place to stay," said my newfound friend.

"Haint it though! The trouble is, it's a good place for a man in trouble with the law to hide out in."

With those words, I almost wemt into a connipshun fit. But Luke, he just went on same as ever with his story. "Tell you why, Mister, if ever I saw a killer roaming in these here parts, I would shoot him on sight, sure."

"Would you now! Well, the law is looking for a man who shot and killed another man, young feller." At that point, the stranger gold-panner bent down and took a close inspection, leaning down to look into Luke's face in the firelight to find some slash of guilt. But Luke, he was a good 'tender, let me tell you. How he could act was a caution. "We both of us be on the lookout for fugitives...I can always tell a killer from a innocent man m'self," said Luke.

"I knowed that to be so," said the stranger.

"How can you know? How to you know?" Luke asked.

"By the way he talks, how he wears his hat ashading his eyes and ifn he's got a weapon on. him. Oh, sure I can tell, mister."

"If you saw a robber or a killer on a poster, would you capture him and turn him in and collect a reeward?"

"You betcha I would!"

"I would double the reeward," I said.

"Good boys. I knew you was honest from the start."

"We keep out eyes wide open for any suspicious-looking ..murderers."

"Call the chief of the Sacramento police if you find one."

"Oh, you just never kin tell who you might run into."

"That's right. Well, boys, I got to finish unpacking this hyere burro. I gotter to feed her, find a stall for her and myself both."

"Colnel Sutter is a generous man," Noah said.

"Y' hear that?" Luke put in.

"There are times when that is a useful provision of God above,", said the stranger, inspecting the pack on his burro. "Blessings on you two boys."

"And the same to you," I said, not really knowing why he would bless us since we had done nothin in particular to earn his blessing. Then I seen more soldiers and some ranchers come apourng into the fort, I dared to identify them as such. Col. Sutter suddenly showed up at the campfire before the crackling wood and smoke and the yellow light flickering on his whitened beard and moustache and patch of white hair. He warmed himself for a short spell , his open jacket with shoulder pins and sleeve stripes identified his rank and service. I knew that much about soldierlng. I sort of liked the man from the start, and why not? He was our protector and savior of a kind.

I spoke up to Colonel Sutter about our plan. He agreed to help us provision a burro. We could forget about the wagon. He would purchase the animal from some of his rescued mountaineers or his sourdoughs who were turning in their shovels. Not every panner was successful and lots of them fagged out with disappointment and the hardships of panning for gold. They returned home with stories about wild Indians, I 'spect, and about the gold they never did find. Someofthem drank their gold away in the zillion saloons lin the mines. There was men who yearned for a excuse to go back to their homes and families. When Mister Sutter struck a deal, he called me over to him in the fort yard and handed me the riens to a burro. I was sure he was glad to get rid of us...and I was afraid a deputy of the law would spot Luke at the Fort and put him in handcuffs and heist him off to jail. Things can happen fast in this country.

Col. Sutter said that me and Luke had done enough work around Sutter's Fort to pay for one mule. I don't know what he was referring to, but I allow as how I did not argue with the man. Shucks, we had done very little, cleaned the stalls like I said, and curried the animals two days ago. We also went out and with our borrowed two-man saw. We cut couple a trees and managed buck them into logs. We loaded up the Colonel's wagon for the trip back to the Fort. The work was hard, but I didnt mind it since I knew we were getting ready to hightail it out of the Fort before a soldier or a deputy of the law recognied Luke and threw us both into jail. That was the heart of the matter for us.

Leave the Fort for American River and the town of Sacramento, where we planned to stop for a night at each place, then on out way from creek to creek and into El Dorado with my new companion. The story he told me showed he werent guilty at all, but that the woman's husband who was my friend's Pa, shot him instead but they put the blame on Luke, the son with a gun in his hand. Still we had to get away, nobody would believe my friend's story noways, because that's just the way life is sometimes when the truth is too dangerous or too uncivil to handle even if it be the truth. That was the story he told me. In my mind I couldn't help going back my own horrible sufferin, the bunch who called themselves the *Forlorn Hope* and had got caught in a blizzard and some died from the cold and starvation. It was cold enough to freeze your breath in the air so it would drop to the ground like a chunk of ice. It was cold enough you could cut it with a wood saw and lt was cold enough so that if you took your hand out of your mittens for just a minute you would lose your hand. That was the suckin unholy truth of the matter, let me tell you.

Soon as the fire died down and we saw they would not put more wood on, I and Luke decided to bunk indoors for the night in one of the soldiers' barracks--there was about a hundred or more cavalry soldiers here in Fort Sutter. They looked like they were getting ready to go east and escort a train of sojourners across where we came from, over the mountains. The soldiers knew the way and had the help of a feller named *Good and Sharp*, a Paiute Indian. We had met with Paiutes back on the Salt Lake who stole our cattle, sure 'nough they did, almost a fifty head and left us with little to eat. These Paiutes were fierce, with bones in their hair and rings on their legs, hair done in knots/ They carried rifles like bows lin their hands...same as us whites...taken off a killed soldiers. They would butcher our cows and dry the meat and have food for a year or more, while we starved. It was just the devils pot for the lot of us. Mister Donner had bought along his entire herd of cattle and *Peavy,* they called him, had another twenty. But those danged Paiutes must have had Mexican *vaqueros* in amongst them to make off with so many steers. But they did. Well, I dont trust them Paiutes here at Sutter's Fort neither.

We got up early, the solders were still snoring away and the hut was hot and smelly of rotten bananas and I was glad to get out of doors. We still had a piece or two of that chicken we had the night before....Mexican miners smuggled in the cocoanuts filled with brandy they soldto panners. And so me and Luke, we went out to the dead coals of the fire ring and had us a little breakfast. Then we spent another hour packing up our mule. Luke...he was still a runaway from the law... he cared not a wit to steal, since murder was his most gorgeous crime.. He stole two shovels and two picks and come walking back with a big grin on his face, showd them to me with grunt of satisfaction. We *found* two pans and I pulled the blankets off our cots in the barracks. We needed more provisions and so me and Luke, we broke into the supply hut and helped outselfes to a huge sack of flour and some cuts of beef and bacon, and a fistfull of luminettes for fires. IL felt real sneaky doing this but Luke looked like he enjoyed the gathering of our stake.

We provisioned ourselves, but the Colonel, he had had us clean stalls and so we did not ask him but took stuff for our pay. We would find our own gold. Before the sun was up, we found the small gate aside the main gate and lt was open. We told the sentry we was going out for the week and we would bring some gold back for the Colonel and if he was quiet we would pan some for him. I give him a gold watch from my pa--it was dead like his body, he shook it, I said it needed to be warmed to run best as it was too cold outside at this hour-- he did not shout. All the watch needed was a little winding. We wished him a good day of sentrying and we set off, by my reckoning, in a north eastward direction. We hoped the sentry would not blab and roust the cavalry out after us like guard dogs, for we were going without the Colonel's blessings and his handshake. We would follow the sun and moon for our compass. Most of the creeks ran east and West from out of the Sierras, and we would have no trouble finding our way. A panner told me that gold has a smell about it you can follow like a hound dog.

THE DIGGINS

Ever since we left the Fort the old feeling of me being abandoned hovered over me...lost, like you know, shiverling to death in the cold and hungry and won't nobody strike a fire to warm our hands or put a bowl of mush on the table, like back at Johnson's ranch. This feeling covered my life like a dark cloud of hopelessness . I tried to explain this to Luke. He pretended not to hear me.

"What more can I ask for out here, Luke. 'S a lonely corner of the world. We be on our way to richess, don never forgit that."

"I'll remember when I see some of that yellow dust in my wash pan."

"If them cavalry back there come a galloping along, you better hide real quick."

"Oh, they dont bother me none. I aint afreared of them heel diggers."

"Well if they got a fugitive they intend to take in, youll be bothered by a rope. You can count on that...after murderlin a man for bad words."

"Shucks, that aint nothing to be consarned about, Noah. Them dudes with the law oin their hands don look for no cheap-shot murder like myself. They want bank robbers and stage coach hold-up gauchos."

"I wouldnt be too sure o that if I was you. Be hard totalk yourself out of guilt for a murder, and you know that," I replied, quick as a squirrel's flash."

So we rode on towards Sacramento until at last it came inter view. " I heard tell there was gold along the banks of the Sacramento River...and the American River also, where that sourdough come from...the one back there at the Fort. They might even get up a vigilantes committee to come after you, Luke. They chase murderers all the time. Hang them, too, you can bet on that. Well, we were safe for the time being."

We were headed towards Sacramento, a town what boasted of a mill and loggers and miners aplenty, cheaters, robbers, murders like Luke here, all on the lookout for vilgilantes. They never run out of business. Thats the skinny truth, the criminals and the suspects alongside with them. Law and order is more the cut of things ln a town like Sacramento. But I 'spect we'll find it reckless and as violent as swarming hornets when y' throwl a rock at their hive'. Gold does it all. We felt secure for now on our two burros. We're jest ordinary panners. I's guess the Colonl and that sntry with the dumb watch was glad to get shut of us back there at the Fort."

We came to a creek with a wood bridge and a sign on t' other side that said *Putah Creek.*

"What the devil does that mean, Luke...Putah Creek."

"See them shacks? Well, when miners come to town, they some of them make a stop...at them whorehouses... Putah is *whore* in Mexican lingo."

"Oh, I didn't know. You sure know a lot about this part of the country."

Noah he said not a word. Some women were sitting on the end of the bridge, dangling their legs. They did not look at us. They were pretty to behold, like those pictures on the coffee can. We ambled on. Our burro needed water, so we walked him down to the creek and watered him and let him browse on some of the grass that was growing at the river's edge. Then we took up the road again.

Pretty soon, we came to the town. First thing I saw was a big pitchur on a paper, a poster that told us about Murietta's knifes and the scalps he had skinned...they were all there in that museum advertising. We ambled past a laundry. The dirt road turned to bricks. A Chinaman named Lee Sun ran the e-establishsment. Next to him was the assayer's office but there was no long line of gold pickers waiting outside to put their gold dust or nuggets to the scales. A connestoga wagon pulled by a team of ox came past us. I didn't expect that, but we were coming near to the town of *Chance. Chance, California*--that was its name. A 'gantuan poster wth a steamship on it welcomed gold prospectors to to El Dorado . Rates were a hundred-fifty dollars or so, pretty cheap around South America. But then many of those miners and gold diggers tripped acrosst the country, and that were fine.   Then I heard the awfullest sound, like a dozen angry bulls stomping their hoofs at the same time. "Whats that noise?" Luke asked me.

"Stamping mill...outside of town...." Derndest racket! crushes rocks so's they can be panned in the sluce boxes of the miners, I explained. Miners bring their rocks down there to be crushed afore they can take out the gold from the crushings. Did you see that sign about Joaquin Murietta, the bandido. *Bandido* means little bandit, but he sure got his loot aplenty by shooting and robbing folks, wagon trains, banks, you kin name it. Noting little about that. Hell aint no little place either to accommodate the likes of him."

"Well, he dont scare me none," Luke said.

"Me neither. We got that there double-ott shotgoun for pertection."

"Dont take much aim to shoot it either. If he wants to stop us, just let him try."

"That s your ol spirit, *Luke I* don't reckon he's aywheres around closeby, I mean. Soon 's we get into town, we got to take in a little 'freshment and go to the theatre."

"Well, I say, you got some mighty ganderish ideas this morning, Noah . We aint got but a lick and a snap 'twixt us to pay for anythin. We better find a place by the river somewheres first and fix our pannin and then something to eat."

"'Taint nothing to talk about them things, Luke. Theys a part of life in this hyer town."

"I guess so."

"But say, the more miles we put twixt you and them who wants to hang you, the better off for the both of us." Luke looked at me kind of funny like. "I mean, I'd sure hate to see a good friend hauled off tied up on the backs of some vigilate's saddle, all trussed up like a branded yearling in ropes...to be hanged from the next tree."

"Oh, I got my druthers, Noah. You can bet on that. I got m' wits for a fight. That dude thought he would get off with insulting Ma like a dog's whelp. Well, he didnt, and may the devil take his soul."

"Look, Luke! See that there big derrick thing... and right here in town...?"

"Gold mine elevaor, I hert tell...frame over a big hole in the ground. It takes the miners and their buggies up and down like a bucket of water on a rope pulley. Wait." The two of them stopped to listen but only the pounding of the stamping mill caught their ears and seemed to tremble the whole ground.

Soon's as we make camp and get some vittles inside of us, lets explore around a bit. Y' care, luke?"

"Not at all Noah. We got to stay on the watch...real careful. We still aint out of trouble."

They missed most of Sacramento, on the river, escept for the miners' brown and gray canvas tents, the panners along the river banks and the carts and wagons and horses on the dirt streets..and the sounds of the vendors shouting to the street crowd. There was nothing for the two of them to engage their time in watching; they had their mission of escape from the law, at least Luke did, and lf one then the ohter, too, as the law went. Sacramento was a supply town for miners, picks and shovels could be bought there at ten times the ordinary price for the askin. Blankets at fifty dollrs, a pair of boots two hundred dollars, a spade fifty dollars, a pick, seventy five. Tent canvas by the yard, at forty-five-dollars a yard. That was all because there was a lot of gold going around and changing hands, sometimes not even gold coins but just a nugget or a smidgeon of gold dust in a tin cup. Those commodities had to be brought across the country, through the jungles of Panama, or around the horn, that was why. There werent no other word for greed exceptomg the word **gold**. They almost spell the same

"Looks to me like folks 've turned mighty greedy what with so much richess around and the miners coming and going in the town for supplies.: I had to letit out.

" We got ours, so I aint complaining," Luke said.

The streets were crowded with a covered wagon passing us now and then. splashing tghrough the mud holes . Or a miner was leading his mules or his urros, now andthen a long eared donkey, loaded on both sides with stuff, the pick and shovels-- the last things he tied onto his side bags. Poor animals.... The miners most always looked down at the road, niver looked around them as they led their pack animals...bearded like they hadn't shaved since they came to California, and smoking maybe a big eastern cigar to celebrate finding gold... or a pipe...mostly they was Eastern gentlemen. Oh, we had all kinds in the gold fields. Even poets...like Pa used to say. Gold 'tracts all sorts of spiders, sidewilders, whores, saddlers, carpenters, doctors and preachers. "Oh, my Pa could go on so."

"Say, Luke, you ever heart of Black Bart?"

"No, was he a nigger?"

No, I dont think so, leastwise I never heard tell of it. Mebe that was his heart. Anyways, he held up the Stage line, Wells Fargo many a tlime and he always was very polite."

"Spoke kindly, sir, to the driver, I 'low."

"You are right, Luke. *Would you kindly throw down that strongbox, driver*-- those were his usual words. Then he would tell all the follks to step outside and he would discombobulate them of their rings and watches and any money they carried. He was so damned polite when women folks took off their rings, he partly turned his back and he said, *Sorry to inconvenience you, sir, but this here robbery has got to be a success. I should like toget on with it...*he told them gents--and some was dressed like miners--to empty their pockets."

"He must a been a greedy son of the devil...Black Bart." said Luke. "Black Bart-- he had *organization*."

"There you go again," Noah said.. "Please comply with my urgent requests, sir." Those might've een his exact words. He'd stack his loot atop the strong box and apologize to the driver for the delay, and the dude riding shotgun and all the riders for his,,,his causing them a consarned inconvenience. Then he'd slap the drag horse on the rump, the coach bucked and took off in a rumbliung, creaking and jingling cloud of dust down the road. He had a horse nearby...course he did... he'd loaded up the loot from the pasengers with what was lin the strong box. Then he'd write a little poem for the sherilff to read when he found out what had happened. He liked to pin the poem onter a tree twig or meybe onto tree bark with a brooch he had taken from one of the riding ladies, a wee pennance for his mideed."

"Thats a good story to tell, Noah. How come you know so much?"

I pointed to my noggin--"I can see it without its ever happenin. It's true, every word of it. You ask any...any sherilff or any person who knows anythin about stage coaching and he'll tell you the same thing."

"Well, if you say so, it must be true. Where'd you hear tell of those things?" Luke queried.

"Oh,I got m' confidential frien's. They know something about stage coaching."

I was flabbergasted by my pal's cool distance. I had up until now thought that everbody thought my words were writ in sacred pages of some holy book. That I was honest. *Its hard to get along midst dishonest folks,* I thought, and then pinched m'self for such a pieeyed thought. I said to Luke tha\t mebe we ought to stop at a wagonworks to have the smithy check the shoes s on our burro. Our sole transportation was beginnin to limp a tad. It warnt a good thing to travel about the country with a crippled burro. Just about then a wildun on a pinto come galloping pastus, stopped a short ways afar and stared at Luke like he was about to catch fire. That frightened me and put Luke into the shimmies of fright, for he was certain that he had been found by a deputy or a stranger from the town who had heard about the murder.   Course there were many murders in this country--usually over a woman or cheatig at cards, a times jealousy but not often a holdup twixt men...'s sfunny that way when ever'body has gold. But every man's murder belongsto him and he takes special care to hide his crime. like as if he wanted to presarve the memory. Luke turned like a frosted jar, all white and sweat breaking out and he turned to me as the man rode past, looking down from his saddle at Luke. I knew something was going on, but I could not figure it out...who was that feller and why did he size up my frien like his buying a new revolver or shot gun or new riding horse. Real kerful and steady with his stare, he was.

> "I think we beter hightail it out of this here town," I said to Luke.
> "That feller...."
> "You know him...?
> "Never seen him afore in my life," said Luke.

We kept these things in our mind when we stopped at the smithy's. A Mister Buckern came out at Smithy's--*All Iron Work & Wagon Care* on the off drag in *Sacra,emp*, 'longside the Sacramento River. He looked at our burro's shoes, one hoof at a time, while we watched him rap on each shoe with his hammer. Some of the nails must've worked loose. While this work was agoin on, me and Luke took us a walk into the town . We saw a crowd and come up close and there, *by snum,* as my Pa used to say, there was a man with this here huge black bear putting him through tricks like staniding on its hindles and lapping for the crowd...and and dancing with a monky in its pws. That was stonishing any way you look at it!. We watched through tlhe crowd as the man had the bear stand on his hind paws and balance a ball twixt his front paws and his nose. That crowd sure did like that one, for they all clapped with a gusto. Then he had the bear...he called him *Sparkey*, this here three-hundred pound bear..."*Sparky* do a couple a somersaults for the crowd...." *Sparky* took him a monkey and he let that monkey jump up on his back and the two of ;m walked about the edge of the crfowd while folks put money into tlhe monkeys cup, atop that there black bear. It was a cautious sight, let me tell you!
\

Well , me and Luke, we stopped for a flatcake at a seller from his wagon on the street corner. Ladies in some high gear and gentlemen who looked like they had never dirtied their hands was walking along the boardwalks and chumming along. That showed that *Sacramento* was pretty civilized. I saw things I never did see back in Springfield, or for that matter anywhere else in Sacramento.... the miners mixing with some high-toned folks.   The rains had muddied the road so 's you had to pick your place to cross. And the lanterns on the lamp posts had begun to smoke, they be lit too long. A sign stood on the boardwalk that said, *blankets a pair, two hundred and fifty dollars...shovels fifty dollars, pans twenty dollars*. Seemed to me the shopkeepers had raised prices because most everybody had gold in their pockets and were willing to pay them outragmg prices. Luke and me, we just looked at each other and neither of us said a word.

If when we get back the smithy dont charge us too much, we can give him a a mite of Luke's gold dust. And if he dont accept that I can give him my Pa's fob to the watch I give that sentry back at the Fort. My Pa was particular, so it is a good fob.

"I hope yer right," said Luke. He was mighty skeptical of my words, Luke was, and that was good in this part of the country. If you believed everthing you see ofr hear, you'd say that there bear talked English like his owner. That's what he tolt the crowd, that *Sparky* talked bear talk and he learned a new word every day, Today it was *play horse. Play horse*--that was the latest.

We passed by the performing bear on our way back to the smithy's shop. When we arrived, there was our burro all right with the tools still lashed to the gear on the his sides. Insead of charging us for hammering back on Cleo's shoes, he showed us a picture poster that had a drawing on it of Luke. It was a wanted poster. The sheriffs in ten counties were hunting for him. He held the poster up to Luke's face to compare the faces. The he went to a bench in his shop and came back with a shotgun that was hidden underneath some burlap sacks and he pointed it at us.

The man seemed skeptical and so I wrote him a IOU in my best handwriting and me and Luke both signed it and...surprise..! Dan pulled a quit of *Red Indian* from his pocket and tried give it to the smithy. The smithy took the tobacco and turned to Lulke and said, while he stuffed the IOU into his shirt pocket,
"I dont know who you are," he said to Luke, "but you look suspicioning like that wanted feller who shot a man anotherr county. I don't want yer business," he said. "Now you'lll be on yer way and y' can skip the charge. I'll have no truck with murderers."

He said these words like as if he knew the whole story and believed what he said. Me and Luke left that smithys shop as quick as we'd come in. Luke looked scared, and I was glad to get shut of the whole matter, and also not have to pay the bill for the repairs on *Cleo's* hoofs. It was a gracious bit of business there in Sacamento. We thought it best we be on our way. About the time we left the smithy's shop, a bunch of them cavalry soldiers from the war come riding hell bent through the town, kicking up dust and and mud and causing folks to scatter. But they were no possee, that's for cartain.

"That was a fine bargain, Luke," I said to him.
"Didnt you strike up a fine bargain yerself with that there IOU?"
"It's as good as we are. When we've got our gold dust, we can come back this way and pay him real honest like." Luke just nodded and grinned. We were learning fast how to *make out*, as they say, when we had almost nothing for grub or tent canvas.

We had our burro and that was about it...and our plan.

We headed for the river. I sure would 'ave liked to take in a show at the *Belladonna Theatre*. Luke, he was a shy feller, and so we skipped that part of our way north. Besides, if we stayed in one place for too long, somebody might see him and cry out *fugitive* and run for the sheriff of the town to take Luke into his custody...and me 'long with him. What would I do without my fugitive pal?-- is all I can ask. Inside a hour we smelled the river and saw th water rushing down from the mountains with flatboats loaded up wlith lumber and such stuff and some empty and figers with long guide poles and smoke from their cabins. It was a real busy rivers cene, I kin tell y' . Along the bank there was planted tents of the panners and a bunch of men here and there working at the water's edge with their shovels and pans and sluce boxes. It was a sight that did not shake me, for I knew about such things from talk of the Donners and Mister Reed back there at the Cannibal Camp. It was always a good idea when we rolled into a new sitiation to watch the cautious good things that was going on so as to know what we ought to do to make ourselves diggins along the river.

"Lets pick a spot and start panning," Luke said.
"Suits me real fine," I said. "We could use a little gold dust right now.".
"Me and Luke from Springfield pulled up to a flat spot along the river bank. We grabbed our tools from out of Cleo's dunnage. We found us a good place to pitch camp and started to panning. It was a caution--panning--it took neither brains or brawn but only patience. Like my Pa once said when it comes to removing tree stumps, 'After yer fuse ils lit,y gotta be patlient fer the ex-plosion.' Bent over as we were in panning, it would be mighty hard for anybody to recognize Luke, especially a bounty-hunter. And there was plenty of them around, just waiting to catch a thief or a killer and take him in for a bounty. Ten thousand dollars. I aint yet found what sort of a bounty is on Luke's head, but it must be a plenty. I remember that feller that looked at Luke like a rotten melon...up there along the road. Y' never can tell.

We watched a bunch of panners nearby, how they did it--a scoop into the pan with some watter, then swirl it round so 's the gold settled into the bottom of the pan. More water, less mud until all that was left was the gold. Sinks cause its heavy....
"Fetch me that oat bag,"
"Right away, Luke." It had a burlap bottom that kept back the gold, when there was any gold, and let the water through. Well, we caught us up a thumbnail bit of gold dust after working this way for amost two hours. It was mighty slow work, and we were gettng hungry again. We had us a fine tessible small amount of gold dust but it would buy us a meal. Up the river there smoked a campfire.
"Lets put up for the day, Luke, and see if we caint catch us a bite to eat."
"Suits me jes fine."
I pointed to the campfire a short ways off, up the river. "We got a hook...leastwise I got me a hook, and we can fish for supper tonight and camp right here on the river."

"Thats a sparkin good idea," said Luke.

"Lets us go get some mediate food," I urged to him. " Leave the burro here and go trade...what 've we got to trade? You got anything, Luke?"

"I got me a knife in m' pocket," he said.

"Well, we dont want to use yer knife for a barter. You got a brass button on yer shirt?"

"Naw, but I got a top with a brass point on it."

"Thats good. Lets have it an' we can smash the point and make it look like a 'normous nugget."

So we done jus that and the plan worked out real fine and the point on Luke's top looked almost like a nuggget. All the time, we were wondering if anybody would recognize him--we had not seen a poster of a wanted man nailed anywheres in town--only the smithy's drawing--and so we felt safe. We were taking our chances all l'ong. Them at the campfire payed us no mind when we walked up, except that they called us trespassin'. Shucks! We 's just walkin' by....I tole one of them that that we were hongry. That was why we came, and we got us a real gold nugget. lf they would take a look at it. Luke fished the smashed point of his spinnin top from his pocket and put it in his palm. That feller flrst, and then his two pals come over and took al look at it and their faces turned to sunrise.

"Help yerselves, boys," the first man they called *Gash* sald to us. He had a big scar on one cheek.   And so we took us a piece of bacon hanging on a wire over the fire. That strip of bacon tasted mighty good, let me tell you.   One of the panners offered us a pancake apiece and so we took us another slice of bacon whilest the first man howled.

"Hey, you blathering kids want to see us starve?"

"We be starving ourselves. And we be done, sir. And we thank you for all your common cursty."

He waved us away with his hand whilist the other two panners took a close look at the brass-gold and   mutters something that sounded like swearing and then they went back to their panning. I coud tell they were skeptical amighty. After this jawing with strangers, we went back to our campsite and staked us out a claim of ten yards eilther silde and begun to pan for gold whilest the sun begun to set. We would sleep cold and safe at our diggins this night. Seemed the days were gettlng a little longer but it was still cold as a rock in the snow.

"I got to hand lt to you, Noah . You sure got a way of getting round things like repairing Cleo's shoes and fetching up food for the both of us."

"Shucks, Luke...'twerent no trouble. My Pa was a go and fetch sort of man. If he hadn't died chewing on boiled harness leather, he'd be right here wlth us this minute. Meantime, m' frien', we just dont let nobody creep up on you from behind."

"You're right as rain, Noah. Soon 's my hair grows long and a little more beard...and what wlth mud on my face...there aint nobody going to find me and you."

"Still, we got to keep moving. Theys enough serious panners and others out here 'long the river so's nobody would care about your murderin that dude."

"I think yer right, Noah."

"But we gott a keep movin. Stay too long in one place, folks start suspicioning things. Word gets around."

"Let me throw out a hook with a stone sinker and let it just be...for the night. Catfish are bottom-grubbers. We just might catch us a fish for breakfast."

"Good ildea," Luke said. He was a real talker. So we bulit us a small fire there on the bank of the Sacramento River and all the time Luke was telling me about how his Pa was in prison and it might be catching for him as his son...to do some reckless thing and land up in jail. I put him off of that idea, I did, since a bad man can have a good son and a rotter of a kid can have a deacon for a father in the church." Luke laughed. I never heard him laugh afore.

So there the two of us was as we sat around our spindling campfire, kept going with dry brush and driftwood we they dragged to the flames from the dry bankment. We spent our second or third night like this, Luke a outlaw figutive from a murder ...that was Luke...and me ...a 'complice and a refugee from the Donner party long past. We made a constabulary pair, let me tell you.

RIVER TRAIL

So we come to all Auburn, and right away, I sensed this were our big 'venture. We ambled up to a stop front of the barbershop. Chckens and dogs was running in the road. Folks did not give is any mind. We began to walk. I thought it would be a good to get lus a few vittles. And so we turmed into a parlor where they was serving barbequed pork ribs and me and Luke had us a good filling of pork ribs at a board table set on saw horses, and we drank some sasparilla and we enjoyed the meal mighty fine. We hadn't eaten for almost two days. Luke's bag of gold dust paid for it all, and the man was glad to get the gold dust let me tell you, I figured hl charged too much for them chops but they sure was good! Well, we had us a good time at that restaurant, watching folks walk by, some with dirty panners clothes, crushed and muddy hats and, from time to tilme, a man witha shotgun for his company. There were no kids hereabouts, and some women but they was dressed for work, and this were a working town. Wagon or two rumbled along the street, they wasw life here in *Auburn.*

Lets go on a sparking good trip into town, I said to Luke. Mebe we can find us another burro. We walked along the plannk sidewalk a ways...it was a small town but it was set to boom when more mineers come into town. We saw no burros, but we did come to a seed and grain stall and we asked the man ilfn he knew where a body could buy a pack urro for a coupple of miners who wanted to pan for gold...meaning us, naturally. He said they was a proprietor who owned a *funnin'* place town the street might could telll us where we could buy a animal. What she meant was the *ITheDiggins Theatre*. Now a theatre is the last place I could 'spect to find a burro, for them actors what cavorts in grease paint like Indians travel by carriage or afoot and sometimes on horseback. l thought we oughter give it a try, the *The Diggins Theatre*. One small thing happened along the main street of Aubusn. We was warned back at the Fort about Aubusn. Sure nough, there rose a gunfight. We heard the shots but did not know the cause. We saw the body of a hurt or killed an on the street outide thetheatre, just as tthe mortition dressed all in black drove up in his cart.. We had other business. We were lin the market for a riding burro. I heard about the usher at the movie theatre.

We walked up to the man who looked like he was waiting for lcustomers like us and we put the question to him. He looked at us like we was out of our noggins. Why you boys want burros for? he asked.

"We be prospectors for gold," I told him. Luke show the man how much gold we found. He pulled out his lather spurse from a pocket and dangled lt afore the man's face. He looked mighty surprised, like we had robbed a panner for his gold.

"We re ready to give a mite of our gold ifn you can hustle us up a burro. He invited us intothe lobby. Luke put his gold bag back into his pocket. We went inside, expectling we were wastng our time. What we saw a couple of actors in tight pants with sword in their hands and they's flailing away and clashingheir swords something awful. "just practicing," ourguide told us, for Henry IV. I never found out who Henry was and why he should be fourth instead of third or first. All that was happening there inside that theatre. ilt was a ltheatre wlith a stage, and so we sat down to watch as the one of the sword- thrashers walked about the ring smelling the air as ifon a scent, and now and again looking around him like he was lost. Then suddenly the other sword player come charging from the side of the stage and they got into it again. One sword thrasher gainst another sword flasher! It was wild and bloody, let me tell you. The miners in that theatre growled and howled and tthe actors they struck out at each other, one of them raking his sword acrost thearm of the other actor. Blood flowed. They took pup their clshingagain. I ;as puzzled I did not know why they fought like death afoot. I should've stopped here ifn we hadnt need for a burro.

Then the most starking thing happened, a man come and tapped me on the shoulder and called us both away from the the blood and the fighting swordsmen. .
"How much you boys willing to pay for a burro?"
"The goin price," I tol the man
"What would that be?"
"Three pinches of gold dust for another burro," I said the the man.\
"Make it five and the animal is yours," he said. He motioned for a men to come to us. We was not outside *The Diggins Theatre*. The man come walking with reins iln his hands, leading out second burros. We thought we had made a good deal.
"I sell this burro to you fellers for a small handful of dust."
"The animal looked a little poor, but we had no choice."
"Luke turned to the man. "We got to make this final. Lulke give the man his five pinches of gold into a open bag the man pulled from one pants pocket. The man walked back ilnto *The Diggins Theatre*. He looked back like we had cheated him. We flipped a coin to see who would ride first, and who would walk. Cleo followed long behind us whilest I let Luke ride.
"Theys a creeks runs through the town. We seen panners along the creek, but first we had to find us a place to camp for the night. We walked through the hills of Auburn. We saw a poster that read, **HORNITOS--REWARD** *FOR HIS CAPTURE*. We thanks God it was not a poster to reward anybody who saw Luke. He was invisible right now, but still, you never could tell. Words gets aroud..
"Theres always bad folks running away from the law," I saidto Dan.
"Sure, like myself. Well, we got us a couple of burros, and we dont need to hang for past things either of us don wrong.
"You ever heard tell of Joaquin Murietta?" Luke asked me.

"Sure...he robbed banks, shot up the town, robbed folks and killed while he was holding up folks."

"This is his killin country," I said to Luke . "Theres plenty of gold around heres...and wouldja look at the prices of them tools, shovels-- fifty dollars... for a pick, thirty-five dollars..., tents three hundred, lanterns two hundred. Land a mighty! Youd think they was no end in sight to the costs of things here in town."

"Mighty greedy is all I can say," I said, to him.

"We got our tools. But at them prices, we could be robbed!".

?Not whilest I got my shotgun," I told Luke.

Right about then a stage coach come rumbling down the dirt street, headed for the stage office someweres 'round the corner. It looked practically full. Wells Fargo hit the jackpot, I said. on the silde. Thetop was loaded upwith grunks and such stuff and the driver cracked his whip smartls to show soff who he was whilst the man at the vack hung to the side rails in ihis seat, a shotgun at his feet. It were a p;aralous trip to ride by stage anywheres.   That night we found us a place beside the Chisholm Creek, it was called. We not had our burros to feed. I had the gumpshun to wanderdown along the creek to the next panning place and ask them man ln he had some animal food. For a litle of our gold dust, I bought a bag of wild apples from the man. I did not know if them burros would like wild apples, but they was mighty hungry and so they began to eat wild apples. Bless my creepin shadow, they was hungry. They didnt puff up with bloating gas. We had ought to in the morning , one of us, find a feed and grain shop and buy a couple a scacks of oats for the poor animals. We unloaded Cleo and prepared to stay for the night. I had Luke go search for some kindling--they wasnt much of that around what with so many panners along the creek, but he found a old fence and dragged it to our fire, and we had a small campflire.

We put up our tent and made do tied the animsls nearby to our fence stakes...so ifnt they was pulled away, we would know by the shaking of our tent. Luke was pretty smart that way. Luke was still in his fears. We fecided ho leave the town of Auburn....

We rattled and scuffed along the river's upper road, hardly a trail that followed the Feather River northwards. Luke, he was always looking behind him to see if there was a possee of some sort kicking up the dust on his tail. We werent alone on the trail. Now and then a ccovered wagon pulled by oxes would hail us from behind so we had to move over to the sie of the road. Spring was almost gone and the level of the river was lower and sometimes exposed flecks of gold in the sun. Every so often we stopped edon the upper road and walked down to the river's edge and give the river bed a close inspection. No sense in passing up a opportunity.   One flake meant there were others. Other panners, by twos and thees were working their shovels at their sluce boxes and ore cradles.   They did not mind us as we watched.

Along one stretch of the Feather there must have been a hundred or more sourdoughs panning for gold.   Ever since the strike at Columa and Dry Diggins, miners had come to the rivers and creeks by the cazilions , like cattle to a watering hole.   Their white and brown tents scattered over the landscape and up on the surrounding hills told me and Luke the hard-rock miners had found some rich veins of quartz--that was where the gold was in the hard rock. Camp fire smoke riz over the landscape as we started towards the Sacramento River. They would have to get the hard rock shovelings the stamping mill in Columa some way, packing it out in burro side bags or on wagons miners shared. Gold had that kind of drilve for them miners, I can tell you. Holes linthe hillsides showed just where they was digging outthe quartz.

One other thing caught our' tention--bootlegging. " 'S funny, but I figered bootlegging whiskey stills belonged down in Kentucky. Not atall...here along the Feather River, hid in the hillsides...and doing a right smart business, unless I miss my guess. Them bootleggers truck their fire-water to Red Bluff and mostly to Sacramento...whilest the governmint dont take no mind of the unlawful business, unless I miss my guess. Me and Luke, we don't drink, and thats a good thing, too, else we would not make it up to the border but would squander our time dreaming along the river and casting a shovelfull of mud into out sluce...we got one tied onto the burro. No, siree, we wanted to steer clear of that devil's contrapshun that robs miners of their gold, like faro or poker. No, we don't go looking for stills. Why should we? All thes ame, you see them sourdoughs tip up the bottle, you know what's going on, for cartain. Unless I miss my guess, them bootleggers and moonshiners are making a fortune from the panners and hard-rock miners. Its all a part of the ...*organization*, as Luke would say. We thought we saw one abandoned whiskey still pn a slide scursion, barrels, some copper pipes, firewoo and the like, but no owner.... moonshiner ...caught and heisted off to jail or quit plum out for lack of potatoes but not from lack of business, ulnless I miss my guess. Potato mash....

Luke liked these side trips. Whilest we were down there on the river bed, he could not be identified. Civil War rangers come into the area--we seen them lin blue scouting on horseack--butthey paid us no mind. In the Civil War battles and just iltching to use their army revolvers agai, perhaps gainst a innocent man like Luke. Oh, I did not put much faith in the Springfield incident; I just took Luke's word for it that he was a wanted man. Al;ong the way we come to a small lbunch of houses, five orsix and a church...a village such as grewup along the rivers iln California. Luke wanted to go in and have alook around, but I desised him. So we traveled on. We started west. The next town was to become Red Bluff.

Let me say a small speech or two about crossisng the Feather River. It was a low tide, so to speak--rivers dont have tides--and we saw some rtocks that jutted out into the current. Me and Luke, with the help of some panners nearby, we carried a couple of logs from the driftwood longside the river to the rocks and two of the panners, bigger than me or Luke, helped to lay them from one side to the other, with some rocks n the middle for a extra span, so that at a narrow point where the water was fast, it was slow enough for us to c-onstruct us a bridge. It was hard, but it was worth it. Me and Luke and the burros , we crossed on the upside of those logs so as not to be carried down river by the current. It was a terribly treachering situation, let me tell you. The miners expected us to give them gold for their work, but we decided that we would not give our gold dust to just anybody, even if they helped us to build that log bridsge. Luke was a better keeper of the gold dust than me, thats for cartain. Unless I miss my guess, them pannners were mighty glad we put up that bridge, since now they could cross to the other side of the river and set up camp there. Everbody gets a piece of the gold when we coooerate like we did.

The mud of spring rains had caked onl the road, so travel was fairly easly for us and *Cleo*. we hadno yet named the other burro, *Lasses*, maylbe. The peaks riz on both sides of us. jagged and white, like Ma's broken porcelain dishes. Cedars and pine trees riz from the slopes. We stopped along the way to chaw with some panners. Always, they were hopeful diggers, wanting to show us what they had panned from the river. Like I say, the Feather River was low in places but most generally it was fast and swift, with rapids where the river turned. At times a dory appeared around a curve and dashed into the rapids, loaded with sacks of stuff, grain, corn, south bound. It was too shallow for any sort of barge navigation. The trail was hardly a road. The stagecoach road left us after Marksville, going on up the Yuba into Oregon. The countryside round about was walled in by high forested mountains, like I say, no rocks such as we seen at Sutter Lake. Snow would fall in another six motnhs. When we stopped to camp and built us a fire to cook what we had bought, a times off a panner...some carried the country store in their tethered canvas wagon, why the air was puffed here and there with white camper smoke and our own campfire was shot up with mosquitors and bugs that was drawed to the fire.

Fallen stuff was floating downcurrent towards Sacramento. Small boats, like dories, usually the they were loaded up with goods like sacks of grain or potatoes...I reckoned... or mebe empty, just a man and a boy to guide the thing with oars down the river. There was more money to be made by traveling grog shops. They peddled bootleg whiskey...they satisfied the miner's thirst...that was where the panners often spent the gold at night theyd panned up that day. Me and Luke, we heard about New Helvitia, another of those quick-start towns...and Colma, first to settle on miners' gold. But for us, we had to keep to the trail northward. It would not be safe to stop and stay any time until we reached Oregon. I asked a miner at one camp, three men shoveling river mud into their sluce, a fourth come out of a tent on the 'bankment and commenced to pour water down the sluce from a bucket he dipped into the river, to separate the mud from the gold, if there was any. Two of the miners inspected the sluce baffles for the bright yellow sparkle.

"How far is the Sacramento from here?" I asked.

"Wal now, if your going to Sacramento your're headed the wrong way."

"The river, sir. The river called the Sacramento."

"Oh, why didnt you say so? Well, now you're practically standing on it. The rest of the river is up there...." The miner pointed toward the high border and what he called "the cascades range: in the distance. ...and to get to it you will have to travel through Indian country."

"Indians! Where'd they come from?"

"The Maidu tribe--they pitched their teepees nearby to Columa. But they're a ways off...and peace-biding. No need to fear them. Just Mexican outlaws like that Juaquin Murietta feller."

"We got ourt gold dust to offer them a peace offering if we have to."

"That wont be necessary. They dig out their own gold. You're safe. But they are mostly the non-shooting kind of Indians." The panner tried to reassure me and Luke, but I was not going to roll th dice on his words. We had to keep our tracking senses sharp and ready, let me tell you. This was dangerous country.

"The town of Red Bluff...if you havent heard? Well, if you will look west, you might not see the river but you can smell it."

"The river?"

"'S what I said. When the sun goes down it turns to gold. You caint miss it."

"West of here?"

"Thats what I said...'bout five hundred yards...." He spat tobacco juice, fixed his dirty hat on his head and called out, "Hey, Spade, hand me that crowbar will y'? A rock a' times has gold in it, under the muck. One discovery leads to 'nother." He dug up a rock and,s ure 'nough! there were specks of gold in its surface. He showed it around to his three friends and then layed it aside like a precious jewel. See, young feller, you never can tell, whats about to happen."

"I heart the Sacramento River has many creeks...."

"Oh, its the creeks yer agoing after. Well, sir, thats a smart move. We be going to find us a creek and stake out a new digging afore too long...what say, boys?"

There was agreement, as the three others stood watching the pro-cedings, leaning on their shovel handles and listening to our conversation. :Well I dont want tos interrupt your diggin," I said to the man. "Pleased to get the information."

"Thats all right, young feller. The ways a stranger gets about in these parts is to ask sensible questions. " He set to with his shovel again, mucking river mud into his sluce and watching carefully to inspect the results.

They's just beginners," I said to Luke. He simply grunted.
 One of the panners slung his shovel into the muck and pitched a gob of river sand into the sluce, followed by a sloshed bucket ofwater.

"You boys think we're smar starter, panners with a frying pan for a sluce, and you dont know a flake of gold from a gralin of iron pyrite."

"Ill just betcha we do," Luke barked in his loudest voice.

\   "Come over hyer then, young feller. See fer yrself...y' see any gold il that there sluce."

Luke and me, we both peered into the sluce past the panner... his friends called him *Sluce*...to see lif they could spot a flake.

"No, we dont see none, as yet. Luke said, "Jes g\live me that shovel and I'll show you how to dig up gold." He was a feisty one. The panner thrust the shovel almost into Luke's face and stood back with a wide smirk. Luke jabbed the point of that spade into the muck, came up with a hefty gob and pitched it into the sluce. The panner, *Sluce,* poured lin another bucket of river water.

"There!...y see!" Luke shouted with a laugh. The three miners and Luke came to catch sight of a peppering of gold dust that lay in the muck.

"Theys mine!" said Luke. "Jes as soon as I can separate them.: He sooped up the sluce mud, dipped in some river water and commenced to separate the gold from the black sand. That didnt take more'n a minute. The panners peered in at the revolving slush and leaned back. One of 'm folded his arms with satisfaction, the other clapped his sceptical friend on the shoulder.

"There, y' see, Sluce. I toldja this was the right place to dig."

Sluce growled and made as if to take the pan from Luke. "Let 'm have it...for showing us where to dig. We got to hand it to you boys. Beginners luck sometimes pays off, dont it fellers?"

\

The miner began to grumble among themselfs.. Noah pulled Luke aside. He poured the remainder of the slush into a small urlapag he pulled out of Cleo's sildepack. The two of them turned their backs on the panners and started back onto the trail, northward along the Feather River road. Their destilnation on the Sacramento River and a small ltown called Red Bluff. It took the lads another three days to wend through the low hills, eating wild apricots as they traveled. Noah caught a fish with a piece of hard tack bread and Luke set a snare for a rabbil or a squirrel. They were unlucky until the third daywhen Noah found a rabbitstruggling to free itself rom his wire snare, aited with a piece of root. . Luke brained the little animal, skinned it with some skill, and the two of them delayed their westward trek for another night as they feasted on roast rabbilt over their small campflire. It was a glriously clear night, the jillions of stars were out, They appeared to light up the dark, shadowy hills against the night sky. There was no moon, and the two boys slept like steamer deckhands.

We no sooner came into Red Bluff, after traveling short ways up the Sacramento than we saw this here poster **WANTED; JOAQUIN MURIETTA**. He had killed lots of miners, some Indians, some whites, as he roamed around the mining camps, shooting when he felt like it. He wanted Vengeance for the crimes against his brother and wife. It was that devil's anger that goaded him...and us...along, not just the gold. Come from Mexico, he was accused in a card game of cheating, tied to a tree and whipped, his wife raped, his brother murdered in the outstretch of the shooting. He became a wild one-- Murietta--as bloody story as ever I heard...unless itwas one about the two fandango dancers who fought each other in a knife fight in a mining camp street while the miners cheered them on from the side. Happenings like that made my friend Luke's shooting almost invisible. Of course, being who he was, he figured he was a mighty important killer to have a dozen posseemen giving up their shops and farms to come chasing after him. But that was Luke. He was sure news of his crime was handed along from one county to the next. There was always the bounty-hunter on the prowl for the criminal on the loose. They were good men, and efficient, too. However, by luck his face wasn't on no poster. He didnt go around killing innocent folks like that Murietta, whose chopped-off head was on a display in a jar of whiskey sent to Frisco. 'S funny how things work out sometimes. .

Their arrival in Red Bluff was marked by a unique scene, neither of them could have expectsed. About mid morning on Sidewinder Street, up throughj town, a gathering of some twenty or more citizens \were watching with laughter a fight between a bear and a bull. Some ofthe town's boys were sitting on the shop eves, others from a lamppost as the crowd roared at lintervals and applauded and hooted to fire up excitement.

Noah and Luke pu;shed into the crowd.
"You boys hain never seen a fight like this." a sourdough shouted through his dilrty beard.
Luke supposed they had not. H saild nothing. "Wal, le' me tell you, the bear ul win. I got to some gravy on thet bear. Thet bull caint use its horns like the bear can use its claws."

Miners in dirty vests, crushes hats, beared and splattered with dry river mud looked mighty happy to see that bear winning out over the bull. They watched and cheered with great gusto. Mexicans were the most enthussilastic--viva the bear-- es mucho dinero--the worth of that black bear to their pockets and their pride. The bull represented a fulll meal and then some. There was not much to say about the fracas except that, when the bulk at last did gored the bear, great moans came from the milling crowd of more than fifty towns folk. A woman had the nerve to throw a piece of bacon rind into the ring. The bear sniffed it, lapped it up with its black tongue and charged into th ebull . The owmer with a whip drove the bull back. The bull shook itshead to shake off the sting of the whip. The owner of the bear applied some cobwebs to the gore wound to stop the bleeding. He enticed the animal with a \dead fish and led lt awayl to its cage out of sight. Less than a week later, after Luke and NOah had canvassed the mliners along the river for clues as to gold in the area, the best place to dig, any recent finds theythought were spectacular, they would hunker down along the Sacramento foir a day ortwo until they had to go north again. Then, wouldntcha know sit, a circus came to town. Noah was determined to make the best of this.
He bragged to Luke that he could do a circus somersault like a trapeeze acrobat only on the ground, and that back in Illinois he performed for a small carnival show. He did a hand spring for his pal.
" 'Y see, Luke...aint nothing to it at all. Just a matter of...."
"Organization...."
"There y go again. No...balance, balance on yer hands, yer whole body. Watch." He did another handspring for his pal who grinned wildely. I say, lets go...even if we dont have the money."
"We dont ."
Good, said Noah, well enter y the sde door."
"Side door...." said Luke, surprised by his pal's solution to poverty.
"Under the tent flaps. I'll show you. On the following day, Noah performed his magic trick of sneaking into the tent under the flaps, the side entrance. Luke followed. When a cop came over to them, Luke blanched with a sudden fright, but

38.

Noah was as cool as a melon in the snow.

"You got good eyes, Mister Officer. I hope I got cher eyesight when I com yer age."

"Keeps it sharp in this job. Didnt I ;just see you two boys sneak under the tent yonder?".

"Oh, No, officer," said Noah. That was a magining thing. My friend here..." --he pounded Luke on the back and whispered, "Cough real big for the officer....go ahead...cough, get it out of yer system." So Luke coughed.

"Ye see there officer, my friend here is sensitive to drafts and we just...well, I just wanted to close down that there tent flap because the tthere cold draft would start my friend here to a spell a coughing. He whispered close ot Luke's ear. "Cough...fer gosh sakes. yer almost sick...for the cop. And so the pal Luke caughed for the officer. He smiled wlth doubt on his face. He turned and left the two of them to enjoy the acts of the circus come to town. They watched, the two of them, captured by the a balancing act of tive acrobats, the elepnant that rolled this huge ball around the ring, fhe trapeeze whiz what did a couple of flips and landed in a net as the crowd gasped and cheered. And, sure 'nough, there was the same act of a bear and a bull, but bear was different this time. It was a polar bear. The two friends enjoyed some taffy, purchsed by Luke for a pinch of gold dust. A blast of horns ended the show as a band entered and struck up a hefty march. More acts, another balancing of a man on a iron hoop...he rollled around the ring, two elephnants that tussled inl a tug of war with their trunks and finallly parted a heavy rope. A tralined tiger jumped through a half a dozen hoops, a clown fought a boxing ;atch with another clown, They wore immense boxing gloves and their antics awed the crowd with laughter. The last two was a man in an iron cage who wrestled with this immense bear. When the bear won and it was sitting on top a its opponent, bear keepers entered the ring and led the beast away. Meantime, rescuers with large red crosses on their backs administered first aid to the fighters.

What me and Luke found was the most thrilling for the crowd, and was a jaw-dropper was a man chased around the ring by a wild animal that looked like a wolf. The human excaped capture by the wolf. Personally the wolf looked like the family dog. Luke and me walked out of the tent with an expression of having been hypnotized by what we had watched. The band struck up another piece as the crowd poured out from under the big top. When we got to where we had tiedup Lasses, the burro was gone, stolen. We looked around in wonder..."I'll be goshdarned and go to hell!" I said. "Our only animal...only animal...except Cloe! That was a ratskillin stunt to pull, alright!" We returned to our campsite on the river and turned in hardly sayin a word. "Steal a body's burro--burro thieving, plain and simple." Luke muttered.

"Well look for the burro in the morning," I said.

We didnt find hide or hair of our burro, *Lasses*. We camped out for another two days at our diggins alongside the river. We worked hard to put gold dust back into our money bag again. I can tell you with our small sluce and bending the shovel handle and our backs under the scorchin August sun, lt was a monster of a job.

But we made some headway. We had to have gold to make out in town what with the costs of everthin gone up from vittles to some new tent canvas. The last tent got a big hole burned it it from a campfire...inside the tent sos Luke could keep warm. That was a fiddler's tune, let me tell llyou.   Luke, he carried his leather purse, and we put our dust into it. Along with river mud. Funny thing about that river. It was fast and deep for a trifle of river traffic, such as it was above Red Bluff, but the spring high-water runoff , believe it if y want to, had left swales of almost still water along its shores,   That was where we panned.

We tried to separate things from time to time by laying the gold dust out on our a tailrace turned bottomside up, blowing the river sand from it as best we could. Gold being heavy as it was, stayed, like lowing the chaff from wheat. Anyway, in about a week, we had us a good purse of gold dust and we was a couple of happy panners. Luke began to relax and to see that he werent no real prize even if he did kill some feller back there in Springfield. Running with a fugitive give me the willys, but what could I do? I was happy to get rid of Pa's eminies and his drunken doings while he was around. I liked my freedom, I can tell you that.

We decided we was so close tothe Oegon border we had no need for another burro, so we dropedthat idea..whichgiveus some spiring comfort. My shoes are eginnintowear out and I'm gettiln a blistering on my foot soles. That means a pair of new boots for me whilest Luke can ford them, here lin Red Bluff someres.

"We;ll keep our eyes open." Just about then we saw a hound dog and a pitt bull iln a real dogfi\lght. . A crowd of miners had collecgted near to one of these travelin grog shops--a tent wilth a swilgn on it that said: **WHISKEY, RUM, SASSAFRASS.** We stopped to watch. Gent panners, who was dressed like going to a party in top hats and starched vests had sat down n a log to watch. Seemed to me mighty strange that working miners wthout beards, wore coats and top hats...but then I guess they were spectators. Them who paid a hundred dollars to come round the Horn in a clipper ship. I 'spect they come , like many, for the show as much as for the gold. I saw one ad: *Children in Proportion.* Whatever the devil did that mean?. Nurses, bricklayers, shoemakers, schoolteachers, cooks and carpenters all were invited. It was a spendiferous time for bodies what wanted to worka and have adventure at the same time, like me and Luke. We get tos the next town, well see if we pickup somegrub and I se ilf we can flind me a pair a boot...trade off the part of Cleo's load for stuff we needed, now that the distance was coming close...save the gold dust for other things.

On a cool day a traypsilng along the rilver, il 'peared to me how Luke had been carrying on about how he once swam acrost a river in his home town in Feaux. And oso, I challenged him to swim acrost the river towhere the big pine tree dipped over the river. ILt was a swarmlin hot day. He could not take any chunk of wood to help him keep a float. But as the contest got going for the both of us, we would see who could swilm the fastist. When Luke suddenly went out ofsslight I called to some panners nearby for help. "Help!...Help! My frlien 's drownin...there iln the river!" One of them had a big old tick which catched thewilnd to inflate, like a baloon and he throwed itlintosthe river. aI grabbed me a piece of drilftwood and Ishouted to Luke to grab the flated mattress and IL throwed iln the drilftwood hard as I could and I shouted to Luk to hang on for there was helpacomin. The log floateddown to Luke and hegrabbed onto it; that mattress tick was a sorryl piece of raftiln. I dove in and began toswlim towards him just as a crowd began t collect towatchthe rescue of a drownsing miner. I grabbed Luke by the hair and pulled his head above the water. He put his hands on the log and we pushed towards the shsore. He thrashed 'round consierable, kicked up the river. But we made it back to shore whilest the crowd of miners clapped. Iwas plum tuckered out, let me tell you, but Luke was safe and I was glad about that. Thet crowd called me a ahero and one or two slapped Luke on the back and a pretty girl likely a miner's daughter who had been watching come up and kissed Luke on the cheek and made him feel like a swell forethat crowd.

The rescue could not have ended any more gloriously for the two of us. We took a invite to visit a nearby campfire . Other miners round that fire filled us with admiration for our mutual 'complishment. We was feasted on bear steaks and spuds. The campers--a family, mostly boys, the pretiest girl, invited us to stay in their camp for the night. Me and Luke took the invitation. That night we listened to tales of gold told around the campfire... a hunter who shot his stuck ramrod into the groundand discovered a fortune in gold. A story where a man , stumbled on finds gold iln a dropped Wells Fagro box and pays off his gambling debts,buys some land with the rest of the gold, 'counter a anmal called *Nugget* and finally runs off with yer gold at night. So y can never be too kerful here in the gold field. Next morning wetold the good folks we had to be on our way...early. Again them campers applauded our rescue story, said we was the bravest boys they had ever seen They clapped at our venturous spirit and they give me and Luke two bags full of vilttles--cooked potatoes, some barvbequed ribs, more bear steaks and thley saw us off soon after sunrise. We were mighty glad we stopped in to visit with these folks for the night. One of those miners had heard about a figutive murderer...abouf Luke's age. HLe hlad some mlighty furious stories totell, about filnding a seventy five pound nugget, in a creek and how the Mesxicans and grilngos filght over diggins...you ailnt Mexicaqns are y? he asked...IL'll swar, tht was a dumbox thing to ask me and Luke. He saild there was somethin called crylstaled gold. Next tlime we come to a saloon and seen all them faro tables, we was to look around for crystaled gold. That was all that miner said, but it was enough to alert Luke and warn me that we had oughter be on our way. Well, I told him we seen all the saloons we care to visit, and water flumes and trading posts and hear skins and such. We 'precilated folks good ways, there was so many robheries and killings. Luke looked over to me whilest I was carrying on.

We set off with flapjacks fer breakfast. They waved us goodbye and turned to their sluce boxes next minute. They two of us looked around and saw that the open countryside invited them to keep moving.
"When we get to the border we can sell off our gear, Luke. I can take

thegold fer the return to Fort Sutter. Cleo willl t᠎ yourn. I\'ll make out...."

"Thats a rippin plan!" he said. "O᠎ly I hate to leave you afoot...." I did not say another word. The plan was set.

"I heard tell burros sometlimes run wile in these parts," Luke said. "Mebe you can catch yerself a wild burro...."

"Well, I aint no cowboy so and I aint got me rope...so we an l just forget about that un...or negoshiate.?

"We got uls a little gold now and we might could make a good buy. Then youwon't have to walk back to the Fort."...

"We'll just have to take the rai n as it falls." I told him. "And the dust and IL can camp alonside the river or in the woods. I'll make out...."

"You keep sayin that." He was quiet for a long time. "Afrter all, we caint be choosey, can we?"

"No, speciailly you, Luke. You dont think any possee is gonna come all this way,chasisng after you."

No, but I heard tell theys a thing called a telegraph, and they could tell the sheriff in the net towns to be on the lookout for us."

"Right as rain, Noah. But how in blazes would he know you was you?"᠎

"Sounds right, but we caint be too kerful, Luke. After all, you killed a man. They kin describe you."

"Well thlen, the law can come after me, same as any other fugitive.".

"We'll make it together. LYou aint been caughsyet. Yer ree, Luke...and we got only afew miles to go, m' friend."

"We can do it. I always wondered what the north country looked like."

About then, the two of them saw what appe4arsed to be the tin roor6tops ashining in the sun a ways off, a village of some sorts.They clanged into the mailn street of a cluser of four or five houses. Luke shouted to a man working his hoe in a garden on the other silde of the road, "What;s thename of this here town, mister?"

"ILt alint got no name....!" That did ilt...a town, a village withsout a name.

"Lets name this place Shinnytown." He was full of wise things to say. So we named a village Shinnytown for its roofs that flashed lin the sun. At least we'd leave somethin behind. We cometo a placewe heardtell was called Mirage Valley. We werent there yet but Luke, I seen, had begun to lose all his fear of being followed and caught. After all, a man's conscience is a mighty powerful thing....

UNREWARDED DREAMS

It got so that my pal Luke could not sleep at night, so itchy and afeard was he about pursuers for his crime of murder. Being friends, I did not enqure about the circumstances until one night, encamped on Clearwater Creek that fed into the American River, isolated from any town except Auburn to the north, and from the diggins of miners who had cheated on their past lives, I saw him rob a panner's tent of cookery and foodstuffs. Luke, I mean. The panner was down at the creek iln the dusk light, tryng for a rew grains of gold before the light failed. When he came back his mouth was full of nasty and profane words/ The pot had a hole in it plugged with tree pitch. We had a skillet for panning. The tongs wuz tool short for a big fire. And the spoons were more like small saucers. I was almost glad Luke had robbed that feller. But it was a take for Luke, like scratching a little place to cure a big itch.   He was pretty slick about the taking of a pan, also some flour and bacon from that man's wilderness domicile. Luke said he was sure that most of the panners and their like had been killers at time or 'nother in their lives, while skaking their fist at religion. That way they could hide behind the sheriff whilest at the same time watching out for any posseemen who might catch up with them. Stealing and killin in the gold country was a parlous matter, I'll confess.

This unspoken camaderie was a thing uppermost in Luke's mind. He even that first night around our campfire, told how vigilantes hanged their victims, and if he ever was caught folks would he remember him with a tombstone. He hoped it would be a big one so that his eminies would notice. He was coneited like a girl that way.   He even said that all criminals he could think of had tombstones.   It was the thing to do, and that suspects had tombstones also, since they were dead and could not object to being dead, which is what a tombstone does--it kills off any objections about the man's past. I saw dying more as a trap to catch a smuggler of guns or something like it. You could die in a trap gasping for water or as a free man shouting for power. I was sick to think either one of us wanted more than to flee north, away from capture and lost in the gold country. My head sometimes hurt thinking about our perdicament.

Luke, whenever he waved a fire brand in the air, signaled to the spirits to come visit the miners, then lead us to their gold. That was a flapdoodle foolish notion, that a flaming stick like a torch had that tumaceous sort of power. We both feared that law and were certailn that other folks plundered and burned the towns where killers lived. San Francisco, he said, was one of those towns. Then he said, my friend Luke, that any ghost we might meet along the way would come from a ghost town where most ghosts lived--exceptilng those too onery even to live mongst other ghosts. We were out in solitary country, where there still roared a rough and reckless sort, violnent, gold-bitten with parades of all sorts. Parades. right down the middle of the street with bands and all, then shooting one tother after dark to spell off the friendly spirit. I could not explain it, no, siree. These mysteries burgled my head as we packed up and left the creek afer one night and headed to Auburn, the wildest knothole of a town, I heard tell at the Fort. Watch out for Auburn. If you don't lose yer socks in a poker game, yer sure to lose yer prayin soul in a slambang shootout. Then where'd yer gold seeking come to? Fact is, we were actually looking for such ghosts when we came to that little berg we heard tell of called Auburn. It was smalll but like a wildcat, clawling and scratchin wild. It had a goin dance hall, and since we were getting bolder and more careless, Luke said, "Lets us go in and see what jin of strangulation and traipsying they offer strangers like ourselfes. We hadnt no other way to spend a good country evening, so we went in. We were gettilng low on gold dust.

Such a shindig as ever you did want to see! The gents was hugging them ladies like sacks a oats, and they were sitting on the laps of the gents--at first I figured there was a shortage of chairs and would liked to call the management-- those cards and gold nuggets were spread out acrosst some of the tables, a banquet such as you could never guess. Well, the long bar was filled with horses drawed up to the condiments and two bartenders were kept busy asliding drinks down the countrer--saved them steps--and was skiddish fun for the drinkers to find a tonic of shiskey come sliding down that bar past their eyes. I seen a game of skitties once...when I was younger. The piano player, when he spotted us turned his piano to playing folks tunes with great shindinging fingers and dancing keys, so that all the miners in that saloon enjoyed the music as much as me and Lulke. Thet jumpin place was named aright--the **Shindig Saloon**.

This was one of them glorious watering holes for the pioneers in Auburn village, a virtual celebration of gold and what all it brought...which werent much here in this small village. Me and Luke, we could handle matters alright...we felt right at home here, at least he did, he confessed to me, his priest. My gawd! Well, he had to have some body to let out for his guilty feelings to.
"They caint find me here...nor you neither, Jonah. Yer Pa might have cursed you for surviving that mountain predicament while he died, or...jus maybe, thet sentry called out a searching party, out thieving at theFort, that no good watch you give the sentry, and the stuff we heisted from the pantry...them causes might have brought out a search party to hunt us both down."
"My Pa died bck there inthe mountains from the cold and hunger. You're the one who's running scared. I got to get you up into Oregon where the laws protect criminals like yourself/"
"I'm mighty thankful to you, Noah for the help."I think they're glad to get

shut of you at Sutters Fort. You could have joined the soldiers and escaped that way."

"No, because then I'd have to take orders. And I'm a free man, Luke...and I 'tend to keep it that way."

"Glad you tolt me the truth, Noah. Well, we might have us a good tlime, cepting for those ladies. You want to bet on the cards?"

"I aint much of a hand at poker playing," I said "But if you can loan me some of yer dust...I got here a fine nugget in my pocket, we can have us a small good time and perhaps make some money if luck comes our way."

"I thought you would 'preciate the chance to grow our pannings into a bag of gold that'd make folks back home zing with envy."

"I dont play for no envy Luke. Thats sporacious and never works, but if you'd play for a good nights rest in a upstairs room, I just might have a go at it."

Luke thought that was a trepsidical idea and he said so and so we commenced at a table where a couple of panners were playing poker and we butted in and said we'd like to get us up a game and would they oblige us. The miners wereheavy players just like they were heavy eaters. Me and Luke sat at a table in the Owl Hotel on the way back to our tent and we saw how the folks there loved their steaks, rare, and roasted chicken. They late high on the hog, I can tell you. And they paid in gold dust, which made the storekeepers and hotel men rich, if I dare say so. There was so many of them, at the bar, the poker table, seemed like miners fested the whole countryside. And now...at the hotel, room only for the crows to caw, it seemed like.

"We could use us a room for the night here at the Owl,: Noah said.

"Wal, yup," one of sthem said...sounded like a good idea.

Another of them asked, "Y better consult the barkeep see if there's a room left. This hyer is a busy season fer poker, what with warm weather and more panners than flies on a dead horse what comes into town everyday. Some of them whippersnappers wear boiled shirts."

"You got a bed for us weary travelers?" I asked a Grumpy fat man with wrestlers arms and a miner'potpie cap and a beard like a snatch of black hay. He stood behind the counter. His clock was wrong by about a hour, I figured by the sun. He looked at a board on the wall and said, yes he had one room but t wouldn't be cheap.

"How much is it?" Luke asked.

"Four-fifty dollars a night." I almost comploded with them words, but Luke, he hefted his bag of gold, which was goin empty awful fast , and said we would take it for four pinches of dust. Mister hotelkeeper, he said that was agreeable to him, but that four dollars was worth eight pinches...depended n how big a man's fingers were. So we give three pinches to the man and we went out to our mules and so 's we wouldnt be robbed, dragged most of our stuff upstairs whilest the drinkers watched us like we's two grave robbers astealin the treasures of death. We put the burro into the care of a shed-master, a black man whose job it was to care for the horses, burros and donkeys of the miners passing through...sort of like animal nannies. That cost us another pinch of gold dust. The sack was emptying fast by all those pinches. We discussed it that we woud have to put in at a creek somewheres and reconstitute our stock of gold dust...there wasnt no two ways about the matter. We riz up early , packed our stuff and lit out forthe gold country again. Cleo was fit, still munching on oats when he loaded her up.

I didnt takeus long before we found a fittin creek. That feller at the Fort who told us we could smedll good was right. We smelled gold here at this creek pronto. We found the Volcano creek on the map--it appeared to be up ahead--lets call it *Eruption Creek* to give it mystery. Anyway, we made ourselves at home in our *Bide A Wile* tent...I told Luke I was afeared of sleeping in a hotel that was more like a reconstituted bar. He said he understood...Luke was considering that way. If we were determined to to reach Oregon without any mishap, we hadnt ought to spend our dust so rapaciously. certainly not on draw poker. As for women--perish our notions--we noticed there was sentiment respect fer the women in that there dance hall, since even il the ladies sat on the laps of the men, the miners took off their hats to usher them to a table to drink with the miners. It was a rapacious scene, and bodacious, too.

We took us a good sleep and were on our way the next morning afore daylight. We never counted on being charged for a claim along the creek. A claim-master, who lived in a shanty close to the creek could watch the miners whilest they panned. His name was Thunder Thomilson. His scrawny wife called him such and so we did also. She thought he was the bestis of the best.
Tomilson approached us with his hand out and told us that if we wanted to stay along his creek...like he owned it instead of Gawd er the government...it would cost us a hundred dollars a day.
"A...hundred...! That's a mighty stiff price fer what's free for the takin," I told the man, whose name was Tomilson, as I said.
"Well, if hit was free, they wouldn't be no room fer real honest-to-goodness miners down there."
"No, I guess not, but couldnt you re-duce yer price just a little We're just a couple of vagrant farm boys trying to make a little to take home to our sufferin families."
"You're a smart one, boy," he said to me. "Whynt you stay home on the farm
'stead of coming way out here to pan fer gold?"
I tolt him we were hungry to get to Oregon to cut logs. My pa owned a saw mill down south and we were diirected to cut logs and raft them south to Moterey.
"Well, thats a likely story," he said to me. "Tell you what...you give me just a ponch of yer gold dusy ever day and wen you quit and I'll see to hit that you boys remain pertected the next day from them riflers."
"Riflers!" Luke asked.
"Cheaters. They muscle in on neighbors and claim their diggins."
"There haint no way to stop them?"Luke asked.
"Not unless you want to shoot them, and law takes unkindly to unnecessary shootings."
"As fer necesary shootings...?" Luke asked.
We saw a dozen or so miners all ganged up in one place." I pointed to

them.   "Oh, they're big showoffs." said Tomilson. "They like to bring in outsiders, so it's no problem to invite others to come to the party...to share their glory gold. Rlight this minute, they're teaching a greenhorn how to roll dice...to max out the pile.: "

"Well, ifn you stick to yer bargain," I said, " I guess me and my pal here can go fer your price...althougvh it's uncommonly high."

The high price is keep aristofats out of the competiion," said this here feller *keeper of the diggins*, I call him. 'They come out hyer from the city thinking gold is fer the picking up. But that haitn so. Soon as they get the smelll of success, they want to push the little diggers off the creek. It goes without argument, boy, that they would do the same to you. Thats why I'm asking fer a small piece of yer luck...to pertect you with uncommonly good advice."

Luke said pertection money was 'gainst the law, but if it worked, he saw nothing wrong about it. Me and him had begun to grow small beards so we dld not look like boys any longer. We saw, in the five days we payed pertecshiun money, nothing more than tents and a handful of panners along Volcano Creek. . I had heard that gamling was done on the levee at Sacramento, but they were no levees here at outside of Auburn. The wild music came to us throuh the fog and the dark from the *Shindig* music hall.

"You spect any Indians driven off by whites 'll come trying to mine along this hyer creek?" Luke asked.

"Not much, fer there wast no Indians we sawt ln the saloon. I don expect there's any Indian-white warfare hereabouts."

"Well, it wouldnt surprise me none," said Luke. We aitn going to stick round here long anyway." Cleo seemed to limp like she wanted a shoe.

"We got to find us a horseshooer pretty soon," I said. "We got to take care of our beast. After all, such consarns ae not just for Clo. We got to make it to the border North."

"We'd best keep our eyes peeled, " Luke said. "I don't 'spect this here community will be leveled with Indian White warfare,as I heartr tell had happened up in Oregon."

"Well, mebe so," said Noah. "But we got to keep on the watch against carnivores--they're wild critters what takes what they want for their food ."

"We'll watch with uncommon curtsey," Luke said. And he spat. He had purchased a couple of plugs of *Red Indian* and had taken to chewing and spitting like miners did. They were short on lumineres for their campfire, and so chewing was the best solution for a trade. Luke liked to chew, and pretty soon he got me started into chewing and spitting. We aimed at a target and got in a goodly practice with our spiitting. I could hit a toad a three paces, and Luke he could land tobacco juice into one of our mining pans at a yard. It was challenge, let me tell you.

Then we found us another spot away from that river boss shack, out of

sigh tof all but one tent of miners. This was on a different creek. We   heard it called
Uncut Creek, but the creek cut into the hillside deep. We shook out some gold by
panning a couple of hours. We found that the creeks were better than the river for finding
gold washed down by the rains and snow melt. We had moved up to the Yuba River,
outside a town called Marksville. We had lost our fear of pursusit--I had lost it but not
Luke--and not ourambition to put distancebetween the vigilantes who might come after us
and the sheriffs who had learnt from their telegraph who we was and what we had done,
or, that is, what Luke had done. My Pa was too drunk most of the time to care, I 'spect.
We was both ejoying the escape north.

When we had reached the Middle Fork of the Yuba River, we met up with a
band of soldiers from the San Francisco Presidio who said they were on the trail of horse
thieves. The captain hailed us to get out of his way, and I saluted...it was the most
gorgous thing to do under the circumstances. Naturally, we had only our poor burro to
account for animals, as if me and Luke looked like horse thieves.

Then this army horsemaqn skidded and wheeled in a cloud of dust. "You
boys haven't seen a couple of riders driving ...fifteen horses from the double-X ranch
south of here-- stolen?"
"We aint seen a horse since yesterday," Luke said to the Capt'n. "We'll
keep on the lookout. But how do we warn you?"
"*Marksburg* has a signal system, telegraph I think it is. There's a telegraph
in Ophia, just a leetle north. Send the message to the San Francisco presidio. There are
courriers there who know where we are headed. We can cut them a slice of pie if they
want trouble...as they already have commenced. Just you keep on the look out. Horse
thieves pertect their prize with guns, boys. You got any weapons on you?"
"Rifle there on the burro sidepack," I said. Luke whipped out his six-
shooter which he showed the Captain. I derned near went into a tuckerin fit o" faint when
I saw Luke's gun. He never told me.
"Well, count yerself deputies in sarch of a bunch of no-count horse
thieves."
"'Twould be our pleasure and high honor, sir. " I said, "to accept yer
deputizing. We aint got no badges though."
" Here,: he said, and tossed us a brand new brass po-lice whistle. "Pertect
yourselfs.   Blow that and they'll run. That'll alert folks and let them weasels know they're
bein followed....'
"Like a sniffin hound dog," Luke replied.
"They's cowards...most of 'm."
"Yess sr!" I said, swelling up as big as a river toad. "We gotcha right, and
we will keep on the lookout, you can be sure of that, Captn."
"Good boys. I can use all the help I can find."
"Were your men," said Luke
"Good, that's the old fighting spirit."
The Capt'n wheeled his big gray around--a fine horse it was--and took off

with of his three men. Me and Luke was powered, invoked and deputized like soldiers...
to find a couple a horse thieves. We were thankful the Capt'n didn't ask us abou the
Springfield murder and the fact that Luke was a fugitve and I was his getaway 'complice.
One lawbreaker at a time, I thought.

        As things went, we came to a little bunch of houses...*this must be Ophia*, I
thought...close to the Feather river and thought we'd settle down here. Luke said he
thlought we were sure to find wanted posters in town. We passed by the freight and stage
office of Wells Fargo. I did not see any **WANTED** posters. We stopped in.
        "You know where we can find us a burro?" I asked the man.
        "We ride only horses in this outfit," he said. He pushed his hat off his
forehead and combed his lon whiskers with a scrubby hand. He dildn nottake kindly to
my asking him about a burro. I could not figure that out. Suspicion, I guess. Got to
remember, folks come to this gold could to get lost from troubles, like Luke, andto run
away from crimes and other bad situations.   Folks learned to mind their own businss iln
this part of the country.
        "Our circumstances do not permit a horse, sir," I said.
        "Well, in that case, good-day to you. We need riders. Now if you're
willing to change jobs from panner to express rider, you got yerself a fine animal out
back."   "Sir, we're headed north into Oregon territory
...timebercutters, ax men, we are, sir."
        "In that case, goodday to y'. We aint got no need or timbercutters around
here."
        "I can see that," I said. I took a pinch of dust from Lukes bag. "Sir, its a
burro we be looking for," I insisted. I held up the pinch of gold 'twixt my fingers.
        "In that case, step right on in here. Inside was a counter with a assayer's a
scale on the counter. He had me place another pinch or two of gold dust on a scale, then
said. "Go to the smithy down the road a piece. See ifn hes got a burro he is willin to sell
you. This hyer gold is good 'nough."
        "We'll try our luck," I said and departed the Wells Fargo office. I said, to
Luke, "Some folks are so stiff with their help they got to drop into their pants from a
rafter come morning." I saw two blurros tied up to the side-rail at the office.
        "He had his reasons." said Luke.   The man told us they were looking for
express riders, but me and Luke were not ready to ride for *Pony Express* mail service,
although it would be a shivering experience, I know that--there was the sign above the
door--***Wanted, pony express riders, single, twenty-three, orphans, good riders and
ready for danger....*** Those qualifications fit us alright. O: wasmt a orphan and Luke was
a fugitive. but Luke was afraid of being caught and jailed and hung, in Texas. And I
would lose my promiset to get him to Oregon safely. We had made a pact , and that was
that. Ordinary citizens were used for such jobs if they could hit a wild boar at five
hundred yards.   Cattle folks had things sewed up when it came to managing herds and
earning money and such like. Along the *Old Government Road*...which Luke told me led
back to Kentucky...how he knew I had no idea. But it 'peared that for now we were on a
neutral property with no soldier, no bandits, no shooting-trouble, just a ordinary town,

Nevada City.

       We found ourselves on the main road through the town of *Ophia*, passed Sun Yee 's laundry, a feed and grain store, a wagon works and a smithy along the main road. I asked the man, who wore a shabby hat and smoked a long cigar outside his black beard and snapped his suspenders, as he put one muddy boot on the horse trough.
       "We be in need of another burro, sir. Would y take some gold dust for one of those animals?"
       "How mucha 're y offerin?"
       "Four pinches, about half a ounce..." gold dust being heavy stuff.
       "Taint nough. Double that and its yourn."
       "Eight pinches. Luke, give us the bag sos I can count out eight pinches of our hard-earned dust. IL'll have yl know, slir, this here dust it aint ordinary gold dust, its blessed by the devil," Noah said. "That gold dust is blessed by the devil," Noah said. The man looked at him like hed lost his tetherings. "It'll give you special powers to overocome bad luck, sir." The man chewed on his cigar, rolling it around in his mouth He looked at both of the boys with squinty eyes.

       We tied the bargain up with a handshake, and me and the man shook hands a second time to close the bargain. The shabby-hat man handed Luke the tether rope and, quick as a cat skinning up a tree, he flung hisself over that burro and we were on the way again. The hull matter was a spankin good bargain, let me tell you.... Then we saw the office of *The Observer* with the sign swinging over the door. That was the newspaper in town. Luke said that maybe we ought to stop by and talk to the editor. He maybe had some news. We decided to take the chance. His name was Pottsman.

       Mr. Pottsman rose up like a puddin pie in the sun from behind the desk when we dropped in. He looked at us with friendsome eyes, expecting us to tell him a piece of news. We shook our hands all round--this handshaking was a pertection thing...no gun, no stick of dyanamite, no knife in at least one hand....
       "You boys got any news to report...no gossip, y' hear. Just the news plain and simple and all's fit to print. Y've come a ways, by the looks of yer clothes."
       "That we have," said I. "And we got us a ways to go."
       "Headed someres?"
       "Timber country, sir," I said. "We're ax men."
       "Y' dont say," said the man, looking the boys up and down with an expression of wonder and skeptical chill on his face.
       "My frien' here..." I began, "...he is a double-bit axe man and I can use a whip-saw with the best of 'm."
       "Firewood cutting season is upon us. If you fellers want to stick around a month or t o, you can make herselves some smart money cutting firewood for folks here in Ophia."
       "We 'd sure like to," I said, but the constraining facts are that ifn we dont keep moving north, the best time for work in th woods will be here and gone."

"I understand.   Well, no news is good news," he laughed.

"We got one stick of news," I said . "We be on the lookout for some strays from my Pa's ranch...fine horses, three of 'm."

That was a mighty fine story to turn the man's attention away from ourselves to another matter.

"Well, we publish small items for the *Lost and Found* column here in the *Ophia Observer.*"

"Three...one sorrel, a paint and a big white," I said,

"They shouldn't be too hard to find. You got some money to pay for the ad?"

"We'll be waiting...meantime, we got to get on our way," said Noah.

I quite understand," said the newsman. The *Ophia Observer* is a worthy paper of record that will, hopefully, lead to th capture of your runaway strays."

"No," I said, "matter of fact, were also hunting fer a lost uncle." I was quick on my feet to find a answer to such ordinary questions.

"A lost uncle." said the editor.   "Ye dont say, and thoe stray horses--was he with them, or cany'   not tell me? The matter was becoming a mystery to the edior, and I felt like I was bei\ng backed into a corner. "And just where did y' see him last?" the editor asked. I looked at Luke.

"We seen him in Springfield, Illinoiis."

The man almost fell baclwards into his chair. "Sprngfield!" he said in shout.   "You're a long ways from Sprngfield. What makes you think he might be in this neck of the woods?"

"Were only guessing, Mister Pottsman."

"You sure he come out this way? This is mainly prospecting country."

"Oh, sure," I   replied. "He liked to travel round the country and he was alway talking about hunting for gold...my uncle. I told him you don't hunt for gold like a wild animal by sniffin the ground.   You pan or dig for it. Theres the only way."

"We could put a ad in your paper advertising he come here to the newspqper office and make his presence known . Then we pop out and I say, Uncle Forger...it's you That wouldlbe a splendiferous idea."

"What do you say his name was?"

Me and Luke looked at each other. I come up with a quick one--"Gregory Gadsen," I offered.

"*Gregoryl Gadsen.* **Wanted.** *Voyager named Gregory Gddsen. If you read this, report to the office of **The Observer**. Two relatives searching for you.*"

"I think that sounds real fine," Luke said.

"How much for the ad?" I asked.

"One dollar and fifty cents," the editor said, and took off his green eyeahade to wipe his brow. "You boys are temporary residents here in Ophia?. Where are you staying?"

I motioned for Luke to open his bag of gold dust again, and, reaching in, I took out two pinches of dust.

"Here." The editor pushed a piece of brown wrap in front of the boys and

Noah dropped the two pinches on the wrapping paper.

"Looks good enough for me," said the newsman. He folded the paper over neatly and stuffed it in his pocket. "The item will be in the next edition...first day of the new week."

Luke started to say the name of a Hotel, the *Owl Hotel,* we had passed, but I nudged him with my elbow. "Were not staying long around here...pannin is out hope...along the Feather. Were headed north."

"I see, and so...your camped somewheres?" the editor asked.

"About four miles from here, alongside the North Fork of the River."

"Good, good. Well, I'll run the ad for two days, and if nobody shows up, well, consider the gamble money well spent...you made yerselves a friend of the editor."

We started to go but the editor called. "You fergot the dollar fifty!" Luke pulled out his leather bag from one pocket and taking a pinch of his dust, he dropped it into the editors opened brown paper. He refolded it and againstuffed it into his shirt pocket. I saw there was more than one way to pan for gold. The Chinese had it right, what with their laundry, their meals for miners, pork fried rice, crawdad soup and the like. Mr. Pottsman looked at us like we were bewitched or out a our minds. Then smiled. "I see you boys have got onto the spirit of this countryside. Gold dust is everhere, not just on the ground. It's gotten to be popular stuff with the natives."

We just wanted to make sure the ad gets around."

"It will, it will. We got fifteen hundred circulation. Come back in two days see if anybody has answered the ad."

"We will....our uncle wants to join us..file a claim to some dilggins for himself."

"That's fine, boys. I never expect more than I get. Glad to be a reuniter of families," he said and went back to his desk where he was working over some news stories in hand-writing.

"Why'd we do that?" Luke asked. "I mean...your uncle and all that razmataz."

"Plain fact, Luke. You cant tell when a hound dog's hungry...same as a editor hongry for news. When theres not much happening around town, he will listen."

"We didn't come here to sell nothing in Ophia . We came to pan gold on the river."

"Listen, Luke, you are wanted...never forget that fack...we put up a face, two voyagers looking for a lost person...and some horses. You avoid suspicion by posting a front. That's called casting off."

"Casting off, my gawd. "

"Disguise...!"

"We sartainly hope so...and w'ere most obliged to that editor," I told Luke. The two sojourners decided not to hang around the town any longer than was necessary to prepare their campfire and consume their supper for the night for the weather had turned to rain and the road was muddy...the canvas tent in one of the burro's sidepacks was just the shelter for the night along the river bank. I identified it as the *Feather*. They would have to cross ln the morning. The boys first put up their brown canvas tent then bulld a roaring fire where they hunched over and rubbed their hands and got warm for the first time this day, it seemed to them.

"We cross the river in the morning, Luke. We spent enough time doing things. We got to get on the road. "

"How do you figure to cross the river, m' friend?" Luke asked.

"Easy. We cut us a couple of logs, tie the packs twixt them, fins a slow place in the current , let the burros swim and push across to the other side. Everthin's tied together sos nothing is lost. Even me and you, Luke...." The plan seemed useable. In the morning the two of them set to work and by noon they were ready to push off. A thousand yards up the river they had found a place to cross, waist high, so it appeared. They set out from the river bank and in less than an hour they had reached the opposite bank, which was mostly rocks and high brush. There they built a huge fire to dryoff themselve and their side packs. They led their animals to a spot where some lichens and ferns were growing and set the burros to grazing as best they could. A burro is not as picky as a horse. Whatever ils green and smells sweet is fodder for their pack animals. They decided to split the load between the two beasts and whenever the trail was straight, each would mount up and take a ride for a mile or two, then give their animals a rest. I was the planner in all of this.

For a pinch of gold dust we had crossed the Feather River on a big flat-boat raft that carried some cows long with us . We set out northward, came to a big open space oif land where we could see for miles. But lt was night and, by now, we didn't care much. We followed some rimtracks...venturers had used the road afore us. We crossed the Feather River without any happenings and re-moved ourselves northards. When theime was right, we stopped tolet oururro feed on fresh grass. Our poor burro found much grass for its hungry appetite, so we did not move fast, but we camped out around a small fire for the night to give the animal a chancet to rest. We always unloaded our stuff. The main Feathe rRiver was west of us. We crossed tributes without any stopping, fer the water was relatilve shallow and our burro enjoyed the spalsh of water around its hocks and legs. We took our time, even though we both knew he Luke was wanted for murder.

Luke turned away. He had lost some of his gold dust for nothing. All the same, we could not take any chances, and we had to appear ordinary citizens. I could never convincet Luke I was right on that score...throw the pursuers off the scent. We traveled on in the morning, settilng out before dawn. By nightfall we had reached Red Bluff on the Sacramento River. We saw under the signs of the cup and R with a cross a warning printed on yellow paper. It said, **WARNING, cholera and dystentery season. Boil your water ten minutes. One doctor on duty to help...hospital twenty miles away...this is the season.**

"Those're mighty fierce diseases," said Luke. "They kin kill you."

"Well, if they be lurking hereabouts, we better not stick around.. We better scratch gravel in the morning. We got to pick us up some biscuit powder, coffee, sugar and such like. We got to do some panning alongside the river whilest were about things."

"I agree," said Luke , who was the real observer. He could spot a gallyhorder of gold from a mile away... He was always watching his slurry for flakes he was quick to pick out. I put my pencil to some paper we'd brung along for a diary and made drawings of plants, and buildings first in Marksburg then in Ophia ...the landscape at the river where we pitched out tent, the snowy mountains around us. Luke knew nothing about the hard times I'd gone through, same as I was ignorant of his situation except that he was a fugitive from the law for murdering a bully in Springfield. We made a brace of rarin culprits, I can tell you that. \

Also, we knew for sure Luke was beilng hunted, by the law or by a bounty hunter...they fested the woods like spiders...**wanted** and me and him would be brought in together if ever they found him. It was a fearsome time for the both of us, here in the gold fields what with disease all 'round us. But we couldl not let our fears overtake us or we would be lost for sure. I had once thought about praying for us, like Pa might have done if had he not gone off the deep end and got drunk and robbed a store and gone to jail. Ma...I lost track of her right after we left...she was back at Fort Sutter, I reckon, which, I remind m'self , was where me and Luke met up and began this whole sploration. Folks at home had a rightteous cause to feel fear. Away out here, they were not much pertection except by the Lord and the horse Cavalry...soldiers. Folks here accepted fear like they accepted the weather. Gold weighed more 'n anything in their scales.

We noticed as we camped out along the river how some panners got themselves into gangs and dug and sluced together for, at times they'd crowd around to look at a nugget that camedown the sluce baffles. It was a mighty exciting and a cautious sitiation. Course they would have to split the dust five to ten ways. This did not seem to matter to them much. We watched them dig out the banks of the river and smash through rocks with dynamite. Like I say, ome of them were Mexlcans, some Chinese or Indians from California, like the Hopes and Piautes. We saw a daguerrotype shop when wegot into the town of Red Bluff. I thought it would be fine if I could send home a daguerrytype of myself and and Luke with shovels and picks in our hand, standing alongside the river, my foot on our slucebox. But neither of us had a home. But we had no home, neither of us did.

And we had no time for such falderal or, for that matter, gold dust to spare. Anyway who would 'preciate the pitchur. seeing as how there was nobody to look at it. I thought the photographer had a mighty fine thing of it, since all sorts of folks, Mexicans, Dutchmen, Frenhies, Indians and Chinese...look real busy in a pitchur with their shovels, standing around on the river bank. The Chinese keep to theyselfs. I heard tell they got into a war...called it a *tong war*...over diggin rights...and clans they were split up into. But then some things in life had to wait, my Pa always said. Well, he is waiting now, in the jailhouse in San Francisco.

We could not have done no better wthoujt trying, for in our circumstances, machinery would be useless. Just plain ol' muscle and grit did the job of finding gold. I heard tell it was mounting up to forty millions of dollars every year...enough to keep the crepacious politicians happy, I'll swear. That's a powerful lot of gold dust--forty million dollars worth. We be special folks to mine it...*get rich very quick* was our tune. Naturally, the man...Levi I think his name was...made a fortune selling denim canvas tents, and then it was pants for the miners. More's the twenty-mile wide gold belt or the Malakoff diggins, I heard tell of, or the wars over gold at Mokelumme Hill and the Frenchies and Chilleans fighting over diggins...those things rattle the bear's cage for cartailn.

"I don't known if we oughta stick round here long," Luke said, when he woke up and saw the frost on the insides of our tent.
"Oh, cold, y' got to expect that when you're a traveler into the north country."
"Not with all that pounding shooting we heard going on."
I listened and all I could hear was the far-off sound of pounding of the stamping mill.
"What's the matter with you, Luke?. That there noise is the stamping mill."
"Stamping mill! What in blazes are they stamping out?"
"They're crushing rock ore brougt in wagons from the mines in the mountains."
"Crushsing it...?"
"Why, sure, else how do you think they can get at the gold whats hidden in the rocks 'cepting they crush the rocks?"
"Makes sense...and then."
"Then they just flush away the rocks and that leaves the gold on the bottom of the sluce.
"Sounds mighty gumptuous to me." I didn't know but what Luke was just putting me on, but she was honest. Whenever we did see the stamping mill, we watched the mill for a day, and then we moved on north'rds. There was a bridge someheres but we did not know. We packed up. We would have to ask questions along the way."
"I sure hope to hell's high water they's a bridge acrosst the river."
"They may have a ferry instead, Luke...."
"That'd be good, too, Noah. Just so's we can cross without having to swim or find us a raft again."
"No, there're e-nough folks living in towns so that they can afford a ferry of some sort. Its only stage robbers who swim the river when they've done robbed a stage coach."
"And that bandido Joaquin Muieta...he was a fierce one."
"We won't meet up with his likes, count on it, Luke."
"I hope not, 'cause we haint got but that one pistol for our pertecshun."
"Well, lets pack up and get outa here," said Luke. I thought that was a altogether ripe idea, considering the skies were clear for travelin'. We had us a small campfire on the river's edge. We panned fer half a day and put a small pinch of golddust

back into Luke's leather purse.

"Telll you what, ol' Pal," Luke said to me, ifn we meet that feller named Black Bart, well tie him into our friendship."

"Black Bart!..are you out of your mind?"

Y know the feller who robs stagecoachea and is polite as a featherduster to folks...lets them keep their rings and watches...sometimes, when he feels moved by their tears."

"He writes a lttle poetry, I heard tell."

"Right as rain, my friend ," Luke replied   "He leaves a little poem after him to commenorate a successful robbery."

"Where you hear about him?" I asked.

"In the newspaper *The Observer*. While you were gollywocking in there, I read a poem that appeared on the front page about a stage coach robbery. This time it was the Butterfield Stage. *Where I lay ;me down to sleep....*" thats all I remmber only he didn't say nothing about his soul that I recall."

"His gold to keep perhaps," I added. .

"That'd be more like it," said Luke.

We both of us had decided to travel by night which was cooler and safer. We had to make Oregon to be sure for Luke's sake, since the sheriffs and governmint in Oregon did not low bad men--which Luke surely was-- to be caught up and shipped south to California to stand trial. Our way was the only safe-way passage to Orgeon. But going by night we were better able to avoid any cavalry from the Presidio or any bounty-hunters who we might come across. Bounty hunting had become a grand adventure and made much profit for its hunters. I know. My pa was brought in by a bounty-hunter, right smart.

We traveled alongthe north fork of the Sacramento River for a concusion mount of miles. The hills were frosted with early winter, and the ground soggy from recent heavy rain. From the trail the forest to th east reminded me of the Sierra ordeal. I saw saw a deer on the edge of the woods but it just watched us. And I had no gun to bring it down, although deer meat would be mighty succulent at this time. Luke tried some fishing and by gor he caught himself a small river trout with a piece of bread on his hook. We enjoyed a o]l-fashioned fish fry there on the banks of the Feather River before pushing on. Pushing is the right word, since there was nobody pulling us or leading us exceptisng maybe the good Lord. We skirted round a low ridge, then found a pass through thle Shasta foothills. It was a struggle, let me tell you! Up and down, up and down through the foothills as we made out way, stopping only to let the burros, our faithful burros, crop on the new grass. It must've been mighty luscious to its taste.

Shasta Clity was a forging stop for us. We didnt want to get 'volved with gambling again. Our gold supply was being reduced by our stravagance. In this town of about eight hundred, we seen posters that advertised Lola Montez,who danced for the miners...at the *Fandango Theatre*.   she did the Irish jig and highland fling...but I dont think she was Irish or Scottish. All the miners enjoyed her dancing in skinnyflints. I saw a spunkin crowd outside the *Fandango Theatre*. I cautioned Luke we ought to give that hole a wide birth or we could be robbed...our pockets picked whilest we just stood round, watching.   That was another way to pan for gold...Black Bart was smart enough to see that...and those cautious skinnyshin dancers. One thing we did counter as we moved through the town was a rip snorting fistfight of a couple of drunks outside the *Golden Belle Saloon*. A crowd was collected in a circle outside the saloon, and dogs were sniffiln round for their masters . We aint run into no gun fight...just yet...but we're neither of us real 'ticing to see one. I got to see Luke safe over the border and I got to return home...safe...to Fort Sutter, I reckon.   Where else?

We come at last to the Pitt River, veered off somewhat west.
We didn't know how close we were to the Oregon border. until a small cabin presented itself to our tired eyes.
"Let go see whats happening at that there cabin," I said to Luke as he pointed to the small square-shaped cabin of a hunter or settler . We knew we couldnt be far off from the Oregon-California border. From the county of El Dorado to the Oregon boarder was a cautious big piece of real estate, I reckoned. Luke's bag of gold dust had payed the way, almost as if by inheritance. We had both worked to keep it full , but our 'scursion had gregantuan costs neiher of us counted on. The Pitt River looked like a babbler. He set down, led our animals to the nearest green and made camp for the night...whichwas clear and sprinkled with stars. We still had us a ways to go. Believe it or not, when we woke up in the morning, we saw we was camped outside a old cemetery....

EL MIRAGE VALLEY

We sighted the valley from a ridge. More tin roofs shone like mirrors under the rising orange sun, cows drifting hither and yonder, a farmer out plowing his small acre, dogs not yet awake and barkingf at us as we come down the trail. It was a pretty settlement for sure, Luke knew it from pase experienc, when he and his two brothers peddled milk pails and farmers tethered their cows to front portches in similar villages. Naturally, this one was a long ways from where he started.

"We found a good place to put down...folks here would not know about Luke's murer of a bully in Springfield."

"Yer far from home here, Luke. Telegraph passes the word along."

" I wisht you would not keep bringing up that murder...like it was fresh news.
I got a right to be skeered."

We been on the move since Fort Sutter?" I said. "That ought to 'moun to something." He looked at me kinda glumb like and saild not a word.

We went down further iltos the town whose name they did not know right off. until they came to a signthat said: **Welcome toMcCloud...Pack train stopover of choice.** We found themselves a place along a creek that ran throughthe town. We had not settleddownfor long efore we heart the ilngle of ells andlooked uptothe road above us.There riding a mulea man led four burros loaded with goods. He waved and sopped andcame down to the creek to fill up his canteen.

We hit off in conversation. :You brilng a lot of stuff for panning gold,: Isalid to the man.

"Panning gold. Tarnation, I'm bringing supplies inter this hyer town. Its so far off the main road they got to have special delivery. I got stuffs, for their butcher, salted pork, barbequed rinds, salt, butter, flour, coffee...you name it".

"You're the supply train," I said.

"Tha's about the size of it." He commenced to fill up his canteeen.

"Them four burros are surely loaded," I said.

"One trlip a week I make the trip," he saild.

"No stagecoach runs through here...."

"Not a one...too far off the main road west of here. There's other pack trains. Folks tell the difference by the sound of our bells. My animals bring in clothes, shoes, hats, guns and the like."

"Its organized," said Luke.

"Very well organized the man sad. "My name's Gad." We shook hands round and said we were pleased to meet up with a man who had so much supplies, as we had next to nothing. He said he might cut loose a small pack for us if we had the gold. Course we did and he went up to one of his burros and brought back a bundle with a spyglass in it, and some pork rinds and a small case of apple cider. "This here glass is good for hunting turkeys...or deer. Spot 'm a mile off...Good for stories, too...like, how you was a cabiln boy and this is the capt'n spy glass.

"Pirates...!"

"I wouldn't go so far as that...but its purty. Don't cost much. It can make a swell out of you in no time," the man said. Luke looked at the spyglass and I saw he was eager to own it. Gad, the peddler, also is brought down some luminettes, which Luke called for...and another canteen, for Luke has been drinking out of mine all the time. "We're mighty 'bliged to you," I said to the peddler.

"I 'preciate the time to stop..gives m' animals a rest."

"You dont come here often," Isaid.

"Like I say--Oncet a week, I take orders and try to bring back what they ordered. Tin of pickles, knives...no guns...knives is the weapon ... the instrument for pertection," the man said.

"You got a right smart jingle with that bell," I said.

"Oh, they know whose coming by the sound of m' bell...who I am. Tell the dlifference in the trade by the sound of m' bell. *Bong, bong*...y' hear that and you gotta watch for hardware stuff...knives, new fangled can openers, candles and kerosene for lanterns, occasional horse collar, tools and some blasting powder...Keeps Lem's Hardware store supplied. if the bell is *Ting. ting*..y' hear that, thats Harv, brings in schoolhouse stuff, books for readlin, slates and chalk, paper and sometimes toys. Other packers comethrough here and theirbells have a differnet sound. Mine's *dang, dang*."

"That so? Well, were glad you stopped."

"You boys think you can use anything to...sorya help your gold prospecting?"

"We can use another canteen," Luke said. "We been drlinking out of the same one." The man went up to one of his burros--he knew just where to look and unknotting a rope and giving a mighty tug, he came back down tous with a shiny canteen.

"Jes in case you fellers get thirsty, I brought a bottle of wine...Care for a drink?" he asked us. We shook our heads and the man twisted the bottletop mightily and took a couple of swllows.

"Sun's sartling to come up," Luke said. "Pretty soon the dogs will commence to barking."

"Oh, that don't bother me none," said the peddler. "I go to places--cabins scattered round and not just to the hardware store--where folks look over my goods. I get used to their dogs. I bring along a bible ort wo, some ginghams, and a little whiskey...but not much of that."

"Trade is brisk, is it?" I asked. Gad smiled with the thought. "I never will

Vigilantsesarodn these parts halitn hd a good gun filght slince Moses was lintown. They go mostglyat ocrruptpoliticians.

How ilsthat done.

Wal, if a politiciansteals from the country treasure, letus say, or stuffas the ballot box swiths nqmews so 6tem whore up there on lboot hill,then thats thetargset for ourvivilaqnte committee. Retired General Gladstone has formed hisself a committee togo after those culpprits. HLe tends to drfaft a constitution for this here Nevada City.

That willbe mighty filne, saild Luke. A book of laws ils the best way to keepa handle on outlaws...

And only cusses called themslves politicians. ZHailt no worth to them whatsoever.

Folkslll have to vote on it.

Right as rain, ml frliend. And when hit passes, everybody intown will grease his gunl to see the law is up held.

LI; lsurely ;hope litis, said Luke and regarded danwlith a hiddle look of concern.

Them Meicans cn vote ilf he wants ftovecome a ciltizen first. Notl many of them arou;nd. They like to be free to come and go to JGuadalahara.

Laws for no ildlel miner. How a man works, when and how lhard are what count around here, strangerso.

Thats sonly fair, said Dan.
``
Wsork puts a brand on a man.
`
Hsilt sure does.. Say, you know a thing or two about work withsthat sack of gold.

Me and myh partner here worked fer almosta year to pan that sackfull.

Well, have a care fore lit can go in ;lno time arfound here. We got some sharep and pretty shady sons of bitches who rolllthe dice. Andcareful ofl them cards, strangers.. They trim theedges, mark them wlith clhalk, grease certali nones...hou nevercan tell yhohor they mark their plahying cards. Poker haitn not what it used to be, a game aof chance. Now silts a game of ...of gettling ready. Thats what they outer call this here town...Ready Town. Thjeyus one called Ropugh and Ready, buReady would suit us jes filne. We take a likilng to ready...and dustrrious miners.. Thge bartender wiped glasses as he looked down at the several drinkers, lminers at his longbar. We learned it had come round the horn, from New England someweres. We was watisng for a game to commence soswe could sep up anddo us a little glambling. Luke thought that would be the est wahy to hide rom the law, just incazs that ketch led to sspicioning.

We're glad you told us these things, Gad. He cocked his ears toward theroad where the four burrows stood patiently, waitingfor their peddlerf master to gove tje order t o move on. The tinkle of the packers bell on a rope aroundthe neck of the lead burro showed the temper and the impatlience of the animals to get moving again.

"I been up here when things are just as quiet. In 'nother hour or so, the tents along the river you see up there...they come to life. smoking fires already, filshing fergit that sixty-pound cast iron stove I brought all the way from Sacramento."

"A stove...."

"A wood stove...cast iron!" the peddler exclaimed. "But the man, the buyer...he died meantime...soI sold the stove to the hardware store.. Lem's place...."

"Y've got to make a living...I understand," I said.

"My burros, they got to be fed also. *Bagdad* has got a loose shoe right this minute. I got to find me a smithy to get him to nail the show back on.

"Thats surely practical," I said. I'm glad yer round when we break a shovel handle. I hope your prices aint too high."

"I asks only what the trade will stand," Gad said. "There's plenty of open country round here, down along the river. You fellas need any tent canvas, got yeself an axe, a good shovel or two, buckets.... I arry all tlhem items and more."

Right now we'e fixed. This has got toe our diggins. Noh Taunton'sdliggins, long the SaramentoRiver. We travel in style, Mister Peddler."

"Y' can be glad its also a peaceful place. Just last week they was one of them tong wars east of here...and folks stayed in their houses...and in their tents."

"Tong wars," I said. "What are they all about?"

"Chinamen...they have their families, their clans and theyre sensitive, yomightsay to who owns what land. They don't talk much, very polite, say little, work hard. But they fight like butchers 'gainst each othelr. They ont use guns... leastwise I don't think tlhey do. Aint seen none. But knifes...knifes are their weapons. They stab and slash each other and cut off their pigtails...dishonor, like scalping a men...like the Indians done afore you come up here. Well, they maybe will want to washs yer shirts. But theyre good folks and mostly honorable and I see they got a store for themselves. stick to the southside of town pretty much. The Chinese know how to handle gold...better than white men. Isell stuff to them on a reglar basis. They alus got the gold to pay for flat irons or stitching stuff. They be around a while, is my guess."

Well.that is good news.

But let me warn you of one thing--stuff costs aplenty here lin town, so ilf youbroughbt your pans and shovels and picks and other geat along, thats good cause the propriletgors,theys uusallyskinflints until this gold strike come alone, theyllcharge you aplenty. Ye can count on that.

Well talke our precaution, said Luke. Hiseye fell ona poster tacked ogto onewall:; ; WANTGED FOR MURDER, young man, age 19, for murder of hostler lin Sspringfield, Illinois. Thought to ve headed for gold flields. ARMED AND DANGEROUS. Dan shrugged when he saw the poster bug Luke looked around him under hidden glancesat the men iln the barrorom. None ofthem appeared to be a threat to thei pailr on their journey of escape. \

I see you strangers lookingatthat there poster. Hailt no picture excepta drawling. You see anybody like that feller, youcall the shrrilff rilght off or come in here. IL know who to call.

WQell do justthat, saild Luke

for bottom feeder...upstream, all them things to lIfe. Miners strt panning, sluce boxes go into action...lose no time...there's swarms along the river bank...You never seen so many excepting in fishing season. Case you boys figure yer alone...well, y' aint by a long shot."

I looked at Luke. "Mister Gad, me and my partner here, we maybe could use some of yer goods." The peddler's face brightened. I knew he was talking so's we could make up our minds. "We need somemore luminettes...and maybe some coffee and that canteen. Like I say, we been drinking from the same canteen. I knew me and Luke would be giving up partnering 'fore long and we need our own canteens of river water. So the peddler went up to his burros again and retrned with luminettes wrapped in butchers paper, and a canteen .

"I brought along a box a shotgun shells for a hunter or two hereabouts. You boys dont hunt do you?" We looked at each other and shook our heads. Chickens are my favorite plate...but theys turkeys...wild as a desert hare round abouts... make good soup, if yer a hunter."

"Not us. Fishs is the bestus....".

"There, ye've hit it. Fish! I haint got a rod or reel but I got some line and hooks lif yer willin to part with some of yer golddust. LYou can make poles out a tree branches...."

"Luke...," I said to Luke. He dug out his bag of gold dust. "How much?" he asked the man.

"Two pinches for the finest lines, lures and hooks y' could 'magine." Luke npdded, and the man again went up to his pack-burro and found the things. He returned shortly, and they purchase took place on a flat rock. Luke took his canteen down to the river and put it under a rock to fill, just as the man retrned.

"We dont know how to thank you, Gad, for yer help."

"That's my business--to help folks," he said. "Why just last week when I come through a couple of miners asked me to help them at their diggins. Ordinarily, I don't want to get 'volved, but they said a couple of Mexicans had somehow gotten a corner on gold in the diggins an they needed some help to drove them back to up-river...to where they come from." Luke and me, we shook our heads. But the man, the peddler, went on. "Seems like tlhey was tryin to reverse things.. gambling, shooting by Maxicans in the saloon in McCloud...and some other fracases. Gambling, it ailnt much around here, bult robberies!..it/s a dog filght...maybe a ikilling a week when times are normal."

"We dont want to cause no trouble, Mister Gad," said Luke with a meek voice I had never heard him use before.

"Oh, you wont have to walk far afore trouble come to you, yes like that." He snapped his fingers. The bell on the lead burro dankled. They alint but one or two women here in this whole town. They take in some of the miners' washing, but other than them, there hailnt yet been yet no fights over women, lole as at Brodie and Hartman and Red Bluff a nd other such pleaces where they's dance halls and night doves."

"We been throughs those towns," I said.

Course with hardly a boat and never a raft or a barge on the river, y dont have drifters coming down the river and stoppping for a drink and a fight in the tavern jes to getrid of the panning cramps.".

"No, thats certailnly true," I said not knowing much about what he was saying. "Listen...the dogs'll come abarking pretty soon. I suppose you got yer business to take care of."

"Rightly so," said the peddler. "And I got to find a smithy for Sarah."
"Sarah?"
"She's my lead burro."
"Oh," I said. Well I wisht we could help you, Gad, but were strangers here in town."

"I unerstand that rightly 'nough, boys. I know my way around. I'm cartain there's a smithy someweres up round the hardware store I seem to recollect." Wilth those words, Gad, the Peddler, climed upthe embankment. His lead burro jangled its bell and he waved himself off headed into the town.

Panners here and there come out oftheir tents. Me and Llulke we went about staking down our canvas domicile. This was to be our diggins...at least for a day, maybe two. Luke was not too ready to stay long anyweres. Luke reached down and took up a handful of rivervank mud.

He puzzled me a times. " Then advertisements are always braggling about how you can reach down and scoop up gold off the ground."

"You didnt find any, Luke. Its all in that there river...washes down with the thaw. Likely buried by now...."

The two of them spent the rest of the day twilxt panning and sleeping until they heard noisecoming from the mainstreet of town, which was nearby.

I think we are in luck,: Luke said. "Just sos we dont get recognized."

Oh, man you're always thinking about being captured and hlauled away to prison. Dontcha ever think....what if they are the bad ones?"

We cant call ourselfs safe ...no tillwe hit that border."

"I wisht IL was as confident as you, my frien."

"We'll stick around here...put some more dust into that bag of yourn...we be going to need it fore this journeys done, Luke. Now, le's hustle up some grub. The fugituves cooked some fish that had started to turn and they slied and peeled potatoes from their gear. They collectsed river grass from nearby into their buckets and fed their animals They panned with rdor, neither of us finding a nugget...but the flakes sof gold shimmered inthe light and so we was able to add to our bank account of gold dust. The evening come on like a juniper shade in the sun. Luke read his almanac...he was always readiang that danged almanac. I Dan whittled for m'self a smart walking stick from a nearbvy willer brake. Campfies sent up smoke all day long and that river was a busy place, y can count on that. My guessils that lots a those men had found the first home in their whole life. I heard tell I-talians come to pan forgold...gutterals...Germans, and Frenchies...and the Dutch come to the gold filelds like coming to a pork rib barbeque. They was all sorts, sfar as ILcould tell. Quartz gold was a mighy 'ticing thing, I can say that much 'bout our circumstantiation.

"These here homesteaders are sure a gambling lot," Luke spoke out.

"You said that right, my friend. I reckon we can do us a little gambling ourselfs. We dont own no rundown shack, but the gold we got is as good as theirs, no nuggets, flakes and dust is all."

"Ifn worse comes to worse, we dont need to pan. We can mebe tunnel into the mountain if we got our druthers.

'You got yer blatherings." I said to Luke. He made me mad.. "Tuneling's derned hardwork...hard-rock mining, pick and shovel and blasting. We haint got us a site and, 'sides, we need blastilng powder. Also, Luke, you know yerself we aint got the time...."

"Tents and and stakes've gotta be our comfert in this sitiation. We can sleep in our ewn cave...made a canvas...."

"You got a wild 'magination, old frien'."

"We can always liven things up.. like then cowboys. After all, we dont have to stay here long."

"I wonder what they call this settlement." Noah pondered.

"*Juniper* mebe. I seen a lot of Juniper trees round abouts."

But you havent seen no rains yet. When the rains come, we cartailnly got to make it further onards. We still got some miles to go...." Noah knew the 'portance oftlime...like gold in the scales.

"Get out of town afore flashfloods."

"Shucks they always come in the spring...lesson theres a heavy rain."

"Well, lets look to our druthers." said Luke. "For my part, no hotel has got the finest commodations in a hundret miles."

Likely not. Theys also a gambling den, theyre called in that hotel, I betcha. And if theys gambling, I think mebe we ought to gamble a little of our gold. What sdo yousay to that, Luke?"

"Ifn there's gamblers in that hotel you speak of, Id give it a second thought. We cailnt be too far from the border. We come this far."

"We come this far, Luke... nobody's going to recognize you."

"How would they anyway, three hundred miles away from Fort Sutter and a good sight ;more from Springfield."

"Well, I just think you got no reason to be afeared...less you got a premonition.

"What the devill is a premonition?"

"It's thinking something is going to happen afore it happens."

"I gota premonition I kin be chased by vigilantes."

"Vigilantes!" Luke dropped his shoel and sat down on the embankment. "I wish to heaven youd fergit yer belng chased. Ue yer gumpshun, Luke. Use yer gumpshun!"

Ifn I had stolen into a mans house, I could. But when I shot that feller what linsulted my Ma, I killed that varmint. I meant it and I knew I had to make m'self scarce."

"Well, you and me, we're scarce alright. We be gamblers right off sos nobody will care if you murdered a man. Say you shot him fer cheating at poker. It would e the same. A dead man is a dead man no matter how he come to be dead...."

"I hope your right, Noah. I jes hope you're right."

"Course I'm right. We can always pertend were cowboys lookin fer work."

"Thee alint no cowes round here," saild Luke. And we caint possibly be cowboys...not leading a packloaded burro and panning along this hyer rilver. No, cowboys are out, Noah...Cleo is a a dead glveaway as to what were up to. ...especially with them picks and shovels stuck in the burro pack."

"Well, who cares what were up to anyways? We can go into a taverm and get us a drink of sasparilla."

"Now I take kindly to that suggestion, Luke. I sure do. This here traveling by burro around the countryside sets up a powerful thirst in a man."

"You're right, Luke."

The two of them spoke but little, cooked a meal of fish and potatoes over their evening campfire. They slept soundly to the rushing near-roar of the river in the night. The next day, so accustosmed were they to their shared thoughts, they packed up and, after feeding Cleo more fresh grass, they prepared to go into town. They still had not yet learned its name, regarding it as a mere settlement. Jawing with the peddler had not changed their perceptions.

"Lets give gambling one last shot, Noah. We come this far without 'gaging any sheriff, and, 'sides, they's so many murders in this neck of the woods, yours wouldnt 'mount to a hill a beans. They got too many things to tend to--like stealing horses and the like."

"Its your money, your good dust, Luke. But I dont play poker real good, so lets jes make it draw-poker this one last time." Another pack train was passing, and a wagon loaded with hay and a cart, more wagons, folks dressed up on the seats, going to church, a clutered street, like streets in Sacramento...folks in town on a brigh Sunday morning.... traipsing about their small-town business, looking, waving to friends, and the like. It was busy on the street, like in all small towns.

"Suits me jes fine, Noah." The two of them entered the *Hightail Saloon* on Arcacia street. They heard wild laughter and the clinking of tumbler glasses and a caution strange sounds. In the dimness of the lantern light, the bartender--he was a tall, fence-post lookin feller, who could reach over the bar and pick yer pock jes like that...he was servin drinks...this time a the mornin. Luke and me walked up up to the long,shiny bar...like walkin into a cave of glass and lights... and I put in a order for drinks. The man, the bartender, who looked bony, a black beard gracin his face, a gent with a pivot scales moustache...he served us two 'mense sasparilllas with straws. Luke paid the man for the drinks. We saw down the bar where some panners and other miners folk had come in for a early snort. It was far from meal-time. The smell of frying pork drifted to my nose. We looked all about but could see no stove or cook who brought up the smellt of frying pork.

"You boys care rto gamble...if you aint too poor." He laughed like he thought we was beggars or somethin. Well, right away,this struck Luke in his pride sack and so he pulled out the bag of gold dust and scattered a little in one palm. "I see y' come prepared," he said. "If y' care to stick around, I might accommmodate you with a job. We got to mop the floor every night...reglar mopper died last night from gunshot wound ...we take care to be clean afore company sets in."

"Mop floors...!"

"They's some pretty women folk comes here Sunday mornin after their church..., and they is mighty perticular."

"What do we get out of it?" Luke asked.

"I'll give you each a dollar and free jigger of bourbon...you drink or you wouldnt be here. when ye have finished the job."

"We'd prefer, sir, if you don mind, that you tell us where we can get us a pork sandwich."

"Oh, tjat's easy 'nough. *Parky* is my chef,,,he cooks behind the bar for me and hisself and sometilmes cooks for a customer. "

"We're powerful hungry Mister."

"Parky...Mister Jonas Parky...cjef gramdee at the *Hightail* saloon...".

"Were glad to know where we are," said Luke. "We sure aint no lost hound dogs....!

This was the Prettiest place you ever did see...gold! Great Scott! ye never seen all thlat gold makes what comes out from the mines and off thet there river! The most gorgeous hotel lobby I ever did see, marble tables, stuffed chairs in the lobby, and thet saloon looked like a kings gambling room, it surely did, what with polished dark wood and glass mirror and the noise and tinkle and racket from gambling tables. Me and Luke, we dont drilk, so we found us a table with two players a slippin their liquor and we settled down. We passed up the mopppin offer but bought us...Luke did...two sasparillas instead. We was set to gamble. It didnt take us long, Luke rented the cards from the bartender, who asked his age...he did not want to become volved with the law. IL dild the talkin. I said we was young cavalry sojers just out of the army and was itching to gamble our army pay away. The bartender saw the wink from the customer and he shoved the cards acrost to me, and... back at the table agin. So we begun. Draw poker is so simple you could play it with no hands...blindfolded, movin cards with yer big toes..

We played a game, we lost three pinches of gold dust. Noah was displussed and we played on, made up fer the loss...only the other two players, strangers, one of 'm had sticky fingers and pulled two cards off the top of the deck and we called him on it, one in particular. He was mad as a cow on jimson weed, and he drawed his gun and was going to shoot me when I said, "I got a knife here that can cut a card edgewise...and ifn I throw it at the ten of spades,I can hit the middle spade with this hyer knife. " He laughed. "Ifn I can do that, you put yer gun away." He said, " Go ahead, kinddo!" I think that loudmouth dude would've shot me on the spot and walked out of thet *Hightail Saloon* without nobody puttin a hand on him or shouting bloody murder. Thet was the long and short a things. Yes,siree. I spsit on the card and stuck it to a wall and, when folks there at the bar and tables were watching with sour and puckerng looks on thei faces, why I threw my knife and I did what I promised. I had done this back home, 'fore that hell trip into the snowrocky mountalis. The man was mighty 'pressed, and one or two clapped for my pe-rformance. And so when I also cut a card like a sandwich. that dude growled. It was a powerful sign of my powers and that feller, he put his gun back in his holster and walked away from the table, probablyly thinking we was just a couple of kids playing hookey from school. IL was a hero lin that saloon...and Luke, he wanted to brag on me and shook me by one arm punched me iln the chest, real frilendly like, and pointed to me and grinned from ear to ear. "Caint beat that!" he tolt the Sunday crowd.

Luke was flabbergasted at my skill and the whole scene. He said, "Lets catch us a ride up to the border...sell Cleo and our stuff here in town. We got no choice, Noah. It's all open country up there. Turn Cleo loose, then."

"That sounds like a fisslible plan a action." So we went to the hardware store, on Thorn street and practiclly give the stuff away...since we was done with gold panning until Luke reached the border. We left the saloon...I seen why they called it the *Hightail Saloon*. Jes about then a hearse passed, with a parade following, folks all gussiedup and going to the cemetery. . We watched like they was prepared to meet their maker in their Sunday best. .

"I sure would like to ride that black hearse up to the border. What a way to go out of the whole picture!"

What in thuneration put that idee into yer head, Luke? Caint do that. They operate twixt the church, the balming place and the graveyard. Y' aint ready yet for balming...."

"Jes one little ride is all. I would pay my gold dust...fer a ride.."

"You aitn yet a dead body, Luke. 'Sides, you got to follow the hearse to the graveyard. Then you got to pay the driver to drive you the next eighty miles."

"I got the gold dust."

"Some things yer dust caint buy, Luke...a ride in a dead mans hearse and a trip to the great beyond."

"Well, then, we give Cleo a break. Shes free now. What ought we to do with her?"

"I'm 'gainst sellin our burro fer its like sellin yer soul to the devil to get rid of our burrp. Cleos got no voice in the matter but a honky tone."

"We might could give her to charity... find us the nearest church and give her to the preacher."

"Geat scott..whatd a preacher do with a used burro? I got a better ildea. Lets give her to the sherilff."

Luke said, "You got to be out of yer everloving mind, Noah Stanton. He sees me... the sheriff...and I'm a gonner!"

"He wont recognize you. We can say we're big hearted fellows who give up prospectin and we see you're in need of a good ambulance."

"A 'mbulance. What ever the devil is that?"

Takes hurt and sick folks to the doctor" said Noah. " They got no way in this here small town t' get to the docgor...lifn they beshot or run down on the street or et inter a knife fight at the diggilns. Its a parlous situation, Luke..."

"Sounds sort of stupid to me, my friend...a mbulance for the sheriff. What if he cuts Cleo up forl steaks?"

"Oh, come on now, Luke. Yer talking nonsense."

"We got to...dispose of her in a...kindly way."

"We mebe can give her t the local missionry so-ciety. Ever small town has got a missisonry society."

"What do they do?" Luke asked, his face as glum as a persimon eater in summer.

"They feed the needful folks and sometimes preach to local sinners. Cleo would be a messanger for them, or whatever. They go out to places and spread their preachin and this hyer burro would come in mighty handy, I ' llow."

"Lets stick round for one more show," Luke said. I could tell he was sorry we had to split up at the border, but I wasnt goin inta Oregon with no murderer, whether he done it or not. Besides, I had my friens back at the Fort. We had come through that hell of a winter and I could noit jes leave m like that. I conidered m'self a fugitive from that winter...jes as Luke was a fugitive from his murder in Springfield. We were escapin....

It was Sunday. I did not want to see another bearr and bull fight .' Stead, we would hunt up the preacher. We done that all right when we heard th church bell ringing. We had packed up our tent and geat from our diggins down 'long the Sacrameto River and in town fer good. We followed the sound of the bell. We found the place, all right,and folks gussied up for church. Me and Luke was short in that way...no fine clothes. But we found a feller who looked like he knew what we wanted. We did not want to be saved. We wanted to be shut of our burro. So I come up to him , Cleo was now freed from her sidepacks.

"Sir," Luke said. "We got us a fine burro here. We give up panning, but we dontg know what to do with our beast.:

"Ah, yes...the illusion of wealth. It is a temptation and a a millstosne...."

"Yes,sir...we done finished the tempttson part and know nothing 'bout a millstone. Only, we got a problem on our hands."

"There aint nothing the Lord caint solve...or one of his wrkers...which is me. I'm deacon Almonds."

"Yes, sir...deacon almonds," I said. "We cane to offer help to you, sir."

"Ah, yes, and perhaps the Lord has bought you to us today. What is your request of me, boys?"

That there's the animal ...the finest,the mostest loyal of burros."

"Loyal, you say...?"

"Will bide with you wherever you go, Deacon Almonds."

Ihear you...I hear you. Praise the Lord. This is ye ranimal?"

"It is," I said.

JJe looked Cleo over, rolled back her gums to look at her teeth, felt her knees and hocks and lifted one hoof to in-spect the shoe. He was a mighty particular feller.

"How much?"

"She's yours." I said, if y want to take ker of her." He looked like he did not believe me..or Luke, who was standing off a ways..

"You sure...you aint trying to sell me stelad of makin a donation?"

"Sir, we both of us re going out of the gold prospectin business. We cant r-main ound long here ln town. Mebe another pannner...."

As if the thought had just hit him on the haid like a rock, "This here burro is yourn...not some other panners?"

"Banker's honor. Sir, do we look like thieves?..she ils ourn for cartain. Cleo," I Lcalled. The animal perked up its ears. "Y see there, Mister deacon. You jes try callin Cleo. The deacon called to the burro but the animal did not show a sign....".

Now ifn seein is believin, y gotta admit she belongs to us. We give her kindly treatmnt. . But...you know the way...."

"The Lord giveth and the Lord taketh away. I got a better use...we go out missionarin round bout the coutryside,and sometimes we walk, sometimes borry a wagon. But if we had our own...transportshun....'

'Perfect...I knew it....shes yourn," I said. "She likes rabbit-ear cactus if you pull the needles...and she's partlicular about her oats, they got to have a littie water...taint to be cooked, y unerstan. And she ...well, mebe I dont mention it to a religious feller, but if you put a tad of brandy in her drinking water, she will guzzle it to the bottom."

"Brandy in yer animals drinking water. She's a heavy drinker...."

" 'Swhat my friend here said," put in Luke. "She haint a heavy drinker...nothing like that. I done rode her many a mile. She don need a saddle, but if y'll brush her coat onct a week she likes that real good."

"Bramd...a bandy-drinking burro...I got to get the preache rin on this un. Any more structions come with this here animal?"

"One more," I said. Luke looked at me real sceptical like. "If you'll toss a feather pillow into her stall, she'll feel right at home."

"God above have mercy. A pillow in the stall of a ordinary burro!"

"Sir, she aitn a ordinary burro," I said.

"No sreee, she aint ordinariy," Luke echoed.

"I suppose we could arrange it...filne a nanny for her mongst the elderly of our congregation. Does she got a pedecree of some ssort?".

"Pedegree...?" I aske.d

"You know...blood-line breeding...like a good race horse."

"Sir, we come from the wildest fort ye could ever magin. Shes a Fort Sutter burro, that means she in'erstands military stuff--marching, drill and the like...and sojering. She can read too." The man looked flumdungoned. I handed him a copy of one of Bart's poms. "This come with the animal...a receipt for the money we give...ten pinches of gold dust."

He read the pom, as to the few parlishoners them had stopped from curiosity --one of Bart's poms:

Here I lay me down to Sleep \`
*   to wait the coming morrow.*
perhaps Success, perhaps defeat
*   and everlastling Sorrow.*
let com what will, I'll try it on
*   my condition cant be worse*
and if thers money In that Box
*   tis money in my purse.*

"Well, we do some of that," said the religious man. "Drill." All the time folks was going into his church and we stood outside dickering over Cleo.

"You say yere giving her away?" The man tugged at his geem tweed coat and tipped a straw hat offn his forehead. He looked at his filngernails like a woman, and he fixed his bible under his arm. *He a reglar*, I thought.

"Thas what I said. "I'm jes leavling some 'structions so Cleo wont get lonesome ... she be not jes a smart burro but a happy burro."

The man laughed. "A...happy burro!" he said and grunted with the notion. "Well, if you say so...a burro what's happy is in the Lord.   She'll be better than a sermon for the morning," he said.

"Or a wild ass like the bible talks about.,": Luke said.

The deacon Almonds, he took up the reins\ and was about to depart when I said, "Luke, dont y' want to kiss yer old frien goodbye?"

Luke looked at me like I had horns. He patted Cleo on the head and plucked a tuft of grass from off the road and fed it to her. I jes patted her on the head and flanks. She had served us faithful. I thought I saw tears come inter Luke's eyes. The town I could tell was gonna turn rowdy even on Sunday. Their religion was mostly conscribed by gossip and gold.

Fate were done with us. We'd missed a gun-shooting...the knife my Pa give me on my fourteenth birthday done the job. But one more thing happened that set us off on the last leg of our trek to feedom for th both of us. Some ignorant panner had struck a skillet fire in his tent. First thing you knowed, that tent-house was going up in flames, with men runnin away from th scene in front of the church, grabbing sacks and pails on th run. There had to be water. It dont take long for a fire to come a conflagrashun in this country. The missionary took our burro and walked away without so much as a *God bless us*. We didn't care. Now we was freed.

We had us a tolerably long ways to walk...eighty miles...we 'd manage somehow. We had put packs into ropes for the both of us before we left the hardware store. That was hard, but we'd make out. I took the luminettes from the pack and a small pot fer food and mebe some coffee. Not much more. We shared a half each man of our tent canvas and would find branches fer the pegs as we traveled. We left McCloud partly in flames, the smoke rising up over the trown, folks headed fer th church, the missionary walking away with Cleo and not a twitch of a sheriff anywheres to be seen! I knowed we had our luck in hand with us. I'll never ferget the dickerin over our burro.

"

PRECAUTIONS

"Hear that rattle a our tin cups last night?" I asked Luke

"I was too dern tired, ol' chum...."

"A huge pack rat tried to make off with our tinware. I hert the rattle...'s what woke me up. They was must enough light coming from under the tent to spot him...half afoot long. Gawd! that thing ever bit you, you'd die on the spot. It makes off with whatever it can find, let me tell you. I hert tell they sometimes come in twos and threes and clean out a body 'f his table ware...make off with skinning knifes...stuff they can drag away. And when they is hongry, they will chew on yer shoe leather."

"Well, thats a surprise to me...field mice is my kind of animal."

"This here was no field mouse...a hug pack rat, almost come into our tent ifn I hadn/t throwed a shoe at him...."

"I caint see what a onery pack rat can do with a tin plate."

"Cover his burrow, mebe."

"Or trade it off fer a winter coat or something like that."

"Now yer gettin silly, Luke."

The two refugees, one of them from the law and the other from his the grisly cannibalism in the mountains, and his Ma's death on rocksnow plain, his Pa in jail, got ready to move . In a hour, they were on the road again. They found a feed and graln shop and stopped long enough to buy oats for themselfs, now that their burro was gone...liberated." That was about all, since Cleo was not their companion any longer, all the time stoppin to browse on field grass...since it was grass most a her sorta like bes'...fer cows on down."

The two refugees hiked the uproad toward the pass all daly, scarcely talk.ing along thle waly, except to point out the aplin glow on MountShata, which they had passed the dayl before and seemed to notilfy them it was time to make camp. The two of them were well-matched in strength. The oats came in handy when they stopped to make camp that first night out of McCloud. Logging wagons, drawn by teams of six and eight horses boiling up dust passed them before dark, headed toward the sawmill at McCloud. Its whine lingered in their ears. They were soon to reach their destination. An empty logging wagon came up from the south, headed ito the Trinity River woods. It was not too much trouble for the man to stop. He sloweddown his wagon and waved us to jump in at the back. We ran and caught upwith the tail-gate of thet there logging wagon. We crouched down and 'joyed the ride. We was surely glad for the ride. The driver teamster turned around anf asked us how far we were going. Luke said," to the border, Mister."

"Thet so. Well, I aint agoin thet far but yer welcome aboard. Nice to have company 'stead a logs."

Yer coming from McCloud sawmill?" I asked.

"Yep, that's right."

"We 'preciate the ride, sir," Luke said. The man did not answer. The mense wheels of thet empty wagon rumbled so we could hardly hear to talk.

We must've rid twenty miles 'fore the man said, "Here's where I turn in... another twenty miles to the operashun. Y take care, y' hear?" he said. I said, "Sir...Mister...obliged for the ride.: Luke waved him away. He nodded and clacked with a shout to his team a eight drays--percherons they looked like to me-- and the logging wagon moved on up the road into the nearby woods. We hert a roar coming from somewheres over toward the river, but payed it no mind. We stopped to boil some oats for walkin'. Luke discovered some wild berries down in a holler and we et till we was full. I caint say our meal was anythin like we coulda had at the *Owl Hotel*, but it was sufficient. Some things in life has just gotta be trimmed down to size to 'commodate circumstances..., like our hongry needs.

We seed no more miners up thisa way...not because there wasn't no more gold in the ground, but cause it was too lonely and stricken without hunreds prospectilng for gold. I remember Pa oncet tolt me that when all the fishermen come to the same spot on the river, the fish congregate for the feed. It's sort of like that way in prospecting. The more sourdoughs panning on the creek, the more gold comes to be found. We was alone, that's for cartain. We walked and we walked until close to dusk we seen some lights in the distance. Another town, Luke shouted. Inside of a hour we set out blistered feet down in a place we come to hear was called Truckee Pass. Truckee...that surely did fit the descripshun of our ride with the teamster logger. Yep. We'd find us a place to bunk down fer the night, even ifn it werent sociable or clean fer out sweaty and dirty coverlins. We haitn bgot built some miles to go, and then, Luke willbe shut of his fears and pursuers and any of them howling monkeys who wants to catch a poor fleeing Cananite like Luke and tie him in ropes and truck him off to jail or something else he don't deserve. Oh, I know the lay of the land by this time. We found ourselfs walkin along the main street in thet town...there was a sign that said, *No Sashayin Round. Drop Your Guns at the Sheriff's* . Some nights it was wilder' a desert hare...the dancin, and boozin and makin out with th' women...

good ones stayed far away, I reckoned. Insults was answered with a gun...like m' frien Luke's sitiashun. I hert tell a handsome dude shot a mocker to his woman one day while they was walkin' along the street and he put a hole in that drunk's head lkie a pevy hook and it were all over. Things was quiet this mornin". The travelers wanted a clean shave in one of the buildings along that street...they would give up that idea. Luke pointed to a huge sign over the board-walk said, *SUMMIT HOTEL.* "Mightn't we get a room with a floor in it for this last night night?" Luke asked, foolish like.

"Or a rundown chickenshed...."

"Or mabe catch us a chIcken and have a roast or the night some'eres outside a town...."

"Thet sounds mighty fine, Luke. " We begun to cast around...no chickens hereinthe middle of town. We passed by thee red brick hotel with the gringy sign...left behind 's they wended along the mainstreet. Folks here had things to do so they wasnt roaming the streets, they was at work, and there was the long and the short of it. We passed by a billiard hall, and the shops 'long the main drag. I could tell Luke was near starvation. I jes countnt let 'm leave me without a dinner of sorts, a meal celebratin' our lastlin' friendship and the journey from Fort Sutter...but what? We ambled along, poking our curiosity here and there. We come to a shop with lights still on and the man...it was a butcher shop and he was closin up fer the night.

I put on m' best proachin manner and said to him, in religious tone of voice. "We hain had a thing to et fer five hndred miles in this wilderness. I don't know what made me say *willderness.*

The man, still wearing his butcher's apron, and a long black beard and bill-cap said to us, perticularly to me, "We're closing up shop for the night."

"Sir," I said again, "Caint you spare a hambone or some other scraps a suet for us starvin younguns?"

I layed it on, that we was almost orphans in the wilderness and he had a 'bligashun to feed us.

He looked us over up and down and finally, he said,"Come over here." He reached down into a barrel and come up with this big ham-bone. Now if you'll take some scraps of fat and boil this hyer bone for a hour, all the commestible juices wlll come floating to the surface. And ifn y throw in some carrots and taters, ye'll have a fine stew."

"We will think on this matter," said Luke in a hightone voice that buzzed me. The butcher wrapped the hambone and suet scraps in butchers paper and said, "Thet be a charge for the paper, young gents...but I can 'sorb it in my working costs. Y' better scratch gravel 'fore the local sheriff finds two waifs without a job and beggin on the streets of Truckee."

"We'll be on our way right off," I said. We left the butcher behind. He snuffed out his kerosene lanterns and hanged up his apron and we stood outsdie on the street awachin'.... this town had no lamplighter or any sort of lumination, so it were pretty dark. "Lets go some'eres to build us a campfire, Noah, and make us a pot a stew. We got the pot and luminettes." So we walked outside a town, which was not but a quarter mile afar and made camp for the night and boiled the hambone as the butcher told us to do. We had no carrots or potatoes--'ceptin some chunks a biscuits I stole-- and so we sipped the hot broth that warmed our insides and brought back the flush of strength to our cheeks...our cheeks with growin beards, and they was looking pretty 'thentic, I can tell y'. It was a gorgeous moment fer me and m' sidekick Luke.

"Say Noah , you suppose the sheriff has got word from the telegraph operator...."

"About what... your murderilng some derned fool!'"

"They put a price on m' head, I spect. Thats usually th way them law folks handle matters...organization.".

"Well, I'm lhere to pertect you," said Noah. "Don never ferget that/" Luke give me \ a funnuy, suspicious and sceptical look. Remember that shop sign we passed...said, *__Tropico Gold, nuggets, dust, flakes weighedc, bought here__*. You think melbe we ought to sell our dust instead of carrin it round like we do?"

"Naw, I be born in hell ifn ever I sell my sack of dust. When we split, I plan to share it with you anyways, Noah. You gotta hike back tol Fort Sutter."

"Assayer would cheat you, count on that. It's more valu'ble just like it is. When it gets to be too bothersons, we can split it up. Put yourn in one a yer socks...."

"Aint no gold that 's ever bothersome," Luke said. He was a wopplin' good philosopher, that Luke. He knowed how to handle ordinary matters like selling gold and philosophizin 'bout pack rats.

"One thing we got to be kerful of," said Luke.

"Yeah, what 's that?".

"Snakes . Lots a powerful poisonous snakes hereabouts...when done pitched our tent who knows but they's a den a vipers hereabouts. We got to build up dirt around ourtentso snakes...and mebe a pack rat or two...caint slither in an kill us both at night...cause they might be snake burrows in the rocks. Rattlesnakes like to hide under rocks."

"Well, I sure don want to set up all night and keep watch. Some things in life, Luke, y' jes got to take a chance on. That 's jes the way nature is, m' Pa tolt me oncet. I don suppose there 's anyway we can clear out the hull countryside a snakes."

"I didnt say the hull countryside, I said here ...right smack down here...where this hyer tent stands. We put down fer the night."

"Our campfore keeps snakes and rats and such away...skeered...I hert tell, They won't come an bother us none...mpt wotj tjet fore/ Sicj crotters are sleered a fire," Luke pronounced with smooth talk.

Fire...they is cautious about fire," I tolt him. We can build us up high a nice camptire tonight and them cretters will take a caution not to come crawling round our tent.

"Think youre right, said Luke. "

"Y' gotta think like a snake er a rat thinks," I tolt 'm.

"Also I hear we piss around the tent they won't come botherilng us none."

"I never hert of that," I said. "They don like dogs none. Mebe we ought to get us a little dog...small soz we can carry him in our pockets."

"Theres a right smart idea. We'll catch uls a runaway dog. Else we got to buy one ."

And so, in solid handshakin' 'greement about most things, we passed the night without a snake er a rat comin inter our tent, and we riz up at dawn and packed our stuff and stomp'd out the coals, and we headed to the town a Truckee, back agin to where we was give the stew ham-bone and the sorry advice a thet butcher, past the town shops.

One caught my eyes, under a shed--farm tools, still useable, on sale, used and some rusting, like a scythe, a graln spreader for small fields, a pot-bellied stove, real cheap. I could not help thinking about them brave folks what died in the rocksnow mountains...they was all farmers and these tools was familiar to them...I'd be seeilng a few of them when I make it back to Fort Sutter.

"How many miles you figure we got to go afore we meet up with the border?" Luke asked me.

"Less 'n fifty I' guess. I knowed it was more'n two hundred miles . "Meantime aint we got to find us a breakfast. We kin 'fore to pay with some of thet gold dust," I said and Luke agreed. Just about then therecome what seemed like a shootin...there was a exchane a gunfire, I knowed that for cartain....Life commences mighty early in a small town. Couln't be anything but dry diggins around here...no soudough panners seen on the streets. This was a good place for them who robbed them miners' sluce boxes..smart, hide where there weren't mining going on. I don see no mules roaming aout...always good for stealing...farmers didnt brand them animals...over by the river there was likely some panning going on. I sort of expected a tent city up here...don't know why when there was no creek nearby. I heard tell there was still a part of a loot taken from a *Ophir* stickup and hid here in the Mountains. Y' caint really tell about such things. Mebe jus' talk.... Well, here we was...aint nobody going to shower us with coins and nugests and fifty dollar slugs like we wuz actors on a stage. We would druther make ourselfs in-visible at this point...since Luke was about ready to cast off.

Luke heard it first. Here wwe was out in the open country, and there came the sound of a thousand horses with hoofs pounding the ground \, mostlikely five or six, from below thebrow sof the hill. First thing we knowed, here come some cavalrymen, ysssir, right out there in the open, and they was riding hell bent fser election. Luke, he looked real scared., but there was nowheres we could hide, no building, no cactus, no boulders. But here they come, thelr riders ben t over the manes of the snorses a flahying inl the wind, the sojilers kicking the flanks a their mounts and on their faces,s the wildest, looks, grilns like, grilm and set as if on a chase. They did not look at us. They onl ran on buyl as slif they was on the trail of aa criminals.

"Well, you can relax now, Luke. They was no vigilantes out after you.

"Still, all the same, we, I caint be too careful. What if they had stopped and asked us our names?"

"W'd a tolt 'em, real straight out, honest and innocent like."

"Mebe you would."

"You got to get one thing straight, Luke. The whole world haint out lookin fer you. You aint that im-portant."

"No, but I kilt a man back in Springfield...."

"Were a long ways from springfield."

"Still, we cannot stop just here. News travels like a flash...."

"You'll make it over the Oregon border and then ye can find a job and go free-- somewheres to yer own liiking fer -it would all be over with your killing that feller."

"I wisht I had yer confidence, Noah."

They went on a short ways and they passed a sign that said. *Clymores Diggins, Glory hole, one mile.*

"You aint never seen a glory hole afore?"

""What in blazes you s'pose that mean, Noah ? I come from farming country. They aitn no glory holes out in the wheat field."

"No, I spect not. Well its like a water-well and the miners go up and down on this hyer elevator to where they was diggin yesterday."

"Sideways?"

"Yep, sideways, after they reached the bottom of the gold they dig sideways till the gold stops." Noah felt confident in his exsplanation.

Well, what you tell me about this hyer gory hole is something to reckon with." said Luke. "A straight-in tunnel is the best way, in my reckoning.   Why they caint jes to go up and down is past good sense, Noah."

Well, if you seen it once, you'd unerstand, said Noah.

"You see that contrapshun?" Luke asked .

"Yep, reminds me a a hog killin farm."

"Thets called the head-frame, ilts has the pulleys and ropes that lift the miners in and out a the mine, like we waz talking about....jes like a water wheel, like I said," said Noah.

They passed some tents and shacks along the way, a small settlment a miners, on a rippling creek. Where ever they was water, they was sure to be habitation.

"Look there!" Luke cried out of a suldden. :What's that there chicken, mad, running down the road?"

Luke laughed, "Thet's a roadrunnner...just like he's a songbird alrunning down the road.   Almostr fast as a horse!"

"Caint he fly?"

"Not more 'n like a wild turkey, mebe up into the trees a' times...when hes scared."

"Well, that is a funny sight, I can tell y'," said Luke.

We rode in close to some shacks whose tin roofs showed like mirrors in the midday sun. The sound of a creek come to my ears.

"Wouldnt this be a good place to put down for a while and hide, in theshade of the mornin'?"

"No, Luke these here shacks contain dangerous varmints...some is miners, others is Indians, but they come way\ out here \to es-cape from somehtin or other."

"Well, I don trust em more than yew," said Luke . We rode up to one of the shacks and in the shade stopped andrested. They pulled off their packs and felt the cool air on their sweating backs. . Nobody payed any attention to us vagabonds who had veered off into their little village.

A man hailed us down from 'longside the road.

"It wouldnt do ye no good to stop here, fer were all tulckered out withs the shisnanigsans of miners here abouts...staking out claims on our property."

"Well, that's a miserable thing, sir," Luke said.

" 'Sides, they's some of then Paiute Indians here 'bouts, and they dont take kindly to 'strangers, no matter where theys comeling from er going to."

"I un'erstand," Luke said. 'But we aint cowboys.

The man laughed. "You see any cows herebouts. :

" They was none...just a mangy dog and some chickens,"I told him.. The man went into his cabn and brought out a shot gun and pointed it at us.

"You got us wrong, mister," said Luke. We don't come to bring you no harm. We be on out way."

"Right soon, if I got my way." He shook his shotgun at us. "Down stream a this village its a place to pitch yer tent if lyer a mind to. Or they's a restaurant...*The Fryin Pan...*"

"We're not robbers. We pan for gold to keep us alive and in boot leather, sir," said Luke.

"Good....well, y' can un'erstand when a man wants to pertect his property and his family....:

"I understand that right smart," said Luke. "We'll be on our way." The man lowered his shotgun. "I be obliged to yew if y' would." he said and took himself a seat in a rocker on his front porch, his shotgun acrosst his knees while he watched us depart. That was all pretty scarry, let tell you. From a distance the man shouted to us, Ifn ye want to gamble they's a saloon up at a place they call Mulkeme Hill. Run by a old trapper and his Indian Squaw. They'd 'preciate yer company...and yer gold!"

We come to the place called *The Frying Pan*, for just such folks like us, on the road... " Lets us see if we can dicker for a breakfast, one for you and nother fer me," I 'lowed. We wheeled into the spot and found us a table close to the door.

"I got me my gold dust," said Luke. "Aint nothing so valuable as a sack a gold dust to them what aint got none. We're mighty kerful up to this point...and we got to be." A man wearilng a tall, black stove pipe hat come up to us where we sat and he said, "What will you boys have this marnin?"

I said, " We're poweful hongry. A mess of bacon and eggs would do us real fine."

"He shouted something to the back of the eatin place...probably the cook. "Adam and eve on a raft and porker fer a pet!"

Now this sort a talk befuzzled me and looked at Luke like he was also out of his gumpshn mind. But the man, in a greasy apron fixed his bow tie and went back to the pantry whilest we sat there in his eatin joint. I 'had pulled off one of m' socks afore leavling our camp and I said to Luke: "Here is my sack, Luke. Ifn you'd care to part with some of yer gold dust, I'd be mighty 'preciative. I'm goin to need providins for the trip back to Fort Sutter."

He took his bag of dust from one pocket and while stretched the sock he poured in a generous smidgin of dust. It was a handy transaction and a pre-caution, lemme tell .

"I'm much obliged to you, Luke." I stuffed the sock into my shirt pocket, and wewaited ferthe waiter iln the bowtie and stove pipe hat to come..which he did right soon. We 'dulged ourselfs in a fine breakfast of bacon and eggs and toast with butter. It was probably the last meal we would ett together, us pals, frien's fer life.

A small short man with one arm and crow-wing moustaches, a crumpled felt hat, yeller suspenders and a tableclothshirt come to see what refreshment he could find from a long journey. He had a stutterin voice like a loose brake shoe. He'd had jes come in from off the man street. He looked like one of them peddlers with a sack of mule-back things to sell. The man showed us his wares...a couple of knifes hewas offerin' fer sale. .

" 'S matter a fact," said Luke, "We 're looking to buy us a couple of ...hunting knifes."

"Hunting knives, eh. Wall, caint be a better pace for buinesst than the breakfast table, gents. I think I just might have what yer a looking fer." The trapper and his Squaw wife looked on wilth interest. Knifs of any sort had a kinda fascination for the trapper...as you can tell. He took us over to thewinder and pulled out from the sack he was totin" two of the finest looking butcher, hunting knifes I ever did see. Scotch my persnaps, ifn they wasn't the shiniest, sharpest and most handsomest knives I ever did see. By the look on Luke's face I could tell he was thinkin the same thing....

"You take gold dust, mister, fer them knifes?

"I can, it aint the kindest thing to do, since I could cheat you boys, but I'm a honest dude and, l gol dern, I got me a pair of scales that will do justice to any man's gold dust, you can be sure. You got perhaps any gold dust on you?

"We got us a sackful," said Luke...enough to buy ten o' them knifes without battin a eye.. Luke pulled his drawstring leather bag from under his shirt and dangled lt front of the man's eyes...and they growed big as saucers. He took us over to his scales.. But first he layed out the knifes real shiny and handsome. He took Luke's sack of gold dust put a paper on the table, and he had Luke pinch out a couple a ounces. Now gold dust is heavy stuff...since it sinks to the bottom of the panners pan whilest the river mud and black sand is washed over the brim.

"Two ounces, one fer each knife, " said the man.

Luke looked at me and then at the peddler of knifes. I looked at Luke and the Peddler shook his head like he could not believe what he was seeiln--a young dude refusing to give his life fer a ordinry hunting knife...it was a beauty though.

"It's s a deal," said Luke. He took the bag, drawed up the strings and put it under his shirt agin.

"Oh, you ailt by chance got any sheathes fer these knifes?" I asked the peddler.

"Glad you asked, young feller. I got a dandy sheathe, with carvings inter the leather and turquoise decorations...made by one a them Piute . I can let y' have one for each o them knifes...all for the 'nificent price of a ounce of gold."

Me amd Luke looked at each other again. Luke nodded his head. He was a little older, so I give him the say in the matter. It took us nearly three weeks t collect that ounce, but they was plenty a gold still out there, so we didnt care much. We took a knife apiece,

We heard a loud racket and in busted a man; in a beaver-skin cap and a leather Wall, sir, to make a long jacket. He was stooped oer lie his backwas loded, he had on fur-coveed boots that I could see and his leather face wilth har\steely blueeyes put one on to a caution. It was z trapper who had come in with his Squaw wife. He hid one hand in his pocket when he spoke. Behind him there 'peared a woman who looked like a Indian Squaw, with a turquoise thing in her shiny black hair, and dark skin and what looked like a blanket wrapped round her. Indians who married whites rarely give up their ways a dressin. The Squaw woman took np interest...she wore stuck in her black shin hair a turquoise thing...a thing like a blessing of a god to them, turquoise... its blue the tears of their god. They sat down acrosst from us, and he right off began to talk. "You boys ever been on a bear hunt?"
 I said, "We be on a hunt right now, but not fer animals, sir. What's on yer mind?" I asked him real impudent like. .
 "I'm looking for a hunting partner. I be a trapper fer beaver skins but I'll need help in hunting. Tis not my business to hunt...perticular fer bears. I be a trapper, like I say."
 "We would be mighty glad to oblige y' sir," I said. I'm thinking 't is queer fer this feller to want help of any sort exceptin from his Indians quaw wife. But he sald , "I'd take Cynthia here"...he had give her a white man's name..."I'd take Synthia here, but she is feared of bears.   I'm going to need help in toting the animal from out of the woods." I didn't hear no horse outside. Jest then a donkey brayed. "Besides, I keep only the skin, not the meat. Somethin fer the wolves.... you boys eat bear meat?..its tough and sweet...you'll be in good luck if you pitch in with me for the hunt."

I looked at Luke and he looked back at me, and we decided that we ought to go with the man on his hunt, not fer the meat but, Luke said, to make sure we don't meet up with no sheriff in the town who got the telegraph message of a fugitive murderer on the loose. "He be armed with a shotgun and dangerous." Luke dangerous? It was a es-cape. I tolt this hyer trapper that we would like mightily to go fer the 'sperience, as hunting bears seemed to be a way to make a livin. He said beaver-hunting on the creeks was a better way. He wanted to shake my hand, and so I shook his. He had two fingers missin but I did not ask how he lost his fingers. The man in the tall stove pipe hat and black bow tie...his shirt was was pink...came to out table and set down a mess of grits and pork rinds and greens from the garden. The trapper said he had a gun, which I did not see--it was leaned up in one corne or the pantry room.
 "I be a trapper all my life and, like I say...not a hunter. You boys look like ye could use some good bear meat. My squaw traps game...she hunts but it's too hard for her to hunt in the woods...woods'er not made fer squaw of any brand." I was thinkin.
You jes never can tell when you might have to use his shotgun 'gainst some suckin fool

who takes us for outlaws in order to collect a ransome.   I said this out loud to Luke.

"A reward," Luke corrected. "Bounty hunters aint partial t' the law er to their quarry," said Luke with uncommon understandin' The trapper-man didnt know what we was talkin about but he 'peared anxious to have company fer his hunt. I could not unerstand why...was he feared a the bear? He had no hound dog like some hunter bring along in th hunt...or was he shy on 'sperience. He straightened his beaver skin cap and slammed a trap of some sort on the table with a loud, craceous rattle.   "This is my lawful game 'strument, the bear trap. *C'est bon ca, Je fabrique le chose pour le gran* ...beast." I did not speak French so I did not understand his boast, which it was, fer he swelled up when he said it.   *I go to hunt. we hunt, me and you...a final escape*, I'm thnking, and 't is all for the good of Luke's crossing the border.   I did not un'erstand right then that the trapper man was supperstitious and that if three hunt a bear, the gods take off the curse of cruel to nature, but if one man hunts, 't is all on his shoulers. He explained all that. Then he and his squaw dived into a plate of grits and pork rinds and greens from the garden. It was a strange 'ccasion, it seemed to me, jes as me and Luke were about ready to finish our 'scape. He would not be found crossing the border in the woods--which was where they alus expect murderers to cross--and I would be lib'rated to start back to the fort...but I did not tell Luke my plan. The trapper and his squaw wife made talk in French with hand signs I did not un'erstand. I saw his right hand with the two fingers missin.   I did not know why he come hunting with his Squaw in tow, unless she was better than him at reading trail signs. That's a caution. Her face had no expression on it...dark eyes, a wanderin' look at us from time to time.

"We got to hit the trail, you boys. Them knifes'll come in handy." The trapper and his wife practically dragged me and Luke out the door whilest the peddler stayed for a mug a coffee. He pushed his wife up onter the donkey. It brayed. He slapped tts rump and it bucked once. She rode off like a discharged gunshot just as a brown floppy-eared hunting hound dawg come arunnin up from nowhere and sniffed at us and at the bear trap he had hung on his belt. We, me and Luke, wuz nervous amd skeered like two crows over a puddin pie. When we left that 'eatin 'stablishment, we wuz really nervous, since we was close enough to almost jump over the border...us two fugitives.

Soon 's we got over Mulkelme Hill, the town was plum gone out of sight 'ceptin fer the headframe of the *Ransome* deep hole mine--what lifts and drops miners down inter th groun....we wuz in th woods 'fore y knew it. Our trapper guide, he waz full of things to say, like a history book back home, alwayls spouting bout happenings, famous folks and such. "Some diggins ar dry...but that's motly cause no booze is tolerated...folks come to dig, not drinkj. Only a dry-goods store...and gold y kin pound twixt two rocks to see ifn its gold. Kept their gold to theyslfes--*Rough and Ready*--'s why thet dadbuned town never joined the Union side...to spensive! Panning gold more 'portant than shooting southern rebels ...many panners rehels, I spect.   I seen that Lotta Crabtree do her Irish jig and highland fling...and believe me, boys...she was the derndest thing on two legs cepting a milkin stool and thats got three. *Rattlesnake Bar*...there wus a place...could buy sluce boxes y' could not rob...*what the devil was the man talking about, robbing sluce boxes!..this was a bear hunt....*mule trains was a' times robbed comin from th mines with rocks to the crusher...but in *Growlersburg*, nuggets said to growl in panners' tin pans...." I don't know 'bout that one. We stopper to listen, the hound run off a ways and come back and whine small and stand froze on the trail. "He's picked up the scent," the trapper said under his breath. We won't fill no tin cup with gold for th' day's diggins, but we suren Lucifer's fire got us a trail to a bear. Jes look at that hound dawg run like he was mad!

"A bear can smell hunters and their dogs fer miles, long 'fore you ever catch sight of him." The hound ran twenty paces and returned..."He's tellin us we was on the right track. When a bear runs in its own territory, it knows where to run and hide-- caves, ravines, small 'croppings." This bear was on the scamper and it was runnin for its life in its own territory. The dawg kept his nose close to the ground, hardly movin from side to side. This showed us that the tracks wuz fresh and we hadnt ough tto worry about bein sidetracked. A bear--this bear is smarter than we figured. It 'ppeard like it is circling back. "A bear will do that--circle back-- to confuse the hound and throw the trackers off the trail. When the dawg comes to the place where the tracks cross in circling back, the hound has three directions it can travel and does not know which one. Then the hunters, we step into the pitchur and point the hound along the trail. Its a combination of man and dog that makes this hunt a success. "The hound there...whose name 's *St Peter*...circled back. The hunter had brok a branch to mark where the trail would circle back to. The dog tracked in silence ,paddin down loose duff and needles...a bear knows how close he is to the hunter aint 'tall sure if we be gainin on him." The hound made some small sounds but the trapper put the dog to silence. We had been on the scent more 'n a hour but it 'peared we had made little progress, fer thet black fur iln the dark a the woods totally hid the animal from human eyes, but not from *St. Peter*. The hound 'ppeaed to sense that the bear was tiring--since a bear to run fer its life fer over a hour was very tirisome fer the aimal. Every time we stopped, we give the bear that much 'ppurtunity to gain a lead on us. It might take us all night until dawn to come 'pon the beast...but our trapper was confident we would. Luke and me, we kept up the pace of the trapper and *St. Peter*. We could not get ahead of 'm, yet they had no more idea where the bear actually was then we did. Of a sudden the trapper give a little cry out, for he saw that' we had come back to his broken branch. The dog stopped and began to run in a circle.

"Y see there, the bear thinks he has fooled the dog and us. He has circled back and now... because the beast had not come that way to start with, the trapper saw that the bear was headed back towards the campfire we had left over a hour ago. When a bear sees that it has not fooled its hunters, it soon tires...fer that is the wisdom of the aanimal--that it instinctly knows it cannot run forever. Tfhe houng give a small yelp and run off at a distance and returned. This told the hunter that the dog had located the bear. But whether er not the bear was waitin to rip the dog to shreds with its claws, or whether it simply paused to get its breath--these options were evident at this lmomelt. St Pter run back and forth till he stopped short and buried his nose in the groun', 'ppeared like, to make a spot then barked, as he lifted hisself up on hind legs and clawed the bark a a particular tree, all the time barking like he was mad with happiness to find the bear, upside the limbs of thet tree...and jumping up onto the bark with its forepaws it barked wildly up into the tree. He had treed the animal we had run to exhaustion. It had no choice but to scramble wildly up into the branches of a immense juniper treee for perteckshun. We had no lantern with us...but a dark splotch in amongst thebranches showed the trapper where the bear most likely had sat, watching us from his height of about 20 feet. The trapper come up close to the tree. He looked up into th branches. He backed off a short ways and fired one round from his shotgun.

We did not expect anything to happen, but his aim was good, fer thet bear come down, smiting the big limb below on theway down, till it landed with a solid thump like a chopped tree into the forest duff. The bear did not move. St. Peter barked at it, then moved in close and sniffed and barked again. The bear did not move but its glassy brown eyes somhow was still open, 'ppeared to stare i[at us. We walked over to the creture and thet trapper leaned down and grabbed the muzzle, then lifted its eyes and then was sire that the animal was dead. Before our staring at him, he took out a large bowie huntin knife and begun to re-move the hide from off the animal. IL was cartailn that its hide and not the meat was why he had come. Indians like hides. This bear hide was for his Indian Squaw. We sat down on the groun and watched the operation fer about a hour.

"You boys can find yer way, caint you?" he asked us. I said we could find our way outta this woods. When he had removed the skin from the bear and 'cluded the head with its mouth and eyes still, open, he jimmied his knife after wiping the blood from it, then he throwed the hide over his shoulder, the head ahangin down over his back. He looked mighty proud of this trophy. He looked round then set off in the direction we had come from, where his Squaw was. I\ said, "Well, Luke, looks like we got us a bear carcass to feed on fer thle night. Ever et bear meat 'fore?." He grumbled no he hadn't. I took a luminere from my shoulder pack, fer I had a thought or two about this huning trip. Precautions was in order. We made us a campfire. There was the bear lookin all nakedwithout his hide, fur still round its paws, and its head plum gone. We had nothing else to do but to take our new knifes and cut us off steaks from its hind rump and first hang them over the fire and then drop them into the coals for a good hour so 's they was cooked good.

I said to Luke, "You aint got but a short ways to go to cross the border."

"I can make it, but you, Noah, what are you going to do?"

This was the first time he has said anything about my sitiashun, er even spoke my name all during the hunt.

"I got me that gold dust you split off back there in town. West a here they 's a stage road."

"How do you know that?"

I seen th wheel tracka when we corsst th road. Anyway, I'll ltake the stage back to Fort Sutter."

"I'll be safe in Oregon."

"I cartainly hope so..." Noah bend down on his knees, chocked with the smoke and with a stick he turned them bear stakes in the coals. "Listen, Luke . brother...y'll niver walk safe from yer conscience. Tha's a promise. It's going to chase after you fer the rest a yer life!"

"How you know that?"

"Just' cause I know its so. If you re-pent and 'fess to the sheriff, it'll all be over and they can do what they want wich you. You have heared 'bout th' consdience?"

"I got to find me a priest and make confession."

"Not a priest. Jes th sheriff...an God be listenin in, y can count on that."

"I don know if I wan ter con-fess...actshally. I done wrong...I kilt a man, but he had il comin."

"That aint the point a yer argment, Luke. Y need to tell som'one in 'thority what can judge y'."

"I aint ready to ne judged, Noah. Tarnation, I sure aint!"

"Well, m' friend, y got blood on yer hands."

"Thet 's from thet bear."

"Naw, y' know what I mean...from thet feller y' snuffed out back there in Springfield."

"Well, if it do y' any good."

"Not me, Luke!..yerself!..'fess to the sheriff, let God do his mighties, and y' be free onct agin."

"I be free already." I had to sigh with wearies.

Luke give me a long look search in m' face to see if I was makin' a joke to him, but I would not lie to m' brother...fer we had become like brothers . I said no more but let my idee perclate in his thinkin fer a spell. I was sure he would come 'round, like a man whats been hit with a log comes to after a while.

"Mebe I don't want to...clear my conscilence."

"Then yew got no choice but to be a fug'tive fer the rest a yer life."

"I'll grow a bearrd then nobody 'll recognize me."

"Won't do y' no good. You got to get rid a yer guilt somehow. Y' jes caint hide yer guilt behind a beard from folks on the street."

"Oh, I'll fergit the whole thing after a while..."

"Never, Luke...never will y' fergit that night...how it happened, the man's words...yer Ma acryin'....Never. Never will y' ferget the time ye shot thet man. Y'll have thet guilt haing 'round yer neck fer the rest ayer life. Yer Ma has most liekly gone to heaven by now and so y've no witness."

"Time 'll help me to ferget."

"Tlime won;t close up th't hurt, Luke....only thing is to say yer sorry and tell the story to a sherif and let him take care a the details. It'll be writ on th' book there in Springfield. Oncc y've confessed, th guilt 'll leave you like a tracking hound dog and ye'll live yer life without a hurtin conscience till y' die. But ifn y' dont 'fess 'nd give up to the law, then yer case is closed so far as God is concened."

"I'm agoin to hell, I s'pose."

"Not fer me t say. I know this, that guilt can be droppped like a load a firewood on yer back when y tell the family of the man you shot y'r sorry and take th conequences. Aint I yer frien t' be telllin you this?"

"Why, yeah, Noah I never did doubt that one mite. Damn me..."

Noah said no more about the matter. He just put his arm around Luke's shoulders, then went to the fire where their steaks had finished cooking.

"Well, then, jes set yer mind thet thet is th road y'll travel." Noah stood up. turned their steaks. "Meat 's done." For forty minutes they enjoyed their feast. When they had finished their meal of bear steaks, Noah stood and gave his pal a big hug and said, "Thata way is north. By my reckoning the border is close to five...mebe les 'n five miles away...thet way." He pointed through the woods in a northerly direction. I'm goin this way." He thumbed over his shoulder. "I got thet gold dust y' gave me, and I'll catch me a ride south to the Sacramento Fort.

"Going to miss you, Noah."

"We been real pals...like brothers... and you aint been caught. But you got to stand up like a man and tell the truth."

"I will, Noah. What you say is good 'dvise. I'll do it for cartain."

"Good! Then I can count on it. Ifn y' want to write me a note at the Fort, that's alright...but don' expect a answer."

"No, Noah I won't." They shook hands and Noah turned on his heel fast and headed in a Westerly direction, toward the main stage road, whilest Luke kicked dirt onto the fire and struck off in a northward direction.

Within a few minutes the snap of twigs on the forest floor could not be heard. Both young men headed toward their separate destinations. Noah hailed down a stage-coach traveling from Medford to Sacramento and showed the driver his sack of gold dust. His comrade made it through the woods into a clearing where he found two hunters. Within the hour he had related his story to them and asked to taken to the sheriff. This they consented, for they had completed their hunt and had not seen a black bear. Luke told them of his adventure with Noah and the trapper in the woods. He showed them the blood of the bear on his hands, like an initiation mark. The two near-brothers never communicated with one another again...for circumstances had separated them beyond all time.

THE MOLLIES ARE COMING

AN HISTORICAL NOVEL

BY

Charles E. Miller

JAMES "McKENNA" McPARLAN,
Detective Extraordinary

I

It was a gray day outside, the Pennsylvania hills were swathed in low clouds. The sound of a factory whistle broke into the room where a small clique of some thirty uniformed men men were gathered to hear the story, imparted to their newest recruit James McParlan. These were the officers of the Pinkerton Agency, and the time was some seventy-two hours after another murder had occurred on upper Chelsea Street in the area of The Flats, a district of impoverished coal miners' shacks in Eastern Pennsylvania, It was a town wise in its cries of distrust of mine bosses and rampant with disgust over mine dangers of dust, fire and explosions, a region sacred to mine owners yet rife with dissatisfaction by the men who tunneled in darkness, sparks of flint from metal on metal, hammering away with eight-pound mauls by candlelight, men who spat coal dust from their coal miners lungs and watched the weird pagentry of maul and pike eat into the black and implacable wall while their eyes flashed a ghoulish stare at the rocky stuff that was the genesis of wealth, poverty and comfort in a town called Shenandoah..

The summons was from a mine owner and his Prosecutor and owner of the Reading Railroad, the black snake that hauled the coal to the middlemen fter having rumbled and shrieked in like an angry monster through the sorter.   .He was Mister Frank Whelan. He was telling his special recruit and the men in the room with the water-stained wallpaper the story of the a group of violent troublemakers who identified themselves as *the Mollies,* the inheritors of the reputation for violence similar to that of the *Buckshots* in this country. Their killings had occurred in Schuylkill County in 1854. Frank B. Gowan, Esq. had come to Pinkerton, begging in the manner of a dignitary due special favors, to see if the Detective could not help him rid his mines--and he owned some five or six in addition to the railroad--of the Mollie violence, that contagion that made strong men shy from the dark and good men engage the enemy of labor without a care. For they, *The Mollies*, thrived on violence, abetted by mine superintendents, bosses, and their cronies who could keep the miners on a wrack of debt for the remainder of their short lives, usually somewhere in their late thirties. The scene was a soporific for God's judgement, not man/s, though the elegantly dressed Mister Whelan sought relief for himself and for no other. Whelan, an Irishman himself, had proved unable to handle the immensity of the troubles in the anthracite coal fields, the killings done by the Mollies of mine bosses, superintendents and their familiars. Many a well-liked man who was not a Mollie had been done lin, "rubbed out, "snuffed out" for some petty reason, often revenge, and most often for the victim's role in mine superintendence and bossism--which the miners linked to their impoverished circumstances.

In the coal fields of Shenandoah Schuylskill and Carbon Counties, the wage for a deep pit coal miner was, at the time of the Civil War, about fifty cents a day. When a miner had purchased food, clothing, household necessities from the company store, with script worthless outside the town, he was in debt to the store. Miners felt, therefore, that they were slaves of the Coal Mining Company with no hope for the morrow. They shared a sense of despair and simmering anger and that rage against circumstances that betray the law-biding man for what he really is, a man of noble countenance, made in the image of God.   Cave-ins and fires and uncontrolled coal dust were another reason for the miners' wrath. It was mostly the Irish who rebelled, less frequently the Welsh and German miners who, themselves, were all too frequently the victims of the Mollies' lawless shootings. The Mollies would put a man down by clubbing and knifing him, then having done a "clean job," retreat through the woods from the scene of the crime to their own communities. In this way, they escaped detection for some fourteen years, until this crisis meeting in which Whelan presented his case, and McParlan presented his credentials of courage, daring and reckless character. There was just this glitch in the proceedings:--Pinkerton had the wit not do divulge his recruit's mission only that he was a new member of their organization. He was there to appraise his backup men, which he would never call upon, and the nature of his mission as Whelan divulged it to his opeaitves. Thus, Gowan, owner of the Reading Railroad. a main transporter of coal outside the mine and mine owner himself, had for personal reasons come to Pinkerton for help.

The Mollie violence germinated its start in early Ireland where revenge began on land owned by British landlords who were often more ambassadors of hell than landlords whoevilced a brittle English character toward their Irish neighbors. *Maguirism,* as it was called, took off during the American Civil War, bringing into the melee the capers of soldiers in the fields, the hotheads of disenfranchised freebooters of the whiskey trade and scalpions who had learned how to silence a rifle with cotton wadding and a horse blanket. It was all in the trick of the Irish, those members of the Ancient Order of the Hibernians that at times furnished a facade of respectability to the Mollies. They were said to be a secret civic order, but the fury of the Mollies in their quest for revenge by shootings required little or no secrecy except in the planning of an ambush, the coordination of an assault, the inception of an attack on a well-known, honest, often Irish hardworking citizen of the town. The common citizens saw these attacks as senseless, and they were. For motives were concealed in the angst of revenge. Perhlaps the vinctm was accused of cheating in the handling of groceries at the Company Store…or paying a scrub to take his shift down at the seam.

McParlan was a short man with a hanging moustache, a mild and round face and small, pudgy hands. He spoke with tact. "I was born in Armagh County, Ulster, Province, sir . And I know ye have a mind where that's at." Pinkerton laughed. . The day had grown surly and dark. The Sargent turned on the lights and the meeting continued. We'd be right to set him telling' his story, Molly's anguish and her pitiless end. But fist, perhaps ye should reconnoiter the way the whole thing sprouted."

3.

Whelan explained the beginning of Mollies in this way: Because of her Catholic faith, a rather fierce woman named Mollie Maguire was the target of attempts at eviction from her rented domicile in Ulster County, Ireland, sited on a piece of property owned by an English blue-blood. Refusing to evict, she resorted to violence, killing the British landlord to defend her station. Like toadstools, Whelan explained, men sprang up like vigilantees to murder British landlord agents in lands acquired by Feudal fiat in the Middle Ages in Ireland.

"The Mollies, as they cast themselves, dressed up as women in pursuit of their victim. Give me your ears, gents...they carried about with them the pugnacious conviction of having been personally wronged. In short, gentlemen, they fought against the British for what they saw as wrongs to the Irish, an old story, an ancient rebellion, a godless task and and a bloody series of reprisals all down through English-Irish history. I cannot change that...but we're going to change their opinion of the Pinkertons, by Gor. And ye know how the kettle boils in that 'n."`

The Sargent paused, opened the door and shouted down the stairwell. "If yer not sleeping on the job, Jakes, me boy, bring us up two trays, would ye, with a load a brood aile from Master Brougham and some fine tarts made by the queen o' the kitchen Missus Shereen. And make 't a running jump, me lad...and ye'll find mahr in yer paycheck next time. Aye!."

With that order he slammed the door to the upper room with the rain-stained wallpaper. Jakes quite soon by all measurements brought up for his cadre of *missionaries*, as he called them, the order "tea and tarts." From two wooden trays the lad served the the men of the agency while they listened to their boss, Harry, tell of the Mollies. as they had come to be called. Having given this brief history, he introduced their newest; member who was named McParlan, James McParlan, or plain *Jimmy*, sitting there among gents The men were trying to summon images of Molly activity. The Sargent said no more about their recruit, and after a decent interval he dismissed the men to their assigned duties of patrol and detective investigation, for there were more cases for the Pinkertons than those generated by the Mollies.

The Sargent also removed himself from the room, leaving the recruit alone with Pinkerton himself, his new boss. He informed McParlan, that only he, himself, Pinkerton, McParlan and Mister Gowan would know about *the arrangement*, as he called the hiring. He was to t ake the name of McKenna. In short, Jimmy McParlan, alias MxKenna, was to become a spy on the Mollies. This role was not to be a romantic evesdropping on Mollie goings on but, instead, to involve McKenna's direct participation with the vicious vagabonds called Mollies, in a word, to become like one of them, or more than one of them, for he had decided that a formal facade would arouse suspicion. Though he was not a heavy drinker, he would assume the role of a ne'r do well, casting about from town to town in search of work down in the mines, yet finding work never on one job for longer than two weeks, in a word, a vagabond and a likeable derelict with the big Irish heart for the murderous crusade of the Mollies.

It was unpleasant work. In a Mollie tavern in Girardville, McKenna was boasting of his prowess with a maul. One of his Mollie colleagues slapped him across the back, then asked him to show his hands, which were almost lily-white, soft, lacking calouses and the hard look of a mauler a the coal seam. He wanted, indeed, he knew that he should demonstrate his new-found loyalty to the Mollies, who were favorites to beat up on mine bosses, to pick a fight and to rub out an enemy, a foreman of superintendant. McKenna bragged also about his sharp eye with a gun, his old deer-hunting pal having gon into the ranks of the Army of the Potomac. This comment angered the several Mollies in Shea's Tavern. And so, without much caution to their words, they assigned to him the job of burning down the house of a mine superintendant in the Transcola mine. He was a plucky bastard, they all agreed, this super, yet he wrangled outsiders to chafe the pride of deep-pit diggers by telling they them fell short in their day's output.. It was a put-up job, this harassment of the miners. Plucky McKenna was treated to another beer, whch he feared, for if he lost his bearings amongst these criminals he would be lost. He pretended to drink,foamed at the mouth and that was all.

"Ave we got a job fer you, me bye," said a bearded man with a high brow forehad, drooping moustache and hands that shook. "He lives just a bump and a hip down the main street where we are at. He works the midnight shift at theTranscola Mine. Wife and three kids, all in school. Just his house, that's all were all after. Take it down."

"I've a better proposition, 'gainst a breaker boss in Summit Hill. Seems he wants to trade his men for a higher wage from the company, layed off two just yesterday. I need to take are o' him;."

Yellow Jack Donahue sighed, looked sharply at the new recruit to the Molies and said no more.

"I got other men can do the job, McKenna, thanks."

"Aye, there's the bye, smart stiff, hard fisted with Irish pride in a job well done.. Lemme help you a bit, me man," said a second advisor at the bar, he with a wave gold hair, black hat and a vest with a jade cravat, though he didna look like he had ever stepped onto a ore car or gone down a shaft before. Yet he was a Mollie, for sure. "I'll use the kerosene he keeps in a barrel behind his house…his, ye understand, not the company's…splash it around aplenty, along the ground like a long fuse to the house. And make with a ladder to slosh some atope the shingles wouldna do no harm."

"Sounds like a easy job." McParlan replied. "Next time maybe we can...coordinate." His good sense had come to his rescue again, a trait for which he was known by both Pinkerton and the Mollies. McKenna explained that he had escaped Lincoln's Civil War draft in '64 by pretending to be fritzy of the mind, even put on a madness act in front of the recruiter for the Continental Army. So he was let go as a prospective solidier in Grant's Army of the Potomac. . It was ten years later, 1873,when he now he had a mission, to burrow like a mole into the Mollies, become one of them, learn their secrets, their plans for murder, mayhem, fires, attacks on mining bosses and bodymasters. They had multiplied, Mollie murderers working in towns where they were not known, firing a home here and there, beating a superintendent, maiming a mine boss, all in the cause of bloody revenge against the "authorities" of the mines and retailiaion against snitches payed off by the mine bosses.

The Civil War as ove but not the bloodletting of the Mollies. McKenna has his assignment, and he had convinced Yellow Jack he was *authentic* by being assigning the firing of a mine boss home. Yet he had slipped the knot of this job and Donohue had appointed another in his place.

"It will be a pushover," McKenna encourased his replacement for the arson job. "Give ye a hint, chicken feathers, her raises chickens for their eggs and feathers, wife does, I seen them, heard Donohue say so. By floating this job to another Mollie, already McKenna had started to undermine the Mollie control. He could counter-order the assignment of a respected murderer.

A pushover...aye, that it is, that it is," came the provoked laugher and Yellow Jack slapped McKenna across his back while the other man drank and enjoyed McKenna's first challenge.

When a man is given a task he hates to perform, and fear mocks his pride and a scolding crimps his energy, he seeks no homage but that of fate, for to flee into the flames of a disaster, even if for himself, alone, is to flee from the fortunes of ones own safety, luck and reputation. ILt would not do to addle a man who fears to perform an unpleasant, if not a dangerous job, for to so so translates into revenge and from revenge to the ultimate agony of retribution which alays in cases of villainy means the falter and collapse of self pride and the image before himself of a man's basic self-confidence .

And so McKenna had become involved in this initial crime, to be performed by another, yet he had had a hand in the planning, and that was crucial to his assignment. His counter-plan had also proved his loyalty to the Mollies as well as the concealment of his fear of exposeure to the Mollies in town. He did not tell Donohue what other plan he had but let the Yellow Jack believe that it involved a murder. Never forget how quickly the hard words passes from man to man when a Mollie had done a job 'right.'

A third man said, as a sort of abettor of the growing darkness, "Ye can fleeinto the woods thereabouts, m; friend. 'Twon't be so hard as ye think." He was talkning now to John McClean, a Mollie of some experience in arson. He had set several breaker fires, but had not yet fired a mine... " And only the old woman is there to look out fer herself...the kids are at school...and she being not a cripple and in her good senses, will flee to safety. We will watch. And when that cursed Super arrives in the mornin, he will know what we Mollies kin carry off to them heathens!"."

Thus duly instructed, admonished and encouraged to perfom his onerous task, arsonist McClean did as instructed. Finding the barrel half-empty, he made a trail tol\ thel house, \with cat's feet he circled the house with pouring from a bucket of the stuff. He found a basket of chicken feathers and placed it near to a corner of the house and saturated the feathers with kerosene, prepared to be ignited like a torch. The entire preparation required an hours to do right. He would have to forget the foor, forl hefound no laddedr. He struck a match, the kerosene quiskly glames, spread along the trail to the lhouse and within miknutes the nouse was stgartilng to burn. He could not be seen and so he fled down a side street that led into an alley opening into the woodsy flat just outside of town. He would go to Summit Hill. McClean possesed experience in methods of escape, that Yellow Jack could count on. McKenna, or his part, faked his concern for the safety of McClean in pulling off "the job." This jpb Donohue saw and understood and applauded McKenna for. The spy never set down details in writing, for to have his notes discovered would mark his end. Besides, he had not only a remarkable memory for details but he was able to convey a man of little discipline, a somewhat disorderly character who had a had time keeping a job, much less finding one. The avaracious Yellow Jack appreciated this rather irresponsible Mollie as a man they could use.

Now that he had he had made a initial entry into Mollie management, which he saw for himself was the only way to undermine their power, McKenna realized that he would travel and ingratiate himself into the *good graces*... "'tis a laugh that...'" of the Mollies in their hotbed in Shenandoah. It was 1874. "Well, I've put it off long enough...." --the very man hired by Mister Gowan of the Phily and Reading railroad and Coal and Iron Company. "He hired us, the *Pinkies* in seventy-three, just last year, to rid the mines of the Mollies gang."

The challenge would be typical of the Mollies, whenever they felt McKenna might be fooling them. "Yer a man, Jimmy McKenna, with cool face and iron stomach. Tell the me where ye was barn, Mister McKenna?" A somewhat short man, handsome of face, long drooping moustache and wearilng a brimmed hat and a cravat, stood and in a few brief sentences identified himself to his new mine boss.

Back in Philadelphia, McKenna had this likely report to make to his Pinkerton overseer. "They'll take a liking to me, since I got me wits without real brains and a stubborn streak to me nature. I find it best to bend and twist with the wind of the circumstances, like a stalk. o' wheat..but I shall bring in what you seek, of course, Mister Pinkerton, I'll report on all the goings on of them scalawags what make brief a honest man's life and turn wages into heaven's holy script, though, they be low. I can promise not to disappoint ye, sahr."
he said, at which moment, Pinkerton saild,
"I'll warrant ye they'll have a time figuring you out," Pinkerton told his recruit. "Ye'll lay low, play detached, find folly in yer own honesty, grow long hair with a crow's nest of a beard, exude memories of the poor Mol;ies whove suffered from mine explosions and one on to thehr Maker...gone in the line of duty. In General, Mister McParlan--now Jimmy *McKenna*--ye'll trade yer fine Irish mind for the madness they admire, those cursed Mollies with their excuses for murder. I'll have no more of that...nor Mister Gowan...his railroad and his mines have suffered great losses....And mind, ye, Jimmy, me good man , niver forget yer Mollie manners, which is to find shooting the fixed table manners of the Mollies and the etiquette from the end of a gun. Fact is, you will most likely be asked on those glorious occasions to murder...to pull the trigger...on a civilian whose crime is to bear the Mollie mark of death, bossism. Resist that temptation, Jimmy, but be such a rowdy, good natured, undependable bastard they won't want to get rid of you and, instead, turn you into the king's jester of the tribe...make no mistake about that. I know their minds. I say these thngs to ye with the sincerity of a Father Confessor. The Mollies find murder the fit penalty for power...some en can be murdered for a farthing.but anger belongs to God and the angels." They both laughed at

this comparison.

A man who enquires into the conscience of another is alway suspect of having a scheme to reveal, a fight with his corrupt mind, if he requires … 'tis a consideration to equip his courage to do a job/ But, McKenna, do be careful, lest yer hands deceive yer brain and ye fail to acquit yerself o' yer promise. Duty is slack to some men, rigid to others. In the Mollie tribe, life is warfare with its leader, Donohue and its hideout Malonoy City.   To a criminal. McKenna, me man, loyalty is everything, especially his survival. in the jungle of pededatory revenge. " Whelan had delivered his sermon for survival in the Mollies.

Let it be known how they operate, the Mollies avoided the Civil War Draft in 1864--when the Patomac Army was running short of soldiers. Some mine bosses had had their mines shut down by armed Nohern soldiers until recruit quotas were met by the government. That did not aid mine supervisors and bosses who appeared to comply with the Federal mandate. In this way, they became men maked for death by the Mollies, murder becoming savagely and inexplicably mixed with patriotism Generally, the Mollies held no liking for the Southern cause, but they bore the scent of danger and the rage of the blast, those Mollies. What they did not give to the war against the States they gave to mine superintendants and bosses-- they beat them up something awful at times, even killing the worst-hated of them. These things Pinkerton heard tell of in the saloons of Shenandoah.

And when Gowan, the lawyer, had come to his office, he was regaled with numerous stories of beatings, arson, shootings and other mahem to make the anthracite coal mining less profitable than they actually were, a major resource for millions in their homes, shops, on therailroad and in burgeoning New England factories. Moving from town to town, McKenna had learned well what was happening in the mining communities of Pennslvania. The Mollies, when they took a notion, would beat up on any owners of the mines, if they could identify them, and on mine bosses, the which naturally included superintendents. No two ways about that, there was no love lost. The Mollies had shown that they were a law unto themselves. They were the anarchists sof the seventeenth century in America, abrood of vipers who followed the only law they knew, murder as retribution for imagined and often real abuses of miners, themselves victims of a poor technology and the greed of company owners.

In Dublin, the Grand Mayor was enjoying a sip of old Irish henna when a womal named *Molly Maguire* walked in. Her hair was tangled, her eyes deep for lack of sleep, her hands nervous and her hidden beauty obscured by the frown of anger.

"I'm not a lookin' for me husband," she announced. There were about a dozen saloon climate addicts of the old school, warming their hams by the hearth-fire and their steeping their gullets with fine Irish whsiskey. Whilest seated there they overheard her. The fire in the pub was ablaze. Men seldom gather to hear good news, they congregate for the bad, the loathsome and the fearful. Her message was none of these. She sought vengeance with a *whip and a flail of her tonue*, as the saying went.

"Well now, me good woman," replied he Mayor, "what ails ye ails us, gentlemen of the auld sod."

"You canna talk but abou what happened, 'tis no jest or gossip, sirs."

"We understand, m' lady. Proceed."

"Me name's Molly Maguire and 'tis the name of me proud parents...and though I not be a damned Brit, I'm as fit as any soul for excitement."

Well, sirs," 'tis the Mayor speakin; now--"this here British Lout comes up to me and he says, says he..."Sit ye down first, Molly, and don't tag along like them other stones, a plavin' about Britlsh manners. " This Harv, he was the leader of the commutation of the pub.

"So she sat, and she went on with what she told to her favorites of the old saloon, o'East Dublin. 'T was her story...."

"I be behind but two months in me rent, and washin I take in don't bring my quarter up to the line."

"Aye, we rightly understand ye," says the major domo of the heap, three, maybe four taking a ear to her story.

He says, ter me, he says, like I was his broom pan. ".... 'If ye don't pay me, I'm going to have to rough ye up a bit.' He says this to me, a layde of old Irish stock, though I not be highborn like some of them pussy dames around London with their airs....But hesays, s ays he, this blueblooded fart on a three-legged stool, let me first give ye the solemn wahrning, that tis not yer Catholic scrapings that bother me and enflame me rage to throw yer skirt out of me house bit 'is yer thnking yerself a mendicant of the faith that twist m' purse so. LI'll out with ye in a fortnight, dame rascal of thetub." Such high faluttin talk I never did hear e'n in the scurviest o pubs."

"We discharged he Pope two-hndred years ago, madam."

"So tis because I'm a Catholic yer raising all this ruckus."

"Ye put it mildly, Mizz Maguire....and a fair pleading for a public whore."

":Well then, look out fer yer skin, ol' moneybags, because I'm defending the faith ...and meself 'longside."

"Aye, I thought ye had a smattering of royal piss in ye, and ;tis a shame, because all them Brits an't worth a fools bleat when it comes to religion." With this remark she smacked that landlord square in his face with her tallywag abacus...she'd bough it to sum her bill for pub ale...and then she scattered the drunken loons and she hefted poker iron from the fireplace and raised it against him, her British landlord. "... If some of the drinking gents there had na riz up to defend the Brit--and he was all boot and slicker of him a Englishman--why she'd have kilt him right then and there,by God.

"'He says them things to you;...bein' a woman."

"Aye, that he does, ye just heard him...and I'm thinking, if me husband were still on this earth and heard such witchery and bloody mouthing, from this bloke that scapegrace of English manners, he'd stir up a bloody brawl on his hands, let me tell y."

"Well, we understand ye well, m'am   Yer not so high barn that chief o the ciserns is gonna report ye to he Crowns of England and have all them rapscallions down on yer little pad,"

"No," this landowner, still in his frothy uppers, he says, bold and brave and sassy he says, like a damnd British toad always ready to hop,   " 'I will send a lady over to. Yer cottage to...lend a ear, , to hear yer troubles, but meantime I be compelled," he said, to remove all me furniture so I don't want ever to come back agin."

"Those wahr his insultin words ?" a stranger asked.

"Aye, that they were ...and mare...he says, if ye don' find a way to make rent on the land that's mine by the Kings title, I'll have ye thrown into debtor's prison and that'll be the end of ye, right smart and quick...an no spalpeen o' Irish folly will stop me. 'Tis me land, fee simple and sure. I hav got a paper fom the King, right here in m' vest." amd he pounded his chest like a trained ape.

"Bloody, like he was God and owned the whole earth, tide, winds and sod. Ye hear that lads? A defender of womaood at the hearth who had taken in the hull tale, spoke out in defense of his Mizz Mcguire.

Molly went on. "First he says its me rent, then me Catholic faith, God protect me life, the one being the excuse for the other. "

Atthis crisis, a true getleman befoe the flame stands up, his ale mug in his hand and he says, "This hyer woman has a good cause for a fight, and all Irishmen are ready for a fight when it comes to rights o' land and life and good things. Hear ye, this ma'm, we aren't jes sittin here sipping our ale without a soul or a care or caution. We will play the part of the Hibernians of old Ireland. We will fight fer the cause of a hearth and home fer this here lady, and others like her--the spirit remains the same, the sceneshifts toPennsylvania coal country--besmirched by them accursed mine bosses and owners of God's good coal who cannot afford a decent wage down in the hole for us:" The nippers listin in to the talk by one of theirs all shouted their cheers to Missus Molly Maguire. They all, as a body, rose up and were about to storm the landlords, carcasses and all like Molly of Ulster County who protected her cottag\e against against arrest, when the barkeep entered, and asked, in a most graciously polite manner, like the way of the King's footman, by Gor, to leave his establishment as she was the cause of trouble, and so she left. . They wished her well. They also knew their words were not empty blatherings of idiots but of good Irishmen who knew justice when its light shone in their window..

"Listen lads, this hyere Molly is in great difficulty and we might do something about it." There came a chorus of manly voices and pounding of fists and such like and I knowed we was ready to defend this fine spoke of Irish beauty. Molly stood only five feet, four, was a lovely round at the hips, but had the prettiest face, clear skin, hair black as Dorchester Coal. So this fellow, name was Harv O'Malley. Harv O'Malley, he 'courages the others there but Molly, she wanted to keep her reins in hand lest the landlord punish her for offspringing at his plot, which mongst them British Lards is a thing to rise 'm into a high dugeon. So, we waits and she says, now she says, "Now, wait fer me signal," like she was real ready to go fer a fight. "I got me own plans. And thank ye for the rye, gentlemen. You have the spirit of oauld Ireland, sure 'nough, sure's Molly's barn a fightin' lass...." With that she left. We followed Molly ag a distance to her cottage, which was nothing to mutter about, on the east side out skis o' Dublin, it was. and she had washing hung out to the Irish afternoon sun. Wall, sires, that ignorant Englishj bloke, dared his threat with English stuffing, come over, sent his agent over to Molly Maguire's house and yet...y' won't believe this, sirs, but that that agent was a woman, me thinks she was a man in womans clothes, and \she roughed this Molly up somewhat awsome, give her a bad blue face and cuts round her eyes and mahap a broken nose, she did, because she was back in her rent by two months. Well, I knowd now why she did not show up, not until the Constable come in one night about a fortnight later and he says to her, he says, shaking his head something awful, I would na have believed it if I had not heard it from her it with me own ears."

Molly was good to her word, she had a plan all right. Her husband, God love his soul, was a poacher of squirrels, retired from the racket, but she kept his poaching gun, and when that British bloke showed up, she shot him with quail-shot right in his face\...Stra\ght-forward lady, that. Gawd, that must've been a awful sight, blood and that Brits face scattered around her outside porch. I don't expect her to come ere again, for she's wanted now on a charge o' murder. Not ever body knows who she is, so you blokes keep yer lids on, no talking, no pointing the fingers excepting for another glass o' ale, understand me?" There came a chorus of agreement this night in the **Rock O Eire Tavern**, when Harv learned what had happened from a police mate of is. She shot him, right in; the face! Gawd what a insult to the holy Crown of England. He threatened her for her religion...and her chattels, her boot. Why, he's made a small fortune selling them! What ever become of common British courtesy and the dignity of a parson at dinner, let me remind you fellows. Smythe, put another log on the flames, would ye."

These good-hearted Irishmen, enjoying their ale, heard Molly's sad story and it angered then not a little, by Gor. They thought long about it, maybe two, three weeks, didna say much but a body could tell they was squirmin' with the story of Molly Magure's plight and the cursed British taking a hold of her skirts and thrashing her with what she did not deserve. That very night Molly, late as the tavern hours go, paid a visit to the **Rock O Eire**—she had no place to go, could not return since the Scotties had the coppers on her trail, and she wanted a a place to stay--like a poor bitch dog out in the rain, she was. Our barkeep, bless his soul, said to this forlorn lass named Molly Maguire,

"Molly, I know yer troubles, and I seen many meself and I fought the police once. And many a battle 'gainst the British 'vaders. When I first come to Dublin from Old Kilarney, I looked like a tramp and I argued with one of them Scotties. I spent ten days in the skillet but it was worth it because me and my brother--I call him that-- from Kilalrney... he was the chief constable at the desk ...we became friends over a game of gin rummy in me locked cell, of course. He was a real bagger, that bloke. But a feller, whose name I donna remember put me up till I could manage to come here to work at the **Slanting Light Saloon**. And though it war no blood spilt in me case, it were hard for a begining. "

"'Well, sir,' she said, this Molly Maguire, she said 'I know I'm wanted, but I call ye me brothers and ask ye to help me out...to do something 'gainst them British pissy cats call themselves the English lions, fer I have me husband's poaching gun still in me hand and I know how to use it like a stirrin stick, and I aim to take out one er two of England's finest,. now that I've made me start. They'll regret them two months of due rent like they was a farthing of rent money when I be done with me wishes , fer Molly Maguire is not one to lay down on me retributions, pitch me that one, gentlemen of the auld sod:"

These words ere spoken like a true spirit of the Ancient Hibernians. And so the Irish Mollies began there in Dublin in the *Slanting Light Saloon*. Truth was they didna always know where Dublin ended and the rest of the world began, fer many a true son of old Ireland went to the new world to make his living and as circumstances would have it, there went with them like Patty's shadow the reputatuion of that woman who changed the face of a arrogant Brit trying to collect his rent and put a curse on her faith, he did...though he wast not a tither but, he was trying to collect his blood money, that' s what, and so she done him well by killing him, for it left the collection in the hands of English royalty, bless me if it didna...fer what is the Crown but fee collectors of us Irish to presrve their high-born ways, old braid,c ariages, French wine and English lace., drink to that, lads. But I cannot tell y' how far this will go when the circumstances change to America. No, sire, I cannot tell ye a thin at all."

Well. just as that Harv O'Malley chap figured, the Mollies did come to America and in them days, there was plenty a Brits in New England to stand up for the crown though they be in their new country.   I know well what yere a-thinking, me friends--that we was trouble makers, but ken ye the sitiation in Ireland, then take them hearaches and hurt inter the New World, and ye've got a potion that'd kill any English lion and put to sleep the gods of Irish chance, let me tell ye. but thayers little to go on in Ameriica. Now ye come to the interesting part, a constable of the village of Hampshire...we be in America this day, he is doing the talking. And he be not one of them arrogant British blokes but a true leaf from the Irish clover. His name is Alan Pinkerton, Detective , and he's in charge of a bunch of men who call themselves the Pinkertons...name of the chap who begun a detective agency. Well mind ye, they was some shooting on in the coal fields a Pennsylvania...had the folks in the hills terrorized with all the bloodletting and gunfire that were done, killings that went on in the name of the Mollies. Let me regale you with more of this group's hist\ory. 'Twas a danger to walk the streets of any coal town back then, for a man could be shot by talking to a Molly, or mistaken fer a Molly. Bend yer ears lads, we've got a roaring, dangerous fight on our hands, and the more you know about the Mollies, the better we'll be able to proceed." He took a sip of tea and a generous bite from his apple tart.

Picture dingy hills with broken and thnning pines rising above, and on stilts, shanties, small houses precariously perched, and along the street, houses, small bungalows covered with coal dust from the breaker of years gone past, and why would anyone paint his house? A broken board fence keeps in the dogs and kids, washing here and there on the line turns gray before it's dried, and an old man on a cane and some rowdy kids on the sidewalk seem like the only life around, the street with broken pavement and recent rain water filling the potholes, a tin livery wagon drawn by a dappled gray headed up the street, the horse in the freezing weather steaming its way upgrade.   Lord only knows where its heading. This is the town of Carbon, and righly named,it was, since soot covers well nigh everthing and when a man takes off his hat at night they's a soot line where his head was covered, separating his face. Down the street a tad there's the country store, sells food and household needs, cleaning things, mops, soap and such. Miners use their pay before they get it to keep in their hands, deductions for the month in rent and life's necessaries to keep their homes runnin. A company store takes pretty near all a man earns down in the mines. Well, in just such a setting the Molly Maguire rage crept over the Allegheny landscape and into the homes and hearts of good solid men of the community. They found a ways to revenge their small pay, which, mind you, was less than a dollar a day, wages such that a Chinaman could count on. This was what fired their revenge against mine superintendents, mine bosses all along for the eight years the Mollies were active. A miner could go from one town to the next and there wouldn't be a tad of difference, except maybe some mothers and wives would try to grow a little color in their window boxes or sport a bright hat or dress their kids in colorfful shirts. But otherwise it was coal-soot gray all round. And the sound of that damned breaker morning, noon and night, cracking coal for the rich mine owners without the government bothering to 'spect things what was going on.

Revenge was the motive imported from Ireland to the Pennsylvania coal fields and evident in labor riots. We referred to Mollies as members of their secret fraternal Ancient Order of the Hibernians, which \have come to take the name of the outstanding Irish washerwoman named Mollie Maguire, who, God preserve us, killed her British landlord and set the stamp and scale for our troubles here in the their new country of America. .

"We have had out hands full nowadays, Sargent, with labor trouble in the mines. Me brother was shot in Suskyll by a State Trooper, them bastards bring in the artillery to do their fighting....the supers of the mines I mean." We had this frightening chatter in the office of the Chief of the Shenandoah Police, who roamed the hills like varmints and knew what a man wanted when he carried a gun. Those were the times. And so they were on the lookout for Mollies, remembering the Molly Maguire who fought off a man dressed in a woman's rags. Aye, there was hell to pay. Well, this is how the Sargent Detective, he was all of that, with three stripes on his tucker. He says to his men, and they was all Pinkertons men, at that.

"We got a fight on our hands. These Mollies think they're a law unto themselves. and so far they've proved it. But I've got gladnews fer them, and for any of you put to chase them dogs across the river. We've got the arms, we got the stuffin and we got the sight o' heaven on ever round we shoot, 'cause we don't care none 'boutl dyin when the cause is right."

There were about thirty of them Pinkies, I call 'em, chanted to that refrain, :"leave it to the Pinkies…!" bless me Irish Paters. They gave a murmur of assent to this assessment. A handful of them had come from mining communities and knew the witchery of the Hibernians and the bloodletting of labor-strikes over low wages, fifty cents per day in some coal regions. It was no secret to them that the Hibernians were no man's fool and that labor superintendents and mine bosses were out to make at killing for their owners in coal prices at the expense of the men who dug it out by measured quotas and watched their families half-starve for want of better pay.

"Aye, and me brother in Hempstead Mines is jammed in fer life by his job...pays most of his check to the company store, he does."

"Thats the root of the kill, gents, the grip of the lines on the miner so as he can scarcely breathe, buy milk for his babes and clothes for his school kith."

"They're obligated to deal with company stores," came another voice.

"Deeper and deeper into debt," came yet another comment among these gathered trouble-searchers.

The Sargent spoke next. Sure and there's endless enmity between mine officials and the miners for these causes, chiefly the stores and low wages."

A man who wheezed spoke up next. Black dust I breathed in for twenty years. If it were not for Pinkerton, I'd be dead."

"Well, God's mercy on you, my friend," said another detective.

The Sargent went on. "Mine conditions became so intolerable that the miners in Schuylkill, Mahonoy City, Oakdale, some of the miners have taken matters into their own hands. Goes back to Ireland. Our brothers there held loaded arms over the heads of the dastardly landlords. Aye, me friends, the price of a piece of bread and a chip of land to lay your weary head on was almost far out of reach for them lads."

There's more trouble afoot, since the Irish--and we're of their kind--pick a fight to find cause to rub out the enemy. And who be they? Usually the English, at times the Welsh and Germans for not cooperatingt....they get in theway of strlkes forfmore money...or work on as scabs. I tell ye my friends, if it warn't for the fists of Irish miners and the weeping of their little ones and the cries of their women there would be no trouble at all and things would never get out of hand. Our secretary here can read the record." He took another sip and a bite from his tart.

The man referred to as the secretary, with a small Irish flag on his vest put in his word. "Tayke 1872 fahr instance, powerful interests seized the anthrax coal fields in Western Pennsylvania -- ye know what that country is like, some of ye--and lawlessnes ran amuck with low wages as always and newcomers following the will of the Mollies. Oh, the record is clare, gents, the Mollies, the Hinbernians, follow their own rules and ways, let me tell ye.

The sargeant had to agree Coal barons stomp on good Irish labor to get their blood money, let me tell you, so folks in New England can have their winters comfy without a thought to us Irish grinders down in the mines."

A Lieutenant, until now silent, spoke up. "Them companies hired scabs, they did when the miners struck for a day's honest pay, not fifty-nine cents, by Gor, what would buy not a quart of milk from the company store. Well, I led one of them gangs, we formed up, we did, to fight the Barons and their low wages and particularly them scabs, hired to keep the coal coming for their profits, they did. In seventy-five, a mob of about a hundred stopped work in Mahonoy City, they did, at the Shenandoah, the same, derailed a night passenger train. The miners, aye and I was one of them, torched a breaker at Carmel, shot two contractors at Oakdale a few days later. It was hot and bloody, by Gor, and costing the Bosses who hired scabs to meet contracts for amount of coal. It was not a lovely sight. The facing off of the miners came when the companies hired possees on the engines that preceded passenger trains through the mining districts.

Another Agency man, small, wiry and graying spoke up, talked about his experience with the Mollies. "On the Philadelphia and Reading railroad," he said, "switchmen, watchmen, agents were beaten and the switches changed, the tracks obstructed--all to keep the coal trains from comin through. Aye, I knew it fer a fact that this railraod was a asset of the coal barons, since it took coal to market as well as passengers to others destinations."

The Sargent spoke up. "Well, we have trouble on our hands, for cartain, gentlemen. The Mollies have dictate to the superintendents who they want hired and fired. And the Irish who've come to America have had it worse'n broken-down breaker. They're takin a long and hard time sorting out their feelings of the situation.

ii

The year was 1874, just last year, when McKenna dropoped to the crowed plaform at the train station in Philadelphia . He had come here to Pennsylvania to work in the mines. He had met and we and Attorney Gowan and Alan Piukerton, of that eminent detective agency, had talked ove the situation of repeated brutal violence and murder in the anthracite mines of Eastern Pennsylvania. N'er-do-well McKenna was planning to become one of the murders, the brutalizers of mine officials. He had already put on the disguise of a Molly--disheveled wavy black hair and bearded, a disguise of fakery, and a searching glance that somehow communicated trouble and a hands-off approach. His was a study in intentional irresolution and wayward behavior, the appearance of irresponsibility attempting to appear one of the respectable townsmen of Carbon in this small community of Pennsylvania, inshort, a Mollie and not to be trusted. His appearance and conduct combined elegance and the suggestion of torn roots, a displaced person dressed in a black hat, bow tie and the hands of an idler which , at present, he could not disguise.

"Where you headed?" a stranger voice asked him.

"I come to join me brother,."   McKenna lied in a convincing way, for although not every Hibernian was a Mollie, ever Mollie was a Hibernan, a member of that ancient brotherhood order of Irish rebels against British overlords. He would in time perfect the acceptable lie of the steady eyes and frozen features of his face. His compatriots accepted that God was part Irish; only they knew that therefore only God could read his mind.

"Come with me, then, we be expecting ye. One of our brothers told us about y'. Year a man of gumption and good faire. Kin ye lift a toast to a Molly Maguire with ease?"

"Aye, that I can," spy McKenna replied.

He seated himself into a two-man horse cart at the station in Carbon and away they went to where there was a gathering at a small hutch of a house on the outskirts of this coal-dusted village, McKenna had arried in town sto observe certain activities sof the Mollies, wherever he should dredge them up, mingle with and interlope into their tight-lipped little gatherings. He was thent to warn Pinkerton of any coming events, as the saying went, *festivities* of sabotage and embrogios and violence and the like. After all, every Irishman knew that their blood celebrated death with a carnival of games, tossing the tabor, flinging the stone, dancing and the like. But he had a deeper job, down into the mines, of experience and trouble, as ye might say. McKenna, the spy, was "ter undermine them Mollies, don't y know, their plans, but he was also to use his brains to avoid being exploded, as the saying went…which translated into… exploited but exploded will do. That were closer to the mark."

"Wha brings y' way out here?" his compariot asked me along the way.

"I be desperate fer work and I hert the mines was the best way to go, don't y' know. Minin' is a hard thing to begin with, so ye might as well find a good job in a good circumstance."

The Mollie assined to pick up McKenna at the Carbon station looked at the newcomer with a kind of odd squint… like the new arrival had sprouted corn in his ears, but he said nothing. The spy was ready to sign in with them in order "to keep me poor mither and babes in food back in Colorado." No old hymn of wealth was lhe to sing, for he did rue the devil--and the world knew it--that the Irish need more than luck in Colorado. "Aye, they've mines there," said his driver, " and good anthracite s coal it is, too, but the miners haven't learned to tell a jack from a ace of spades when it comes to fightin' fer a good day's pay down in the shaft. If yer a fightin' man, , ye've come to the right place," he boasted. They spoke not another word until they arrived at theshack.

"Now let me tell ye right off, there's many coal town here in Pennsylvania, Auburn, Pinegrove, Tremont, Newtown, Schuylkill Haven, Middle Creek…then there's Donaldson, Raousch Creek and Tower City…aye, they're a pack of them and all mining coal.? He finally told McKenna his name…Clyde , He was a winner, he knew all about everyone of those towns.

Like it was told to McKenna, there was a gathering…a gathering to a rebel Irishman can mean trouble, for it meant either to pray, play or to lynch. They stood as if on wires, loudly bellowing greetings with a sharp clap or two to greet their spy in residence, aka McKenna, Mollie extraordinary, or what they had yet gain--a suspicion, sniffing like a dog in a hog pen. Why he should be so hardily welcomed he did not know until he learned tit had been bruited about that he was an expert in explosives. This skill bore the same honorarium as a celebration for a Dublin Mayor. The railroad would funishs the dysamite.

McKenna's escort invited him to give a speech, and he did the same. "All ye good Maguires, let us not fergit our…landlords." There issued a wild cheer from the assembly, a rattle of tankard lids and a one-pound pewter tankard thrust into his hands. McKenna responded by saying, "I heard Broad Mountain is yer stronghold."

":Aye, that it is," said his host…a ball of a little man with arms as long as his legs and a face like a ruined crumpet…"and likely, too, every Mollie is a kissing member of the Order of the Hibernians, though, let me warn ye and ever one of ye scouts out there, not ever member of the Ancient Order is a Mollie." The pub crowd raised their tankards and fell into disaray; for they were not capable of clewing to each other for longer than one refill of scrungy potato beer, not these devils of disaray and disruption. They knew their enemy and his name was boss and his work was depression, deprivation and coal dust.

Things went along right well. The next day, McKenna was taken down into the Colbert mine, a tour ye might say. Then the badge'master assigned him a tin number off the rack and he became one of the miners. He be a working miner back in Colorado, and so he worked down in the shaft at Carbon, hearing the miners grumble about their wages...which were seventy-five cents a day. May the good Lard bless them all, and bottle their sweat for His angels, "that weren't enough to putty a broke jug, it warn't, and most of that went to the company store in Carbon." The pit super had McKenna's work cut out for him now. He was offended by the scrabbling wage but careful of the Mollies, ye might say, some wast German, a Welshman or two. He didn't not stop to sort 'em out. He listened to o thir complaints with a sensitive ear, between metallic lblows of the mail on the pike, he caught many awhispered agony. Once, in the poor candle light down at the bottom of the shaft, the maul misstruck the head of the pike, yet drew blood from the pikesman's hand. Still , he went on with his work, for if he stopped to nurse a broken or bloody hand, he would lose his Chinese wages for the rest of the day. McKenna saw this and commiserated in stoney silence.

McKenna told his host, who'd put him up until he found a place, that jr thought he might move on to a more tidier place than Carbon--"me mither taught me to fear dirt." And so it was. She would roll in her grave if she knowed I was a coal miner. But that's the way life spins out a' times. Me midwife was a cleaner dame than me mither in that coal town.""

The miners at the end of his shift tipped their bonnets and said goodbye to McKenna, for they were mighty sorry to see such a hail good chap depart, Lor bless 'm, a Mollie strung true to the Hibernian tune by the hand of God. Huzzah, huzzah!" Next week found the spy ensconced in Pottsville, to which town he walked most of the way. McKenna wrote to Pinkerton, dropping his letter into the Horse-Carrier for the United States Post office at sthe railroad tracks in Carbon : "I could no' afford a horse. I was given a lift by a feller in a wagon loaded with small barrels of moonshine he called milk he had dropped off at the Carbon Constabulary, whatever the devil that meant. Their booze and their politics is mixed in coal country. I knowed that there were no cendary action in Carbon, not for now...and I had not yet seen a cow in a pasture in the town, though some folks might have kept a cow to beat the price of milk at the company store. Anyway, this bloke, he tells me--his name I don't recall right off-- he was in the jar for shoving *queer*--that's counterfeit money--he and me we hit it off right smart. He belonged he said to the Order of the Hibernians at Buffalo but here he was in Pennsylvania, he sayed he'd not return for fear of being discovered as a murderer and counterfeiter. Well, now I was getting someplace. I was gettin in touch with the soul of the Mollies, which was a part of me mission. He was supporting the Mollies with his counterfeit paper...for what purpose I was yet to larn, for they were active to steal gun powder from the railroad, and fer guns and ammunition --collect bills of charity yet cover them with comon grace...one a orphanage.

From this meeting grew the assignment described, in which the new recruit, McParlan, alias, McKenna, was chosen to set fire to the house of a mine boss, but he was able to slough it off onto another Mollie named McClean. And he did a fine job, clean and without whiskers, as the saysing went. Now McKenna was enmeshed in this most violent tribal war of the anthracite mines.

The Mollies held meeting whenever there was a job to be done, like a shooting, coffin letters to selected bosses and days off from the hole to protest. McKnna's work as a secretery gave him excuses to travel about for the pinkies. He was grateful lfor the appointment.   For a while He worked in the Suderman Mine, hacking coal from a eighteen inch seam, not a man grumbled this time, since the work left no energy to do much else but cut and shovel coal all day long.

Being appointed Secretary in the small coal town of Carbon, McKenna had to stay in touch with the different branches of the Hibernians, which meant travel. He got himself a gig, a mall cart with a roof for the heavy rains in Keystone County , and a dapple horse she warn't much good but to travel him about. It was safer on the open road than on a train, and, besides, where he got the money of course, nugt've caused some whiskers to rise….McKenna received his pay from Pinkerton…he was to be a Mollie in Shaunessy's saloon… a counterfeiter…and that seemed to settle the question of source for his folding money. At least that alibi did alay suspicion. So a pony cart, he called it, there he was, traveling about the countryside like a doctor making house calls.

A silent Pinkerton told him in a letter at General Delivery by way of the Pottsville Post Office, he was to watch carefully for Mollies who shot double-barrel shotguns at engineers from ambush alon the tracks from Carbon to Schuylkill Haven. When he heard about this he was livid. To gun down a defenseless man was the height of cowardice. This gave him a fresh insight into the Mollie :Maguire mental trappings, since the hereintofore revenge and anguish over long hours in the dark, coal dust, no ventillation, black lung, and company-store debts had been the achieving reasons for the Mollie anger.   Such a tactic by the Mollies as ambush of a train enginneer was not only cowardly but inhuman and of inequitable and dangerous "exchange of a man's life for a buckt of coal!"

There was one Mollie who was notorious among them all, and that was Jack Kehoe. McKenna was well aware that his residence in Shenandoah was connected to petty thievery assault, arson of breakers, mine bosses houses, and Coffin letters sent to authority figures, mine bosses and superintendents in general, that warned them against retaliation opposing the Mollies. McKenna had heard such talk in a cheap-down saloon in the town, set upon stilts above the main road, there being a stables and a coal shed on the lower road under the saloon. When the grog was flowing strong and the miners were letting off steam was when McKenna heard about these letters, signed with a skull and crossbones and intended to be real personal and dangerous to the recipient. No mining boss ever took one of those letters lightly. When he ,himself, received one of these coffin letters, McKenna called a pow-wow of "my fellow allies" at Kehoe's house. He told his brother Hibernians over grog at the *Stilts Saloon* that he had gotten "a skull and crossbones threat last night," He showed the Mollies his coffin letter. It warned him against taking sides with mine bosses. That was the worst of the crimes charged against him. . "Ye see this here scar on me forehead? It were not a birthmark, no sire, brothers. When I was a little younger, them Mollies surrounded our house...they thought me Pa was a superintendent, and they wanted to force him out to club and shoot him to death…like thet there slave owner in the Civil War.   It didn't happen\ because he was absent that day, thank the good Lawrd, for they would a called it a good business day if they had done what they come to our house to do." McKenna showed the letter He had received in the mail , a letter to the Hibernians, and they laughed and said it was to in form me that the Mollies issue invitations like regular folks, but that I, being a secretary and a good Mollie meself, was exempt. They--and the sender kept his face hid--simply wanted me to know what was their method of operation, for two of them in our tribe confessed to our secret meeting--all the Mollie meeting was secret--a :La Cross Superintendent in Shenandoah was targeted for penalizing a miner coming down into the hole late. That Boss be a lying in; his coffin right this night ..the *Roadside Tavern* clan gleaned the story about McKenna's Pa gettin a warning. He told them he understood such goings on "from me own experience. " This niht at the *Stilts Saloon*, this meeting was to be a general business meeting, for now the Mollies had pegged me as a scatter-brained kind of bloke… dependable but no fist in me mouth, not for Jimmy McKenna, "Well, let me inform ye bretheren, that coffin notices of skull and crossbones come up, like leaves in the wind, to warn a party to leave the community or become executed. I can tell ye it happened more 'n once". He told them straight out and proceeded o get drunk to cover his intelligence.

There was lawlessness, aplenty in Schuylskill, Carbon and Northumberland, right near to where we sit. Most of the terrorizing violence was done by the Mollie Maguires. Eight showed up. There was mood lightner passed around and some of the best in the county's armory of moonshiner whiskey. McKenna demurred, said it gave him a ore-hammering headache when I drank while cogitating violence…a true test of his loyalty!   He confessed to his bretheren he was wild enough without the booze. When men of violence gather, they tend to want to share their better natures to offset guilt feelings for having done wrong. It's natural. Spy McKenna knew hat truth of mahemandinsolence and ravishment of another man's life and family.

This was a strange meeting for McKenna , since miners and their associates considered him to be shiftless, not long on any one job, a bloke who hated mining but had to make a living somehow. The fact that they saw he had money was dismissed by his excuse that he was a counterfeiter. He made out that the Hibernian Society could afford a good secretary, if no other officer, and so the Mollies accepted his alibis. His instability combined with his seeming affluence no longer aroused suspicion, but he had managed to explain the contradiction.   So Jimmy McKenna moved around, thus he let it be known there would occur another meeting at the *Stilts Saloon*--so it was called for the reason of the saloon's location on a hill, one side supportsed by unmilled trees..
    An Irish Pinkerton man with a full beard and black hat called at the roomin house where McKenna had put up. He showed the spy-operative his effectual badge.
    ""Come in, come on in, brother," McKenna addressed him. "We Mollies have got to stick together!" N|McKenna said in loud tones and shut the door.
    "My names McPherson. I come from headquarters. I come to remind you

of how dangerous things can be...what with guns in some Mollies' houses, and a bear hunt for sympathizers. They've got secret signals, McKenna. The boss just wanted you to be on the alert...a hat with a visible hole in the crown means that Mollie is the gunman for a kill. Watch who he mixes with, the superintendent of that perticular mine crew is the marked man. A Mollie who wears a close-cropped beard has assumed the honorable job of clubbing a Boss to death and harming his babes."

"What does that mean...?" McKenna was appalled.

"He waters the milk, he poisons the food somehow. Oh, its risky and inhuman, but consider them what works for fifty cents a hour, their babes are half-starving a times, and the women are crying in tears all night long...."

"You expect me to put a stop...:"

"Look, McKenna, if you know of something in the works, I want you to put a letter on the midnight mail train to Philadelphia--Kelo Steiner works in the mail car. We'll beef up our manpower out here. It will take some doing but you can handle it. Even if they figure we're onto their tricks, that's a start."

"Just havin the slant on them things is not enough...."

"You've got to be the messenger of death, Mc Kenna."

"Meaning....?"

"Warn them ...warn them...the boss families. That's enough...if not just to petect the kids. The Supers are not stupid. They'll take precautions, you can be sure of that. The Mollies have Civil War marksmen, eh. Death is cheap and easly. Ever consider?" The two men shook hands.

"Count me in ...I'll do me best, and... expect a letter in a few days, very soon. There's more than Irish whiskey brewin here in Shenandoah." The Pinkerton operative vanished like smoke in the wind, departing like a phantom.

McKenna heard a horse and wagon pull away from the boarding house. A Secretary of the Mollie Society needed a place to write, did he not, and a sort of settling down. What could be better for a Secretary of the Order than a saloon corner in Shenandoah? .

"Who be ye?" said Mauff Lawler, "in the *Erin go Braugh Saloon* that night. He was the *bodymaster* at the Shenandoah division. Mahoney Valley was squirming with Mollies, as their chief hangout, so to say. Lawler saw that McKenna had made this here coal maining community his headquarters, for it was a crawling nest of Mollies, he saw that right off. "I hear ye say yer name's...McKenna ." said Lawler, keeping his own identity a secret, as did not Mollies in he business of death to mine bosses.

"That it is and a good Irish name it is...Jimmy McKenna." Tonight he was in Shenandoah.

"I wouldn't be too cartain of that if I was you," Lawler warned him.

"And why not? "Tis as good a name as Flaherity and ready to cure any spalpeen of his discourtesy, right off."

"That's what I like to hear...the fightin spirit of us Mollies. I'll drink to that," he told me. We was in the *Erin go Braugh* saloon down in the nugget town of Shenandoah. Mckenna had met up with him at Carbon and his pal at the old *Stilts*

Saloon. "Well, I be the secretary," McKenna told him...I had a official card for identification which McKenna showed him. But his guide, Dormer, when he introduced McKenna to the *bodymaster*, he squinted at McKenna and told him he looked too dirty for heaven and too clean for hell. He needed to freshen up with some coal dust in his crown. He took me by the hands and looked as the palms for calouses, but there were none and he threw them down.

He said to me, "Who are ye, really?" Then here was the *body master*.who came up with a fresh whiskey from the bar. Dormer looked a frightened a tad.

"I'm here to record events," said McKenna. "I aint no spy if thet's what yer a thinking.":

"Thet's yer notion of goodness, not mine." this Dormer fellow says to McKenna. "If ye be not a spy, then yer a renegade."

"Ah, I know to what ye refer. I have not bolted from no crowd, no covy of pidgeons, no herd a squirrels. I got me rights. I be a miner fron Shenandoah."

"Yer hands look like a pussy cats, yer a milk maid by them forks," he said, meaning his hands.

McKenna began to lie in earnest. Amid a brood of vipers it is couth to act like a viper. He lied with a vengeance and skill. He told the inquisitor had left the mine in Shenandoah, " 'most a year ago"...which was a lie, "and I'm here with me new assignment fer as lng as they can use me...minin' for coal is not my idea of salvation. I also make funny money," McKenna added, and gratuitously handed his tablemate a magnificent Civil War note with Abe Lincoln printed on it. I counterfeit...a hobby of mine...keeps me busy most of the time, that and ...Secretery...when not downin the hole."

"By whose say...?" Oh, he were a testy one...meaning *Secretary* of the Mollies.

:"By the say Pat Dormer from Pottsville.: McKenna thought he would try a little flattery. He had learned long ago that no matter what the world thinks, flamboozlers like flattery. He called it "stirrin the brew. in a man's skull."

Dormer's face brightened a little and he said. "Sir, I take all me precautions serious. You being a sportin' Irishman, not a rogue like them mine owners, not a pidgeon like them superintendents....aye, and two contractors were shot in Oakdale just a few days ago."

"They had it comin' to them, what with old cables snapping and the dun of dynamite not goin off and drill bits wore out and the men's wages less than a dollar a day. Fightin to make a quota.... '

"Them scum thought all was fine and dandy, they did," said Dormer. :Gangs have taken up the cudgel, Mister Mc Kenna, and more power to ye if the gangs don't get to the armin of the men first and the violence to harm our wives and babes. Oh, they's a testy lot and vicious howling, snappin' mad dogs, roaming from one mine to the next trying to flush out company recruits for their mayhem, and most don't know a whisker from a gold toothpick when it comes to mining. They re just claiming territory for themselves, Mister McKenna, and ye right well know that I'm sure."

" I do, I do, and ye speak with a good head on yer shoulder, sir, and I keep me eyes on things happinin around the mines...for tis me business as secretery...." The conscience of even the most violent, wayward or scoundrel of men works to their disadvantage at times, to expose them and their skullduggery, and so it had done this night in the *Erin go Braugh Saloon.*

McKenna put on his best shipboard collar, and weaved a bit with fine Irish whiskey, though he was as sober as a toad... fer he knew he was in a squirming lot of Mollies, here in the town of Mahoney Valley. Over all McDuff Lawler was the one bodymaster at the Shenandoah division of the colleries. McKenna put on a good show and escaped with his scalp. This was a bloody business of narrow escapes and clan rivalry, despite the Mollie name. That rivalry, McKenna found, was especiallyv vicious when a Mollie snitched on another Mollie so as to gain approval from his own neighbors, but the warning had gone out and the snitch was liquidated by a shooter from a neighboring town.

Some curators of history may wonder how McKennagot any news back to Pinkerton. He could tell you it warn't so hard as he thought. Every spy has a system to relay information back to the major domo of the operation. McKenna claimed as friends a smart man or two in the railroad business who worked for the mails in the postal railroad cars, where letters from town to town were sorted. One one such name was was George Mahon, a good Irish Catholic. When the two-fifty-one train came through the town in the Pottsburg, McKenna would try to meet him with a letter to be delivered to Pinkerton back in Philadelphia, the last one intelligence all about a Mahaney Valley ruckus...it was a strong-hold just north of Broad Mountain. Scabs took over the mine. McKenna's own coachman, he called him, the letter carrier on the Reading rail line, he delivered this letter in which McKenna described the conditions, generally, of the miners and the scabs at the Mahaney Valley mine and the gangs. He knew right away it was twixt hell and high water that he was to hand McKenna's observations to Pinkerton. Jimmy McKenna had a good grip onto the helve end of the mallet at this point. He had yet to figure out a way to derail the Mollie violence. That was a part of his mission.--no just to warn the would-be victims, to deter the instigators, but to deralil their schemes.

He saw the mobs were out to cause trouble, even a thousand whohad brought work to a stop at the Carbon mine one afternoon. And why was that? It was a strike to force the owner, a Jack named Pitton, British bloke, who wanted the men down in the deep hole to produce more coal and less rock. Well, what was the rock sorter boys for if not to pick rock from coal? They were earning even less than the miners. It were a scramble, I can tell ye, to lay a hand on good common sense.

Iln eery town, Carbon, Pottsbeurg, Shenandoah, Middle Creek, Northumberland, Mahonay Valley, the Mollies he consortgsed with took the spy for a shiftless yet likeable lout,, who bragged about being Secretary of the Mollies \of Hibernia Society, yet had trouble staying on a job down in the shafts and pits for more than a few days or weeks.Ten he would move on. Mollies who looked at the man said he was fired by the superintendent for being drunk or not reporting in on time. The first was for the Lord's forgiving, the second earned condemnation for old-dog laziness. That was a caution, let a man tell you. In Schuylkill Haven McKenna the spy and sometimes miner found for himself a fine roof and a bowl of hot soup and a rack in the town. He came to the fine stone house owned a man named Malvaney, a former Super who, feeling for his miners, joined with them in their fight for better wages. Yet he owned this mansion fit for a squanderous English duke, it was. Most of the furniture he'd sold for cash to pay off company store debts ...of some miners, by Gor, but; here he was...to go to a invited meeting at Lawlers. He was a lawyer as well as a confirmed Mollie in disguise. He selected shrewdly those to surround him, Mollies who did not believe in murder or violence to achieve justice, but in accommodation. Being a landowner, he should have ben a prime target, according to the history of Molly Maguire's fate. But placating Mollies were among his friends. Ont his night,to erase his doubts, he swore in McKenna as a Mollie in good standing, although, still unbeknownst to Lawler, a spy for Pinkerton. The swearing-in was brief. Only ten Mollies came to witness the taking of the Hibernian oath. .

"Do ye take the oath of affirmation and loyalty to the Ancient Order," Lawlers asked McKenna.

"Man, I wouldn't be here if I did not take a shine to yer *bloody* Order" I thought but did not say it.

"It is a noble Order of Ancient time--the Hibernians are them whot made wrack and ruin of the kings in olden times, let me tell you." There were ten of us there to take the swearin in oath, and we did so, amid the scarce upholstered furniture, a broken table and empty dinnerware cupboard, which he had not sold. We would soon be sitting on benches if he redeemed any more miners. He was a fellow with a good heart, though, and I did not blame him for once being a Superintendent.

I said "I do so swear."

He said, "Raise your right hand." He did so. He gandered them scurvies sitting about, Hes suspected why they had all they come to be there--by open invitation like McKenna..

So the spy raised his right hand. He was a lucky one by the devil of the Irish. "To this strong and respected Order do ye 'tach yer kin of soul and yer blood of faith?" McKenna heard and answeed, "I do."

"Do ye think of old Ireland as the best of countries for God's order?"
McKenna said, "I do that, too."

"Do ye wish to God the British would kick in and come to shake our loyal hands?"

McKenna said, "that would be fine if they did.".

"And do ye swear to keep the secrets of the Order?"

Jimmy McKenna said that he would abide but first I had to learn what those secrets were.

"Then do ye swear to keep secret certain duties of the Ancient Order of the Hibernians?" Again McKenna said, "I do so swear."

"Then by the power vested in me, I pronounce you Brother in the Faith and keeper of the secrets of Hibernia."

Jimmy said that he was muchly pleased to be those things.

The Hon. Lawlersm Esq. finished when he said, "'Tis done. my good friend McKenna."

Not just the Master of the Bodies. so called the *bodymaster*, but other members of the order came up to McKenna and shook his hand and said--"*the followers of the Irish way be with ye, Brother Mollie...careless as the winds that blow and wayward as a goat out ter pasture and unpredicatable as the waves on the shore of the Emerald Isle. "* He took these as complements and grinned, for they surely were. The last thing that McKenna wanted was to be pegged as being too smart, over-confident and steady without Irish grog. He wasn't about to marry into the Order but to find our about the Mollies and send his spy details to Pinkerton in Philadelphia. Were it not for F. B. Gowan, a lawyer and wealthy mine owner. himself, and owner of the Reading Coal and Iron Mining Company, coming to Pinkerton with his problem of Mollie violence and troubles , McKenna , already a diligent and productive detective on independent prowl, would not be in this situation. He already had a reputation for dependable work, and had fingered for the Pinkies a number of murderers now behind bars in Philadelphia jails. , while his reputation had recommended itself to Pinkerton.

There occurred a long strike, at a tremendous cost to the coal companies from paniced suppliers, miners being forced to return to work not just by company police but because of the intimate needs of their families. The company always kept iuts sown police foce for...distrubancesand mob conrol...and insurrections. The scene was familiar to the miners and their bosses at the Pinegrove Mine. The local town sheriff and his two deputies, who were also Mollies, did not attempt to break up the violence when one shift met the next coming up from the mines and , sorting out the scabs, layed into them with ball bats, sticks and rocks. Many a head, some fifteen, were, gashed and driven from the shaft headframe back to their homes. There was much angry shouting, curses, the air was thick with angry shouts and open rage and intimidation and courage, as some fought back for their wives and babes. The Mollies, however, took the day, and the mine boss, bloodied, his clothes torn and himself limping was led to a place out of sight, behind a slagheap, where with a gun shot, he was disposed of by an invisble assailant, a murderer. Nobody knew exactly who had pulled the trigger. In his assigned character, McKenna, rushing to the Pinegrove Mine, greeted a club-wielding trio with a loud curse and a boast that he would have done the mine boss in sooner if he had had his chance. This swell-headed boast brought Mollie grins and assents of encouragement. They hung together, these troublemakers, so McKenna had observed. Nobody would identify the murderer. He could not draw the murderer's name from those who knew. He would have to put the mine-boss's name down in his record as having been killed in a mining accident. The irony was clear to the detective from the Pinkerton Agency. A warnings shot sometimes finds sits mark.

At another mine, the Auburn mine, the miners had run out of company script for the purchase of food. McKenna was there, and armed hirelings of the company, with British rifles, aimed at some two-hundred miners on company land. Shots rang out. Two miners fell dead. Their wives and children would not greet them this night or any more. McKenna, stooping over the bloodied forms, found them certifiably dead. He learned that they were both family men. There was a need for police, McKenna saw that. He appointed a non-Mollie captain--his name was Jasper

O'Hara-- to go Philadelphia with the message of impending violence at the Auburn Mine.
. The mob stormed the Auburn Collery and some twentys five of the Pinkerton agents
with Winchesters halted the mob at the gates. McKenna, the snitch, was there, but in the
mob. he could not let himself be identified as a having broug ht in the law. The
Pinkerton men advanced toward the mine head, while close to a hundred miners, sweaty
faces black from the dust of the mine, still wearing their head lanterns, yet armed with
chunks of coal, advanced toward the Agents. The coal flew, the agents fired rounds above
the miners, then advanced with their small shields and billy clubs. There came an open
clash, the sounds of wood on flesh, hard curses, miners falling to the ground, the Agents
taking their blows as well, bloodied faces and hands, scuffling, dragging the miners out of
the fray and handcuffing them. After almost an hour, the Pinkertons restored order. The
mine superintendent was nowhere to be seen. In fact, no collery person of authority had
appeared, their lives being in great danger from the start, and suspected, anyway, of
having called in the Pinkerton men.

There was much confusion of bodies and reasoning that morning.
McKenna's thought was that perhaps he had only excerbated the wrath of the miners,
whose grievances had not been addressed for an entire year. Yet he had, nonetheless,
done his duty as a Pinkerton hireling. Who could know?. It was a miracle hat more of
the miners and the Agency men were not killed. As for the plight of the miners, they had
suffered, some gone hungry, due to the strike the a general panic caused by exhausted
food supplies iln he company store. A man could not work if he was hungry, and the
mine owner, a man named Sorrenson, a Swede, did not appear to understand how hunger
affects a man's work and attitude.

Not a fortnight later, a mob marched to Mahanoy City and they drove off
the sheriff of Schuylkill Country . McKenna had seen this fracas coming. He sent his
warning to Philadelphia as hastily as he could, when he had sniffed out the intent of a
small group of miners to fire he breaker frame . Others, he learned, planned to wagon
their families away from the violence, to abscond from the town to the sanctuary of
relatives outside the coal community. Mollie possees took over the town, they threw
open the jail and released the prisoners, none reckoned as murderers but trouble-makers.
It took the sheriff's appeal to the Pennsylvania Governor to muster a regiment of militia to
restore order at the mines in Mahanoy City. As soon as the militia of about a hundred
men in military dress entered the mine compound, which included the dwellings, a
school, the stores and the like...and they ground into the silence of that aftertnoon in half
a dozen vehicles bearng thearmy white star, the silence of death settled over the
community. Who could tell what might happen. Those miners who still labored in the
dust and dark and damp of the mine did not earn a dollar day, and more was the pity for
not a few would have to quit due to lung black lung disease. That was long before the
owners even thought to take any precautions with ventilation, dust control and sick leave.
Many a miner suffered horribly. For a time felt the Mollies were doing good to fight the
Mine bosses and superintendents of the colleries. On this particular day, the militia did
not fire a round, but, surreptitiously, three miners were put into a truck and the entire
outfit left with a roar and drifts of dust.

McKenna was a witness for George Major of Mahanoy City, who was shot during a disturbance at a fire, set by Molly arsonists, the Pinkerton spy agent was certain.. He fingered one suspect as the would-be assassin, a bloke named Dougherty. He sat at his trialooheld limpromptu, almos vigilanee syle, at the towns courthouse…empty symbol of justice lin those days, where he, McKenna, without revealing his identity in this community, tried to furnish exonerating evidence to conceal his identity. Yet the accused, a Molly named Frank O'Connor, was acquitted. Many a miner thought he was also guilty of that fire to desroy hearsay that McKenna was complicit in arson. .Chief George Major needed to be killed. McKenna had no mind-control and certainly no authority to deter the crime of murder. He could not regulate those who felt O'Connor was guilty of Major's murder. For he had ventured out and was fired upon by Mollies who were, as yet unknown, having escape through the woods. In the hasty court trial, the victims assailants were referred to as *unknown parties*. They escaped. McKenna's testimony as an uninvolved Mollie, was as a character-witness for Major. He wrote, however, in his letter to Alan Pinkerton that he thought Dougherty, the acquitted man, was a the murderer . He had two brothers, Gilliam M.Thomas and Jessie Major, who were the brothers of the murdered man. They could, perhaps, enlighten the Agency as to motive for the murder. Major, a mine boss, had refused to improve on the conditions in the mine.

McKenna sent set the whole story to headquarters , that Michael Clark's hotel in Mahanoy City was where the plotters had met to discuss Major's murder. "Why not postpone the job until Major goes...fishing...make the job look like drunken boating accident." The plotters looked askant at McKenna's suggestion, sniffing the air for favoritsim and grilling him hard with their eyes, behind which he detected a trace of suspicion. So, he said no more at the meeting. There came to this little confab a slink known as John Kehoe. Kehoe urged more mob violence, but; Dougherty blocked it, the suspect. Dougherty said that the murder of the brothers Wm. Thomas and Jessie Major , brother of George Major, would be enough to satisfy the thirst for revenge. McKenna pointed out to Pinkerton how "murder incorporated" had almost no connection to the complaints coming from the colleries' manned by tired and half-starved miners. He sent back that he understood, but law enforcement was his plan in life and he had to obey the law.

Then in the very same hotel, the Clark, where the assassination was plotted, the officers of the Hibernian Order met yet on a different night, a double-murder was planned. McKenna attended the latter assembly. He was astonished to see that the Order members. with murder on their minds and revenge in the souls, opened with prayer. Thomas would be the first of the brothers to go. At this same meeting the question of filling the ranks came up, and Kehoe suggested recruiting 19 to 23 year olds for the killing jobs. McKenna alerted Pinkerton to that prospect, so that his agents could scout around schools and in town for posters that hid the murderous purpose.: *Come join, adventure, excitement and learning*...all promised by the Ancient Order of the Hibernians to gullible youths. McKenna had learned that the violence committed by the

Mollies' were acts almost solely for revenge, lawless criminal murders of retaliation, one leading to the next and so on. The facade, promoted by the Federation of Miner Labor, was intended for better working conditions, higher wages and mine safety. It was a case of the end justifying the means, for the Mollies that meant murder. McKenna realized that the justification lay in the minds of the violent Mollies and not in the law. It was his duty, in order to keep his front in-tact, that he also play a part in the schemed murders. Thus, he warned Thomas of his intended assassination by four Mollies, and that the other brother Majors might elude the Mollies after his, McKenna's, warning. In this way the threat was resolved. McKenna was able to deter more bloodshed by warnings consistent with the secret of life's sanctity, a part of the code of the Hibernian Society. Indeed, the murderous Mollies stood implacably in violation of their Society's secret code of conduct.

McKenna attended a picnic for the Hibernian Society, a more formal and respectful reference.. All was going well with the wives of Mollies and others living it up at this picnic, with good Irish whiskey in abundance. McKenna had an argument. A certain Gomer James was cursing the Mollies for their violence , and telling them they that their crimes did more harm than good. The Pinkerton Agent heard gun shots, saw the crowd gathered around the body of Gomer James and, approaching close, saw that the viction of the gunfire, evidently, had been struck in the chest and fatally wounded. Thomas Hurley, whom McKenna recognized at once from school-days, would you believe it! was there and standing still with a pistol in his hand, which, unmindful of McKenna's presence, he replaced in a shoulder holster. This happened outside the town of Shenandoah, McKenna's boyhood stomping grounds. McKenna ducked out of the crowd with haste least Hurley unmask his identity as McParlan. Mollies on the prowl for vengeance were quick to opick up on mistaken identities, whether used for crime or protection from crime. In eilthr case, McKenna did not want to find himself re-united with an old school mate and associate of a murderer before this crowd of stranger Mollies. He fled, therefore, abandoning the party of drunken Mollies. McKenna reported the murder to the Shenandoah sheriff, as a good Molly should, and he learned that Hurley h ad been ordered by the Society to be killed. He also overheard Hurley boasting of his murder even while the body of his victim, Gomer James, was still warm and was being transpsorted off the picnic grounds. Before I could get away entirely, by a hand signal Mollie Mat Lawlers called me to another table at the same picnic and urged me to go to Giarardville to see Kehoe about the killing.

I knew that the Society would not take Gomer James' death lightly, and who is Hurley?--he ought to pay ..! .This was where McKenna almost tipped his hand. as explained. Hurley ought to be paid five hundred dollars for the "clean job." That was the Mollie Lawlers' attitude. McKenna passed these details along to Pinkerton in Philadelphic, but McKenna came to learn that the money for the "clean job" was never paid, although it was authorized by the Society through Kehoe. . Nor had the murder been particuarly "clean, since at least a dozen witnesses could testify against Hurley in a court of law. The less often a Mollie appeared in court, the better it was for the good health of the Society and the success of their lament against pitifully low wages, violence and mine safety. McKenna supposed that even the Hiberians were feeling the pinch of the panic about that time. McKenna could not tell any outsider how many prominent men in the coal regions met death at the hands of the Mollies. The numbers were hidden in morgue records, delayed discoveries of the bodies, the fear of one for another should the a body snitch, and the inefficiency of the mining-town police. There was always the woods to blame for the loss of a body, despite the searches by the sheriffs and their dogs. The families of the slain suffered the most. A miner could leave the mines and go to New York, Boston or Savannah. The wife and children of the slain were virtually prisoners sof the coal mine. Common sense and community compassion came often to their aid; but those remedies had their limits. Thus, Jimmy McKenna found himself increasingly involved in the work of violent Mollies, posing as henchmen for their disenfranchised clan, and flaming torches for justice. Theirs was usually justice at the muzzle of a gun or of a lighted dynamite fuse or a torched breaker, the last of which which put mining for that community out of business for six months while the townsfolk scrabbled to bring food to the tables for their families. Above it all, the women, usually the voiceless victims, stood strong, staunch, defiant and resolute, with the determination of frontier pioneers, to see the bad days through and to keep their families well, fed and cared for.

At two in the morning, a Frank B.Yost and a fellow officer Barney McCarron both lamplighters, were on their rounds attending the street lamps in Tamaqua. At one particulart street corner, where Yost lived, he started up the ladder to extinguish the street lamp. A bloody chap, a Mollie of course, waited across the street. At the exact instant when Yost was ready to descend on his ladder, having turned off the light, a shot pierced him in the back. He fell backwards onto the boardwalk. The Mollies knew not the word *coward*. Strangely, they had convinced themselves that they operated in the best interests of their suffering humanity. McKenna wrote to Pinkerton: "He was shot good and fell in his own blood," So calloused had McKenna become to wanton murder that he saw his description as reported facts, exclusive of the cowardice and tragedy involved. McCarron, the brother of the slain lamplighter, saw two figures running away and he, McCarron fired on them, but they disappeared like ghosts. Yost, mortally wounded, had crawled almost to his home nearby, when he expired. Three days later, a crowd followed his popular corpse to the grave. There was a favorable public sentiment that urged respect for the lamplighter in the patch. McKenna had to tell Pinkerton that Yost was a member in good standing with the Society in America. He was one of them. With the Mollies there never had to be a reasonable motive for a killing. Random kilings were a kind of blood madness.   A murder of a mine official almost always carried with it the tinge of justification, for that official sided with the hated collery owner. However, for a Mollie to kill another Mollie was totally irrational a prompting of whim, personal dislike, some small offense or a paranoic fear by the murderr of his victim. At tmes the mere act of climbing a ladder ignited a fear of surveilance, charged with guilt for some unseen crime. .

In this case of he murdered Yost, lamplighter for the town of Tamaqua, the colliery police were, however, more efficient than McKenna had presumed. With the help of local officers, they arrested two Mollies, Hugh McGeghan and James Boyle of Summit Hill. But the plot to kill Yost was more complicated than anyone had a right to assume. James Roarty of Coal Dale, James Carroll of Tamaqua and Thomas Duffy of Reevesdale all were arrested on the charge of complicity in Yost's murder. Taken to Pottsviille for trial, with the help of collaborative witnesses, the accused McGeghanand Boyle remained in jail while awaiting trial. The court convicted the two men of first degree murder. The Court ordered them all ot be hanged the same day as their judgement, that was June 21, 1877.

Despite this immediate justice, shootings gained in intensity and number. A Thomas Sanger was killed at Raven Run coal patch just before noon, that was a community on the line of the Lehigh Valley Railroad, not five miles from Shenandoah. At Raven Run, Thomas Sanger, then an inside boss at Messrs Heaton's collery, was shot to gratify Bucky Donnelly, ex-bodymaster at the Raven division of the Society. Kehoe in Girardville had to okay the murder, therefore August Charles, James McAllister, Michael Doyle and Thomas Munley all left Gilberton and walked to Girardville for Kehoe's official blessing for the murder to come. When they returned to Raven Run with Kehoe's okay for the murder, Donnelly invited them into his house, There they exchanged hats and coats with each other and stationed themselves near Heaton's colliery. They were observed by hundreds of men and boys at the collery, where they waited. McKenna was one of those witnesses. At the right moment, Donnelly fired on Sanger, who emerged with a friend named Uren, just as he was leaving his house. The other assassins in the party fired to keep the local miners at a distance. As Sanger headed toward his house, Munley headed him off. The retreating murderers fired on Robert Heaton, with no hits. Reaching the Lehigh Valley Railroad, the would-be assassins exchanged their clothing again. They had some whiskey and ,haing exchanged clothing and polished off a bottle of *Old Erin*, they dispersed over the mountains to Shenandoah. Mckenna was in the saloon when the murderers entered and to him and to Lawher, saloon owner, they told their story of the presumed murder Robert Heaton.whom they had not hit and was still alive. This recital came not as hearsay but as sworn evidence by Lawher at the trial of the assassins Doyle, Munley, McAllister and Charles.

"It was a clean job," boasted Friday O'Donnell, "We shot two when we only expected to shoot one."

"Yes," Munley added, "and I shot the first man, Sanger bloke, just as he was trying to get into a house."

"Well, you are their savior, sir," said the tapster. "Dont ye know that many devout followed the funeral cortege, more than to Christ's tomb. I'll warrant ye, to Odd Fellow's Cemetery in Girandville...many friends from all parts of the county who was without cause...:

"Fairness, justice, that's all we seek, Tapster...but some times thair's a reason to knock down a few more to get yer point across." Again, for the Mollies the end justified the means, so McKenna saw, in pursuit of his mission. Munley went on with his his story.

"Well, we stayed a mite at Lawlers chap and then we parted our separate god-fearling ways. But we kept in mind a meeting of Shenandoah Division. Munley come along to question the killing and John Jones... Oh, he was a rascal at times, he raised a question. To tlhis I saild, 'I'll go. I got my hand in now.' See, that's the heart a dedication--I muscle up to the task."

But the party weren't over yet. Munley, Darcy and McKenna, they went as a body to Tomaqua to to kill McCarron, the seond lampligher, but at *Carrolls Sal*oon McKenna told his fellow plotters it would do no good to carry out their plan, because since The Big Chief Kehoe wanted him to come to Gurardsville to do a job, and thus floating this alibi, McKenna put up a Mollie-argument, almost always listened to, to stop to the killing party by the sheer logic of *no-lawful-cause*/ This reasoning prompted the two men to return home. Pinkerton had urged McKenna to stop any would-be killings if he could and if he got the chance, fight with his fists as one of his salaried duties as a detective. Not until February of seventy-six were Munley and Charles McAllister arrested and charged with Yost's murder. Now don't ask McKenna why, He was the spy and interloper, but there were times when there was no motive except to see Irish blood spilled in the name of self-righteous anger. That was all, that was all. The authorities, they tried and convicted Munley and he was sentenced later that same year. Community patience was about to give out, proving there were good men nigh. Five months later a Vigilance Committee of two, the McAllister hrothers, paid a visit to the house of widow O' Donnell, mother of McCarron and Yost, her house situated in the notorious den of the Mollies in Wiggams Patch. The result of their visit was that Charles O Donnell was killed and Mrs. James McAllister was also killed in the melee. Charles McAllister and James McAllister got away, Unluckily, and green to brown it were, the Charles McAllister did come back but the latter never did.

There's a relationship ye ought to know, that Mrs. O' Donnell was the mother-in-law to Jack Kehoe, County Delegate of the Mollies. The eventual murder of Kehoe gave impetus to a return to a more peaceable state of affairs that had been lacking for some years. Pinkerton knew this and McKenna, his prize recruit, cerctainly did. He was one of the many who had received a *coffin notice*, making him a marked man. How could he escape his fate? A marked man had little chance to survive. McKenna told that to Pinkerton and he agreed. Seems that not five minutes after Khoe left his house-- this happened was in September of '75 and McKenna had been in the works two years or more--five minutes after he had left his house he was murdered . At noon on the same day, three men were arrested for the shooting--Doyle, Kelly and Kerrigan. The law held them for Kehoe's murder, they were jailed until the case was called early the next year. The prisoners had one option, they elected to be tried separately. And that was a square thing to do because a killer will make himself out to be more innocent than his cronies, right there in the courtroom. Do not mention about perjury. Michael Doyle was the first to be tried...lasted two weeks, 122 witnesses testified in such a way as to leave no doubt of the man's guilt, who having shot Kehoe at point blank range was charged with murder in the first degree.

Aye, there was much bold gun play in those days, like pirates aboard a captured ship they were, and the blood flowed freely. Kelly and Doyle, they were hanged at Maunch Chunk mid-year, in company with Alexandrer Campbell, who was also implicated in the murder of Kehoe. Apparently no case could be made against Kerrigan. The Society got rid of some of its troubles that day. An accomplice means complicit in the planning of a murder and therefore an active participant, as if he had pulled the trigger. Pinkerton saw this McKenna's way. He, the extraordinary spy, was as willing as any man to exoneratge a Man, be he a Mollie or not, if he made no contribution whatsoever to the murder. For his own code of f justice, there was no such thing as a plea- bargain once a man's guilty involvement was proved.

In early September , William Sanger left his house and only a short ways soff he met his killer who shot him in one arm. He ran around the house whereupon he met a second villain, gun in hand. He turned, fell, stumbled, as a third man appeared and shot him fatally. Yet a fourth came up to the victim, turned the body over and tried to deliver the *coup de grac*. Robert Heaton, an employee, heard the shooting, rushed armed to Sanger's side. The dying Sanger told him, never mind me, give it to them, boy. The killers had fled. Heaton went at once to see McKenna, where he lived and told him all the details of Sanger's murder.

By this time, after two years and longer, the Mollies had begun to suspect McKenna of complicity with the enemy, or at least of criminal participation in the murder of old friends. There was among most of the Mollies this hunger for a causal person, someone whom they could blame for their troubles, a figure to slay, an authority to put down. There was an insolent and contagious fever to this temper of the day, which, it seemed to Mc Kenna, had to run itseif out by exhausting the remedy for the miners sufferings--he murder of heartless and greedy mine officals. A doubting Molly friend, not convinced of McKenna's treachery, said simply that he was a wild card, ought not to be paid much attention to, often did his own thing, could not keep a job, wanered like mad bull, and participated in rat-killin/ Playing the roe of worhless baabond, he successfully threw the Mollies off track of suspicion. They had no proof, only suspicion. McKenna left for Philadephia, the enemy within their ranks at about this time, when Sanger was murdered.

At first McKenna could furnish evidence only that this and such had happened, but;then he agreed to appear as McParlan. Jimmy Kerrigan confessed cleanly, broke clean from the Order. He told all he knew about the Mollies. Kerrigan., jhe of all the Mollies, had done the most to corrupt the trade societies of the coal regions. He squealed to save his own life. An informer, he did not see justice done but, all the same, he saved his own life. As for his apologies, he referred to the Mollies' as drunken malevolents with evil natures. At the Court on the day of their trial, the court spectators were dumbfounded. The Judge and jury could not square the cool, resolute, gentlemanly quiet McParlan with the wild reckless overboasting McKenna He had playe his part well, He cast a spell on those spectators and the legal array during the four days that he was on the stand, the colossal surprise of murder trial history. The entire bar of the county was present, listening to the ghastly, dramatic revelations from a spy's own lips of the evil and methods of the Mollies. On cross-examination, the Counsel failed to find a single flaw in McKenna's testimony. " 'Twasn't that I was so smart, it was that the Mollies were so bightedly stupid in their antics. They had surrounded themselves withs the charms of innocence, conjured up by their insane imagnations."

Never never before was a Mollie convicted but now they were found guilty by the wholsesale. MePhearson was under constant guard, he himself feared he might be killed in the courtroom to prevent his testimony. With the sudden arrest of the Molly ringleaders, they were arrestsed and thrown into jail. One mauy ponder a to why there why there are so many Irish cops and why that profession is their fair choice.

Jack Kehoe, the high constable of Girandville County delegate of the Hiberian order did not escape death, but , Michael Lawler of Shenandoah, Frank O' Neill of St. Clair, Patrick Butler of Lost Creek, Patrick Dolany, Sr. of Mine Run, Michael O' Brlien and Frank McHugh of Mulhaney City, and Christopher Donnelly of Mount Laffee--- there was the lay out of Molly authority. The acts of the Mollies for some 14 years, from before the close of the Civil War, from 1863 to alboutl 1877. They in large part had failed to realize and understand that an accessory to a crime was as guilty in the eyes of the law as the perpetrator. The attitude of putting *their* rights first, without reason or respect for the rights of other was typical of their conduct in Ireland and it carried over into this country. For this trial on the Mollies, the entire bar of the Shenancoah county was present, hearing the ghastly dramatic revelations of the crimes and methods of the Mollies. The Mollies in large part failed to understand either the notions of *accessory to a crime* or *tolerance*. They did not always win the shootout. They said they had no enemy but for their own kind, but many of those chosen by the Mollies for death were beloved by the entire neighborhood and also by some of the Mollies. There seemed to be neither sense, judgement nor justice in their violence.

A great throng gathered on a Pottsville holiday for the hanging June 1877 of six Mollies. In jail, they heard the construction of the gallows, hoped the governor at Harrisburg would reprieve them. The ringleader, Jack Kehoe, boasted he would not be hung. Priests came to give last rites from Pottsville, Minersville, Hecksersville and Port Carbon. At first, the plan was to hang three at once, but the plan was changed to two at once, the Sheriff's choice. At almost eleven, a great moment was about to become a reality. At first, from the doorway at the end of the yard, came James Boyle and Hugh McGeghan, with the Sheriff and two priests and prison officials in the group. The condemned mounted the gallows in firm steps and positioned themselves for the hanging. The condemned, came in common clothing, priests in their black cossacks, whiie surplices and black stoles bound with white with white crosses on either end and praying fervently as they walked.

McGeghan was a large burly man. Boyle much lighter. The former gave close attention to the priest, the latter paid more attention to the cross he carried that held up his robe. At eleven o'clock, a distant shot rang out, the court house clock rang its toll, died down, men shook hands with officials and prepared for eternity. Death comes to the Mollies. At 11 19 , white caps were placed over the heads of the condemned men, a sharp click, a deadened fall and two Mollies dangled and twirled about on rope ends beneath the platform. The noose about McGeghan's neck had been poorly placed, not directly behind his ear and so it slipped toward the front. He shook with convulsions for four minutes after his fall. Boyle was dead in ten minutes, McGeghan in fifteen. The traps were reset and close to noon, the next pair, Carroll and Roarity dropped into the well. Again a shot was fired at a distance from the town. No one ruffled; prayers to ask fortiveness were carried out as with the others. The trapdoors sprang at 12: 21 and 12 23 Carroll was deat at 12 37 Roarity minutes later.

Next, from the jail, Munley and Duffy walked to their gallows. They appeared just as one ten, one of the priests spoke to Duffy, heard him to say, "those lose by saying anything." When the Sheriff whispered to Munley, he replied with a shake of his head and in a low voice muttered "...too late" The drop came at 1 18. Again the knots were bungled but both men were dead at one thirty-three. Five of the Mollies were tried in their own neighborhoods, a special train assigned to their families by the RR to the scene. Munley was buried at Harrisburg, Carroll and Duffy taken to Tannaqua, and the bodies of McGeghan, Roarity and Boyle were taken to Summit Hill. Mauch Chunk saw four Mollies hanged. In the quiet, picturesque village, Michaael Doyle, Edward J. Kelly, Alexander Campbell were all convicted of murder of John and alias *Yellowjack* Donahue for the murde rof Morgan Powell.

A crowd gathered at the site. Easton Grays, a lcader of soldiers in full uniform, with ammunition and guns marched up the street to post as guards in front of the jail. A scaffold had been erected in the corridor, the jurors and deputy sheriffs were placed behind the scafford and at the entrance to the jail. Newsmen were assigned to plaes in front of the upper cells. Alex Campbell came first, with a firm step, then Doyle, Donahue and Kelly, each carried a crucifix, each closely followed by one of the priests in attendance. Doyle muttered that if he had obeyed the priest and kept out of secret societies, he would not have been in that predicament. Four hanged together. Men were already manacled, white caps put over their heads. Campbell and Doyle dropped two feet and six inches. Donahue and Kelly somewhat over three feet..

The trap was sprung at ten forty-eight and Campbell and Doyle died without a struggle. Donahue struggled violently for almost two minutes. A priest stepped up and annointed his hands as if to ease the physical pain by a religious ceremony. Kelly struggled as if in agony, but died in eight minutes. Campbell had trouble, his pulse could be felt at the end of fourteen minutes. Campbelll and Doyle died without broken necks. Donohue and Kelly met death by strangulation. At eleven thirty the four were cut down and taken to the train for removal to their former homes. Thomas was hanged for the murder of Mogan Powell and James Donnell, and Charles McAllister and was hanged for the deaths of Sanger and Uren within the year at Pottsville. Pat Hester, Tully and McHugh were hanged at Bloomsburg, Columbia the next year, 1878. The Mollies had put their cause before the law,\ as the average person, came to understand the history of the day in which the Mollie Maguires were on the loose.

iii

Jimmy McKenna stepped into a pothole on the dirt road from Schuylskill Haven to Auburn and Pinegrove mining communities, within sight of each other. Muddied from his fall on his face, he swore. He stood up,
brushed the mud from his clothes and ambled on, just a path, for another six miles to Pinegrove. The skies were dark with more rain, the slush ominous to the foot-traveler and deep, bearing no traffic except for a vagabond like himself, who scurried along with boots slushing in the mire, the mud having penetrated under his torn slicker. He kicked up the mud and water and soaked his feet in his heavy shoes, until at last he arrived, shivering and wet to the skin and hungry at the Cockleburr Saloon, The saloon, he reasoned, was the best place to continue his investigation and his spy work. He racked up rickty steps to the closed doors and found two miners inside, it being a Saturday night in stormy weather. He greeted one of the saloon sojourners with the hand in fist and fist in the palm as the accepted Mollie salutation, so he had been informed by Allan Pinkerton before he left Philadelphia. To show he was a Mollie and could e trusted, he used that greeting. He carried on his person a wad of bureau money, from which he peeled off a bill with an elaboralte gesture, green, the pride of old Erin, and. shoving it across the bar, ordered a short beer. He did not wish to become drunk, although t this would be one of his disguises.

"Mine closed?" Prete4ndin to be a little tipsy, h plunked down on the bench and, lealning in close and personal across the table, he enquired of one of the as yet unnamed miners, identifiable by his long, black, uncropped hair, a shaggy beard and a rawboned look to his hands and face and his movements .a man hardened by the long hours of physial labor with a miner's tool like a maul, down in the hole.

"Mines 're closed?"

"We don't work on Sundays...just the company store."

Silence. "Miners all at home."

"I 'spect so, name's Horace. You a newcomer."

"Just floated in," said McKenna. "My name's McKenna." He slopped a little splash of beer on the table by accident, apologized. "I'm here lookin' for work."

"They's a plenty a gaff... if you can stand conditions. Gotta be sober."

"Conditions...?".

The miner named Horace cranked up his frown, batted blue eyes, grinned a knowing grin to his partner, then shifting his billed cap on his head, confronted McKenna. "Coal dust, damn near work in the dark...ore carts need maintenance. You maybe hadn't oughter ask fer work, stranger."

"McKenna's ' name, from Schuylskill...."

"Glad. Nothing's new around here exceptin' the morning sun, and right now, Mister, there haint much o' that."

"No, I come from Schuylskill...not much doing over there. I'm not hurtin' for a pocket full of gold, but a job with a pick would do me better.".

"I seed you got a roll a flire starter." McKenna was puzzled, then realized that

Horace had observed his agency bankroll. "They got l need of powder monkey...last one disappeared in ' exploshun. Miscalculated...snake come back to bite him, it did. They found only his gold watch in one piece. Damned fool went back to check and th' charge went off. Gawd!"

"I always thought they waited a day."

"Not this mine boss...in on top o' things. No waitin'. Mine boss ...he haint got no are for his men, not one of'
'em. Most mine bosses thata way."

"You wouldnt expect them to hire sunday school teachers."

"No, just fellers with the smarts not to test a fuse 'til time passes.Damn glad he didn't send in any men with that monnkey.

"I never set fuses."

Don't, they's a short life for powder monkeys...and plenty a other jobs. They get the same pay as t'others. That don't make sense," the miner went on.

"Lots a things don't make'sense here, Horace. I cain't go long without earning my keep. Drink keeps me steady."

"I seed that. Case yer lookin' fer a rack fer the night, they's a janitor owns a boarding house up the road. He's the clean-up man fer the mine, he picks up any left tools...dynamite, stuff maybe left behind. Ever' shift hes got to go down there. He's got smarts. he'll rent ye a place to stay."

"That's mighty fine of you," said; ;McKenna. Miners don]t mind the rain none down in the hole. So ...how much he charge?"

"Hell, ye'll have to ask him," said the second miner, name of Bonnard. "Naame'sBonnard. That cat's pretty sharp, he don't howl nonbe if ye skip rent, but he's sur as God made little maggots take yer scalp if ye don' ferry up with the rent. I know. I come crost him twicet. He don' want ter see me round no more. They's like that up here...kerful o' two things, their shaftin tools and their green shoves."

"I think I'll be kerful," McKenna promised. Silence. "Beer in here is thin"

"Waters it down he does, to make a little extra." Bonnard pulled a small sack of wheat germ from one pocket, sniffed it and handed it to McKenna.. "Smell o' it...It's th' wheat he took from th' beer...though,bless me, I think it were the potaters. Pour a lettle in wid chyer beer will give it body. Cain't blame him" said Bonnard.

"No, I guess not. Well, I gotta fnd me a place to rack out, and I'll check out that mine boss in the morning. He got a shack?"

"Just inside th tunnel hole...like a gate checker. He gets there early, 'bout five er so, ifn you wants ter catch him, men and boys start arriving at 'bout seven....and they be gone by eight, sure. First crew...."

McKenna mounted stilted steps to the "Clenency Boarding House " to talk with Casius, the keeper and clean up man. The old white haired Negro had nothing but suspicion of McKenna, a scowl and a squinty look under his eyebrows. He told the agent he would lend him a room for a week for four dollars. McKenna coughed up with the rent and stowed his one kit-bag in a corner and, shedding his muddy clothes, lhe dcraped them over a cranking, popping steam radiator. He fell asleep across the rope bed.

The spy extraordinary had agreed that Pinkerton was to supply him with money via a courrier, a trusted member of the Pinkies, by way of horseback from Philadelphia, to be

36.

used lin part to pay for his services, for bribes, payoffs, impressment and jail bonds. The making-go money was to arrive y this courier, who would also deliver any mail McKenna had rceived, as well as first aid such as a healing salve and bandage roll. Allan did not want his finest to be exposed to the hungry eyes and evil tides of Mollies on the hunt, always, for defectors, of which McKenna might appear to be one. Even the one doctor was a confirmed Molly in Schuylskill. Solidarity with the Mollies was the catchword for the Pinkerton employee. McKenna would get his "grub money," Allan called it, on a regular basis. If any Miner, even casually. was to wonder about his bank roll, the agent was to inform him , in a practiced whisper, that he was "pushing the queer," that he was passing counterfeit bills to the company store or wherever, even to meet a bribe condition or payment to a bail bondsman. This,by he way,was a huge source of income for the Mollies, they being able to find suckers in the mining towns to liberate them under bond. The Meerschaum Bank in Phylly was also a contributor to the Mollie largesse and "freedom money" as they called it. It was agreed that, for want of a steady job, he would push the queer, pass counterfeit bills, by way of an operation he had contact wilh in Philadelphia, for which funds he, McKenna, would supply intelligence, inormation, by return courier, a well as by way of an agent postsded on the Reading Coal and Iron Railroad mail car, whenever it was convenient for McKenna. These contacts were adequate but lacking deohad his tag issued to him, a hat with a skerosene lamp and a small pick withn a short handle for working incramped space. The boss was a gargantuan of a man named Honore, as Honore de Balzac, although he was Irish to the core. He wanted to pat down McKenna for a gun, he garbled something about bigshots from the city, and with hands as soft as putty, a back untrained for bending and crawling, knees tender and eyes that were unfocused and unaccustomed to the pitch dark of the hole, McKenna descended with twenty others on the mine shaft elevtor , to a level of three thousand feet, over half a mile into the bowels of the earth.

The morning following his saloon chat with Bonnard and Horace, McKenna encountered the mine boss. a trundling short man named Honore. He walked like a diseased duck, with a waddle, he was as powerful as a steam engine, huge shoulders and biceps, a small face out of proportion to his frame, with a cultivated moustache of blonde color and a face turned by a corkscrew. His hands worked like powerful grips as he handed McKenna his brass tag with a number, instructing him to hang it up each night or they would have togo down and make a search or him. His tool would be a pick, right off, since that required no skill. One of the men could show him where to cut into the seam for best outtake. O'Malley turned to his paper-work on a podium stand outside his office. He furnished McKenna with a hat and a lamp and instruvcted him not to turn the flame up too high as it would soot up the glass and he would run out of fuel during the shift. McKenna marveled at the close calculation of every move.
"Yer pay will be fifty-cents a day fer a nine hour shift. If ye got any complaints...I don't want to hear 'm. The men all make the same, 'cluding the powder monkey. I make a tad more bcause I'm the boss. Is that yer un'erstanin', Mister McKenna?"
"'Tis mine, sihr. As ye can see..I got me no objections."
"Good...lemme see yer hands. McKenns showed him his white and soft palms/
"Ye'll have a hard four 'r five days, but ye'll toughen up, McKenna. Just be sure ye don' s'teal 'nother man's gloves. Ye got to suffer like t'others. We all got to start some time."
"I un'erstand, Mister O'malley. "

"Omalley. Mister stuff is fer the big shots." The men and boys og the morning shift began to arrive, all of them afoot. :Ye go wid them...and ask questions. Things change down there from one day to the next." He looked MxcKenna rom head o toe. "Ye hain't got no booze on ye, ave y' ?"

'No, I hain't...O'Malley."

"Good...We beglin to keep a tan on yer output after the third day,...when ye've got the hang o' things."

"I comprehend, O'Malley." The squat, powerful mine boss wrote some figures in his ledger as he handed out a tag here and there, calling out a name. "Here, Maser Watson, ye cain't pick stones without yer number." The miners were accustomed to serving themselves by plucking their number tag off the hook and wiring it to a pocket on their jacket, some slipping it under the lantern band on their hats,. or into a pocket. It was all so routine, the agent observed. The men and boys appeared, joking amongst themsselves, and sharing coments, anecdotes and thoughts, as they crowed into the cage in preparation for the trip down a mile into the ground. A bell rang once, and the lift began its descent into the blackness, there being no blackness to total and saturating of the air in a mine shaft. They emerged into the bottom of the hole; the lift gave a slight jar as it met the bottom of the shaft. The descent had taken almost fifteen minutes. The first sound McKenna heard when he stepped out of the cage was of a dripping of water. On his face, he felt the stiffling chill of the shaft itself. The men scarcely murmured a word, grim-set as they were for their job of working a 30-inch seam of coal. McKenna wondered why in hell the owner did not supply his miners with some kind of a boring machine. He had heard that they existed. "Too expensive," he thought. They were just coming onto the market. He pretended he kinew what he was doing and humnkered lown, crawling into a space lighted by a larger map-lamp placed to light the area generally.The faces of the miners, now whitish and clean-washed, within an hour, were covered with coal dust, settled onto their sweaty faces and arms and hands, and that rendered them the appearance of masked animated puppets, a wierd and ghoolish aspect that was as frightening as it was awsome. The dust generally remained placid in the still air of the shaft, accumulated by their picking and shoveling and that caused them to gasp when they spoke and laughed on occasion, their teeth like whitish pebbles set in black stone. The coal glinted from its fractured surfaces. The man they called the "drag man" swept the coal out of the way while the miners progressed further and further into the seam of coal.

McKenna expected to hear murmurs of angry dissatisfaction. but he he heard none. Theminers went about their work, their faces were indistincgt cadaverous whitish skulls of eye sockets and mouths under their pale head lam[s silient figures who now moved about in the gloom wlihout apparent direction, their headlamps like glow worms against the darkness. Did they hold an   internat rage? He had to remind himself that one or more, perhaps several of his comrades down in the pit caried about with him inside an anger that was an incipient violence and that, given the opportunity, they would murder the mine Boss, and; further still, they would cremate wilh gunfire the mine owner sand his agents for inflicting this unrelieved misery upon them. They were the Mollies, and they kinew and could instantly identify their enemies.

McKenna was ;ooked aougt fo that glimmer of still water, collected in pools or trickling from an undergound spring, that cold threaten the miners' lives. There was no water where they worked. Of the twenty-seven miners who had begun to strike at the coal and shovel it to the rear in heaps, ready to be loaded into three ore carts that stood their still forms in the shadows, allbllu two of the men woked near McKe;nna. He realized why he held a short-handled pick, for the light of miner lamps disclosed the depth of a ledge that represented back in there the coal seam. They had picked away an amount of coal tlhat created an opening of only about three feet high. The crawling forms of the miners hacked away at the coal like prehistoric worms at the open spit of the coal seam, marking their advance only by short cascades of loosened coal and swirls of deadlyblack dust. They advanced, as if in phalanxes, further each day into the seam. The men soon turned into black caped figures,their hands and faces almost indistinguisheable from the live coal of the seam. The powder monkey, a man by the overheard name of Wasserman, a German miner from Ruhr coal region of West Germany, worked behind the driller and the maul hammerman, the team that bored holes for the sticks of dynamite amd the fuses that draped down the carbon walls like threads, ready to e connected to a flame. Themen worked on while the sun, unseen, passed on overhead, a drag of weary men whlo would reurn in the morning to load up the loosened chunks of the blown coal. Last night had een Sunday night.

There was little talk among the men. What was there to talk about. Theirs was the exhausting labor of carvers into the earth. All their energies were directsed to extracting the coal, as if the flesh, the claws and fur of a live beast thlat had been entrapped for eons of time were now squirmin and clawling at the earth to escape. McKenna had forgotten to provide some kind of lunch, sowhen the Pit Boss called time and the miners layed down their tools, they hopened lunch pails, canvas bags,old whiskey bottles of water and began hungrily to consume lunch, to renew their strength with a piece of fruit, a slice of pie and gargantuan sandwiches of whole slabs of steak and fish. One of the miners, observing McKenna without a lunch, proffered half of his sandwich to him. Thee was an elemental compassion in the offer which McKenna greatly appreciated; he could not have continued the day with any sign of vior without food. And so he had learned something else about the Mollies, that their rage bore the seeds of reunion and pacific comradeship.

"Your first day down here?"

"May be my last. There must be a better way to make a living."

"Not here, not in the hull town o' Pinegrove."

"A lamplighter would be better."

" 'S a picked job...favorites o' the Mollies get them jobs...." He lowered his voice. "...They rule the town...their word is law.. put their favorites on sech jobs."

"Company store...?"

"Mostly women....and you don't look like you're no school teacher." McKenna devoured his half of the man's sandwich without speaking another word, then... "I cain]t promise how long I be here but I thought I'd give minin' a shot."

"I don' know ifn yer a Mollie, but if ye hain't, watch out. They come down hard on them what don't like mining...sees 'm as spies, suspicioning alus, no thought a the man's source...y un'erstan' what I mean?" Them's the ones what makes the laws."

"There cain't be much in the way of law," said McKenna. fully aware that there were ears turned to lisen in to the conversation. "M' name's McKenna, Jimmy McKenna."

"Sullivan...I track fresh pawprints...help 'm get used to the grind... a times have a say who gets hired and who gets fired. Pit Boss trusts me...."

"I been hired, I guess."

"If you get by Honore, yer safe...fer a while."

"I certainly hain't going ter fight another man fer this hyer job."

"That's death; if ye do...them Mollies..." he dropped his voice to a whisper..."they don't take no caution from nobody...if ye know what I ;mean."

"No stoppages."

"Not less they say so," said McKenna's informer.

"Ifn I be too drunk I jes won't report in. There's a end to it."

"And a end to yer work, sir. I don' know where ye come from but I'd caution ye to pay a heed to the Mollies, fer they got the power...aside from the Mine Boss and company agents...they's alus a fight goin] on 'twixt 'em. Shootings...Gawd!" He pointed a finger to his temple, his head. "Ye ken?"

"I ken," said McKenna. Two of he miners were boring holes for the explosives and the powder monkey was bushy setting the sticks, tamping them in with their fuses and leading the fuses off into the darkness to the cage. There he would ignite the ends just before the cage moumnted up into the blackness of the shaft. Lunch finished, McKenna, down on his knees again, crawned to the seam and found his pick, almost invisible in the blackness. The mauler picked up his maul, the driller his drill, and the incessant strike of metal against metal filled the silence. He looked up one time and saw the sparks from the eight pound maul head vanish into the black air. He hoped he would not be asssigned a driller, for it looked to him, but a mere detective, to be a dangerous job, a way to be broken-handed for the rest of his life. He had prepared an excuse. "I got me shiverin' hand...a disease," he would plead, "gives me the tremblins, so I canno' hold a drill steady and the mauler, he canno hit the end o' me dill. Takes a tall glass o' Irish whiskey to steady me hand, it does, by the Saints o' th' ol' the auld sod, it do."

The rest of the day was routine for those hard-rock miners, and the work was insufferalyh hard for a new-comer, so that when the shift ended with a whistle from Honore, at the top of the shaft--the whistle carried down into the hole a half mile like a funne of a trumpet, why McKenna set down his pick, adjusted the flame in his lamp, and with his accomplice in discovery and comraderie, he crawled out from under the rock ledge to where he could stand. He and the others, some twenty in all, crawled far enough so they, too, could stand . Exhausted, carrying their picks, mauls and other tools,edges and apair of aze heads, they walked, physically drained, the hundred yards to the lift, which waited for them-- beyondthe three pre carts. The miners' fist task inthe morning wouldbe to fill the ore cars withs the ebris from the blast. The location of the lift was marked by a kerosene lantern on the gate. Themen crowded lin, scuffing on the metal floo. A draft of cool draft air came own the shaft onto their heds. With a a rling of a bell and a pull on a rope by one of the miners, the lift started its assent. hen they were a bout halfway up, they heard the sound of the explosioniln the distance. McKenna resolved to make better peparations the next day, but luck would not have it so, for Mckenna fell afoul of the bottle and was late in climbing the stairs to his room on the boarding house stilts. The next morning, he reported in late. The Mine Boss Honore was angry but said nothing and McKenna finished the day as before. This time he had packed two sandwiches at the Saloon, and and he used adrink bottle for his water, putting this lunch into a canvas bag. The tenure and size of the operation did not change from day to day. Weary as he became, McKenna was gathering details about the mood, the complaints, the actual working conditions of the miners.

It was hard for McKenna to believe that a man, any man, could spend half his life breathing in the black dust and not rebel. Therefore, he decided that it was this spirit of rebellion over working conditions that animated and fueled many of the shootings. Personal animosity was a second factor. Whenever the miners learned of a defector from the Mollies, which meant for them a man's siding with the management of the mine, that miner becasme an object of scorn that amounted in some cases almost to hatred. He became a potential target for a shooting by unidentified Mollies, often from another town, They liked to travel in wolf-packs of four, making positive identiication of the actual killer impossible in a court of law. Also, by this time McKenna realized that the Mollies possessed as one of their secrets a secret web of communication which he had not yet figured out. How could a man, a miner in Auburn, say, comminicate with another miner in Pinegrove, to such a degree and complexity that the victim in either town ould be fingered and shot? There was, therefore, a certain lethal and fearsome accuracy to the Mollies' identification of those to be murdered-- agents. body-masters, mine Bosses and owners, not to mention engineers who knew too much. There were the names of miners whom Mollies kept on their lists--employees marked for exterminatiton. The process was one, not of conspiracy so much as of summoning the help to commit the job--the recuited use of fellow Mollies, foresworn and foreknown as members of the Order before enlisting them as willling gunmen. Thus, McKenna counselled himself, recruitment and not collective conspiracy was the deathly tool the Order used.

At the Pinegrove mine, captained by Mine Boss Honore, McKenna was careful not to be late again, and n fact showed up early, took his tag fom its row of hooks and attempted to engage Honore in chatter.

"How many men ye got down there, Honore? Do ye have enough to kiver yer needs?"

"Oh, we got men aplenty,,,the Mollies can assure us. When some quit they's others to take their places. It's nery a tangle but always a rush. They's much They's much can be done to improve things down there, as ye know." The Mine Boss looked McKenna over like he was inspecing a shipment of dynamite with too much sawdust or a crate of overipe melons. McKenna got used to this kind of intimate inspection, including Honore's near pat-down for a hand-gun.

One thing Honore told him that proved invaluable to Allan Pinkerton. This pargticular mine at Pinegrove kept back money from the miners' pay to buy off politcians in Harrisburg, the State Capital, where Governo Tompkins, who was known to all Mollies, followed the fortunes of the mines very closely, and, in fact. kept his personal inspectors on the scenes of certain mines. The result was that a bill passed the Harrisburg House that rewarded a man named Jack Kehoe, for his diligence in selecting Mine Bosses and his efficiency in distributing state taxpayer largesse, such as it was, to agents of certain mines. The miners, some of them, knew of the extortion for favorable legislation, but out of fear for their lives they said not a word, either to their friends and even to their wives. One of the things the Mollies hoped for, although to their destruction, was the unionization of the miners. As members of the Ancient Order of the Hibernians, they had no real power, just vengeful acts of violence to get across to the authorities their message of legitimate grievances.

McKenna wrote down on one page what he had learned about conditions in the mine at Pinegrove, the Mollies' activities, their secrecy and the reasons for their brotherhood bonding, the actual conditions of the one mine and the cruelties of the kind of work he had undertaken, picking away at 30 inch coal for fifty centa a hour, ten hours a day. Those circumstances were enough to cause a miner to revolt, especially since his pay for that kind of grfueling work was only fifty-cents a day. he response of the MineBoss ws that he,the miner, was snot being force to work in the mine. McKenna sent this message bylthe postal agent in the ReadlingCoal and Ironrailroad with a request for more queer. He would be moving to Schuylskill Haven next and would pick up the operating moneys at the post office, general delivery.

The rains had left us, the road mud hardened somewhat, so that he was able to walk to Schuylskill Haven without the previous muddy handicap. McKenna wanted to meet a mine owner, but they made themselves scarce. The coal miners in those communities that the detective had visited, allost literally held their rifles over the heads of tlhe mine owners. There were plots ot kill tlhe agents, mine owners and pit bosses, but McKenna had yet to run into one of which he was linvited to become a member. Time would change hiacircumstances and his role within the Mollie Order. Although not all members of the Order could claim active membership, whatever that consisted of, most Mollies were Mollies of the Hilberian Society, but not all members were Mollies. Mining conditions would not mprove. this he wrote to Pinkerton. Only the miners could conrol the dust, the cause for black lung coughing, but they hd to hve coopeation withthe mine owners to prevent cave-ins, the danger of falling seam roofs and methane gas in the mine.

McKnna and his shift gang of miners entered the tunnel or crowded onto the lift in the morning...or evening, fresh and vital, and they returned at night or by dawn light; pitaiable rags of men, their energies depleted, exhausted by the grip of the labor below ground. Their coal besmudged faces showed the level of the labor lthey had put out for eilght to ten hours. Their faces bore reminders, in tension and anxiety, of the experience ofbeilng alwalys under the swsord, coatnually under the threat of ine dangers, of many kinds--drowning by unforseen expossure of ground water, injuries tolimbs, expecially the hands, eyes and legs, and prolonged exposure to the weather lin the mine of constant but deathly chill and the ever-present floating on air of coal dust, itself explosive like grain dust in silo explosions, and of methane gas from the coal seam. The lst incident \ inevitably trapped al the miners at work behind the fallen rock. There they often died of their injuries or satvation, despite frantic efforts outside the mine to rescue them.

McKenna spelled out these realities of hard-rock coal mining. The German and Welsh miners, in conradistinction to the Irish rebels, did not appear to suffer to the same extent as did the Irish Mollies. They were neighbors in the town, houses to house in the valley mountainside. They greeted one another as familiars. The Irish chose to pick a fight or to find cause to rub out the enemy, real or fancied. The Irish became the bosses of one level or he next. English- men from the mines of Britain were shrewd in their silence, learned in their prudent and thrifty waysin their shires. They came most improbably with no grievances toward coal mining, because the English miner was cousin to the land-serfing lives of past cenuries on that tilht little Isle. Their brogue, their accent of speech reminded the Irishs of their own heritage and their struggles in the new country.

Oncea Mollie, alwayls a Mollie because the mantra of those most severely crippled by mining labor, and closest to the end of life were also closest to the spirit of murderous reprisal. They had lin he past seized the anthrax coal fields. When this ultimately event had shoud occured, lawlessness had ecome excepiionally rampant, more sothan McKenna could imagine or had found in the battlefields of Europe. These cataclysmic temporary changes in land-possession simulated what McKenna knew about the European war, yet invested with a certain ritualistic execution that was baronial and Medieval an detached from the everyday life in the mining community. Indeed, he mine owners were knowns as coal barons, like the timber barons, the railroad barons, suggestsling a Medileval society with classeas of the elite and the serfs. Of course the fighting Irish were the serfs. It could no be so otherwise in the tenure of the time, where survivals required miners to labor for their living and for their families and the agents to thrive on the profits gotten therefrom. High prices and Medieval control came like a packaged deal in the mines of eastern Pennsyslvania and Kentucky. When the coal companies made cuts in wages, evem by a few cents per hour, the miners fought the temporarys scabs whom the barons had hired to continue the mine operation. Thus there existed a continual warfare between the latter synergistic battleline and the management of the mine for control of the mine, this rabid and volatile confrontation making of ownership a chaos in the lives of the suffering miners, both retired and actively down in the hole. The barons depended on the miners for their wealth, and the miners depended on the availabillity of work for their survival. Indeed, a thousand milners stopped work at Mahonays City in 1875 at the Shenandoah mine when they struck and refused for several days to work. The miners fought pitched battles against the scabs with clubs and rocks, some of scabs were also Mollies but deperae for work. The rage of their dissatisfaction led the miners into other acts of vandalism, street fights, single assaults on sight, robbery of homes and store lifting. These attacks were accompanid by attempts to derail the night passengerr train of the Reading Railroad out of metropolitanl New York. One such successful derailment occurred at Mount Carmel. Thereafter, the Pinkies rode an engine that preceded the following train. Rioting Mollies torched a breaker at the latter town. The breaker broke and sorted coal into various sizes for consumer uses. Its loss meant that the owner had to shut down the mine until a new breaker coulde built. Long trains of coal cars rolled from operative breakers onto the main line, some as long as one mile, pushed and pulled by locomotives in tandem, bellowing their plumes of black smoke as they labored with their tonnage. The output staggered the vision and the imagination. At the mine-head, in every instance where a miner failed to show up for a day's work, the mine owner permitted the Mine Boss to hire a scab in order to maintain a production quota. McKenna was often mistaken for one of these scabs, and for that reason he was tolerated withs contempt. Some of the Mollies looked upon the Pinkrton agent as a scab because he worked for such short lengths of time, he appeared and disappeared without excuse. Others saw him as a drunken ne'r-do- well who could not hold down a job. Thus, McKenna walked into his ready-made role at the Schuylskill Haven mine.

This grungy coal town, blistered by black coal dust and neither colors nor whiteness ansywhere, even in the laundry on the lines, was typical of anthracite coal towns in eastern Pennsyslvansia and in Kentucky, prticularly if there was a breaker and loading operation going onand tlh prevailing reeze lin the valley blew the dust everywhere. McKenna walked the distance from his last Job at Pinegrove. The road was long, but he endured, stopping to pick wild berries and sip from a spring along the way. The mountans conceal their gifts for the weary. A farmer of sargum with a load for the market was rumbling his way. MKenna looked around and with his tumb made like he wanted to hitch a rilde. The farmer in a dowdy felt hat pulled his dapple horse to a stop and signaled the agent to heist himself onto the wheel then the footboard for a ride to the next town. The old horse, indeed, the wagon had collected a settlling of coal dust from the ailr, vissilble on the harness and on the footboard of the farmer's wagon. The farmer glanced a penetratilng look at his passenger, snapped the reins and the wagon rumbled on. McKenna was grateful for the ride, and observilng the taciturn nature of the farmer, who looked straight ahead until tlhe wagon pulled to a stop at the first house on the outskirts of the town. McKenna dismounted and thanked the farmer who had picked him up and taxied him into Schuyskilll Haven where he would sell his load to local maker of sugar. The common size of such enterprises limited profits but did modestly supply local needs, as did the farmer's ride. He had a wry mouth, chewed a cud, squinted in suspcion under the brim of his hat, and gargled words to his horse when McAKenna hopped off. The sleuth soon discovered differences lin thle appearances of the various communities in this part of Pennsylvania. Not all minining towns were the same, a patch consisting of a few houses, and a town of two dozen or more, that included the company store, the school house, a row of store fronts on a main street and, usually a church tucked in somewhere. .For these folk were religious. In most real-life instances their religion gave them strength and establlished warnings for moralconduct, not the least of which eas muder, thendrunkenness and dissolute ways. For the last reason, McKenna would and did stand out, for a part of his disguise was the drunken sot demeanor and habituation to the local saloon. Most miners had neither the time, money nor inclination for such a pasttime, not when they could, as they often did, purchase illegal whiskey from a local moonshiner for the morrow.

McKenna this time did not go to the saloon but to the company store. A man of rotund proportions, blue eyes, regular Germanic features, a straw hat and wearing a bib-overall grinned through broken and stained teeth to ask what he could help him with.

"Can you tell me, good sir," McKenna asked elaborately, " where me boys can find their schoolmaster?" Of course McKnna had nosons,but the ruse was useful.

"They's a schoolmarm lives just two houses to the end of the block, with a leaning board fence. She can tell ye." With that exchange of intelligence, McKenna walked to the pointed-out house and rapped on the door. Of course, she was not at school. And so what now? The storekeeper had supplied little information. He turned toward the business part of the town where he met a man in a pony cart on the street. Stopping the carter McKenna made the same enquiry.

"Well, sahr, if ye'll go to the sanctuary...'the what?'..the sanctuary...ye perhaps can get yer question answered." He meant the Saloon, since there was no eatery in the town. Thus, onward to the The Breaker Saloon. ildentifiable by its breaker replica over the facade, where any young and masterful Irishman with a drooping black moustache, the same as his, and fast hands stood wiping the bar and then, turning from his glassware, greeted McKenna with a broad grin.

"I see ye've come at just the right hour to avoid trouble and try a sip o' me favorite tonic."

This greetling did not go unnoticed by the agent spy. He layed his cards flat out on the bar...he needed a place to stay, and he was looking for a job. These things the young Irishman could supply. Why the young artender was not down in the mines slightly surprised McKenna, but then he realized that mining was a fool's end, if he stayed, and he usually did, but a young man had other venues of enterprise and self-sufficiency, such as, that he might tend bar or even light street lamps or perhaps become a town policeman.

"Mister Haggerty owns a boarding house down the street. 'Tis the third floor accommodatsions are cheapest, a dollar a day, me thinks, and a tad less if; ye'll pay in advance."

"Well, sir, I've got me dry soul the price of a beer. So if ye'll furnish me palate with that tonic I'd be much obliged to ye." These ends accomplished, McKenna, with some remaining Pinkerton money in his pocket, went to the appointed boarding house--The Flotsam Inn--and greetsed a woman in her sixties, her hair raveled curls and her face puckered and discolored by the coal-laden air. She had lived here for a long time, a very long time , an old-timer,who wore the same look of dispassionate resolve not to be cheated or robbed orswilndled, but to trust only the dogs on the streets wths their barks. It was at once apparent to McKenna that the Mollies, by their method of vengeful warfare, had also corrupted Shuylskilll Haven wlith distrust. "However, on with the mission," he thought.

He paid his tarilff for two days. In order to promote his dtunken and worthless state, the Pinkerton spy did not remain any longer than the two days, and the one full week at Pine grove. These brief residences as an litinerant miner had served him well for his mission. Mster Talmadge,the boaardilng-house keepers name, seemed to toady to a black man who was mopping a hallway, and to lisp his warning to McKensna--"Ye'll keep clear o' the downstairs...they be dogs of Irin that come roaming in the night and I've a care for me guests. I'll take yer two dollars for as many days and come to ye for a longer stay."

"I understand what ye say," said McKenna. "And where, in which direction is the coal mine?" the agent asked .

The keeper laughed until McKenna thought he should have to douse him with water. Hain't ye seed thet there mountain?"

"Yes, truly pile o' slag...." siad McKenna.

Well sashr, thet there is a big lump o' coal and they's a hole to the side of hit and a li'l house outside. And i f ye'll go to that shack, 'tis called so, the Haven Coal Mine, ye'll get yer queries answered." The inn keeper walked off, handing MKenna the key to his room. Inside, he found it clean and spare with broken furniture, a rope bed, a shaky writing desk and chair and a chamber pot. He flopped out onto the bed and was aleep within minutes.

Down at the Haven Mine shack, McKenna went hrough the same process sof signing up for a job, asking first if the boss had any work.

"Do ye know how to work a short-handle pick?".

"Surely, er I wouldna be here."

"Le'me see yer hands." McKenna showed them. " 'Tis a sorry mess yer in, me lad. Here, here be a pair o' gloves ye can use. And they cos me aplenty, so jes ye make cartain ye don' leave 'm down in the hole.. I can use another man to drill and to stuff with the powder monkey."

"I'll take any work I can get. I think I can handle th' job, sahr," said McKenna.

The skinny foreman, the Mine Boss. said: "Ye'll see no extra fat on yer body after a week down ther. 'Tisi a tad chilly... the men 'ave got their ways, sihr, and they's a right smart bunch o' coal miners."

"I expect that, sihr. I like men who know wot their stuffin's worth andc can perform a job good 's the next."

"That's the way I like ye to talk. Be 'ere at six tomorry and I'll give ye a tag and a drill."

"A Drill?"

"Ye cant be too ignorant...'tis to drill holes for the blastlin' powder, kiddo. Ye've got to 'ave a steady hand or the maul-man, he's the monkey willl break yer paw at the wrist. Tthen ye've got some time in the 'ospital."

" 'Tis dark down there. I hope he can see." said the novitiate McKenna.

"He can right off. 'E's a good un, ten years on the maul and stuffin crack inter t' holes. But e's worth his wages, count on it."

The boss presented a fist to McKenna, to which the agent presented the flat of his hand, then reversed it with a fist to the Boss met by the man's palm. This was the secret greeting of two Mollies. At six the following morning, McKenna walked into the mine tunnel, a mule was pulling two carts, one of which was filled with a barrel of what appeared to be water in which were soaking several dozen burlap sacks. This arounsed McKenna's curiosity. He observed a string of four ore carts in which the miners for that shift had found squatting positions for the two-mile trip into the mountain. While on the way, he tried to conceal the gloves he was given, because he sensed that the miners scorned this elementary protection or one's hands, theirs being rock-hardened by their labor. Caloused, had hands ere a mark of long labor, dedication and milner pride. When the shift of miners had arrived at the coal face, McKenna removed the cutomary hat with the miner's lantern and turned up the wick, as others did the same, to lighten with an eerie flickering, yellow glow the indistinct surface of the wall of coal at the terminus of the mine shaft .

'To yer sites, boys...out with ye and a good day's work from ye. Any complaints?" There came none.

McKenna clutched his drill and looking about him, ecognized the looming form in the half light. He asked. "Where do we plant the steel, Brody?" For that was the mauler's name.

"Over here," said the stocky miner with the hammer in one hand. He cracked a spot in the coal face, casusing chips to fall to the floor. McKenna placed the star-point of his drill on the spot Brody had indicated, and the hammerling process began. This was all new to McKenna, as betokened by his gloved hands. He turned his face and squinted to keep dust and chips rom striking him in the eyes. The mauler repeatedly, and with a backward arc, struck the head of the drill with an uncanny precision, for McKenna could not discern in the dark the precise spot of the drill head. This was a dangerous business, McKenna thought. The hammerilngwent onfor ove half an hour in the soft coal. "Over here is where we set the next charge. Hold yer drill down a foot... 'tis better in case I miss me blow."

"I'll try sihr" said McKenna with anxiety and a fake apology. The ringing blows of metal on metal, steel again steel began as sparks flicked out with the sounD and the other miners picked away at thle face, disloding small a nd great at chunks of coal. :Ye see thet there man...well see how he picks at the seam. 'Tis layered...was spead down long ago in layers like sludge...like scum on a pond it was, with all sorts of living things adyin' in it. Thet's the coal wots carbon in due time. Ye'll get used to it." Thus the day's work began as the other miners, their tools striking the vein of coal and chunks falling to the floor atthe seam were mostly the sounds for the day. The labor of removing the coal allowed for little conversation between he miners. McKenna was contented that he could stand while he worked. Oher minersworked on their knees, and they swung their picks precariously close to one another inthe semi-dark. After a while, several mines came to lwhere the burlap soaked in the barrel ofwater and sloshing the fabric, they took the pieces, heavily drilpping,to the floor beneath the coalseam and spreadthemdown like mats on the floor. These mats provided protection for the miners by keeping the dust in the air to a minimum.

"The mauler, Brody, a Welshman said, "Thet's our best answer to coal dust. Water don't stahy' long wit' men's bookts kicking up dust...but them gunney sacks soaked in that barrel o' water do the trick. cartain."

"The mule, where be the mule?" McKenna asked.

"Oh, 'it's taken ter fodder and hits coral. They ne'r leave the mine, Mister McKenna. They born here, work here and die here. They be part blind, don' ye see, outside they would get lost."

This was news to McKenna, as he renewed his grip on he drill and the maul man, Brody commenced once again to hammer on the metal. He onluy stopped to breathe and to get a new grip on the handle of his maul. .

"If ye'll go fetch the dynamite, I'd be much obliged ter ye. 'Tils lin a box lin the secondore car yonder...." McKenna did as he was insructsed, returning with an opened box of dynamite sticks and spools of fuse line. The day was approaching noon, and the two of them had managed to drill four holes in the soft anthracite coal, easy enough compared to solid rock and deep enough to permit the insertion of three sticks of dyamite. "We don' load up the holes jest yet, but we drill some more,and thenwe load them up so's at night we can tetch off the batch...we come down hyer in the morry an' we load up wots been broke off the face. Yesterday, we drilled in another place...they be levils neath this level...thets why there not be any coal today where we stand."

"This light...can you see by the light on me hat?"

"I can right off, I got me cat's eyes ter help. Hit takes ye a while but ye can grow yer gloom-sight fer th' job down here. Ye'd be surprise at how steady and right onter target me maul is...hit has a will o' hits own and she hits the tab o' the drill just so ever time."

"I'll try ter keep me hand steady on the steel, sir."

"That's th' most...appropriate," he said, to show off a little education, most miners beginning their careers at sixteen or so to help support the family. Before that, they are breaker-boys who pick stones from the belts of coal that come their way. In another hour miners repeated the soaked- mat routine that covered the floor entirely where they worked. As a conseuences the tunnelloor before the face became coal mud linsed of coal dust as hey worked at the Pinegrove mine. <cLemma did not want to become a patient black lung case on pulmonaary ward in order to finish his assignment for Pinkerton. The blows of the maul kept coming, the drill dug in deeper and deeper, the novice miner withdrawing the drill it from time to time clear debris from the drill hole. After each hole, the powder monkey, Gory, tamped the usual three sticks into the hole. They would need a total of some twenty holes in order to knock down the seam for the next tday. He and Gory moved along the seam, from one side of the tunnel to the other, working around the miners and their wild, lethal picks that swung and cracked and wrenched, metal to coal wlith filne squeeks in the ever-present darkness. McKenna's hat lamp quavered as he moved, the light shifted, the face of his powder-monkey looked strangely sinister in the unsteady yellow light. He had not planned on becoming this much involved in actual mining. After all, it was information, ntelligence he was after.

"Sihr, Mister Gory," he managed between mauler's blows. Gory stopped his hammering. 'Tis a rest that's good for the soul from time to time." he said as he leaned on the handle of his maul. "Wot can I do fer ye?"

"Are there any kilt by the explosion...ever?" He paused, "Eight last year in the the Rausch Creek Mine...killt by a cave in...but as fer powder explosions, I think not since I set them off when the men aire ready to leave."

"Yet,'tis possible...."

"A' times, sure...a' thing's possible down in a coal mine....depends on how the rocks fall', strength o' the roof.   Ye seed them timbers inthetunnel? Well, then...."""

"Wot sets 'em off?"

"Wot...cave ins...? The gound trembles from time ter time, Mister McKenna, fer cartailn...me thinking about the matter is that we get a earth shake from time to time."

"Earthquake...?"

"'Tis the same , and when the owner he don] supply enough shoring timbers, we can go a scratch and then its bound to happen...a collapse, a cave in. Thet can make widders right smart," he said. The two ofthempicked up heir ools in hand and commenced their lborof boring holes.

"Ifn we stop fer too long the boss over there he will complain. He don' trouble er hurry me none because I be the powder monkey." He hammered away, then stopped to say, Gas canexplode,Mister McKenna. Gas...'tis called methane...blows up in yer face, specially wit these hyer coal lanters."

"How can ye tell if there's gas?"

"Well,sihr, we got a s songbird, a canary were best, a pidgeon from the pond 'll do, 'nd if it keels over from theg as, we partake out o' here wit our tools in hand case we got to dig out ifn there comes a splosion."

"I don' see no canary."

"Boss fault...but hits there most times." The mauler began anew, pointing out to McKenna the next spot where he was to place the drill bit. "Them sacks soaked--they sure keep down the dust and that keep me from coughin."

"Them bags o' water air best ventun since kerosene," McKenna said.

"Men don' 'ave ter stop ter cough an spit...cuts n on production like a tin shovel. Course, ye caint tell the owner nothin bout sech things. We 'preciate the wet floor, we do, 'nd so do the owners....Coal dust can splode also... not jes the gas," said Cory, and Stompy agreed...he ws a miner oerheard our conversation.   "'Splosion at times willcarry a man half a mine jes from thet fierce blow a the blast. :tis a caution...I kin tell ye...take ker...."

McKenna saw owner greed compared to miner innovtion in solving the menace of coal dust,bringing inincreased light to the seam, a put in of first aid forlinjuries down in the hole, aeriation of the the still lethal air and dispersal of methane gas, shorter work hours, improved cutting and cartage methlods for the dug coal...like their wet burlap flooring to reduce coal dust and work stoppages caused by choked lungs. McKenna saw other dangers, the incidence of broken tools, careless handllng of dynamite, warning whistles precedent to a cave in, better communication with the outide surface world, the incidental danger of underground water flooding the mine, work breaks to derail miner exhaustion... he thought mightily on them for the rest of the day and that night as well. He would write the intelligence conerning conditions down in the Schuylskill Haven mine, among others. When there was talk going on among the miners, he listened. On his second day working alongside Gory, he thought he heard the dripping of water rom somewhere. He cupped his ear to the mauler and pointed to the source of the sound.

"Aye, I can tell ye, sirh, in the Rausch Creek last year, pit men broke through a

wallseparatin' th' old milne from where they was cuttin' inter the seam, My Dawd come such a gush o' water 'twas a fearsome river riushed out onter the men 'nd damned near drow'ed most o' them like rats...by His mercy, them blokes climbed to a upper tunnen or...fssst...they'd be dead...a good man knowed the mine like his hand...old-timer, showed 'm the way."
McKenna was impressed with this account of the miners' near-death at Rausch Creek mine. He wroteof these things in detail. He held onto his letter until the following night, when he deliberately got so drilnk he could hardlhy make it to his third floor room. Naurally, he did not show up for work , for which transgression the pit Boss fired him, turning his brass number tag front side back and assining another man to he job of holding the drill for the mauler. McKenna staggered that night in the street as a railn and lilghtning sgtorm drenched the town in water and lihtning flashes. Soaked and lost, bumped into a policeman, who told him to go home. H saild he was lost, the cop led him by the arm to the stairs sof his rooming house. McKenna stood in the shadows of a doorway, pissed then watched the lamplighter ignite the rising glow of a street light. The next day, his two days were up. He packed his dowdy canvas bag. pinched the neck and circled it with a length of rope. He snugged the knot and, bumpling down the dimly lighted stairs, McKnna hit the road for a coal town named Swatara.

He walked through Newtown along the way. A trash picker caught his eye, two boys on their way to school in the next town, a drayman delivering store goods and a lamplighter up on his ladder, turning out his last street light...these were the singular silns of life. He guessed, shrewdly, that he could learn nothing here that he did not already know; and so he passed on, observing one neat fences, a thin tendril of smoke rising from one chimney, the barking of a dog as he passed and in the far disance the wail of a train whistle. The problems of these folks were nodifferent from the problems he had already encountered. He decided not to stop as he could not learn much just from the street level. Besides, the saloon was closed at this hour in the morning. He decied that he was hungry; there was no eatery. He would have to go wlithoutfood for the remalinder of miles, which he had no way of calculating, for,afterall, he was a stranger in this part of the country. He was grateful lto the gods there was no violent action going on, no shooting, not a hint of impending trouble or mahem. The screech and crackle of the breaker was missing, as was coal dust in the air, so that the coal. he imagind, had to be wagoned to the breaker in Schuylskill Haven or to Carbon at some distance. The breakers were spotted to coincide with the railroad tracks for transport to the big city, to Philadelphia and New York. All apperedto McKenna to be orderly and regular. Swatara and Middle Creek were close by each other, proably mining the same or an adjacent vein of sot coal. It was a guess to him, a novitiate in the business of extraction, which way theseams ran. Old-tilmers could tell by the curve, the avrupt ending,iln rock,the rise andfallof the layered blackstuff, nature's contour of her treasure. Other miners had to guess at the configuration of the seam.

But Swatara town, just a patch of about five houses and, agalin, a company store, a church and a saloon, had inheritedan exotic name for a coal town. McKenna went through his routine. He could use a beer for sustenance and breakfast, maybe a flat twist to appease his gnawing hunger. He entered the saloon. He was alone, a black man was mopping. MKenna presented his problem, he was thirsty and hungry. He showed the color of his money. The janitor served him. "Bartender, he come 'long soon. Stay lf ya wants tuh, I tell yum suh, you got t' hang 'hyer lone ."

"That's okay...okay. I'm on the road. Just a rest." He took his bottle of beer from the bar and sat down at a table. When at length the bartender came onto the scene and spotted him, he appeared to recognize him.

"If it ain't Jimmy McKenna the kindly tamp of the road...back iln town." McKenna wa asonished that the man knew his name; he had seen the agent somewhere else, under differen cxircumstances. He was becoming known to the mining communities, an accepted as a town fool. They were always around. He was glad that the bartender had shown he was frilndly, not angry. That made a huge difference to McKenna, in his trade of detecting Mollie misconduct, so-called. When they saw his of his sloppy figure, his dilapidated and untrustworthy lifestyle, his drunken orgies and his late show for work--that was good. Natsurally, small-town gossip had gotten around, like the presence of the town fool Everytown had a fool whom the people could rely on to hang around and to give local color to their town's life. In Schyuylskill, the police had had to pick him up off the street his third, unsecured night, after being fired, They had deposited him at his door on the third floor of the rooming house. One such town fool, other than McKenna, had roamed the town streets lin Pinegrove. McKenna learned that the man was a retired miner and frustrated musician. He liked to play on a stick, pretending it was a banjo, thus to entertain any kids who watched by playing for their laughter, a self- made comedian without stage. Sage was his name and he was a village fool of the lirst water.

At Swatara. McKenna establshed himself at the usual boadling house for a three-day stay, then he about for the saloon on the main drag. He heard of t the recent cave in...sixteen men still trapped in the mine, the church bell sounded in the morning. He saw relatives and friends going to the church to pray for the rescue of the trapped miners. This scene was commonplace,
McKenna realized. Such disasters were a part o the miner's life, irrespective of conrol by the mine owner. The detective mulled over these things, wondering in the silence of his soul why they had to occur. He applied for work at the Mine Boss shack but showed up drunk. Back in the comfort of the town's cheap dive, he overheard talk about hatred for the bodymaser of the mine and his cohort, the pit boss. Later in the day, when a crowd had gathered and remained at the mouth of the mine, the Pinketon agent got an earfull from miners and townsmen about their labor, their working conditions, their coolie wages...not even a Chinaman cold exist on what the mine owner payed them.

When he had sobered up at this scene of confrontation with tragedy, McKenna listened closely to the heartbeat of the people of Swatara. He heard of plans to stop trains by ambush, by obstructions across the tracks...any method to get the owner's attention, to transmit the message of deep dissatisfaction, while the miners put money into the pockets of others, they were kept in a state of impoverishment that was not due to drinking in the saloon...that was only a symptom,...but to the greed and penury of mine owners and their refusal toreduce quota demands of the miners slavilng below ground. McKenna overheard plans to stop trailns, to ambush train engineers, to corrupt enough politicians and owners in cahoots. To his dis;may, the Pinky spy listened in on planned shootings!!! Names were named.

He had gleaned new ilnomation in Swatara. He decided he would amble on to Mahoney Valley, north of Broad Mountains. McKenna now knew about the Mollies at

Swatara from the locals. Those folk were engaged not just in mining their patch of coal but also in farming, from which half-ace veetable patches they brought thei products to the local market on week-ends. There was, also, among the citizens of this small Pennslvania towns of no more than 5,00 souls a certalin contentment withs their circumstances, for it was, at first glance a clean town, having no breaker to spew coal dust into the air, the white paint on fences and houses remained white. Not until the Mollies should come into town to corrupt the two dozen or so miners would there ever occur a change iln community life. For these hopes, mixed with anger, McKenna, personally, was mighty glad. For the time being he could scratch Swatara off his list of discontentsed towns contaminated by the Mollie vilence of revenge.

He thought the time had come when he should visit with Pinkerton in person, thus he took a train from Schuylskill Haven to Philaldelphia to speak with Allan in Person. There was no incident of stoppage or attempt of ambush along the way. The Pinkerton head treated his prime agent, not to another general session with the other Pinkies...Allan could handle that himself...but to a bluegrass concert on the knoll outside of town. There McKenna reveald most of what he knew about the Mollies, in particular their spirit of vengeance against the bodymasters, the company agents, the mine bosses and owners, and certalin engineers...just about any who did the Mollies a bad deal by buckng their disssatisfaction with the way the mines were being run. The agent also described the wet-bag flooring at the Swatara mine, the prevalence of coal dust in the mines and in the town air surrounding the Schuylskill breaker. Most pathetically and with horror on Pinkerton's face, McKenna described the wanton shootings of any authority figure who seemed to be against change in the conditions of the mines . The blue grass bands played superbly. The two Pinkerton men could enjoy their company, as Allan and McParlan, aka Jimm MKenna, took a breather. McKenna told his boss all that he knew about the Mollies. They were usually good family men, paid their tithes at church, bore a certain show of religiosity, were focused on their work and had often many friends in the community. Mr.Pinkerton informed McKenna that he was to set up his headquarters in Pottsville.

When the two men separated, the agent took the train to Pottsville, where the screech and howl of the breaker pervaded the day's air and natural quiet. There he met la man named Dormer, a county commissioner, meaning a sort of judge. This Dormer fellow also owned a low-class drinking establishment, a saloon called the Sheridan House. Dormer had influence and he also tooka shine to McKenna, The result of that liking was that he appointed McKenna to serve as Secretary of the local division of the Ancient Order of the Hiernians, a Medieval organization of comradship that was proud of its Irish roots. He now had an office; Pinkerton furnished him with survival money and instructed him that if anyody questioned the source of his funds, he was to make out that he was a "pusher of the queer," a handler, a distributor of counterfeit money. That would be his excuse for seeming always to have grogmoney yet scarcely ever working in the mines. Dormer connected McKenna to another chap called "Muff" Lawler, a bodymaster--the keeper of the count of Mollies on any one job--these two men also hit it off, Lawler taking a liking to his new friend. McKenna exploited this new frlendship, and he often in a drunken state, posed for real, began to brag to Lawler, a Mollie, about the man he had shot, a mine superintendent, and the house he planned to burn down to wreak vengeance on a snitch. Lawler was immedilately impressed by McKenna's sense of vengeful retribsution, and was therefore drawn to the man. Lawler invited him to Sheridan House where the sly gent poured out his venomed fakery on those who refused to heed the Mollies...calling them were proud, arrogant, vain lot of men for whom money meant more than humn lives. ILt was for this reason, McKenna explailned, that the Mollies felt justified in rubbing out such obstructionists and tyrants of the fine craft of mining. After all, the Ancient Order of the Hibernian Society had its centuries-oldreputation to pertect.

From Pottsville, McKenna would have a straight track nto Pennsylvania as a route for the prosecution of what the detectives and their extraordiary spy had umncovered amongst the Mollies. Since he now was one of them, he had long ago begun to think like one of them. Pinkeron ordered that Jimmy set up headuarters in Shenandoah the followin year, for then he would be ln better touch with the activities of the Mollies in the different mines. Shenandoah being rife with Mollies on the prowl. The murders had become quite commonplace, McKenna wrote to his boss, so much so that "gunmen are brought from other towns to 'clean up' a situation" in the affecte town or mining camp. Mollies for hire was the signal for close attention to their murderous progran to exterminate all impediments to their rule over the mines and over the local police and town officials. McKenna had had many a hearty talk with Lawler at his tavern, he was had gained a reputation for being reckless, dissolute and shiftless, yet wild and capable, all of which endeared him to the Mollies. He was at last sworn in as an official member of the Ancient Order of the Hivbernailnas. A long strike at the Shenandoah mine prove to no avail, creating futher depression lin the local economy, since the miners were not at work, until finallythey had in 1874 to reject the plea of their long strike for higher pay and accept the terms of the coal company. Meantime, the Philly office had asssigned an assistant detective to help McKenna, a man named Linden, R.L Linden. It was still McKenna's game. He armed some twenty men with Winchester rifles when the Mollies stormed the colliery and tried to stop work at the Shenandoah mine. Mollies drove the sheriff of Shuylskill County and his possee from the town. There was gunfire over the heads of the miners, horses mingled in the melee, ttacks by ;Mollies upon the mounted possee, representing the law, and shouts and curses and whineying of the frightened animals. The Mollies, in a violent rage, threw open the cell doors to the jail, releasing prisoners of various ik into the town of Shenandoah, a patent example of the Mollie perversion of justice.

The same possee rode to Mahanoy City and took over the town, ousting the sheriff and patrolling the streets, Naturally, folks stayed indoors. Back in Shananoan, the Governor's troops appeared to quell the distrubance . putting the city and Shenandoah under military conrol. Then, in another disturbance, at a house fire in Mahanoy City, an unknown alleged killer shot a man named George Major, legislator burgess of the City. like a Councilman. The assassin drew a bead on him and murdered him at the scene of a fire. By virtue of witness testmony, hearsay evidence unsworn to, an innocent man named Dougherty was pointed out and arrested for the murder of Major. Dougherty, it happened, was innocent. However, he wanted revenge for the false accusation. Knowing where the blunt force of justice lay in the general region, Dougherty, acquitted of murder, paid a call on the major domo of the Mollies, big shot of the Mollies in Shenandoah, Jack Kehoe. The acuitted shooter said his life was in dangere but would he be safe if the two brothers of George Major were eliminated. Jack Kehoe was the commissar of the Mollies in Shenandoah and so he summoned officers of the Order, including secretary McKenna, to Mahanoy City where he,

Kehoe, assigned "the job" to murder Willliam Thomas, one of the brothers. to gunmen from a neighboring town . The conspiracy meeting opened at the Mahanoy City Squire, Hotel with a prayer:

Kehoe, being irreligious, asked the accuser Dougherty to open the meeing with a word of prayer.

"Oh, Lord," Dougherty began, " place yer hand on the gun of Willie Cranston and may the bullets from his muzzle bring vengeance down upon the heads of the killers fer the death o' wicked obstructionist, Thomas. You are the Lord o' Mollie justice and we Mollies walk in yer shadow o' retribushun. Thy will be done, thy Mercy stay close to us Mollies, ferever 'nd ever, amen." This premise by Dougherty of the invulnerability and sanctity of the Mollie cause was a part of the their widespread delusion of the righteousness of their cause, the invincibility of the Order's members, and the justice of cold-blooded murder to remove one of satan's own, the mine owners, mine bosses and bodymasters--all of thlem being Satan's invisible helpers.

The Big Man Kehoe failed to bring off the job. McKenna was unable to warn one of Donahoe's brothers, Thomas, of his intended murder. Thomas was shot but not fatally. However, McKenna did warn Major, the other brother, in time. Meanwhile, a Welslman named James Gomer was murdered by a Mollie named Hurley at a picnic outside of Shenandoah. Before his death, Gomer had been too loudmouthed, boasting of his proficiency with gun and confessing to the murder of an unknown mine boss. Proving the unproveable was the result. Gormer, at the picnic, had loud-mouthed about his exploits. Mollie Lawler urged Kehoe to reward the Hurley with 500 dollars for the "clean job" at the picnic. The web of interrelated Mollie associations and urges to kill any unwanted obstructionist and allie of company power would continue for at least another year.

James Gomer, with his characteristic blunt words, at a gatherng of the members of the Order, said to them:
"So ye think ye be the gods of this hyer county, do ye now. Well, being a proud Welshman, I deny yer obligations and yer assertions. Ye Mollies control the gates of hell but not the portals of heaven." These words were delivered with lyrical precision. "And, furthermore," Gomer went on, "in Wales, we don't see ourselves as Englishmen, or Irish by Gor, but as free men-- which is why I come here to yer 'Merica. Ye do no control me, Irishsmen, for I be a man fromWales and as doughty as any of ye. So partake of that, ye sons of the devil hisself." He sat down, and he felt the wave of hatred rise up against him, like a tidal surge, and so he left the meeting hall, leavling the Mollies with expressionson their faces of astonishsment, wonder and anger . He was slated to be killed: that was how the Mollies handled their outspoken enemy The men shrank back when Kehoe, pulling out a revolver, shot into the chandlier to   demonstrate his contempt for the establishment, He then and there walked from man to man, demanding allegiance with these words:
"Do ye, Jack Aremy, swear to abide by the secret rules of the Order and to respect its magistrates--meaning me, JackKehoe?|
"I do, I cartainly do, sirh... else I would not comne hyer ."
"And do ye, Henry Kleister, fa int German though ye be, agree that the Ancient Order will exist forever 'nd ever and that I, Jack Kehoe, shall be itsliege master wit power to appoint subaltern officers fer our affahrs?"

"I do, sirh, despite the long words and me short wind."

"Good!...and do ye, Sampson Calcutty, swear to abide by me orders and all th' rules o' Killarney County o' the Ancient Order, so help ye God an' the Saints fer if ye've God in yer soul, ye canno' 'ave the devil there at the same time."

"I do, sihr, Mister Kehoe, eminent Headmaster leader of the Ancient Order.

"Well, spoken, Sampson. Let no spalpeen claim yer soul."

Thus for almost twenty men, Jack Kehoe renewed their allegiance and loyalty to the Ancient Order of the Hibernians, neither comprehending the words nor forfitting the power, imaginary or not, that it brought to an unprincipaled man like Kehoe.

Only because of Dougherty's deadly paranoia against his half-brothers did Kehoe and "Yellow Jack Donohoe" another recruit for the reprisal murder become involved, assigning three additional Mollies, anxious to earn a reputation, to do the job or rubbing out Thomas. McKenna was able to forewarn Thomas, but his warning was not effectual. The four fired at random at Thomas who was not killed, while McKenna did warn Major, Dougherty's other brother in time to enable his escape from death. These motiveless attempts at murder were typical. The gang of four, having had exchanged hats and coats, returned to Shenandoah to reverse the clothing disguise. They came to the saloon for a bracer, exhausted by their ordeal of travel, where they related their story to derelict McKenna, Secretary of the Order. The famed sleuth providenially sat nursing a beer in the saloon at the time when the gang entered, ordered drinks, and let the assassination spill out in broadcast arrogance and loud boasting language. McKenna had a windfall of evidence he would use later in court when the time came.

In the coal town of Tamaqua, Frank B. Yost, a policeman and lamplighter of the town,was murdered in cold blood. No other method other than shoting was ever was used by the Mollies. It was on the morning of July 6, 1875 that Yost with his fellow officer Barney McCarron were extinguishing the lamps along Rampart Street in the pale dawn light.

"Keep yer wick snuffer in hyer pocket, Yost," his pal remine him,"If ye try to climb thet ladder with one hand yell fall fer cartain."

"I"ll mind my handling o' things, Mister McCarron. The town wastes money on these lamps wi' th' cost o kerosene. Half as many 'd do."

"Aain't nothing be done at this point. These old globes need cleaning...waste o' light is a cost."

"Well, we done our job. We got 'nother twenty, McCarron, so we better not waste time atalkin'."

Yost snuffed out the light with a small knob at the base of the reservoir and the light died down. He took a rag from a hip pocket, and he tried to clean some of the soot from inside the globe, tipping it on its hinge. He flinished, stuffed the rag back in his pocket and his snuffer in the other and startsed down his eight-rung ladder. He had reached the third rung from the top when the quiet of that dawn morning was shattered with the sound of a rifle shot, andYost took a bullet in his chest. It did not kill him right away, he let his hands slide downs the rails of the ladder and he slumped to the ground at the foot. McCarron came running over to him, his pistol drawn. He first looked his fallen friend and saw him bleeding in his chess. He lookied around, saw two dark forms running off between the houses. He heard another shot and took a bullet in his aisw. Both men were now wounded, McCarron emptied his gun at the fleeling figures. Yost lived not far aways and, draining blood on the round, he began to crawl toward his house and refuge. After a hundred yards, he could hardly drag himself any further, his strength fast ebbng. He did reach the sgteps to the front of his small wooden frame house where he lost consciousness. McCarron, not in much better condition came staggering after him and reached his friend just as the middle-age yost, wilhs an Irish burr il his voice and a manley smile always for others, expired on his front porch steps.

James Carrol of Tamaqua went to his priest, Father O'Malley, efore the next mass and said to him, "I done a dastardly thing, Father, night fore last. I think I kilt a man."

"You...murdered a man?"

"Yes, Father, and me friends were with me, and I canno't say whose bullet killed the man."

"Who, who was it ye murdered, me man?"

"George Yost, he be a policemun 'nd lamplighter. He was turning out the lights fer the night."

"Yer confession...come to confession. 'Nd Carrol', I would ye go to the local police, make a clean breast of the matter."

"They be a hanging in store fer me if I do."

"They be a hangin' if ye don' fer they'll filnd ye out, 'ye can count on thet."

"I cain't say fer cartain if it was me bulllet that hit Yost."

"There was another man?".

"They was four of us in all."

"Did ye shoot?"

"Yes, Father, I shot."

"Then ye'll all have to stand trial. Yer a 'complice, Caroll...tain't no better a sarvin' up o' justice fer th' 'complice, same 's th' killer." The priest studied the confessor to read his honesty of confession and the fear on his heart and, to see if a speck o' remorse existed for the murdered man. He saw only the fear. "Do ye ken who the others were?"

"Frien's o' mine...."

"The devil's frlends, they cain't be friends of yours, Carrol."

"Question is, will I be found out.

"Oh, man! don'tcha see? Ye'll be found out fer cartain, God help you. Yer a triumph o' satan and a prisoner o' the crime of murder, Carroll. Ye can count on that" said the Priest. "Come to confession, James Carroll, Thet at least is a start. I canno' pertect ye, man."

"I'll be there." But Carroll did not ever appear for confession, since the local police, with the help of Coal and Iron Police and local vigilante officers of Tamaqua captured Carroll and jailed him. Also one of the Mollies in the town fingered others involved, for it apppears that he had observed the murder, alerted from his sleep by the gunshots, and had watched from behind the blinds of hisr house the deadly scene that unfolded before hissleep-filled eyes. As other Mollie feigning to be witnesses, they had found life more sacred than their friendship with the Order, Hugh McGeghan and James Boyle from Summit Hill. But tey kew too much to be innocent witnesses, the shrewd townsmen soon concluded. The people learned of the murder through the Saloon keeper of the Barbed Wire Saloon in Tamaqua. The two men appeared on the next night after the murder and bragged that they had turned out a Mollie light unfaithful to the Order. The Bartender was not a Mollie and reported their braggadocious mockery to townsmen who reported the matter to McKenna at Pottsville. This prompt reportage resulted in the arrest of

lanky and sourfaced Hugh McGeghan and pudgy, arrogant, fat-fisted James Boyle, who
claimed to be related by blood to the British monarch, this madness making of him the
laughing stock amongst those who heard him boast. These twos men were put under arrest.
for their loudmouth revelation at th Barbed Wire Saloon in Summitl Hill, a berg township
that honored the law and the sanctity of life. A burly ex Mollie named Todd Hampden, a
former Mollie until he learned of their muderous program, put James Carroll, complicit in
Yost's smurder, under citizen's arrest and witha drawn revolver led him instead of to the
priest for onfession, to the local police station that had been set up in the small storefront of
a former pastry shop, headquarters, to be sure. Carroll was locked temporarily in the chill
cabinet.

Thomas Duffy of Reevesdale began to loud-mouth his exploit of   snuffing out
another deviate from Mollie protocol...disloyalty being sufficient cause for murder. One
night in the saloon, he thought of himself as witty. The local preacher overheard his boozy
confession of murder. A former wrestler lin the profession at Piladelphia he, the preacher,
wrestled the accomplice to the floor of the barroom and tied his arms behind him with his
necktie. He boldily picked him up like a sack of gran, tossing the murderer over his shoulder
and walking five blocks to the local station in Reevesville, where he dropped his sack upon
the floor lefore the astonished eyes of Jim Hampden, the local sheriff, self appointed. Thus
began the capture the four men complicit in Yost's murder and the attempted murder of
McCarroll .

The Coal and Iron police with the help of local officers not in the pockets of the
Mollies, with local help were able to srrest all four men for direct involvement and
complicity in Yost's murder. They were all Irish; they were all Mollies yet they lived in
separate towns, a trick of the Mollies to divert suspicion--Summit Hill, Reevesdale
andTamaqua. This fact alone shows the nature of the networking between the Mollies, their
customary meeting place for intrigue, plnning and sabotage being the local saloon, the
breeding ground for murder. Four were eventually found to be involved lin Yost's murder,
ranging in age from eighteen to thirty years, were hanged alMOST TWO years tos the month
in Pottsville.

These four languished, one might say, in a Pottsville jail for almost two years.
The town carpenters, within earshot of the jail, in the courtyard to what was once the
mansion of a grower of a sargum and tobaco. They hammered awayl for a month to
construct the gallows thehammerlig and shouts which these four felons were privileged to
hear. Each nail meant that another timber was added. Their collusion in the brutal murder of
the well-liked Yost dug into their souls, as it should have. The trial was swift, a week only.
Pottsville citizens hd been aroused by the killing without reason, ruthless to advance the
Mollie power in the town. The jury would not be intimidated, Judge Casper O'Toole was
strict in his admonitions, the defense was waged by a Molllie, sworn to get them off and the
prosecution by Samuel Harkins, a British lawyer, swamped the jury with both hearsay,
constructive evidence and the evidence of the killers, whose table-talk was overheard by a
witness at the Barbed Wire Saloon. He had come forward with what he had overheard during
the plotting phase of Yost's smurder.
The morning of June21, 1877 was fetid with warm air and anunseasonably warm
spring. The jurors, ancious to leave the sultry courtroom, showed thier impatience with the

defense's argument--that deputy policemana and lampsighter Yost was a thief in disguise and that he was attempting to dismantle a street light...for what purpose the defense could not prove. In fact, Yost was opposed to the M ollies, he beling an officer of the town of Tamaqua and fiercely hated by the Mollies for what he knew and his power of arrest. Many Mollies, having dispensed with pride in the Order, were scarcely able o conceal their sense of guilt for the crimes committed in the name of the Order of Hibernians. And so, up there on those gallows the deathshead mask was placed over each murderer and the death trap was sprung four times on that June morning, at high noon, each man going to his eternal reward in the noose of a strong half-inch hemp rope. Not oneof he ondemned men strangulated or choked but each had his neck snapped in the name of justice.

One other culprit hanged with the four, his name was Thomas Munley, who, like the Yost murderers, wasa Mollie and was jailed withs them. On the same June morning, he, too, swung with Yost's murderers. He had shot to death a well-liked man named James Sanger.   Munley, with   three other Mollies of ill repute--August Charles and James McAllister, Thomas Munley and Michael Doyle had conspsirsed to snuff out the life of a man named James Sanger. They never shared among themselves any suchnotion as a justifiable,even a clear motive. In fact, the lack of a motive, instead of convicting Mollies of murder, was often used actually to exonerate the Mollie. Counsel or the defense reasoned before the jury and judge that the alleged murderer could not have done the man in because he, the Mollie, had no reason to murder the victim. Thus was the jury hypnotized by the details of the murder and fearful for their own lives, let the felon escape the rope. Because of the lack of a lawful motive, August Charles, Michel Doyle, James McAllister and Thomas Munley figured they would escape the gallows if they appealed to Jack Kehoe in Pottsville. Expecting to presen themselves as petitioners for clemency to another of their kind, a Murderer, Jack Kehoe, they trapsied to the two-storey house of   of the Big Man Jack Kehoe in Pottsville and appealed to him to supply them with a motive for killng Yost. His word alone would be the motive. Kehoe, a supple, thin man with shaggy black hair and heavy fisted hand, a vile tongue and a black heart, grinned and winked at the four as he bade them good luck. He said, "Do yer deed, with dispatch. 'Tis the kernel of this business, gentlemen"...gentlemen murderers. "But take care, boys, lest ye be followed or found out. Clew up yer tongues when ye go to The Cracked Nut Saloon. 'Tis a gatherin' place for officers and the law, ye know."

And so he shook the hand of each of the accomplices in the Sanger Murder and they sped off in their borrowed hay wagon that had stood outside. Kehoe returned ot his game of single-handed poker while his wife, Angie brought in toasted cakes for the bodymaster. These four had set out on the darkened road from Gilbertton to Girardville. They were guests ln th house of a culprit named Donnelly, where they exchanged their hats and coats. They wlked to the mineentrance in full iew of hundreds sof miers and reaker boys, antipating Sanger's appearance, he having emerged with a friend guest from his home not far from the mine. The crowd represented men and boys ready to go on shift. Sanger appeared, at the same time as his four assassins emered fromtheir partial concealment. They fired at the unarmed man, who,with his guest, Uren from England, fled back to his house amid a deadly hail of bullets, Munley thought to head Sanger off and emptied his gun, felling hs vicim at the man's front door, while the crowd, some of them followed the one-sided gun battdle to Sanger's home. The fallen manwas helped into his house where his wife tended to his body, by then was closing its life.

The four were not finished. Characteristc of the Mollies being Irish
braggarts s protected by the violence of their Order, the four went at the start of their bloody
escapade to the Lehigh Valley Railroad statuion stop where they again exchanged clothing.
After this delusory attempt at disguise, they called on the tapster of the Coal Dust Saloon for
a stiff glass of ale each. Their thirst duly quenched, they headed up over the mountain to
Shenandoah where, again, they they barged into the rank and dowdy watering hole of "Muff"
Lawler, a felon in an apron and, sweatling, out of breath and partly drunk at Lawlers, they
plunked their faitigued bodies down and began to blab of what they had done. Spy McKenna
happened to be sipping a short beer in their vicinity. Believing him to be the reckless,
good-natured derelict of the town--his greeting was, "sit down, sit down, comrades"--they
accepted his courtesy and began to spill to him what they had accomplished that morning, the
singular murder of James Sanger.

The confession to McKenna by O'Donnell, nicknamed "Friday," was the murder
of Sanger and that the deed , by O'Donnels revelation, had been had been " a clean job,"
They had shot two men, the second being Uren, when they had expected to shoot just one,am,
Sanger. They had wantonly murdered his guest. This was violence, a first hand confession
that McKenna relayed to Pinkerton as soon as he could find and pay a courrier to deliver his
letter. A vigilantes posse had, meantime, killed the mother-ln-law of Kehoe in the O'Donnel
houe, den of murderers and a source of evil by Mollies in the community.

A large crowd followd the bier of JamesYost to the local cemetery in Pottsville.
There, after the graveside ceremony, his friends opened another ceremony, a tradiional Irish
wake. With dancers from the community wearing black arm-bands, dressed ln Irish pinafores
and leather pants nd pantaloons, the dancers committed themselves to a wild Irish fling, first
,and then an Irilhs reel, while fiddlers, horn players, a bagpiper and drums kept the beat of the
music. The crowd who had come to the graveside were joined by villagers, knowing of the
celebration going on. A man named Massey O'Rourke wagoned in several kegs of whiskey
and beer for the celebrants. The wilder ones began to play games, apart from the dancing.
They threw huge rocks for a prize of ten dollars to the winner. The celebrants danced, they
played a race called skip-rope dash in which the runners skipped a hemp rope from the
starting line to the finish. The men, anxious to particiate, took part in this race, as did the
numerous children amid their laughter that lightened the hearts of all. The cemetery had its
own tables and benches. Women with their menfolks and children began to appear at the
cemetery with baskets of food--corn carkes and berries, while one man, from his wagon,
lifted down a cask of wine and another of water. Some of the clebrants had walked out from
the town or come by horseback,   Wthin an hour, almost a hundred celebrants were engaged
in an Irish wake to dispel the gloom and sorrow of losing a dear friend of the community.
As he band played, more and more of the celerants formed rings and danced away their
sadness....

iv

The Yost celebration of life after death only awakened anxieties of another trial that would pove as fiercely contended. For a well-lliked man by the hame of John P. Jones was killed with the same disregard for life as the murderers of Mollie Yost had shown. Jones was the harbinger of peace in the mining communities, the bellwether of trials, the ultimate step of Pinkerton justice and efficiency. Of course, McKenna was the ostrich that refused to put its head in the sand, as had law enforcement in most of the anthracite mining towns. The ordinary people did not want to become involved lest their loved one be victims on the Mollies hit list. Faithful wives did not enquire too deeply into any involvement their husbands may have fallen into. With Darcy and Munley, McKenna, pretending to be a close abettor to the two men, went to the Saloon to discuss the killing. However, McKenna, who was sworn to deter murder if he could, talked Darcy out of the job while Munley went his own way and became the shooter on that cold winter morning inTamaraque. He, of course, was not alone.

A clammy day, with a cold sun and ground fog marked the early morning hours in Pottsville, where, encarcerated for months, a three felons accused of murder, awaited their trial efore a town that literally trembled with anxiety and fear of repisals. Their victim had been the miner, and a Mollie, named Jones, the last name barring him lin the popular mind from Irish ancestry while making of him the sniff-dog for Irish retaliagtion against the mine officials. The only factor of disclaimer was that Jones had no authority eher iln the Order or in the mines. He did, nonetheless, harbor certain dangerous sympathies...to wit, that the mine owners could not keep up quotas with work stoppages, whaever their cause, and that the price of coal had fallen, that wages so deperately low as they were might be cut another penny, and that conditions down in the mine could not be corrected immediately, proof of that fact being that engineers brought in to modify the mine environment inevitably finished their assignment without makine any changes. Therefore they were seen by Mollies as complicit in keeping the mine conditions unchanged as a part of the overall operation status quo. No owner ever shut down his mine becaused of miner hardships.

The company store had its place, and it was a regretable yet necessary mishap, so called, that miners went heavily into debt to the company store. Only if the mine shut down and the town burned to the ground would salvation come. Otherwise, miners and their families bore the onerous debts accumulated over years with their patronage of the only marketplace they had, the mining-town store where credit was king and debt, deep debt, the condition of virtually all miners of that one mine. The milners' debts became a kind of enslavement. From time to time, a member of one family would add to the clan income with a job outside that town, traveling, say from Carbon to Philadelphia for a real job. These families were regardef with mild contempt,for a any miner and his family who did not share in the debt-to-credit relationship with the mine was a suspicious outsider. The Mollies thus held Jones to be one of these.

In order to prosecute the murderers of John P. Jones in a relevant way, McKenna insisted on a reading of the testimony at the trial of Yost's murderers in order to acquaint the jurors with the motive, means and anger behind the murder. The prosecution of those mad, bloody killers o was about to begin. The jury was chosen after both sides had, for three weeks, sifted through a hundred or more community citizens to find those who did not know Jones personally or the murderers but who had lived iln the town of Lansford for many years. Half of them were grayheaded and wheezed with black lung; they held the Mollies in fear or contempt, often both and they possessed a sense of righteous justice that was due to the murdered man and his family.

"Would the clerk be so good as to read the transcript of the confession of the murderer of Mister James P. Yost." A lythe and muchly animated man, small in stature, with ruddy compexion , blue eyes and gesturing hands stood before the jury to begin the trial. McPalan was his name; it stunned the pathetic figures of the accused to see that McKenna was not the sodden, irresponsible n'er-to-well they had met in the saloons. He turned to the jury, "I give you this not to extend this trial but to furnish you good people of Lansford with a perfect example of the way the Mollies work." There was in his words a strange calm, a regulariy, a perfection of speech and control of manner that once more astonished not only the jury but the packed court as well. For here was the slovenly McKenna, filled with bitter rage, once so comradely, sloppy of speech and filled with profanity and adulterous language, now speaking n this morning like a Father of the church, a sqire of the law/ This visible transfomation befuddled one of the accused, who sat at defense counsel's table, as it amazed most of those in the courtroom that day. For McKenna's reputation for being a wiseacre drunk half the time, a derelict who could not keep a job was revealed not to e his true character. The accused had been bamboozled, an they resented having been fooled.

"Would the clerk read the transcript please," McKenna repeated, after the Magistrate, Harry Shannon had introduced him to the court and especially to the jurors, as James McParlan.

The court clerk began his droning recitation of the trial record:
"Has Mister Yost ever come to you asking for help?"
"No, sir," said the accused (murderer of Yost that night on the dawn street as Yost turned out a street lamp.)
"Has he ever revealed to you, by intention or incidentally,that he was a Molly?"
"No, sir."
"And has he ever shown toward you any suspicion of your sintentions?"
"No sir, he has not."
"Did he ever threaen you."
"He never did, sir."

"Your answers are clear as to their meaning...he did not ever present to you a threat of any kind?"

"Not that I can recall."

"Let me sharpen your memory. He once told you that anybody who was a Molly had better watch out. Do you remember that occasion?"

"Not clearly, sir...it mighta been at the saloon."

"But Mr. Yost was not a drinker. He had never gone into the saloon. He was a churchgoer, a deacon, a teetotaler, and as I recall, a member of the local constabulary. Were you aware of those things?"

"No, sir...just that he minded his own business."

"That's right. So Mr. Yost kept largely to himslelf. He never caused trouble."

"Not that I can recall."

"Then why, why did you pull the trigger that killed James Yost?".

"I never...."

"Stop! Your colleague in murder said that it was you who drew a bead on the murdered man while he was atop his ladder turning out the stret lamp."

"Then he lies."

"But the other man in your trio said the same thing. You were the shooter, by the confession of two of your conspiators...the shooter of an innocent man. You are all equally guilty nder the law."

"He had a big mouth, Yost did."

"Big mouth...don't you mean that he was...sociable, that is really what you mean, and that you distrust sociable folks because they might spill something...unlawful... about you. Is that not right?"

"No, sir."

"Stop! That is right. You are a Mollie, is that not right?"

"I am a Mollie, yes, sir."

"And the Mollies have a hate for anyone who is either in power over the operation of the mine, its miners and its economy. Is that not right."

"We have our ...druthers, sir. The mines are a disgrace, the wage is low, too low, the debts we got to aquire cannot be helped. We are prisoners, sir."

"By your choice, I might add. You could move to Philadelphia, you could leave the state... is that not possible?"

"Not after we got homes in Lansford...and work."

"And work!..., just so. You do benefit from the mine, then, dont ye?"

"Yes, sir. "

"But to murder another man, even if he be a Molly, for being a part of your misery--that is justifiable homicide?"

"No, sir. It's just...."

"Yes...Just...?"

"Yost had a big mouth."

"But the jury now sees him as a rather quiet man. Is that not right?"

"They got their 'pinions, sir."

"All the same, you pulled he trigger. You brouht down a innocent man that morning. You had no accusation against him that would sand up in this court, and yet, yet the admission of on-the-site witnesses, sworn to tell lthe trlth, the eye-witness evidence is that it was you who murdered Mister Yost."

"You got yer 'pinion."

"That is not my opinion, sir, that is a fact."

The clerk reader of the transcript looked at McParlan. "Is that all, sir?" he asked.

McParlan said, "The accused felon of this transcript was found guilty because of and despite his answers. Other evidence was bought in. The judge in the Yost case simply dismsissed the witness, the accused. Counsel for family of the slain Yost appealed to the jury for the death sentence, under the circumstances and in accordance with the testimony of the shooter just given.

McParlan turned to the present jurors, five women and seven men from the town of Lansford, waiting to hear the facts in the Jones case at hand. As he turned there was a wild commotion at the back of the courtroom, and a small man with disheveled hair, black hat, in dungarees and wearing a bandoleer that read, Mollies for justice, entered the double doors. Sheriff's deputies, two of them intercepted him, seeing he meant to do harm. The man suddenly wielded a long barreled cavalry pistol and fired six shots presu;mably at the judge. The judge ducked on the first round and the others went astray. He emptied his gun in the general direction of the jurors. He killed one of the women jurors and wounded another. The violence, distress and bloodshed of this confrontation was appalling to all, frightened by the gunfire and seeing the body lying between the jury chairs, blood coming from her face; she had been struck in the head by the felon's bullet. The deputies, in consort with Pinkies standing within earshot, hastened to remove the body to a Pinkerton horse-drawn wagon outsside, and the wounded man as well, sending them off to the samll infirmary in Potsville; for the town had no hospital. The shooter at the back of tlhe courtroom was knocked to the ground and pummeled, his hands tied behind him, as the entiure court stood, ducked, hunched forward, thinking the shots were meant for them. The juryhadreacted in he same way, hiding behind their chairs. The culprit was led out into the corridor, the double doors slammed shut and the incident was ended, in actuality but not in the imaginations of the courtoom witnesses..

McParlan said to the judge, "Your honor, the Mollies are at it again. For the very reason that that madman came in here to seize justice with a gun, we are trying to mete out justice by the law." The judge rapped hard three times. "Order! Order in the court!" he ordered with a heavy, authoritative voice. "Settle down, settle down!" he boomed to the spectators and the jurors. There came a moment of stirring about and finally order spread over the assembly. McParlan turned to the jury again.. "The law, as you can see, ladies and gentlemen of the jury, is not a passive thing. It is the monster that keeps society together and operating." He paced back and forth before them in a meloidramatic manner,lookng into the face of each member on the front row, as if to detect the degree of his or her interest and sincerity of motive for serving. "I have had this testimony read because I want, not to see and to umderstand by similar circumstances the brutal madness the Mollies usee to bring about reform in the mines.. the devious nature of Mollie murders. My agency has estimated a number of over one hundred murders in the region of the anthracite mines..." jurors and audience members gasped. "That's right, many, many...members of the jury... remain and will forever remain unsolved murders of men held in contempt and hatred by the Mollies because they held a job that...supposedly, supposedly. I say, put down, harmed, killed hard-wsorking the miners such as are seated on the jury and in the court this day, in favor of the bodymaster, mine owners and mine bosses. Think about it...the wanton murder of good men, many of them Mollies themlselves, who did not kowtow to the Mollie renegades in towns where Mollies live...and often il other towns where the killers did not live. The Mollie killing apparatus was and is a deadly web of fiends who shoot, who gun down innocent men on the town streets, in open daylighgt, often, and at night when hasty escape is possible. They escape, jurors, not into their homes but through the woods into other towns. That is why they are so elusive, so desperate, so deadly and bloody in their mission to murder mine officials." Again McParlan let his words catch the consciences of any in the court, the jurors, and the witness on the stand, a Mollie named Harry Munley. oyle and Kelly sat at the same table. Four burly miners as deputized sheriffs stood nearby, their folded arms ready to grapple with the accused Mollies should they try to escape .

He paused to let his charges sink into the consciences of the jurors. "They are a brotherhood, jury. They are related, it is their belief, by ancient blood to an Order called he Hibernians, a society of Medival Irish mendicants, it turns out. who practiced a form of religious worship of ancestors, but lived lives of the devil, as they have demonstrated in this town by the accused. "Let me move from Mister Yost to Mister Jones. The manner of their deaths is similar. Both men were killed by a coward with a rifle, firing at his victim from ambush. The murdered Jones kissed his wife and babes that day and left his house...to go where, to a clean job in a building that looked down on the miners, he was headed to join them iln a hard day's work. He wore his bib overalls, he carried his pocket watch, he was early, he brought his lunch bucket packed by his loving wife for his hard day's labor. He had every expectation of returning that night to the dinner table to be with his wife and two boys, a good night's rest, a morning's sit to read the Lansford Tribute, and then off to work. In fact, jurors, he had managed to eek out enough for a down payment on his small frame house, and he was ardently, like a good workman, trying to pay off the mortgage. He was like a thousand others here this town, like you, members of the jury.
"But he would not pay off that mortgage and he would not return to greet his wife with a kiss and to pick up his two boys with a father's love for his sons. No, he did not get one thousand yards away fom his home when a bullet from the gun of that man sitting there, brought down an innocent, a good, a loving and faithful father and hardworking miner in the Lansford Mine...brought him down with blood on the street, stretched out, while other citizens came rushing to his aid. That man sitting there in full view of you, jurors, was the man who in a cowardly act of angry vengeance, shot another man in the back, the most cowardly of acts.

McAllisier arose from the defense table and mounting the steps sat in the witness chair. He was was sworn in, with a grim, cynical snicker on his lips. He did not believe in all this folderol of pleadings and rtestimony and charges, for beling a Mollie through and through he believe in the justice of thegun, and for this reasonthe vigilantes of the town, largely unknown, unidentfiable, were the trel heroes of this drama of hardship v. power.

"Mister McAllister , would you state your name,
James McAllister .'
On the night of February 9th, you were at a meeting at the home of a man named George Lawler, is that not so?"
Yes, I were.
There was adilscussion about rubbing out, rubbing out another soul named Jones.

Do you recall that discussion.

"Hardly."

"Hardly, you say. The bullet from your gun was hardly a shot, is lthat notso.

"Objection, yer honor. The counsel presupposes what is not established as fact."

"Sustained."

"McParlan rephrased his question. The alleged bullet from the gun you allegedly held could have been the bullet that killed the deceased Jones...do you see him here in this court room today?"

"I cannot say, yer honor."

"The judge is His Honor and there he sits. So there was a discussion about putting down a man mamed Jones."

" do not recall."

"Then let me remind you of this." Prosecutor McParlan brought out a paper and showed it first to the judge and then to the witness. That, sir, is one of your coffin letters. Do you recognize it?"

He glanced at the letter McParln held out to him. "I do not."

"Do not lie to this court, Mister McAllister. That is what you murderers call a coffin letter. Every man you killers fingered--that's yer crowd, fingered fer death got one of these...cofflin letters." McAllister shook his head with a careless wave of his hand. McParlan passed the letter to the jury and they inspected it one after the other. As you can see, jurors, the skull and corss-bones atop the coffin was a threat. Can you see that? Can you ask yourselfs, 'What else could this letter mean but a threat to the recipient, death to the miner, to another living human being, death to his faith, death to his debt...thank God for that...death to his family?' That was a possibility, jurors, but that's the only kindly thing l can say about the Mollies, that they marked their man as one, not his family or his friends, just him. These coffin letters, members of the jury were circulated among those the killers fingered to be murdered."

Back to the witness who listened to this appeal to the jurors. You heard my witness to the jurors,sir. What do you say to it?"

"I hain't got no words to add."

"It is good you don't, fer there are no words to add. You're a Mollie, is that not true?"

"Yes, sir."

"And Mister Jones, was he not a Mollie?"

"He was, sir."

`But are not he Mollies supposed to stick together. What then happened? Why did Jones suddenly become your enemy?"

He snitched on Mister Kehoe to the mine boss, said Kehoe wanted the trouble at the mine, a 'sposion or some such to happen, to brilng in the gover'mint."

"How did lyou learn all of this, sir?"

"I hart it from Jack Kehoe hisself."

"I see. So, acting on hearsay, on mere gossip, you took the life of a innocent man."

Objectin. Counsel presumes a fact not yet established."

"Sustalined."

"But you did have a attitude of, let us call it, vengeance?"

"He had it coming." This remark astounded McParlan. He turned to the jurors. You hve justheard his words...the deceased ...'had it coming.' Vengeance was the motive, if there ever was a fitting word...vengeance. Are you aware Charfles McAllister, that your twoaccomplices sit there in this courtroom, Misters Doyle and Kelly, there. " McParlan pointed to the other two arraigned Mollies. The jurors looked at each other, exchanged a comments , wore grave and squinting expressions on their faces as they regarded from a distance the men referred to. Their looks were troubled as they regarded the accused wilh sidelong scrutiny. They were emotionally involved.

"I never heard of him."

"You, sir are uner oath. Do you perjure yourself?"

"Ojection, Yer Honor. Counsel is tryin; to intimidate the witness."

"Objection overruled," the judge responded."The Prosecutor's statements were made without animus...for you,sir, that means without anger and intent to intimidate the witness."

"Mister McCAllister was seen on the very day he shot Mister Jones. But he was sot apprehended at the murder scene. by the crowd. No, he was arrested at the Briar Patch Saloon the next day. He sits there before his court and this jury pleading innocence because he was found far away from hif victim." McParlana turned frm the jury to the witness McAllister.   Now that you ahve perjured yourself that you do not know about the coffin letter, and that you did not kill Jones, let me point out to you the two who were with you on the day of the murder..." McParlan pointed to Kelly and Doyle at the Defense table. They are Mollies who feel the same as you about the mine boss, the bodymaster, the owners of the Tamaqua mine. They are your accomplices."

"I got me frien's."

"Indeed, you do, sir. Let me name them for you and for the jurors. Doyle, Kelly and one more not here, Kerrigan. Haye you heard of those names?"

"A little, sir. There's lots a folks I don' know in Tamaqua."

"They sit right there before you. Would you, Misters Kelly and Doyle, raise your hands." They did so over defense objection that the men had not been sworn in. "Well, sir, let me tell you that you will be the first to go, as the gunman, but you will not go alone. You have no retaliation witness and there is no chance for you to take vengeance out on another citizen of this or any other town."

he defender of the trio, who raised few ojections, now cross-examined the witness. The defense council was named Conrad O'Leary.

"Remember," said; O'Leary you are still under oath. Would you tell this jury what your motive was for killing Jones?"

"Motive. sir? there was no motive... to kill Jones er any other man...."

"You have hit it...Jurors, you have heard the witness accused of murder...from his own lips, the witness confesses he had no motive for murder. A motiveless murder must therefore be a accident." Of the witness, he asked, "Was the killing of Mister Jones an accident?"

"I do not know, sir."

A motiveless killing is a accident killing. Motivated killin' is a murder. That is the way the Mollies think. But let me tell you, McAllister, you will not get off the hook, you will not slip the noose so easily.

The defense lawyer named O'Leary took over the floor to question the wiltness. "If his demise was an accident then there could be no motive. Is that correct."

"I cannot say. I am not a lawyer."

"We cannot establish motive, yet we can establish doubt as to the cause of Jones death." He paused o let his words register in the minds of the jurors.   "Did you know...or perhaps you had now way of knowing...that Mister Jones was a frail man. In fact, he dropped over one day down in the mine." From his table, Counsel fetched a paper, which was a medical report from the town infirmary, where Jones was taken one day, complaining of heat ehaustion. "This hyer paper says that Dr. Hansen, James D. Hansen of th Pottsville Informary, examined Mister Jones on January 4th of 1876 and found, that he had suffered a slight spell of blackout. The question then occurred to Doctor Hansen, did Mister Jones collapse down in the mine from a heart seizure?" The lawyer dropped the report back on his table. "Could not the man in question, Mister Jones, have fallen to the ground from a heart seizure and, striking his head a blow on the rocky soil, sustained bleeding to his skull?"

"I suppose he coulda...but I hain't a doctor."

"No, you are not a doctor and you are not a lawyer, Mister Doyle, but you have common sense...as do the jurors." He came over to them and faced them directly. He began his plea to their reasoning, their common sense. "Does it not strike you, jurors, that the so-called shooting is a cover-up by the prosecutor for the very real possibility that the deceased Mister Jones, who is no longer with us or with his family, who no longer is a faithful toiler at the coal seam, died of a heart seizure? Eh? think about that...and if you doubt..if there isl the slightest doubt in yer minds, then ye must judge Mister Doyle as innocent...and McAllister, whose testlimony you have heard, as a straw man who did not gun down Mister Jones. But, instead, you must consider whether or not the deceased Jones may have succumbed to a bad heart and died that very; morning for that reason and that reason alone. Remember, if there is a shadow of a doubt, you must acquit those three men of the heinous crime of murder." Defender O'Leary reurned to his table and through his black beard and fine teeth, smiled a smile of confidence at the three men who sat there. He appeared confident that he had established a means for acquittal, regardless of the overwhelming testlimony of citizen witnesses. He had focused on the manner of death, not on the sene of a shooting, and that foclus made all the difference in the world in the outcome. Or did it? Judge Shannon, looking over his court, its few spectators reduced by the shooting incident, and at the weary jurors, ordered the sheriff deputies to remove the accused prisoners and return them to the Pottsville jail. Tomorrow would be another day befor the jurors were sequestered for deliberation, for McParlan and O'Leary, each, had presented his side of the case. The judge rapped his gavel. and prepared to dismiss the court for that day. He was metilculous about his desk land was setting things in order...,

The people of Pottsville were aware of the trial. They also knew that Mollies with guns roamed the streets sof this a;nd sother mining towns. They carried guns, the citizens, many of them feafful townsmen. It was mid-afternoon. Some of the citizens cruised around the courthouse, expecting what did actually occur. A bunch of thug Mollies, with clubs and guns, when the court was dismissed, bashed in the side door amd stormed into the courrootm.   The women screamed, the jurymen who had scattered several remained concealed to watch the action. They would be the witnesses. The entire courtroom was in a panic, pandemonium was everywhere. The judge had quit the bench and run for cover iln his chambers in a small side room. Thje thre on treialbraved thle clubs,l; among them frliends, as the insurgent raiders attacked any who stood in their way of seizing the trio. McParlan defended himself with an upraised chair. The brutish thugs grabbed the three prisoners, Kelly, Doyle and McdAllister and were pulling and dragging them to the side door, while the rest of the courtroom had fast emptied.

McParlan and Allan Pinkerton were prepared for just such an occasion. As the bunch of thug Mollies, eight in all, started for the door to exit, they were met by\ a counterforce of Pinkies, three dozen in all who swarmed into the court with batons and visored caps, several wearing side-arms, and, tackling, banging and clubbing with their pistol butts, they brought down the three Mollies and their rescuers. Still, the mahem was not over. While the Pinkerton men were handcuffing the three accused on trial and their Mollie pals, townsmen, thinking the bruhaha involved lawless renegades also attempted to storm into the courtroom, shooting their way in. McParlan, braving gunfire stood sand tried to head them off.

"We got 'em! We got 'em!" he shouted at the top of his lungs to the townsmen, who slacked off. They saw McParlan wavilng his hands wildly. The Pinketon men had their captives under control. About this time,the Judge reappeared, his hair and his necktie askew, and without his black robe. He shouted to Pinkerton and McParlan, "Thrown them in jail for contempt, assault and battery and attempted murder!" The overwhelming force of Pinkerton men next led the rescue gang of Mollies to jail in commandered wagons and at gun point, just as the judge rapped on a counsel table.

"Bring the three accused to court tomorrow. Court adjourned!"

The Pinkies took all of the Mollies, the accused trio, their defenders of eight, and a bunch of the rowdiest and most violent of the citizens to jail...for using firearms agailst unarmed persons, menacing the general body of the trial court for that day, and disturbing the peace.

Judge Shannon was sharp and succinct. "Yesterday, we had trouble in this courtroom. It will not reoccur." With the help of the local police Pinkerton had placed a cordon of his men around the courthouse. Judge Shannon announced gavely to the crowd: "We shall begin with my condemnation of the violent confrontation yesterday in my court. The citizens and the Mollies, who began the ruckus, will be fined for contempt of court. I have already so informed them at the jail. The matter is on the docket, reserved for another day. Today, we continue the trial of ..." he looked at his register "....of Misters McAllister, Doyle and Kelly." He rapped his gavel. "Court is in session."

But the powers of justice were scarcely begun again, for within a week, other miners, Mollies all, were arrested and jailed, their names being Jack Kehoe, who was the chief of police in Girardsville, Frank O'Neill of St. Clair, a man named Lawler, Michael Lawler of Shenandoah, Patrick Dolan, Sr. of Big Mine Run, Frank McHugh of Mahonoy City, Patrick Butler of Lost Creek and one or two others. They would have their day in court. The charges against all of them was the singular charge of murder. Other charges might have been layed against them as lindividuals, such as breech of the peace, threatening violence, robbery of the company store and homes, rape--one of them-and general threats to a peaceful and law-abiding community. The charge of murder was, however, the most viable and sustainable charge, and was the most effective way to put these thugs and outlaws out of business, their business of murder of convenience. They were captured by the local police, in several instances with the help of the citizens with guns, and with the help of miners who lived constantly under the threat of the Mollies' murder for the asking.

"While your accomplices in murder--Doyle and Kelly-- sit there in ropes and under guard, you have the blessed freedom Mister McAllister of listening to your indictment in a free society of honorable and peaeloving men and women.: With these words, McParlan continued the court's prosecution the day after the assault. In the interest of brevity, I will ask you three leading questions. Your answers will provide your defense...or your execution. Rememer that you are under oath. What was your motive in shooting Jones that morning?"

"Sir, I did not shoot Jones. 'Nother bloke shot 'm. I heart the shot and I come arunnin' to his body. I seed who it was. We miners suffer fer the likes o' him."

"Somebody else shot him?"

"That's me figurin."

\   "Jurors,cn you not see detect as a matter of common sense and human compassion that that man, seatedthere before you, does infact lie? H has no alibi that is worthy of consideration. In a word, the man lies. He perjures himself."

"Objection, the charge is hearsay and without evidence."

"Sustained."

"How do you suffer, any more than other miners." McAllister was silent. "You imagine yourselves--all of you Mollies with guns-- to be redeemers."

"We got to make changes."

"By the use of a gun, McAllister! How can that be? You changed a man from life to death. That was the only change you made."

"He was in the way." McParlan was stunned.

"In the way, was he. Thas is me second question. So ye removed him, and what did he stand in front of?"

"Of changes to the mines."

McParlan, stoic in his delivery, faced the jury. "You have heard this man's confession...on the witness stand. He had no power over the mines. He was a miner, the same as you. What could he do to make changes, any change? He had no power. That is me third question. What power did ye think to possess...if ye did not possess the gun that killed Jones?""

"I canno' answer ye that, said McAllister, not because I hain't got me wits together but because he niver tot us what changes he would make."

He had no power to do anything...do ye not un'erstand...no power but to wield the pick and shovel down in the mine...same as you, Mister McAllister. Jurors, y' have heart the testimony. Y' have yer senses. Was not the shooting a savage murder for no reason, by this culprit here on the stand?"

"Objection. Counsel concludes what the whole purpose of this trial is about, evidence to convict for murder."

"Overruled. The prosecutor characterizes a man only accordilng to the charges, not according to a conviction. Proceed."

"I have nothing to add. Yours for cross, defense."

Council for the three charged with murder and complicity asked a single question of McAllister: "Did you shoot Mister Jones on the morning of February 14th?"

"I did not, sir."

"There you have it, your answer from an accused man under oath." The colossal naivete produced a frown and then a grin on the face of McParlan. For he knew the jurors, whom he had helped to select, were not so naive as to think the Mollies had no program for muder, and were invisible, potential culprits with guns, and railed against the mine owners and all the powers that brought the coal to market, including the Iron andCoal railroad monopoly on passenger and freight .

James Doyle was the next to testify. The questioning by McParlan was similar, except that with this man the Prosecutor concentrated on the means, the presumption being that he had the right man.

McParlan, lead off with this assertion. "Jones fell after he left his house, and we already assume hat it was McCallister who shot him in the back, a fiendish scheme cooked up by James Munley whom you had visited the week before the shooting. You were the enabler, sir, the gunman, even if the plan was Munley's...you, Mister Doyle, and your cohorts, Kelly and Kerrigan, foresworn to murder the innocent Jones because he sided with mine authority...having pumped more bullets into the fallen body just to make sure he was dead. Do you recall the scene?"

"I don't know whatcher talking about, sir."

"You don't, eh! Let me refresh yer memory. He said to Doyle, still on the witness sand. "Did you have a motive for the murder?"

"I did not, sir. Fact is I thought Mister Jones was a fine Chris'ian man, sir. 'Nd I honor church-goin folks."

"Except if they do not protest 'longside of ye.... or ye send them to heaven i'stead of to hell before their time's up."

'It were not my regular business to put down a fine man."

"You made it yer business. If you had no motive, did you encourage McAllister...because Jones had money."

"I hain't a robber, sir. "

"Did you goad McAllister because Jones threatened to fire each of the three of ye, or cause the mine boss to fire ye?

"I did not, I did not. I niver had a say as to hiring. Me job was me master, not Jones."

"You leave us to wonder..." He took a breath, "Jurors, does the man there on the stand not leave you--he leaves me--to wonder if he did not in fact have a motive for seeing Jones dead, the motive of job hate and job replacement. Jones was headed to become a mine boss, not Doyle. Job jealousy, I submit, was a part of that man's motivation for complicity in the murder of an innocent citizen of Maraque. Your witness for cross," said McParlan.

Defense Counsel O'Leary asked the witness one pivotal question: "Mister Doyle, where were you on the morning of Feb. 14th?"

"I was at home in Rausch Patch jes finishin' up me breakfast."

"Breakfast...and so you were nowhere near Mister Jones."

"Objection, Yer Honor. The defense poses a question with a presupposed answer. The question is loaded with implications."

"Sustained. Rephrase your question, Counsel."

"Mister Doyle, since you are under oath, you will tell the jury where you actually were on the stated morning."

"I was at home, as I said. Then I went to meet Kelly and Kerrigan."

"And what was your plan...for the day?"

"To meet this heyr Molly named Jones and persuade him to come over over our side."

"Our side. What does that mean, Mister Doyle?"

"It means that he 'come a member a Hibernians like us."

"Old Comradeship, is that what you mean?"

"There was That also, sir. He was a Mollie but he was not pert o' the Order."

"I see, a Mollie in name only."

"Like that, sure. We drink and we do some cards together and we hunts from time to time."

"I see. But on this morning you had finished breakfast and you met your pals. What was your plan then....to go hunting?"

"You are right, sir."

"You had guns...?"

"Yes, sir."

"What kinds of guns?"

"Rifles, shots gun, like fer hunting."

"Quail, turkeys, let us say."

"They's good game birds. Sometimes a deer with them rifles."

"I see, and did you see Mister Jones at any time of that morning?"

"No, sir. Not one hair o' his head."

"Do you stick by that answer?" The witness nodded.

Your honor, this man is guilty of perjury. I will bring in witnesses to prove it."

"Defense may cross-examine the witness," said Judge Shannon.

Counsel asked three pointed questions. Mister Doyle, are you a hunter, that is, hunting a sport you practice?"

"Wherever I can, and hits in season."

"Are you left handed?"

"No sir."

"Your honor and jurors, the missing fingers of his right hand indicate that if he had used a rifle, the murder weapon, he would have to pull the trigger with his left hand but he is right handed. He has only a thumb and a little finger. So that means he could not have fired on the victim? Wrong. He used a pistol in his left hand, the fingers are all there and they work. But he had no pistol. A search of his person on arrest showed he had no gun of any kind."

"Objection," said McParlan. The defense is presuming what he has not proved. He was not a witness to the murder....or else he must be sworn in."

"Sustained," said the judge.

The Defense, another lawyer by the name of Lacross, had no more questions. Judge Shannon motioned for Doyle to step down from the witness stand. The last man was Kelly, accused of complicity in Jones' murder. He was ignorant of the nature of compliciy--that it bore the penalty of death. Called up to the witness stand, he underwent similar questioning and scrutiny, accompanied by denials, challenges, accusations and presentations of witness evidence. McParlan next brough to the stand one of three townsmen-witnesses to the shooting, who had volunteered to testifty. A male juror went into a fit of coughing, as might have been expected. Four of the jurors were active miners and they could not be expected to sit quietly for hours without the effects of coal dust affecting their lungs, their quietude, their presence, their attention. The affected coal miner exited the jury box and went out of the courtroom with loud coughing, The Judge rapped, suspended the testimony for five mjinutes while the audience conversed and the jurors, admonished not to converse, sat in stoney silence regarding one another with silent, uncomfortable looks while they waited for the trial to resume after the brief reprise.

McParlan had the first citizen of Tamaqua sworn in.
"Give the jury your name."
"Malone, me names Jonas Kelly."
"Mister Kelly...You say you heard shots on the morning of February 14'
"I did, sir." "
"How far away were you?"
"About hundred yards."
"What else did you hear...or observe?"
"More gunshots, sir."
"Like, how many?"
"Oh, seven or eight, sir."
More or less than seven or eight?"
"Objection. the witness is being coached."
"Sustained."
"All right then, there were more shots, gunfire coming from the same direction?"
"Yes, sir."
"Did you see anything unusual?"
"Other folks...miners on their ways to work, some breaker boys, and others, running in the direction of the shooting."
"And...?"
"And so we run and we seed three men afrunin' away from a body thet layed there on the groun'. Hit didn't get up so we figured he was the one been shot. We picked him up and took him inter the closest hourse...but he was already dead."
"That man...do you know...did you learn his name?"
"We heart, I heart he be called by th'e name o' Jones."
The Jurors gasped, the judge perked up and learned forward at his bench, gavel in hand, and the jurorymen regarded each other with concern.
"He was dead, very dead, and somebody had murdered him."   "Let me ask you, sir, did you have any ill-will, bad feelings against this Jones, the deceased?"
"He was a squeeler."
"A squeeler. What do you mean? Explain that to the jury,"
"He tells the 'mine boss 'bout things go wrong down in th' mine."
"That's all?"
"Yes, sir."
"Your witness," McParlan said.
The Defense asked the witness who was there when he and Doyle and Kerrigan had reached the body. "Hun'reds" came the answer. The Defense followed up, there ils the possiblilty that amongthem there might ave been the killer who, believing himself concealed, came up to the body of Mr.Jones...."

"To see if he really was dead."

"I don't know, sir. I cannot say why they came. Most folks would come jes to see the blood."

No further questions, said defense.

The trial dragged on for another two weeks, another two jurors were swosrn in to rplc the wounded and killed jurors, witnesses to the action that day, testifing as to the presence of hundreds of witnesses, and the existence of a slain body, that of Jones on the ground. Nobody wanted to expose himelf to Molly revenge by testiying that he had seen any one or more of the three men--who sat at defense table-- shoot additional bullets into the inert form of Jones. Yes, McParlan was certain that that bizzare cruelty had occurred, because he learned from the coroner that Jones' body contained at least a dozen bullets in addiion to the single shot in the back. The gallows were already built inside the jail at Mauch Chung where there Kelly and Doyle, guilty of murder in the first degree, could be hanged two months later. Kerrigan, who was a corrupter of the trade societies of explosives handling, tool fabrication, breaker overhaul and locksmithy, turned to informant at the trial. His testimony went like this when he took the stand: He knew that the explosives were too old and therefore unstable, that the smithy had cut keys to the house of themline owner and the mine boss for Mollies' use, that tool fabrication had been delayed by months, and,finally, that breaker breakdown was bound to occur when pulleys, rollers and the main belt were not inspected and changed on a regulart basis.

"So you saw all that happend that day, Mister Kelly?"

"I did, sir, all of it."

"Did you see those two men,there, Mister McAllister and Mister Doyle on the sceneat the day Jones was killed?"

"I did, sir."

"And what were they doing?"

"They com over to Jones body and hey look a him ."

"To see lif he rally was dead?"

"I think so,sir. The two men who had eden question turned viciouslhy angry and threatened to rushs the wilsness, when deputy sheriffs lintervened and tied them to their chairls.

If you distub this court again, let me warn you, we shall have to rope you tighter into your chairs. Continue, M\ister McParlan.

"So you and McAllister looked over Jones' body. Did you fire any more rounds into him?"

"Ob jection, Yer Honor! Counsel is presuming evidence not yet discovered. The coroner report is not finished."

"They was too many people astandin' around.

"Fear held them. But where were your Mollie friends...
before the crowd arrived?"

"They was there aside Jones."

"At his body?"

"Yes, sir."

"What were they doing there?"

"It look like they was...disposing of him: Again the two men a the Defenders table started to stand up, one of the deputy sheriffs with a couple of lengths of rope tied the

Kellyand Doyle's feet to the legs of their chairs chairs.

"Will the witness tell this court, if he is not certain as to why the two of the accused were near the body, what he saw happen. Did the crowd try to interfere with those two men who are sitting there at the Defenders table?".

"No, sir. But the crowd. they seed everthin' that happened. They knowed Jones...they liked the man. Them two hated his guts.

"Hated Jones' guts? Tell us why, Mister Kerrigan."

"Because he snitch on things go wrong down in the mine, fist- fight with mine boss one day, run out of kerosene 'nother, dust, always dust, powder-monkey he set charges too soon, put th' other miners afeard of splosion fore it were planned."

These things went on...and Jones...snitched...told the mine boss?"

|"He snitched, he sure did."

"That was the motive for Jones' murder." McParlan turned to the jury emphasize his conclusion, ad to make his closing statement.

"The witness may step down."

"You have heard the real reason for Jones' murder..he revealed the downside of things happening in the mine. He put his life at risk. He told these things to the Pottsville Tribute. Those three men, bound by ropes to their chairs all gave different answers to present an unfriendly but not a murderous slant on their relationship o the dead man.Jones was a favorite of the mine boss, he was ambitious to become a mine boss, he was a innocent fine, devout man but a hypocrite. He was iln fact, an informer, which the miners call a snitch. He was against higher pay, he played cards and socialized with those trio there.... I ask you, ladies and gentlemen of the jury, whose story are you to believe? Indeed, good citizens, their alibis were just that, alibis for murder to lighten, to mitigate the sentence of death. I ask this jury to find the defendants, all three of them, guilty of murder in the first degree, and that they be sentenced to hanging by their necks until they are dead for the wanton, unprovoked, cruel and savage murder of one of their kind in name only, a Molly who did them no harm and was not in the slightest a threat to any one of them. I have finished my closing statement." Judge Shannon called on Defene Counsel O'Leary.

"Ladies and gentlemens of the jury, those three men cannot be the killers because the were in other towns on that fateful morning, Doyle was in Maraque, Doyle in the saloon and McAllister was sitting at his breakfast table a full hour before the murder occurred. I ask you to find these men innocent of the crime of first degree murder because they were absent from the scene of the crime, one to finish breakfast, another to go hunting and a third to drink his beer at the Briar Patch Saloon. A big story appeared one day. Let me show it to you. Let this, Yer Honor, be an ex-interrogatory exhibit, tsogether the coffin letter. O'Leary read the newspaper article to the jurors:

> On Fourteenth of February, a man well-liked in the
> towns by the name of Paul Jones, was brutally
> murdered within yards from his home, as he
> went to work. This is the alleged work of certain
> Mollies, who will be found and brought to trial.

> This paper does not know they names as yet. The
> of the name of James McParlan of the Pinkerton
> Agency is working on the case and has

told this paper that the guilty men will be
hanged for the murder of Jones.

James Munley is alleged to be the man behind the
murder of Jones, the others his accomplices.
Under the laws of this state, the accomplices to a
crime bear the same guilt as the perpetratorr. This
equality of culpability will beome apparent as the
trial progresses.

We here at the Tribute are hopeful that the
ommunity will take to heart the death of this well-
liked man to such an extent they will not only
protest the numerous murders of theMollies, but
witness where they are involved, in good
conscience to put an end to the wanton murders of the
now infamous Order of the Hibernian Society, the
Molliesas they are commonly called.

 May Mssrs. McAllister, Kelly, and Doyle   be
convicted by a jury of their peers. Only
then shall this town rest easy. The gallows await
them at Mauch Chunk. May they go to their
deaths in June of this year, 1875. And good
riddance, we say!

        McParlan considered that he had virtually snuffed out the Mollies as a warrlng
clique of violent lawbreakers, more of the anarchist breed, for the law to them was onerous,
oppressive and wrong.

        One more event had to occur at this time, a commitee of vigilantes formed up at
the request of Kehoe lin Girardsille, as a posture of law senforcement, ofwhich he was chief
officer,to stormed the jail alt Mauch Chunk, where the rio were encarcedrated afterf their trial
at Pottsberg. To this distant and parly hidden redoubt the con victshad been trundled,there to
stay foranother two syears before their hanging. This lapse iln time, this lacks ofvigilance
gave rise to the bold plan tostory the jail and frfee the convictsed men,McAllister,Dole and
Kelly.

told this paper that the guilty men will be
hanged for the murder of Jones.

James Munley is alleged to be the man behind the
murder of Jones, the others his accomplices.
Under the laws of this state, the accomplices to a
crime bear the same guilt as the perpetratorr. This
equality of culpability will beome apparent as the
trial progresses.

We here at the Tribute are hopeful that the
ommunity will take to heart the death of this well-
liked man to such an extent they will not only
protest the numerous murders of theMollies, but
witness where they are involved, in good
conscience to put an end to the wanton murders of the
now infamous Order of the Hibernian Society, the
Molliesas they are commonly called.

May Mssrs. McAllister, Kelly and Doyle be
convicted by a jury of their peers. Only
then shall this town rest easy. The gallows await
them at Mauch Chunk. May they go to their
deaths in June of this year, 1875. And good
riddance, we say!

McParlan considered that he had virtually snuffed out the Mollies as a warrlng clique of violent lawbreakers, more of the anarchist breed, for the law to them was onerous, oppressive and wrong.

One more event had to occur at this time, a committee of vigilantees formed up at the request of Kehoe in Girardsville as a posture of law enforcement, of which he wa chief officer, to storm the jail at Mauch Chunk,where the trio were encarcerated after thei trial at Pottsville. To this distant and partly hidden redoubt the convicts had been trundled, there to stay for another two years before their hanging. This lapse in time, this lack of vigilance gave rise to the bold plan to storm the jail and free the convicted men, McAllister, Doyle and Kelly.

One last flourish to this ignorminious chapter in Pennsylvania's history occurred when , having learned of the hangings, the Captain of the local militia of cavalry veterans of the Civil War, polished their harness and saddles, their boots and holsters, and on spirited steeds, twenty-five of them rode their mounts through the streets of Pottsville, reminding the folks of the Great War Between the States they had endured and suffered through. In the twilight, with torches held in the hands of several of the riders, this brilliant cadre rode through the town, leavng as they had arrived on prancing horses and shooting their revolvers into the air to show the power that could have been brought agalnst the Mollies, had Pinkerton called them in for reenforcements. With that show of military force, the days of Mollie vengeance were over.